Of

Aion

To Connie,
Hope you enjoy the
characters! Enjoy.
A. M. Mars.
Joshua 1:9

Star
Of
Aion

A.M.Mars

TATE PUBLISHING
AND ENTERPRISES, LLC

Published by Tate Publishing & Enterprises, LLC
127 E. Trade Center Terrace | Mustang, Oklahoma 73064 USA
1.888.361.9473 | www.tatepublishing.com

Tate Publishing is committed to excellence in the publishing industry. The company reflects the philosophy established by the founders, based on Psalm 68:11,
"The Lord gave the word and great was the company of those who published it."

Book design copyright © 2014 by Tate Publishing, LLC. All rights reserved.

Book and book cover design: Paul Muncey

Cover photography: Wyatt Davidson (sunlight thru the trees)

Cover image: © Maksim Shmeljov /Shutterstock (woman)

Published in the United States of America

ISBN: 978-1-63185-791-1
1. Fiction/Romance/Science Fiction
2. Fiction/Science Fiction/Action Adventure
14.03.05

Live, Laugh and Love to my husband, Daniel, who is my inspirational hero.

And to my friends who were brave enough to tell me the things that needed to be improved.

Interruption / Chapter 1

Inside the castle, spotlights shone on the encased weapons along the hallway that transitioned from old, engraved maces and rifles to futuristic weapons, showcasing their design and use.

Shelby loved the walk down this hallway to the solarium. It reminded her of the evolution of her own life and the power she now felt she had gained in knowing self-defense and weaponry use. Yenti called to her.

Even though she was not in view yet, she would not miss her session with him on the mat. Just as he suspected, she was there and entered the room, ready to start her exercises. Her ardent concentration and commitment to her training was as precise as her punctuality.

"Let's begin." Yenti was concise in his instructions and expected his students to be ready for anything he decided to present. He looked at the intense, deceptively feminine-looking woman as she took her place opposite him on the mat.

Older than most of his students, she was plainly dressed in loose gi and void of jewelry and makeup. Still, her skin was clear and her eyes of amber looked almost gold. Her braid could not contain all the curls or riotous colors her lush hair held. Simply put, she was beautiful and naturally strong.

She concentrated on her warm-up moves and pushed herself until she was sweating and limber. And so it began. She took her stance opposite him and bowed with respect. Today, she was being tested on her hand-to-hand combat and reflexes.

Yenti kicked and deflected, yet she was able to strike him in the solar plexus, hard and fast. He swung and missed her. Her agility required him to anticipate her next move, which often enough was not correct. Again and again she buzzed around him, deflecting his strikes and ducking his blows.

Yenti struck out at her again and even though she evaded him, he caught her thick braid with his quick hand. She was stopped cold. He used it to throw her off balance and across the mat.

She pushed herself to a sitting position. Crestfallen, she pouted. "Crap Yenti! You almost pulled my scalp off!"

He chuckled. "That tail of yours, in a real fight, will be your demise."

Shelby just rolled her eyes and lifted her braid, flipping the end of her hair around like a pretty fan. She batted her eyes over the tip of it at Yenti.

"It's my feminine attribute."

Yenti shook his head, clearly not amused. "We're finished for today."

Shelby was solemn. She knew she had disappointed her instructor with her flippant attitude. He was serious about his student's learning and took no excuses for failure. Still, she stood and saluted him with respect.

Yenti nodded. Dismissed, she turned to leave but he called after her, "Shelby, did you get it?"

A pleased smile broke over her features. "Want to see it?"

"Absolutely."

Shelby pulled a non-futuristic .45 caliber stainless-steel Desert Eagle handgun, sporting an alabaster handgrip, from her bag. With her pinkie fingers up, she tipped it back and forth delicately; point to end, like she was showing off a pretty shirt. She grinned.

Yenti smiled back and whistled appreciatively at the pretty little thing.

~*~

At home Shelby, dressed in white pants and shirt, left the luxury of her bedroom and walked into the open living room where her youngest son admired her new purchase. She finished fussing with her pearl necklace and ruffled his hair.

"How long did it take?"

"Not as long as before," he admitted proudly as he handed her the Desert Eagle.

Shelby examined his work and then expertly disassembled the gun and laid it out before him. Her eyebrow lifted in challenge and she laughed light-heartedly when he sighed.

She was not surprised at all to hear the doorbell ring. As she calmly walked past the black grand piano, she paused to smell the red roses displayed on top of it. The color contrasted starkly against the soft, warm whites of the continuous living room and entry.

She opened the door to unexpected intruders with futuristic rifles. They forced their way in and pushed her back, quickly overcoming her resistance. She was strong-armed to the alabaster floor by her assailant and held there by her braid with black-gloved hands.

From her pinned position on the tiles, she saw her son stand with the gun in his hand, confused by the commotion. He was not even aware he held it, but the intruders were.

Before he could relinquish the pistol, even as it slipped from his hand in surrender, he was shot by the invaders. Her son's body hummed and then transformed into a translucent watery look and dissipated. There was no evidence of him left. He was just ... gone.

The vase of roses crashed to the white tiles and sent red petals adrift like blood on the shards of glass and water. Shelby stared from her prone position motionless. There was no fight left in her, but she was knocked out by the assailants anyway.

~*~

The invasion was swift and complete. One of the multitudes of times the same process of conquering had occurred. It was like clockwork. The planet for all intents and purposes was under Alker control.

This was his first full world empirical assimilation. They were near the stage of expediting distribution of goods, including human cargo, to cities in the realms of Alkernian supremacy.

Sir Kerrick Torrell turned to Doctor Orlie and spoke in Alkernian as he always did when talking to his men. "All these women have been checked for fertility and diseases?"

"Indeed, Sir Kerrick. None have any health issues that are going to be a problem."

"What does that mean, Doc Orlie? Are you hedging some problem I need to be aware of?"

Doc Orlie chuckled, clearly not intimidated by the handsome young man before him. After all, he delivered this leader into the world and had by familiarity and kinship to the family been asked to accompany his godson and give him council in his endeavors in accomplishing his orders from Iritain headship.

"No, no, Sir Kerrick. It's just that some of these women are very young and have never had children and time will only tell if they can. There are a few who are older and have had babies, but..." he raised his shoulders.

"The same could be said for the older women. Maybe they are past bearing." Sir Kerrick looked past his godfather to view the women. "They say that life-expectancy on Earth is only sixty to one hundred years. It is possible that none of these women will suffice."

"So you see my dilemma? Too young or too old, who knows?" Doc Orlie chuckled again.

Doc Orlie would be going with the captives and Alkernian men to Aion. He welcomed his time to study a new planet with all its complexities and structure of life. Aion promised to be a mystical and lush planet with differing continents and regions of varied weather and...so much more that he gushed like a shy teenager when he thought about the endless possibilities of this new adventure. He was scheduled to leave Earth and head for his new home soon. His excitement was barely contained.

The Alkernian conquerors were at an advantage, their number of years being one of them. Their lifespan was in the hundreds, even close to a thousand years, so they had the advantage of being patient and thorough. The process of inserting Alker men into positions of power was done on a world-wide timeline, thus allowing domination and control from the top of world powers.

The other power the Alkernians had was seemingly endless technologies that were thus far insurmountable weapons to use in seizing control of world nations. This included world-to-world transportation and area-to-specific-area maneuvering. With the technologies they had, the usurpers could seize currency and in time bring the forces set against their military into a subservient and weakened state of compliance.

The Earth world was no different. It took less than twenty-five years to send high-ranking dignitaries off-world or to terminate and replace them with their own power.

The Alker goals were simple. The point of taking a world was to bring wealth and prosperity to the great and honorable and blessed nation of the Alkers and all their compatriot nations on the planet Iritain; ruled by the greatest realm of all, the Alker Nation.

This was done by converting cities, states and nations into prosperous but controlled realms that needed the guidance of the Alkernian high ranking Lurts and the now much desired power of their technologies and knowledge.

True assimilation was done by replacing all known leadership with the invading army of leaders and militants and diverting loss of life by quickly and efficiently suspending radical or guerrilla power. The Alkernian power dealt just enough death and destruction to prove complete and limitless domination prowess.

Sir Kerrick Torrell was satisfied with his accomplishments, but he was aware his leadership skills were only part of the successful campaign. His military band and commanders were dedicated and determined, and why not? Once this campaign was over, his whole unit would be decommissioned and sent to live the remainder of their days in oblivion; which was exactly what he wanted after fifty years of military service. This was how it was done for Iritain. All men were expected to serve their nation for at least twenty-five years. Then they were allowed to mate and raise a family. He would finally be able to complete his family lines and settle into one place.

The problem was healthy women were scarce on his home planet. It was not that they were not around, but women of his home planet for the last fifty years almost always had a boy. The scientists outsmarted themselves when they genetically altered and devised a way to ensure an enhanced male child. That alone was not the problem.

Fifty years ago a band of Alker militia had come back from a planetary coup, and had brought with them a disease that was detected in the male body of the returning armed forces. The military males were successfully treated with not a single adverse problem and cleared for reentry into their homeland.

The disease mutated, however, and became airborne to women who mated with these handsome and welcome men. Though they were treated, there was the adverse affect of women bearing one child and then never again. And it had passed on to every woman on Iritain, Alker or not, to become one of the greatest tragedies of all time.

To live to be a thousand years and to possibly never have a child was horrific and one perfect way to see to the demise of all Iritainians. It was possible that with the natural course of life and fatalities, the population could come to a dead stop, extinction.

So there was a quick reversal of genetics to try to balance the sexes and return females into the fold, but the Gala generation as they were referred to, was a lost cause. So the mighty conquerors had no progeny to brag about or to pass on their highly prized genetics to.

But, Sir Kerrick Torrell came upon an idea that he had brought to the Elder Lurt Board. Conquer Earth and transport women, fertile women, disease free women, who could bear children and give them to the undamaged and never infected military men. And do so off Iritain to ensure no continuation of contagion to the next generation or thereafter.

It was a mess for a while on Iritain. He and his men had been on a different campaign off-world and were refused entry until all contaminates and people affected had been sent back to the originating world of the disease; to be forever exiled from their loved ones and families.

Many had lost their lives trying to return, not believing the reigning government would prohibit patriots of their own country from entry and not yet realizing the severity of the ripple effect the disease had on the women. It went on in ways that eventually affected every citizen on the planet.

Maybe it was their Ultimate God's way of punishing their arrogance and lust in wanting more than their own planet, and thinking they could do whatever they wanted to the less powerful and knowledgeable. But, Sir Kerrick and his men had never been allowed to return to their own home planet in over fifty years. All their communications had been through physiporting.

He was commissioned to bring Earth under Alkernian domination for one purpose; to ensure the well-being and longevity of Alkers and the assurance of continued existence.

He looked at the men surrounding him, tall strong men. They were loyal and had been at his beck and call for these many years. Compared to the men of Earth, they looked like they all were in their thirties. A few looked younger.

He looked at his abiding doctor and though he was over four-hundred Earth years, he appeared to be a young sixty year old man with white hair and the body of a tried and tested forty year old.

They were in an underground port preparing to send off the collected women who were now in transport cages awaiting medical preparations needed to undergo and arrive healthy and unharmed in transport.

Sir Kerrick was still pondering over the women when one of the collaborating Earth men brazenly joined him and his guard circle. He personally knew this man and did not like him in the least. He was an arrogant and power-hungry badger and had traded his family for surety for himself and a position of clout when the eventual Alkernian supremacy had come into full force. He stood almost up to the shoulders of his men, which for Earth men meant he was taller than most. But he had a corrupt and dark demeanor that Sir Kerrick Torrell could detect even without the telltale sign that colored the Alkernian men's body when emotions and thoughts were heightened.

He heard one of the women from the group yell for the messenger-man by name. Apparently she knew him and was hoping for his help. He watched the man and saw the red that rose to his face. He was angry, but he ignored the woman and addressed Sir Kerrick with resolute determination.

"I was sent to see if you required anything else from my Lurt Paul before you are deported to Aion--I mean transported to Aion." He spoke terrible broken Alkernian, and yet Sir Kerrick did not miss the deliberate jab at his discharge from the military ranking and status that was always given him.

Sir Kerrick looked at the messenger of Lurt Paul with a degree of irritation that made the man look uncomfortable and step back.

"We are commissioned to return to Iritain, not Aion, before we are decommissioned from our duties."

He sensed his men's ire rising as they deliberately stared the small man down.

In the background the woman was still yelling, trying to get his attention, which he dutifully ignored.

"The woman is persistent." Kerrick lifted his brow and gestured in the woman's direction.

The detestable man ignored her with a shrug and ignored Sir Kerrick's unspoken query. "As is Lurt Paul, who is determined to send you on your way as soon as possible with all that you require."

"I require nothing more at this time. I will not be leaving until all the necessary changes have been accomplished. And since you are the errand boy...I mean assistant for Lurt Paul, you will express to him that I am to be addressed as Sir Kerrick, his Superior and Commander for the duration of my tenure on this planet. Remind him that I and my men are High Lurts on this planet and have not acquired Earth for his command, but for the Romantis who have helped us. They will continue to reign long after we are

11

gone." He saw the smaller man's face redden yet again.

The woman was indeed persistent. With all the commotion going on, she could still be heard above the noise, her voice ripe with desperation. Her hands grabbed the bars and shook them vehemently.

Kerrick could feel her mounting anger and her realization that she was abandoned to whatever fate held for her with no ensuing help from Lurt Paul's assistant.

She finally turned her back to them and slid down with finality to hide her face in her knees and arms; her shoulders set.

He was indifferent to the woman's feelings at present, but he knew soon enough, those women would be mates for bearing progeny and continuing Alker family lines. They sure seemed small for full grown women.

Shelby / Chapter 2

Shelby had already undergone intrusive body checks and examinations. How had it come to this? No one had even been warned about the infiltration of aliens or the eventual demise of their own culture and way of life.

The Alkernians, as she now knew them to be, had systematically accessed their Earth propaganda and realms of power to deliver the message that her entire planet was now ruled by them and they had the technology and prowess to control every aspect of the human race's lives on Earth.

She felt a swell of anger and determination now as she sat in the darkness and listened to the sobbing of others. She could feel their primal fear and hopelessness.

Shelby groaned into her hands. How was this all going to play out and what did the Alkers want from all these women? Even in the dark there were no crying children or deep voices of men.

Shelby spoke out loud into the darkness to the others in her carrier, "Do any of you know where we are going or what they have done with the children?" There was no answer, but then a woman spoke up.

"I think we're being transported off our world to some other place called Aion."

"What? Why do you think that?" Shelby was incredulous, how would she get to her children?

"I heard men talking about the separation of women, men and children. Most of the children are being kept here until they are grown."

"Who said this?" Someone else in the darkness questioned.

Shelby heard the first woman whimper before she replied.

"The Alkernian men spoke in our language and made sure we heard. They deliberately...made sure we heard."

"What's your name?" Shelby was curious.

"Amy Gonzagats. I am from Misza."

"Amy," Shelby tried to probe, "why are we being shipped off Earth?"

"Not all the women are being transported, just some. I'm not sure if they were referring to us. I really don't know." In the darkness her final words hung over the group like an executioner's axe. There was quietness now as they waited for the final blow.

Shelby looked out of their carrier to the men beyond. Who were they?

~*~

Men outside the carriers waited for orders from Sir Kerrick Torrell, the High Lurt Commander of this mission and planet. His concluding directives would finalize the past twenty-five years of intrigue and suspense.

The men who stayed behind two weeks here would, by the accounting of Aion time, be following only a week or so later. Time was slower on Aion.

They had been warned of the real possibility of being younger than their children if they stayed too long there. Not that his men had to worry about that. They had none.

On Aion they'd be prohibited on most accounts the use of superior technologies. Though they had sequestered some advanced equipment and devices for emergency use, they would for the most part be limited to fairly simple and rudimentary weapons and technology on a daily basis. Those were being crated on board the platform for transport.

Previous settlements on the planet revealed Alker technology was useless on Aion. Something in the makeup of the unique planet rendered their weaponry impotent. But, it was also a 'pure' planet, or unpolluted because only organic or low-radiation equipment worked. Thus it was deemed an Eden planet.

Aion, however, was not the most suitable planet to live on in that it would separate the men from the advancements of their own home planet. Though it might actually be a blessing to grow old slower than the rest of their home world, it would render them at a disadvantage eventually.

Sir Kerrick would stay behind almost six months on Earth to settle the affairs of transferring powers to eligible candidates. He would not be the one to choose who would get what, since he had already declined the position to remain High Lurt here.

He was no longer desirous of power that changed civil men into corrupt and uncaring persons of lies. He no longer wanted to be charged with the duties of dividing families and killing enemies of the Assemblies of State. His final orders were too despicable to retell to his own mother and father, so he chose to delegate and withdraw from the position he was entitled to.

The women that had been selected to travel to Aion had no choice. They were captives from the war and the reasons they were chosen were varied. All Sir Kerrick knew was that Doc Orlie had, for differing reasons, secured these four hundred or so women to be the recipients privileged to leave this planet and travel to Aion. They would live the duration of their lives in a new and less-populated planet with vast degrees of weather and climatic changes. And of course, live on a planet whose length of days was longer and yet somehow slower in variable time connections to his home planet of Iritain.

"All the women are secured and the remaining carriers of freight are being loaded and transferred as we speak," the messenger from Lurt Paul reported to Sir Kerrick.

"Fine. Do what you need to do to prepare yourself to go."

"Yes Sir. I meant no disrespect Sir Kerrick Torrell. I am only the messenger and have been instructed to acquire your permission to leave with Lurt Paul's troop."

Sir Kerrick grunted and Commander Rockdurgh spoke to the messenger.

"We require no more from your Lurt. Take the entry portal and leave when you are ready." They exchanged fisted salutes and bowed without taking their eyes off each other as was customary.

"Follow his every move until he and Lurt Paul leave this planet." Sir Kerrick said this to Commander Rockdurgh. "I do not mean to have any surprises or unscheduled mishaps. Get them off this world. That Lurt has been nothing but a pain in my backside."

Commander Rockdurgh smiled. He knew it would be a while before the remaining three hundred of their squadron would be released, but this was the easy road now. They would be peacemakers between exchanging powers, which would happen in far less time than the projected two years.

Finally, they would go home. But what really worried Rockdurgh was the probability that he would spend the remainder of his days alone, without any children to call his own.

The women they sent to Iritain could very well exhibit the same child-bearing problems as their own Alker women, and there were few enough of them that they had become powerful and selective about whom they would mate with.

The fact of the matter was he was not sure that the planet itself did not cause the infertility problem. Doctor Orlie had assured him that it was improbable, but Commander Rockdurgh just wasn't convinced. He subjectively thought that going home was a bad idea for this reason, and so did other men.

Time would tell. Only, he did not have the faith to wait another fifty years for a chance to mate and have children of his own.

Six months later…

It took months of negotiations before Sir Kerrick and his men were finally done with the last of their duties on Earth. Before they even caught their breath, they were assembled for a physiport conference with the Unified Delegated High Lurt on Iritain.

"Sir Kerrick of Torrell, I am so pleased to finally meet with you."

"Thank you, Honored One. I am content to at last see and hear from you personally." Sir Kerrick saluted the High Honored One, known as Bestoch de Lurt Proh. She was a hermaphrodite, born into a position of power and known as a Discerner. Her lifestyle was known to be impeccable to any who witnessed her daily proceedings. She was studied in all manner of disciplines. She was the Leader of all on Iritain, and her appointment was secondary to none.

Her power was wielded with such knowledge that some had disputed whether she could read minds or even read closed books. She was admired and greatly respected for many other reasons, and Sir Kerrick was truly in awe of her.

She possessed a grace that accentuated her position. But if she wielded no power at all, Kerrick was sure she would still be charismatic and respected, and thus honored enough to always be admired. She was one of the rare Alkers that had lived over a thousand years, and her knowledge and clarity were vast.

"Sir Kerrick Torrell, I have lingered over your reports and …" She stopped and smiled at him.

"This surprises you?"

"Yes, Honored One."

"You thought I didn't really know you. I want you and all your men to know that I am very proud to have men like you, who do their duty with honor and precision. I am also aware of many things that you are not Sir Kerrick, so I want you to trust me when I tell you the things that I must. Do you agree?"

"Yes, High and Honored Discerner." Sir Kerrick saluted her as did all the soldiers who stood behind him, all three hundred of his trained and true men.

"Sir Kerrick." She sounded irritated and Kerrick was concerned that he had misspoke. He looked at her and saw softness in her wizened amber eyes.

"You believe I am a discerner, and so I am. What I tell you next, you will not like, nor will your men, but it is necessary.

"You and your three hundred men will not return to Iritain now." She waited for some protest, but Kerrick's men had been trained too well to show any discomfiture to the outside world or to balk at any command from Sir Kerrick or his superiors.

"Your men are as well trained as the reports have said. I am more than pleased with your squadron, Sir Kerrick. Please sit." This she indicated to the men behind Sir Kerrick.

"As I said, you will not return as you thought. There have been other reports coming back from Aion that are not good to my ears. Your Lurt Paul has made a mess of things already. My confidant,

19

whom you probably know as Lurt Paul's messenger, has reported his concerns and it seems that Lurt Paul has been wounded, quite severely and will be returning home.

"My dear comrade, will you and your men go to Aion and settle things there? I will not make you take this assignment, but at the present I do not want you or your remaining men to come home."

Sir Kerrick's scowl could not be hid from his face as he contemplated the predicament before him. They would not be returning home for a hero's welcome. He wondered if Lurt Paul's assistant had something to do with this.

"May I ask High and Honored One, if the women that have been sent to Iritain are acceptable?"

"You would not have sent them if you believed them not to be." She continued to smile at the handsome man before her.

Sir Kerrick feared a resurgence of the horrific Gala virus. "I want my men to be able to return at some point to their home planet. Will they be allowed to in due time?"

"Sir Kerrick of Torrell, some will return, but none will ever stay here again. I foresee this new planet you go to, to be one in which any who stay will prosper and be fruitful. I believe you will even call it home someday.

"Iritain is no place for your honorable and just men, and Aion needs you. Make your home there."

There was an awkward silence, but the Honored One did not go and waited patiently for Sir Kerrick to process his thoughts.

The men behind him waited for their commander to reflect his position to them one way or another.

He turned his back to the Honored One and looked over his men. Their eyes connected with his, each and every one of them. He thought about the twenty-five some years that these particular men had given to him and their National pride and he counted himself very fortunate to know them and to have a community of men he respected.

"I believe you have given us no other choice. But, had you done so Honorable One, I believe each one of my men would have agreed to go as one to Aion."

In unison, the men behind him saluted their respect, two fingers pointing to the heart and stomped their feet loudly once.

When he looked into the face of the hermaphrodite, he knew she had already anticipated his response.

When she spoke, he was sure she could see into his soul. "I did not say this for your men, but for you Sir Kerrick. For I am very aware that you have a betrothed here on this planet, which I know you will need to pursue before you can settle any future you wish to make.

"Go to Aion, and when you need to return, send word. Your request will be honored. Take care, Sir Kerrick of Torrell. Remember all that happens on Aion you will be accountable for. Set the standard to live by and fight for.

"This is something I have thought long and hard on. I know you are the one to bring a new city into being and to bring culture to such a wild place.

"You are an intelligent and patient man, Sir Kerrick, and you have already far exceeded the expectations of the Unified Delegated High Lurts on Iritain.

"I am impressed by your qualifications, Sir Kerrick. You are not quite two hundred years are you?"

"No, High Discerner."

"Your ability at squelching plots and intrigue are borderline miraculous. Are you sure you are not gifted with sight?" She laughed.

Kerrick tried to enter into the humor, but was still swimming in his own disappointment of not seeing his family and his betrothed in person.

"Morrell Orlie has been given his request to accompany you to Aion. He is one of my dearest friends and I'll miss his wonderful humor. Tell him his children will visit soon, so he is to prepare for their arrival. Of course, soon to him could be twenty years to us and is barely a dent of waiting compared to his age. Tell him I said so. He will love the jest of that." She was chuckling to herself as she left without a good-bye.

As if on cue, his parents and other family members of the men approached the physiport screen. It automatically expanded and wound around the room as each man touched the screen and gestured it to scroll past them. Families had been brought into the physiport from other rooms than the secured one of the High Discerner.

The Physical Equivalent Spectrum Picture Port, as the physiport was short for, represented a life-size image of each person to and from each port of reflection that allowed men and their families back home to actually see and hear each other in almost real-life.

His parents were saddened by the outcome. They were stoic and kept their disappointment to themselves, however.

This had been a regular way of communicating over the years, but it was disappointing to not be there in person, to walk with them through their property and to smell his mother's pies baking or the aftershave his father always wore. He tried not to be too sentimental about it, but his regret was tangible.

He looked for his fiancé but she did not appear, and the knowing looks in his parents' faces told him she did not make it, yet again.

"She had other engagements she needed to keep. Your older brother also had his reasons."

Sir Kerrick grunted.

He visited for over an hour with them, knowing that once he left for Aion he would not be able to communicate with them through the physiport because of the time difference. It would distort the images and not be in real time as he would appear to be moving very slowly compared to their point in time.

"Son," his mom called to him in his mind. "Your betrothed is not with you and needs you to remind her that you care for her above all else."

He looked at his father who was talking to him about the relatives and was totally unaware of the separate dialog he was having with his mother.

"I do not believe that Ashanti Pieriota is that insecure in my absence."

"What does that have to do with Marita and Jacova?" His father queried with a drawn brow.

"It is time for me to leave. Father. Mother." He bowed with reverence and trust by lowering his eyes as he saluted. His abrupt closure was typical of his manner.

Kerrick signaled for the physiport to wind down. He saw most of his hardened warriors with long faces and many with tears in their eyes as they realized their loved ones would not be seen for many months to come. Their long awaited return to Iritain would be even longer and possibly non-existent in the future.

Kerrick took one last look at his parents and watched as they forced smiles upon their faces. They both gave him looks of pride swelling in their eyes. He too was proud to have such a noble family, not because of their lineage, but because of their ethics.

In some ways, he knew if they had any inkling of the things he had done to secure the planet of Earth for Iritain, they would have been more than disappointed in him. For this reason, he was anxious to finish his work on Earth and be decommissioned from his post.

He would have to wait to start his family, but he hoped it would only be a while longer until he returned to Iritain.

In the Beginning / Chapter 3

He had been sent to this planet to straighten out the mess that Lurt Paul had created. When he got here, Sir Kerrick had witnessed horrific treatment of the females that had obviously been going on for several months. Deprivation of basic captivity rights as set forth in the Traditions of the Alkernians had not been followed. Granted, the planet was new territory for the Alkernians, but the laws as set forth by generations of conquering and assimilating the conquered had strict protocol.

Too many unsolicited complaints had been sent to the Lurt Elders to be ignored any further. He was ceremoniously given the prestigious command of discovering the truth of the transplanted colony that had disappeared years earlier; and the misconduct of Lurt Paul's transgressions that had been happening on this planet called Aion.

What he was ascertaining was heavy-handed controlling of the captive women who were sent to work the mines and engage with the Lurt's company of men. And the missing colony was still missing.

"Sir Kerrick." Commander Rockdurgh saluted his High Lurt. "Apparently the female that attacked Lurt Paul and left the scar on his face has been in the box for over three weeks."

"What box?" Sir Kerrick was not aware there had been any kind of jail or torture instituted for women. He felt his anger rising against the already hated man.

Commander Rockdurgh pointed toward the outside to indicate the direction of the misguided form of detention. "They don't think she's even alive."

"Get her out and if she is alive, I want to see her." Sir Kerrick was incensed that Lurt Paul would mistreat any woman that could possibly bear children.

The intended reason for bringing the captive women here was to match them with Alkernian men who would otherwise have no children due to the lack of healthy Alkernian women. He himself was betrothed to an Alkernian woman with the possibility of birthing only one child.

It was known that all these Earth women had born children already with the exception of twenty that were still young. Thus, these women were highly valuable to the Alker nation.

Sir Kerrick was surveying the documents of what some of the women had been scheduled to do in the mines. What they had accomplished already was impressive, but at what cost? It seemed the number of women had gone down, and consequently exponentially affected the production in the last months.

He heard the rattling of chains before he saw the uncaged woman. She was filthy and the color of her matted hair was obscured by dirt. She was smaller than an Alker woman, since nearly all were over six feet tall. She might have been just over five feet. What stood out the most was her ability to look dignified and poised in chains, dirt, and three weeks of being in a box that was not large enough for her to stand or sit up in, or stretch completely out in, according to Commander Rockdurgh. Her shoulders were pulled back, her eyes defiant and she was, even now, stretching her body up to full height. She looked at him directly and then surveyed everything her intelligent eyes saw.

"I see Lurt Paul did not manage to kill you." She was studying him with a frown and showed no sign of understanding what he had said. "Why did you attack the commanding Lurt?" He was speaking to her in Alkernian and decided she didn't understand his language.

She was not as smart as he gave her credit for if after these many months she could not engage in some communication with Alkernians. He said so to the men in the room. While they chuckled, he repeated the question in the Earth language and waited for her reply.

She tilted her head slightly to the side and looked at him with deliberation. "He tried to force one of the young women to stay with him, but she refused to mate with him. He did not take her refusal well. He hurt her more than once, so I made sure he couldn't harm her for a while."

A huge man leaned forward and whispered in his ear presumably what she had done to make this so.

His eyes widened comically and he got a satisfied smirk on his face.

"Gentlemen, this petite woman is the one who almost castrated Lurt Paul and put the mark on his face." To Shelby he bowed a semi-respectful acknowledgement. "He will most assuredly give anyone in your care a wider berth. As he has requested leave of this duty, you will not need to castrate him any further."

The other men shifted their firm stance as they chuckled at what she apparently thought was not so funny.

More directly he said to the woman in Earth dialect, "He is sure you are a demon come to take his very soul. He said every woman in the compound has threatened him on your command. Is this so?"

The woman flexed her jaw and looked away but spoke quite softly to him. "I have been without water to wash or clean clothes for three weeks, so I need to go and bathe and I am hungry. We can banter some other time. The chains need to be taken off."

She was so succinct it caught him off guard. After a moment of reflection, he nodded to Commander Rockdurgh to take her chains off.

She turned to leave.

"If you threaten me, woman, I will put you back in the box." He meant to deter her aggressive behavior.

She stopped in her tracks and turned back to face him. Walking slowly back toward him, the unfettered chains fell about her feet and lay still on the carpeted floor. "If anyone dares to put me or any other woman in that box again, I will kill him. So be prepared if you have any intentions at all of doing so."

Sir Kerrick could not believe he had heard such defiance so soon after her release. But maybe she really hated the box. He nodded to the men to grab her and put her back in for another hour or two.

The men stepped up to apprehend her but she ducked so gracefully she looked like she just bowed. As she straightened, she was a step behind them and easily took a weapon from both their belts. With warrior grace she cut a gash on a leg of both men so they teetered to the floor with blood letting over the rich carpets.

In sudden motion she lowered one of the swords to the neck of a downed man, who now comprehended the threat, and menaced the words, "I will not kill you this time, but if you ever grab me again I will attack with severe intent. I do not like Alkernian men."

She looked at Kerrick who held a hand up to stop the other men from engaging, as they intended to do, in a full blown attack. She looked around and saw their obedience to their commander was absolute.

"What do you plan to do now, my small captive?" She had to be insane to lift a sword against his warriors.

She poked one of the men again with her sword as he started to move. "I will maim you if you move a muscle. I'm not very controlled with these swords, and they are sharp."

She was so nonchalant that Kerrick relaxed a bit. He crossed his muscular arms over his chest and leaned against his desk studying her.

"So what now, little warrior?" He smiled and in spite of his men watching the spectacle with apprehension, he enjoyed the spirited sprite.

She thrust one sword into the floor between the men lying there holding their cuts and looked at the one now in her hands.

"I believe I have made the point that I will seriously fight to my last breath if I am confined again." She lifted her eyes and in the place of defiance there was softness that melted him a little. "With ten men around me, I realize you think I will be overcome eventually if you command it…but I would like to go to my cubicle without being threatened at every turn. I am tired."

Sir Kerrick scoffed at her being tired. "It does not appear as though you have learned anything while you were in the box."

He nodded toward Commander Rockdurgh, "Woman, he'll take you to see Doc Orlie. He is in charge of the well-being of all the women. You, I believe, are seriously in need of a mental check-up to take on my skilled men. You caught them unaware this time, but they will never make that mistake again. Be forewarned."

Shelby just looked at him with defiance back in her eyes or was it a challenge? She tossed the sword in her hand toward Kerrick and turned to go with Commander Rockdurgh. The sword landed just shy of his feet.

Commander Rockdurgh looked to Sir Kerrick for assurance he was still to escort her out, not sure what to do now.

Sir Kerrick was not finished. "What is your name?"

"Shelby." She did not even look at him. She walked toward the exit like nothing happened seconds ago to warrant any kind of punishment.

Sepoy Bordog, a by-the-book administrating sentry, stepped up next to him and said with repressed awe when she was gone, "Did she really get Korit and Talig's swords and strike them? So much for military show, she used them for real."

"If all the women can handle themselves as she does, we need to make sure they have zero access to weapons. Make sure the sentries Korit and Talig are punished severely." Sir Kerrick had a smirk on his handsome face. "I never would have expected that from someone who was so weakened. You're sure she was in there for three weeks?"

Sepoy Bordog nodded to Sir Kerrick as they watched the men she accosted limp to Doc Orlie's place to have their cuts bandaged. They followed a safe distance behind the woman and Commander Rockdurgh.

"I do believe, Sir Kerrick, that if she wanted to kill them, she would've inflicted more damage. Korit and Talig will not easily live this down." Sentry Biat was scowling at the thought.

"Make sure they do not."

Shelby was led to the other side of the Lurt's dome which connected to another expansive dome.

A full length hallway ran between the High Lurt's dome and the one that housed the doctor's laboratory and examination areas. Inside the medical area, there were two soldiers observing the doctor's activities with reserved respect. They were apparently there to keep things in order.

The dome was a magnificient example of Alkernian technology and beauty. A touch to the wall would turn on a light with one finger, or two fingers would produce another panel of information. A whole hand to the textile wall of the dome would allow the user to hover the information over their hand until a closed fist through the lighted information would crumple it like a wad of paper, which then dissolved to black letters and fell like ashes to the floor; absorbed somehow back into the matrix of the dome.

In contrast to Sir Kerrick's lavishly adorned dome of hanging fabrics and comfortable furnishings, this dome was sleek and neatly utilitarian. Lighted tubules of plants formed pillars that reached to the heights of the dome visually illuminating floors of storage above.

Shelby observed all this as the grey-haired physician squirreled things into their place. He was another new face to Shelby, one who seemed more like a book character to her than real.

He was a cheery doctor who seemed to be harried and distracted, but when he looked Shelby directly in the eyes, his intelligence was unmistakable. He seemed to enjoy his occupation with complete enthusiasm.

"And what lovely creature, pray tell, did you bring me today Commander Rockdurgh?"

He was obviously ignoring the smell of fermentation that reeked from her and the unkempt hair loaded with dirt. The twinkle in his eyes made Shelby want to smile, but she felt numb, like she was in a fog that made her emotions vague.

Shelby heard them talk in Alkernian, but at the same time she was aware that her knees were weakening. She closed her eyes as the room began to spin faster and faster around her. Strong hands caught her, but she was too weak to open her eyes as she floated to a resting place and lost consciousness.

In and out of her stupor, Shelby heard unfamiliar whispers as she lay quiet on the medical table.

"She is just very weak and dehydrated, Sir Kerrick. We will get her cleaned up and well in short time."

"She needs a thorough examination, as do all the women. I want to know their health needs and weaknesses, any diseases they may have or ailments. I need the report of any discrepancies from the last time they were checked."

"Sir Kerrick, how many women are there?" Doc Orlie was curious.

"Three hundred eighty-eight according to the records." He only knew because he had counted the crews divided up to do the mines and chores.

Doc Orlie's intake of breathe was audible. "There should be over four hundred. What happened to the others?"

Sir Kerrick just stared at the doctor for lack of words. He had yet to surmise what exactly happened to the missing women, over one hundred.

"While you are checking their health, determine what occupations they had previously and what they qualified for before they were apprehended. I want them reassigned to jobs that are more suitable for women of their stature. Most of the women I have seen thus far are not going to last the winter here if they are any more bedraggled than now."

"Yes, yes." Doc Orlie looked pleased with Sir Kerrick's concern for the people in his care. "I will get on it in short order. I will take care of everything." Doc Orlie's hands were gesturing.

"Good." Sir Kerrick bowed his respect to Doctor Orlie then nodded toward Shelby. "I believe she will need a mental exam." But he smiled at her motionless form. "She is quite feisty for her size."

Doc Orlie looked at her and then the two soldiers still waiting for his attention. "So I see."

Later, when sleep released its grip on Shelby, she woke to a dark room heavy with the sound of quiet.

She looked down at her body and saw a monitor on her hand which she carefully removed. She swung her legs over the side of the bed before she realized her clothes had been removed and she was now in a clean wrap. She took a deep breath and felt some of the heaviness that had been in her chest ease.

She slid slowly off the high cot until her bare feet touched the floor. Earlier, her body betrayed her weakness when she slumped to oblivion. She was determined to get her equilibrium and not faint again.

She tip-toed to the exit and went through the hall between the two large dome tents. To her surprise there were guards at the main exit talking back and forth in Alkernian. Shelby determined the best course of action was to walk casually by the guards.

She waited for just a moment, and then ducked out the doorway while their attention was fixed on a woman at the fire. In the darkness, it was easy to move past the men without being noticed. She followed the decending ramp-like pathway from the strategically placed domes of Sir Kerrick's and the doctor. From this height, she could see the firelights glow in the whole encampment.

She hurried down the path to her cubicle, the small space each woman occupied in a large community dome. Around her dome, other domes were connected or raised to accommodate the rocky terrain. Fires were interspersed in the center space, created by the circular placement of the domes. Outside of the camp ring, sentries insinuated themselves into the woods and were not seen unless they wanted to be.

As she walked, she thought about the bleak hours in the box and cringed at the time she had been in the dark hole. So much fear and anger had mixed inside her that she had worked hard at keeping her mind off the claustrophobic nature of the box. She hated the man that put her in there. He was an egotistical tyrant that had made her rage at the cruelty he had inflicted on the younger women.

When Amy had come back from his dome with her body bruised and bloodied from his abuse, Shelby had determined that Lurt Paul would never have the ability or the desire to hurt any woman again.

She still remembered with pleasure his surprise of her slicing his face and then plunging the makeshift sharp instrument into his groin. She had determined to slice his hands next, but only one wrist was marked with her stroke before his co-conspirators halted her quick, expert thrusts.

Someone had swung his fist from behind and knocked her down, hard. She felt the kicks to her stomach, but had the presence of mind to open her eyes toward her victim who was screaming like a girl and bleeding profusely. She had done what she came for, to put fear in the tyrant's mind and to make him lose face before his colleagues.

"You're not so tough when a woman fights back, are you Lurt Paul?" Shelby had endured the beating, but her determination to dig the mental stake of fear into him was strong. "You need to know that when the other women hear that you are still walking, they won't be satisfied until you are maimed permanently."

"Well, you have just sealed your fate, woman. Kill her." His harsh voice belied none of his hate toward Shelby.

"Sir, we have a mandate that we are not to terminate any of the captives under any circumstances."

Those words and the adherence to Alker traditions saved her life.

"Then put her in the box and let time deal with her. Give her nothing but water and one meal a day."

Lurt Paul was methodical in his cruelty. He bent down and grabbed her bloodied jaw. "One day soon you will remember that you are not so important. You should mind your own business and not involve yourself with my affairs."

His breath was stagnant, but Shelby smiled knowingly up at him. "The day you put your filthy hands to my sister was the day your life was nearing the end. The scratches I gave you are just the beginning of your problems. The moment you put me in the box, the women will know that I struck back and you will only have problems from this time on."

And she had not given him an idle threat. He had been poisoned and rejected and the progress in the mines and city had almost completely halted.

The women purposed to take the men to task and severed all communication and dalliances, which in turn, made the men turn their attention to the man who had caused the problem in the first place.

Lurt Paul was thwarted by the women. His soldiers' respect lessened because he could no longer control the sect of women. To compound the problem, his men were not getting their usual sexual dalliances, which created hostility in the day-to-day operations of the work on the planet.

This was relayed to Shelby while she was in the box. The updates sustained her hope during the agony of being isolated under the suffocating box enclosure.

Now she was free, but before she even got to the safety of the other women, she had caused yet more problems with the new Lurt. She felt dismayed. She was probably going to have repercussions from the fool-hardy tactics she'd displayed earlier today, but when he threatened to put her back in the box she instantly lost her sanity.

Shelby was so lost in her personal rebuking for the moment, she was alarmed by the deep voice behind her.

"I thought you would sleep through the night." Sir Kerrick's baritone voice belied his amusement at catching her off guard. He heard her intake of breath and noted her quick positioning for attack. He laughed and stepped out of the shadows to let her see him.

"Are you always ready for a fight?" He looked at her disheveled appearance and lingered over the soft curves that were outlined by the night fires. He wondered if she knew that the wrap was not as figure camouflaging as the uniform she had been wearing.

"You shouldn't sneak up on people," she stated sourly as her body relaxed somewhat. Her eyes boldly took stalk of his calm stance. His arms were crossed over his muscular chest and he was smiling at her with indulgent amusement. She crossed her arms in mock rebuke and tilted her head.

He could not help chuckle. She was a woman that, in spite of her recent abuse and lack of judgment, was still able to be saucy and spirited.

"Do you always talk to yourself?" He watched her lift her chin higher as if she would deny such a thing.

"Yes, I do. All of the women in our family..." She turned her face away as if to hide her blushing face.

He noticed she was uncomfortable with revealing personal matters.

"Why were you in the box, Shelby?" Kerrick was using his infamous genteel voice to soothe her miffed attitude.

"I threatened the Lurt. Don't you have the details in that stupid book he writes in?"

She started to walk away, but was stopped and jerked back in mid-stride by the pull of her braid. As soon as she got her balance back she snapped her hair out of the new Lurt's grip and glared at him.

"When I am talking to you, Shelby, you need to be dismissed formally. I am the ruling Lurt here and I expect you to recognize my authority. I have ways that will make Lurt Paul look like a baby."

"Then, Lurt Kerrick, I will make sure I stay on your good side and avoid you altogether. I am prone to defy authority, especially arrogant Alkernian Lurt's." She mockingly did the salute she had seen his personal guards do as they carried out his commands.

"Shelby." His voice had a calming effect on her and she lost some of her irritation when she heard sincerity in his voice.

"When I make my report, I want to include the reason you felt the need to put your life in jeopardy. Explain why you were in the box."

She paused for a moment and rubbed her bare arms to warm them. She felt that to tell this man what Lurt Paul had done to the younger women would only be scoffed at as trivial, but she would give him his due chance as the new Lurt.

"He was cruel. Some of the women felt his belt or fist if they even dared to reject him or annoy him. When Amy was slapped around and tattooed with his knife, I decided to give him some of his own marks and leave him with something to think about next time; if next time came for him." She shrugged her shoulders and looked away so that her facial expressions would not give away her lingering emotions.

Finally, she looked him in the eyes, drawn out of her reserve and asked, "What I don't understand is how the other men could let him continue to hurt women who were helpless against him. What is wrong with Alkernian men that they would let another man do such cruel things to women? Isn't there some tradition that would call some kind of heroism up in the hearts of Alkernian men that would want to protect women? No. Instead they watch as if they are cowed by one man's anger. How is it possible that warriors would allow such stupid cruelty? I blame the soldiers as much as the Lurt."

She was fervent at the end of the dialogue.

He could see her passion and unmistakable determination to have an end of the matter. "I

40

believe you are mistaken about the Lurt. He and his men are not Alkernians. They are from a different continent called Mophan on Iritain.

"Basically they were given their own nation within our nation. They have their own traditions and laws. Lurt Paul was being given a chance to redeem himself from the mess he created back on Iritain, my home planet.

"But, you need to know that I am High Lurt Sir Kerrick of Torrell. Not just a Lurt or a Pretain, which is why I am called Sir Kerrick, the High Lurt part of the title being understood.

"And for your understanding, Shelby, the reason his men would not defy him, besides the fact that he is one of the highest ranking Lurts and could and would send their families to prison, is that he is reported to have the ability to cloud people's mind so that they do not see what is happening if they are within visual contact of him."

Shelby was stunned at such a claim. "Is that true? Can one man control the minds of many men around him? Then how could I get past that mind control?" She did not believe the possibility of such a power, no matter how much Sir Kerrick asserted it to be true. She also was amazed at his fluency in her native tongue.

Kerrick was surprised by her ignorance of the possibility that Lurt Paul was able to probe her mind. His experience had been that Lurt Paul was one of the few Lurts able to work the thoughts of men around him to do his bidding. It was rumored that his father was Alkernian and that was why his ability was heightened. It was also one of the reasons he was given any credence at all in Alker politics.

"It is true. Why you were not controlled is possibly because you have some ability to block probing of the sub-conscious or maybe, because you are a woman, he didn't think you were any danger to him. He is somewhat arrogant in his opinions."

"It's a man thing." Shelby acknowledged.

Sir Kerrick grunted. "Seems to be something women are just as capable of."

"Could I have been sub-consciously controlled and not known it?" She was suddenly fearful of the intrusion she may have experienced.

He smiled at her ignorance. "The fact that you attacked him is one indication that he did not invade your mind. And that you remember him doing the things he did is another. The fact he was bleeding at the end of your attack, is sure proof he was not able to enter your quick mind, Shelby."

"That is not necessarily true, Kerrick."

"Sir Kerrick," he corrected.

"Maybe he wanted me to attack him so that he could be sent somewhere else. And since I am a woman, he may have felt I would do the least damage."

Sir Kerrick considered her point with interest and then a smile came to his full lips. "Well, that was a miscalculated tactic, one he will be sorry for all the days of his life. The scars on his face and the damage done to his manhood will not be fixed with Alkernian technology. Because he failed in his methods here on Aion, I will see to that." Sir Kerrick scratched the back of his neck and ran his hand through his hair. Her conjecture was decisively arresting. Lurt Paul was a conniving snake and he would not put it past him to have contrived such a plot to get back to his homeland on Iritain.

"You may finish your conversation with yourself now, Shelby."

She rolled her eyes.

When she started to leave, he thought to tell her of the changes made while she had been in the sanatorium.

"Your cubicle was gone through and all instruments that could be weapons were confiscated. I don't want you up at my dome complaining that you have been stripped of personal belongings. All the women were dispossessed of sharp objects. None of my men want the possibility of being maimed, and they want to sleep with some kind of assurance their throats will not be cut, or other parts."

He surprised himself and bowed to Shelby with respect when she turned her back and left in a huff. If all the women were like her, it was going to be an interesting tour. Her shapely shoulders were exposed in the wrap that the doctor had put on her after cleaning the dirt and grime from the weeks in the box. The two moons' light shone across her clean skin so that she looked like a faerie from one of his childhood fables. He sighed and watched her seductive sway as she plodded in her bare feet down the path to her private retreat.

The reason he knew that Lurt Paul did not tamper with her mind was because he had slid into the murky, depraved mind of the antagonist and knew his frustration at not getting Shelby to comply, as he had some of the other women, with his sexual perversions. What stunned Kerrick was Shelby had no idea Lurt Paul hurt the women around her to force her to comply with his wicked desires for her. But then again, maybe she did not want to tell him this was the reason she attacked him.

And why would Lurt Paul want to go home now? What if Shelby's innocent assumption was correct about his motives to use the attack as an excuse to be summoned home to Iritain?

Well, that was a long way away and he had enough to reside over right in the here and now.

After the box / Chapter 4

Shelby found her things had indeed been gone through. As she looked around her cubicle, she saw new clothes lay on her bed. She wondered what fabric the garments were made from. Obviously, some of the women had bartered for fabric to make new clothing.

Though she had sneaked into the back of the large women's dome to her private cubicle that did not stop the women from realizing, even at this late hour, she was free from the prison box.

Many of the women came to welcome her back and let her know she had been especially missed. When they filtered in and out of her small domain, they left tokens of appreciation. She lifted up some of the delicate foods and carefully wrapped soaps. She felt overwhelmed with their concern and unchecked tears slipped down her cheeks.

Shelby plopped down on her covered mat and touched the soft fabric of the new apparel. She looked around her cubicle and felt claustrophobic. She needed to get out of the small space, she longed to feel the healing waters and breathe the air among the trees. Quickly, she grabbed a soft towel and some clean, flowing fabric to wrap herself with after her swim. It had been a long while since she had been free to do as she pleased.

She walked past the group at the common room of the dome with some acknowledgement that she heard her name passed between the women in hushed tones. When she opened the tent exit, she noted the many fires that burned this night while people milled around the different areas talking and enjoying the evening.

Shelby turned sharply to follow the trail beside the women's dome that led down to the lake. She picked up speed and nearly ran the last few yards as she came to the lake's edge.

She was antsy. Undressing quickly, she waded into the clean, soothing water that glowed with the two moon's lights. Like a mermaid, she plunged into the refreshing deep, swimming as fast as she could. When she was to the middle of the lake, she dipped deeper into the water and swam as far as she could toward the small fall that emptied into the larger body.

Shelby floated on her back for a while not caring that the cold water was chilling her body to numbness. She thought how strange that she felt so much more alive in the water than in the confined cluster of tents and fires. She looked at the sky and thought about her surroundings, so much like her own planet and yet so different in the way it seemed feral and new. It was a mystical planet with strange creatures and sounds, but she melted into the wildness as if she was part of Aion itself.

She felt something touch her leg and it jolted her out of her relaxed contemplation. She stilled her movements out of caution and looked around. It must have been one of the small fishes she saw at the edge of the lake some days. There was nothing she could see coming back to do her harm. Nonetheless, she decided to return to the bank.

Diving down with underwater strokes she felt her body gain strength. The freedom made her aware of the stark difference of the box. She never wanted to be enclosed in a small space again.

She reached the shore out of breath and her body tingled with cold. Grabbing her wrap, she sat at the edge of the water with her feet in the soft waves. Her hair hung in a tangled mess down to her waist, partially covering the scars of her husband's unpleasant rage when he'd found out she had learned self-defense and weaponry skills.

Why did her mind think of such a thing now, after she sat in this quiet, peaceful setting? Was it because she realized that Sir Kerrick Torrell of Alker could have beaten her when she picked the swords from his guards and struck them? She pondered the idea that he was a self-controlled man, a man who was not reactive to things that would have enraged her husband. Could her enemy be a better man than the one she had married? He would still be her enemy.

Shelby shook her head. She was thinking foolishness. Her hands came to her face and she hid it there for a while. Tears for the second time this day came unbidden. She was emotionally and physically worn. How was she going to get back to Earth and find her three children? They were young adults, but she wanted to know they were safe. She felt she could not go on and be happy without that assurance. She wondered if off-planet communications were something that captives were allowed.

In some ways she realized that her time in the black, empty, soundless box was like a rebirth. She came out of the darkness with a fighting spirit to cut the connection to her womb of despair and fear.

She had wanted to scream at the pain of light in her eyes and the shock of her brain seeing things that she wanted to be different. But, she was alive and endured something that instilled in her a determination to live the last years of her life doing more than being a conquered victim. With every breath in her, she was going to keep her soul strong and fight for her freedom to find her family. Maybe then the nightmares would cease.

She still did not know what happened to her estranged husband, but she had seen him with the conquering Alkernians from her waiting cell. It was the first time in a long time she was actually glad to see him. But, when she called out his name he looked at her with disgust. She was so stunned, she felt a physical hit in her gut and even now felt hopeless rejection as she remembered that day. How betrayed she had felt, how doomed. She knew then; there would be no one to rescue her or her children.

She also realized, as she continued to look at her husband with the Alkers, he was someone she did not know. He looked small next to the bulk of the Alkers and so in awe of their power. In her mind, he sold his birthright for the expedient thing of the moment. He did not want to be a captive so he willing gave up his inheritance, including his children.

How long had they been in this new place? Was it almost a year? Time was different here. The days seemed longer and the nights were too short and filled with terrors that haunted her dreams.

Shelby shifted from her thoughts to the coolness of the night. The small waves lapped silkily over her feet. A chill went up her back. She looked behind her and saw nothing ominous.

She sighed and looked up at the night sky. The stars were bright here, but there was also a rainbow of colors that appeared on some nights. It reminded her of the aurora borealis on her home planet. Tonight she didn't see the colors, yet the calm was contemplative.

A couple of people had a small fire going on the beach, so Shelby walked down further to give them and herself some privacy. Not many in the encampment ventured down to the water at night. Shelby supposed it was because it was nicer around warm fires talking with others than swimming in a cold lake.

She looked back at the couple. They were leaving and she would be alone. Most of the time she was very relaxed and preferred to be unaccompanied when she was here, but tonight she was tense because of talk earlier of large animals in the area. Her imagination did the rest.

The lake itself was fairytale like. There were sheer cliffs of white rock with plant life and flying birds living there. At one end, close to the trailhead a shallow but wide creek cascaded into a small waterfall. If she had more time, she could probably swim all the way across the lake to the other side, but it would take some work.

Protruding on both sides of the lake were rock formations opposite each other that formed what looked like a broken bridge that narrowed the lake and then opened it up again creating the shape of a small waist on a round body. If someone wanted to, they could construct a bridge; though going into a sheer cliff on the other side would be pointless.

When she stood to go back, something jabbed into her hand and made her gasp in pain. At the same time a man down the beach yelled something at her and pointed. She looked behind her but, there was nothing. As she raised her eyes to the forest line, she became aware of a large creature she had never seen before inching its way toward her. The immense animal stalked menacingly toward her.

Her mind raced to contrive some way out of the meal she was sure to become. Her eyes never left the glare of the animal inching closer to her. She had very little faith in her ability to outrun it, so she retreated backwards into the lake.

The water seemed like a vice around her arms and legs, sucking at her body and putting her efforts of escape into slow motion.

She fell back and let out a choked scream. Out of sheer terror she grabbed rocks and jumped back up to brace her body for the animal's blow. It was like slow motion for her as the animal leaped toward her; claws, fangs and hair filled her view and blocked all else out.

The man in the shadows of the trees could not believe how fast the animal was or how it changed color as it moved across the beach. It was no wonder she could not see the creature, it blended so well with its surroundings. It flew at the woman. He could not move fast enough to get his weapon free to kill the creature before it reached her. He watched in dread as the animal landed and pinned her underwater.

Sir Kerrick saw the attack and took aim from where he was; aware he could miss and kill Shelby instead. He shot at it anyway. The animal creature was absolutely motionless, but it was not his doing.

Was the light playing tricks on him? He saw a bloody hand shoot up out of the water and reach for air. As he strode closer, he realized Shelby was stuck under the beast. He pushed with all his might, but the monstrous creature barely budged.

Behind him people appeared at the trailhead and started toward the commotion, but she needed air now. With all his might he pushed hard and almost freed Shelby.

She panicked and thrashed her arms above the water with her face below.

He took a deep breath and gave her a kiss of life.

Air poured into her lungs and she opened her eyes to look into the face of the giver of her life-saving air.

51

She motioned she was all right, but she was not in the clear yet. He heaved again. This time more men were at his side to roll the beast off and pull her to safety.

She coughed and sputtered while she managed to crawl away on her knees and hands.

Kerrick went to her side. She was visibly shaken and had wounds that were bleeding. He quickly wrapped a couple deep gashes with the torn fabric of her shirt.

"What is that thing?" She muttered incredulously. "I could barely see it coming."

"A Bilboa. I have never seen one of its like. I am sure that Doc Orlie will be very impressed with it." Sir Kerrick took a deep breath of relief. He looked at her and then at the beast and wondered how it had been killed as he surmised it was clearly already dead when he shot it.

Others asked if she was alright. She only nodded.

Sir Kerrick noticed her clenched hand held something and opened it to take a closer look. It was only a jagged broken rock.

He looked over at the men dragging the beast out of the water onto higher ground.

"I want to look at it." Shelby was wobbly, but she needed to see the creature was dead before she would rest.

When she got to the animal, she sank down to her knees in the sand before it. The creature stretched out over nine feet. The hair on the animal was beautiful. She reached out and touched the fur. The luxurious softness surprised her.

"You shot the beast." She looked at Kerrick accusingly.

"I wanted to make sure it was dead." He thought she sounded disappointed with him instead of grateful.

"Well you took your sweet time getting it off me."

He started to get irritated when she turned her head toward him and said, "Thank you for the kiss."

"I was not kissing you, Shelby love. When I kiss you, it will take your breath away, not give it." He grinned at her with a raised eyebrow and she rolled her eyes.

"I believe the reason we've not seen many of these creatures is because they are so well camouflaged." He bent down to touch the fur of the animal.

Others stepped up to touch the creature and marveled also at it softness.

"I don't know how you killed it without a weapon, Shelby. Amazing!" One of the young men was inspecting her work. "The blast shot didn't kill it."

Shelby didn't know how to answer.

When the animal jumped, she pushed forward as hard as she could with her body and with the sharp rock she had miraculously discovered in her fall. She shoved it toward the animal, hoping the impact would break its nose. She missed and to her horror, her hands and arms went into its wide open mouth. The sharp edge of the rock lodged back in its throat far enough to lock the jaw and choke it to death with its own blood.

Shelby looked at her arms now and reasoned that she was very lucky to have them still attached to her body. She had punctures and abrasions on both of them, but she was so glad they were not missing.

"It looks like it choked to death, if Sir Kerrick is right about it being dead before he shot it. There doesn't seem to be any other injuries," the young man inspecting decided.

Shelby involuntarily shivered. She was ready to get bandaged up and take something for the pain. Her adrenaline had taken her just about as far as she would go.

The young man looked down the throat of the monster-animal through the bloody fractured bones of its head. He reached forward and gingerly opened the broken jaws of teeth. Just as he surmised, the stone was lodged in the back of its throat, but it was also jammed into its upper palate. The animal's own clamping down had pierced the rock through its breathing cavity into its skull.

She looked up to see others coming down from the trail. She moved gingerly away from the downed beast and fell clumsily back. She was very weak. Awkwardly, she stood up and again fell to the ground with a hard thud, pushing yet another rock into her palm.

A man helped her up while the other men moved past to the beast and gazed at the lump and then back at her. That was enough for Shelby. She turned and tried to leave, but fell once again down onto her hands and knees. She struggled to get up and away from the creature.

She started to stand and unwittingly faltered back off balance yet again. She landed on her rump in a thud that pushed air out of her lungs with an ugly grunt. Once more she was down, humped over and too weak to support herself.

Strong hands helped her up and sturdy arms lifted her barely clad body off her weak legs. She looked up at the welcomed aid and was taken aback by the green eyes of Sir Kerrick.

He wasted little time shouting orders as he held her limp body. He looked young to Shelby, but his facial features held a determination that bordered on intimidating. His hair was free and shoulder length and accentuated his angular jaw.

She started to wiggle out of his firm hold, but he just heaved her up and looked down at her with a quelling look. His long strides took them past her tent and she frowned at him. His full lips were set in a crooked smile.

"You passed my dome." Shelby wondered where he was going. She was getting spacey and had a hard time holding her head up.

"Yes." He did not elaborate any further, but kept his steady stride.

She realized he was heading toward the main dome where meetings for the settlement were held-- connected to it was Doc Orlie's medical quarters. Sir Kerrick kept his private cubicle enclosed in the area also.

Her head was too heavy so she rested against his muscular chest and closed her eyes. She could hear the steady rhythm of his heart beat and was alarmed that he was so human. She preferred to think of him as the enemy, Alkernian, but his concern let in doubt and confusion.

Shelby was surprised when she opened her eyes and there were men standing over her waiting with expectant looks on their faces. Her eyes rolled from one side to the next taking in her surroundings. Wasn't she brought here just a minute ago? She tried to sit up and felt reassuring hands help her.

"There you go. You gave us a good scare, Shelby dear." Doc Orlie patted her shoulder.

"What happened? How did it get light out so quickly?" Then she remembered the beast. "What happened to the creature that attacked me last night? Sir, what...happened?" Shelby was disoriented.

"Doc Orlie, to you, my sweet lady. Before you left here last night, you'd been given a medicine that accelerated your healing from being in the box, but you went beyond the medicine's capacity when your adrenaline excited the healing process. Sir Kerrick was aware that you'd be spent when your instincts to run kicked in. One of the main things Alkernian warrior men know is that any drugs that are administered when the body is weakened, have dangers of their own."

"Did I have a reaction?" She looked skeptical at the doctor.

He just smiled at her and put his arms out and shrugged his shoulders. "I suggest rest for your weary and weakened body." He motioned to the other men to get back to work. He himself wandered over to a counter to examine something there.

Shelby lay back down, her head spinning with confusion just before she dropped into darkness once again.

"No, no, do not worry, Sir Kerrick. She's not bleeding to death, she just fainted. Granted, she does have some serious lesions, but nothing life threatening." Doc Orlie chuckled.

"We do not know if this creature has any kind of toxin in its bite or claws." Sir Kerrick was not leaving until he was sure she was checked thoroughly.

"Yes, yes, but you need to realize that most animals have nasty bites and I will take the necessary precautions to see that she heals well," Doc Orlie reassured him.

"And no scars. She has enough of them. Do that thing that you do for my men."

"Yes, yes, no scars for Shelby." The whole time Doc Orlie talked to him he moved around effortlessly grabbing equipment to work on her cuts.

"Where do you want the animal, Sir Kerrick?" One of the young men of Sir Kerrick's brigade asked.

Doc Orlie answered. "Put it in the second room. Here, I will go with you to lock it in a cooler container."

Sir Kerrick stayed with Shelby, but he could hear Doc Orlie's exclamations of joy and marvel at the creature's size and shape.

He moved closer to the table she was on. There was no bed in this lab, so she was on a hard cold surface and it reminded him of a morgue. A sheet covered most of her body; still it did not actually conceal her womanly shape.

He reached for her hand to make sure it was not cold and she really was alive. He looked down her swathed body and saw the blood of deeper wounds tinting the fabric. He knew that if this was one of his soldiers he would not be as concerned, knowing they could heal. But something inside of him just did not think a woman should bleed. He laughed at himself. Women bled on a regular basis and did not die. She would be fine.

He put his rough hand on her forehead to feel her temperature. He smoothed the strands of hair that clung to her face and neck, and then slid his hand down her arm to the palm of her hand and spread her clenched fingers open. The rock had made a unique impression in the palm of her hand.

The image tugged at the back of his memory. The shape reminded him of something; he just could not remember what. He pondered it for a while; then it hit him. He needed to check the Book of Prophecies to be sure.

~*~

Shelby swung her legs over the edge of the makeshift bed. She took a deep breath and pushed herself off the table. She was a bit dizzy and sore. As she examined the cuts on her arms, she realized she was not in her own clothes. A clean robe replaced her torn clothing.

Doc Orlie's laboratory was neat and open with lighting. Clear tubules of plants grew to the ceiling of the dome. He was obviously interested in the planet's organics as much as the animal life. Shelby watched him and his helpers, noticing they stole looks at her in what they probably thought were non-conspicuous glances.

"I'm going to my own dome to rest," Shelby stated flatly.

Doc Orlie absently nodded when he perused her standing strong at the side of the table.

Behind her Sir Kerrick appeared at the doorway and quietly watched the waif woman take her leave of the services of Doc Orlie. Sir Kerrick crossed his arms over his chest. One of the reasons he was in the lab was to check on the woman and get Doc's Orlie's opinion of why the creature attacked her.

Sir Kerrick saw the surprise in Shelby's face when she realized he stood at the entrance, blocking her way.

"I need to know more about the animal she killed, Doc."

Shelby cringed at the way he insinuated she was in the wrong.

To solidify her suspicion he looked at her and asked, "Why did that Bilboa attack her? That has not happened here before." She understood him perfectly even though he spoke in his own tongue.

"Well, you would have to actually be on the planet for a while before you could really experience the wildness of all the animals and know if they are aggressive now, wouldn't you?" She retorted in her own language, irked by his whole demeanor. Her body stance displayed her disapproval of his insinuation.

These Alkers arrived just a short time ago; the women had been here almost a year. How would he know if it was acting out of character? It was the first time a creature like that had been seen. Basically, it sounded as if he was accusing her of provoking the animal to attack her, almost like it was her fault.

"What were you doing down by the lake last night?"

Shelby just looked at him. He spoke to her in her language now and she was listening to his accent. It was actually pleasing to hear, but it was so contrasting to the way she felt about this arrogant man that she was irritated with herself for even giving him one ounce of humanity.

He looked at Doc Orlie and talked to him in a strange dialect, ignoring the fact she might understand. She started for the door, but Sir Kerrick gave her a pointed look and stood in her way, arms still crossed over his chest.

She looked over at Doc Orlie who seemed irritated. She was not sure what Sir Kerrick said that made him angry, but he dropped his sample study and went to clean his hands, nodding and talking to Kerrick with exaggerated gestures. She didn't comprehend the whole exchange of the banter.

Sir Kerrick smiled condescendingly as if the conversation was something she wouldn't grasp and physically turned her back to the make-shift bed.

Doc Orlie shooed Sir Kerrick away and patted her shoulder to assuage her confusion and soothe her.

"Sir Kerrick insists that you are given a full examination for the up-coming Alker Birth

Celebration. All the women are going to need one, but since you are here he has insisted that I do the blood work and such now."

Shelby went stiff. She looked at Sir Kerrick and scowled at him. He had just a glint of mischievousness in his look that troubled her.

"This is not a good time. I'll come back in a few days, Doc Orlie."

Sir Kerrick affirmed, "Now."

Shelby shook her head 'no' but Sir Kerrick with his bulk, stepped right up into her space and leaned over her, making her step back to get out of the way. He used his intimidating size to prove that she would do his bidding. When she bumped against the table her hands came up to his torso to prevent him from coming any closer.

He stayed in close proximity and waited for Shelby to comply. She pushed futilely at his chest, unable to budge him. He lifted his hands to the edge of the table on either side of her and leaned even closer, bending her to his will.

She pushed again at his chest and looked at him with unmasked surprise.

Beautiful, full lashes covered her deep amber eyes and hosted brown flecks of color around the irises. Her skin was clear of blemishes, except an old scar above her brow. Her pert little nose and cheek bones and jaw line were exquisitely proportioned to create a perfect place for her full lips.

He smiled at her. She went still and frowned.

Doc Orlie reprimanded him in Alkernian and Sir Kerrick said something back to him, then they both looked at her hands on his chest. Doc Orlie said something back to Sir Kerrick in disgust and walked away from them. Sir Kerrick laughed and the rumbling from his chest made her pull her hands back in surprise.

Sir Kerrick lifted her bodily up on the table top and just as quickly Doc Orlie did some kind of scan over Shelby's whole body. It was over in seconds and Shelby was visibly relieved and shocked.

"All done, dear. Now you can assure the other women it will be an easy procedure. I already took a sample of blood while you were sleeping, so you are all done for now."

Shelby pushed hard with her shoulder against the intrusion of Kerrick's bulk and managed to free herself from the stifling predicament. She was livid. She whacked him on his arm as hard as she could and stomped out of the lab.

"I guess you are right about her being just fine, Doc. She seems spirited enough to fight back if need be." He rubbed his arm mockingly.

"You deserved that. Sir Kerrick, may I remind you that she has been through some stressful ordeals that have probably done havoc on her mind and physical well-being? Instead of provoking her, why not try being gentle or nice to her? Hmm? She is always fighting something so when you anger her she bristles." Doc Orlie's hands were fingering the air with expression.

"I have no intention of courting her, Doc. But," he acquiesced, "there are at least five men who have gone to the elder board and put in their request to do so during AB Celebration."

"Then what was that about?" Doc Orlie queried.

"I do not want my orders questioned, by her or anyone else."

"You mean it is a battle of wills? Come, come, Sir Kerrick. You know better than to pit your will against a woman's, do you not? What is there to gain if you belittle and badger a woman to obedience, hmm? To woo a woman now, that is not so easy. To be friends or to be lovers, that is always the goal."

"I told you already, old man, that I do not desire to court her, but I do desire to make her obey."

"So, you want her to be like all the other women and fall at your feet with desire and obedience."

Sir Kerrick snorted with derision. "Obedience is not breaking anyone's will or spirit."

"Maybe with other women it would not take that, but with her you might be wrong. Let me ask you a question."

"You mean another?" Sir Kerrick shot back.

"Yes, yes. Have you ever met a woman that was not attracted to you? Or one who was as strong-willed as you?"

Sir Kerrick looked at Doc Orlie as if he was crazy.

"I thought so." Doc Orlie concluded.

"What has that got to do with her? And yes, there have been women that did not find me attractive."

Doc Orlie looked at him as if he was daft. He swatted the air in dismissal at Sir Kerrick and turned around to get back to work.

"You will have to discover that for yourself, Sir Kerrick Torrell." He shook his finger in the air again, "But, if her will is as strong as yours you might have to kill her to get her to comply; and if her will is stronger than yours..." He paused and looked Sir Kerrick in the face, "she might just kill you."

Sir Kerrick laughed at that and Doc Orlie shook his head and went back to his studies. How could that small woman do such a thing? Immediately, he thought of the animal she just killed with a rock, and then it did not seem so funny or unlikely. She was a wild thing, and had been badly mistreated, so she was not likely to trust anyone, especially anyone of his Alkernian tribe. What he needed to do was to keep her busy. He looked at Doc Orlie and thought of a plan.

"I think, Doctor, that I have the perfect person to send up the mountain with the survey team for your plants and rocks."

The Cubs / Chapter 5

Shelby woke in a strange room with a woodsy masculine allure, lacking the floral smells she was accustomed to in the women's dome or the medical lab. She sat straight up, but as soon as she did she remembered the deep wounds in her arms. She gasped and tried to breathe through the sharp pains that impaired her body. Her head was woozy and she felt grogginess tugging at her brain. Gently, her hand went up to her eyes to soothe them from the throbbing pain. Finally, after some minutes, the sharp twinges quieted to a dull ache that allowed her to move slowly.

Shelby pushed back the lush covers and waited for the ensuing pain to subside again. It took her a moment to comprehend she had no clothes on. She tried to figure out why and where she was, so all this would make sense. Then, she remembered the animal she had killed. How long ago--a few days, a week? She remembered Sir Kerrick ordered her to stay in one of the personal rooms connected to the infirmary dome so Doc Orlie could monitor her over the next few days.

Yes, she was nearing the end of a third day of rest. As for her missing clothes, she remembered they were torn and used for her wounds. Her head cleared and the fog lifted.

When her feet touched the floor she felt soft fur, but very little light in this room made it hard to see the layout of it. If this was a typical Alker room, the light could be turned on by a stroke on the textile wall, but where was the wall? She moved forward in the darkness and bumped into something on the floor. She felt her way around the room until her eyes adjusted enough to see a large, long counter that held personal items. Light came from the counter as soon as she touched the top.

She was startled by her own reflection and it took a moment to calm her racing heart. She chided herself for her idiocy and turned from her image to look around the room.

The bed she came from was huge with fabric hanging around it in a romantic fashion. Most of the Alker rooms, she was told, were lushly appointed with fabric and richness that compared with some of the wealthiest estates on her planet. She went to the end of the counter and spied what she needed, clothing.

She looked until she found a beautifully embroidered white shirt among uniforms and men's shirts that would cover her body nicely. She pulled it over her tousled hair and searched for some kind of belt to keep it in place. She found a dark sash and wrapped it a couple of times around her waist. Her legs and feet were bare, but she could now make her way out of this room to see about the animal she had slain.

She found the doorway to a main hallway that led to a large room, actually the very room she knew to be the meeting room for the Alkers. She recognized where she was now and made her way back to the infirmary room to see the trophy animal.

She checked a couple rooms before she found the beast. She was horrified when she came upon it. It was gutted and lay out in an ungainly way that made her feel like crying.

She had a deep-seated idea that the Bilboa was female and after forcing herself to look more closely at it, she had the sinking feeling it had just given birth to a cub. It was late, but she needed to go back to the beach and see if she was right.

She walked right past some men who where stationed at the front of Sir Kerrick's dome. They were in deep conversation around the fire and when she looked up into the night sky she could tell it was late. Probably one of the reasons she was able to slip by them unnoticed, or at least she thought so.

He noticed the waif slide by his men and he was disturbed by their ineptitude. That would be dealt with. Right now he wanted to know what she was up to. He just happened to glance back at the compound when he noticed the woman's exit from the dome. She was given a heavy dose of medicine and Doc Orlie assured him she would be out for hours. That obviously was not the result.

He was too far away on the rocks above to get down to her immediately, but he watched for a while to ascertain where she might be headed. It looked to him like she stumbled. He put his eye-glass up to take a closer look at her.

She blended with the reflection of the moonlights off the pale rocks in his white shirt. He smiled in spite of himself. She was wearing one of his ceremony shirts tied with a belt like a dress. Her hair was loose from its perpetual braid and flowed around her in constant movement so that the whole effect of her stealth was lost. He would make sure from now on that she did not have bands that bound her hair and cooperated with her covert activities.

Into the women's dome she went. He watched, not believing for one moment she was done. Just when he thought he was wrong, he sighted her movements down the trail to the lake. His reaction was swift and fleet. He was down the rock wall and to the beginning of the trail before she made it to the end of the dark, beach trail.

He could not imagine what she was doing, but interrogating her would not yield one thing. He needed to see for himself. He watched her closely and glimpsed a flash of metal. The cloud cover only let shards of moonlight through, yet when it did it was enough to see her. Why was she traipsing around in the middle of the night after she had been attacked by an animal? Was she looking to be attacked again? Then it struck him. She was looking for another animal. Why?

He listened as she made noises. It was a poor mimic of the animal she had killed, but she kept calling. The woman was stupid fearless. He should have her beaten and chained. She never did as she was expected and certainly did not care what she was told if she thought otherwise. He almost moved forward except from the corner of his eye he caught a movement in the brush at the edge of the trees.

At that moment, clouds parted enough to send moonlight down on Shelby. She turned toward the trees and stuck the long blade in the sand before her, hands clasped to the handle seemingly for balance. She waited with her head down, he was sure, listening.

Slowly, a smaller version of the animal she killed made its way to the edge of the forested front. It sat there and she made another mewing sound to draw it out further. She looked up and it immediately turned away and loped back into the forest. To Sir Kerrick's surprise Shelby jumped up to go after it. He pulled his knife out and followed her in pursuit. This was crazy!

He heard Shelby whoop the animal call; the one he now remembered hearing before it attacked her. Another call echoed distinctly different from hers and she was off in that direction. He finally saw her running swiftly through the woods. He caught sight of the animal yards ahead of her blending more and more into the surrounding. Did she think she could outrun it?

He caught up to her and she gasped with alarm at the sight of him.

"What are you doing here?" She hissed at him in a squatted position. Her eyes were luminous, looking like water that glowed.

He stood over her and looked down at her upturned face. "The more appropriate question is what are you doing here?" She looked toward the path of the vanishing animal.

Completely ignoring his question she chided him more. "No wonder it ran. I could have captured the creature without hurting it, now I'll have to hunt it down and risk possibly injuring it. You should not have followed me."

Sir Kerrick knelt down and surveyed her appearance. She was breathing with difficulty and her wounds seeped blood through the white sleeves of his shirt.

"You are going to attract all kinds of unwanted beasts if you stay in this forest bleeding. Come with me. You need to get some…"

"No. I'm going to get that animal tonight. It won't last long alone in this forest. It's a cub of the Bilboa I killed. There may be more. Either help me, or let me alone."

"You will do as I say." He growled with complete conviction. How had she gotten another weapon? Was it only days since she had been caged and now she was running through the deep woods disregarding the real danger of being eaten by one of the nocturnal creatures? He should have left her in the box. She was a danger to herself!

So quickly did she hit him that he was completely knocked over, even as he grabbed for her. When he righted himself, she was fleeing deeper into the woods after her quarry.

He swore under his breath and paced after her. It was going to be a long night.

Shelby accidentally spotted a paw print on a leaf that glinted in the moonlight. With luck, she might wear the animal out to the point of it turning to challenge her. She really wanted it alive. With even more fortune, it might even lead her to its den and other litter cubs that might be alive.

She felt such an urgency to protect this cub that she was facing her fears of the ominous woods and putting herself in grave danger at the same time. She probably was putting the cub in danger as well, leaving a trail of her blood for other animals to follow.

She heard noise behind her and positioned herself for a quick response. Her pulse beat loud in her ears. She sniffed to smell what was coming at her and waited. Her fear made her want to run.

She saw hands before it registered---Sir Kerrick was the one bumbling through the bushes toward her. She did not want to be stopped, so she moved on toward her prey; trying to discover the animal before it escaped her.

She halted at the edge of a deep, rocky ravine that created a steep gully with trees spaced widely apart. Shelby was not sure she would find the creature before sunup. Her true fear was that she would not be able to hunt the creature in daylight. She was sure it was nocturnal and would bury itself deep in the planet before light.

She heard a familiar noise ahead of her. She crept closer and realized that the noise echoed off the other side of the rocky gulch. With minimal effort she pushed herself along the ground and peered up and down the walls of the gorge. There!

Shelby could not believe her fortune in finding the opening to what she hoped was the lair. She would wait now and let the animal think it was safe.

When he noticed her, the white shirt was no longer pristine, but covered in leaves and dirt. She had accumulated debris in her passage to this place and now lay prostrate on the ground sleeping in a blanket of camouflage, barely discernable except for the small amount of leg exposed.

He moved beside her and was seriously unnerved when he looked into her muddied face. Her eyes spoke a warning and directed his gaze toward a small opening across the ravine. She was so unexpectedly intense that his senses were heightened to a predatory level. He had found his quarry, and now he was experiencing the thrill of anticipating her find. His adrenaline still surged from the romp through the deep night forest.

He looked at Shelby, or whoever she was at this moment, and wondered how she was so adept in tracking any animal in this unknown land. She slowly turned her head to smile at him with contrasting white teeth out of a face smeared with mud and debris and leaves tangled in her unkempt hair. How could she look so dangerous and appealing at the same time? They waited.

The first rays of morning glimmered on the tips of the ancient trees and the dew on the scarce underbrush reflected the hint of seldom penetrated light. The forest turned slowly from one sound to the first sounds of early morning. The crescendo of animal movements and birds came alive and so did Shelby.

He must have dozed because he did not hear her get up. He watched her move slowly toward the cave and bring out a net she had apparently scavenged. He started to move, but she glared at him and signaled for him to stay where he was. He was not having any of that. He saw her roll her eyes and shake her head. He smiled at her distress.

Shelby made her way down the gorge. At first Kerrick was certain she was going to enter the den, but she motioned above and he understood her intent. She climbed above the opening of the den and held her netting out, ready to catch the fleeing animal.

She mewed a forlorn sound and almost immediately a reply came from within the cave. She made no more sounds and just waited. The small creature crept cautiously as another animal of similar markings and size followed it out of the lair. Still Shelby waited.

With alarm Sir Kerrick saw a completely different kind of animal stalk behind Shelby. He knew she was not aware of its presence; she was intent on the small cubs and anticipating their capture.

He whipped his large knife at the creature. His movement caught her and the cubs' attention. She tossed the net in her hands trying to use the diversion to her advantage.

She realized the stalking animal was close as she leaped and turned in mid-air to view it. A groan of anguish came from her as she landed hard on her side. The larger animal was almost on top of her. The cubs tried to go one way and Shelby rolled another.

To Sir Kerrick's dismay the beast was still after Shelby, even with a knife in its thick neck. By his cursory glance, both cubs struggled to get out of the tangle of netting. His main concern, however, was the black-skinned animal threatening Shelby.

Her arm was bleeding; the gluing of her previous wound had given way from the force of her fall. The animal swiped at her. He ran at it to distract it from its intent, but he had nothing to stop the animal with.

Shelby's arms were out from her body; blood ran down one hand and dripped off her fingertip. The animal's intent was to kill the wounded woman. Sir Kerrick jumped up to push the knife deeper, but the beast batted him away and he went flying onto his back with a loud thud.

The animal's attention was distracted long enough for Shelby to run back to her makeshift bed to retrieve her forgotten blade. The animal pursued after her. She fell to her knees on the ground and searched for the sword with determination.

Sir Kerrick recovered quickly and yelled after the animal, determined to use his bare hands to tear it apart if necessary. For a second, the terrorizing beast stopped and growled at him. It was long enough for Sir Kerrick to witness Shelby fly at the creature from her spot. He thought she had jumped off-course; instead she was using the momentum of the beast's movement to help cut off its head.

She struck it with such force that the blade flew out of her hands and she rolled over the top of the creature and kept flying down the rocky side of the ravine. She finally came to a stop at the base of a larger outcropping of rock.

The preying animal was decapitated and very dead by the hands of his warrior nymph, but she lay in a heap; and the cubs, still tangled in her net, were wailing at the top of their lungs, calling for help. He did not want to be here when the larger beasts of the forest arrived.

He quickly retrieved her blade and went to her side, vowing to himself he would never be caught again without a real weapon. He lifted her up and to his amazement she whimpered he had to save the cubs.

"We need to get out of here! You are bleeding and bringing every living, breathing, carnivorous animal here."

"We need to save those cubs!" She was crying and he swore under his breath. He lifted her to her feet and would have left, but she shook her head and hit him hard on the chest, "Save them, Kerrick!" She was so weak that she fell back to the ground when he let go of her.

The animals snarled and hissed at him while he managed to wrap them more tightly in the netting they tangled themselves into. But the trick was to get them free from the undergrowth of the forest. He used his knife, which he mused to himself, was of little value in killing any foe, and cut away the offending obstacles.

They were heavy, but he dragged them back to Shelby and helped her to her feet. He wondered how he was going to get all of them back to camp, when he heard more noise coming toward them.

"This just gets better and better." He looked at the dread in Shelby's eyes and took her face into his hands. "Woman, we will get home, have no fear."

Hours later, Shelby woke to find herself ensconced in the very same bed and the very same room she had been in before.

At first she thought she was dreaming, but the way her head spun made her believe she probably had a concussion from the fall down the ravine. It was lighter in the room than before. The evening rays of light seemed to scatter across the floor and bounce around the room walls.

She ached all over her body so she made an attempt to examine her arms and legs for damage. She was cleaned up and wearing a woman's nightshirt. She remembered the mirror and decided to take a better look at her injuries.

Getting there was harder than the last time. A huge bruise on her leg hurt so badly she limped more than walked to the counter. Her reflection revealed she was roughly battered. She had a lump on her forehead, a black eye and scratches on her neck and face. She looked at the gashes on her arms and was relieved to see they were once again glued back together. She raised her gown, taking care she didn't create more pain, and turned her back to the reflection to peer over her shoulder at her back and down her legs. She was bruised and the mirror reflected a couple new scratches. She was a mess.

Sir Kerrick watched as she examined her body in front of the mirror and made faces. She was obviously unaware of his presence and he smiled at the fact she was totally preoccupied with such a womanly action.

Doc Orlie insisted she stay near the lab so he could monitor her wounds without trekking all the way down the path to the women's dome. Sir Kerrick only agreed so he could keep a closer eye on her and keep her out of mischief.

Tonight he needed to rest and since she was in his bed, he sat in his chair for a while. Admittedly, he rarely slept in his bed because of his propensity to sleep in short naps or a few hours at a time. It was part of his military training and something that was hard to change.

He continued to watch from his chair as she sat back against the counter and lowered her head. Her loose hair fell over her shoulders and shielded her face from view, but her hand came up to move it back and Sir Kerrick heard her wince. Apparently, her shoulder hurt as well.

He watched her stand up straight, take a deep breath and check her neck movement out. With that done, she moved slowly to his clothes again and looked through the ensemble of uniforms and casual clothing. She found another shirt the same color of soft amber as her eyes and carried it draped over her arm to the bed. She sat down on the bed and must have decided against putting it on because she groaned in pain when she lifted her arms just a little. She opted instead to scoot back on the bed and pull the covers back over her. A few minutes later, she was sleeping again according to her soft sighs.

Kerrick was puzzled by his pleasure in seeing her so unaware of his presence. He knew other women who preened to be noticed, but Shelby rarely took a concerned look at what she presented to the men of his company, or at least he had thought so.

The thought occurred to him that she knew exactly was she was presenting, her whole attire down-played any beauty that she possessed. Her clothes were always loose and heavy. Her face was never completely clean, nor her hands. She never let her hair down or wore any jewelry or feminine clothing at all. And yet, she still attracted attention.

Several of his men made attempts to get her approval. She was either stupid about their desire, which he doubted, or she ignored them with the sole purpose of discouraging them.

He got up from his chair and crawled over the bed to peer down at her relaxed face. By all rights, she should not have been able to get up off the bed yet, let alone be awake. Doc Orlie assured him she had been given a sleeping derivative that would knock any one of his men out for a full night.

It was late in the evening and he had gotten very little sleep in the last two days. He slipped his garb off and lay back on the bed. She was cocooned in all the covers, but he was still more comfortable stretched out than sitting up. He lay awake for a while thinking about how Shelby was so different from the other women in her desire and her aptitude.

She was evidently trained to hunt, and use weapons. Was she one of the warrior women he had heard about on her planet? They were supposed to be spiritual soldiers trained to protect their leaders and religious rights. Or was she just athletic enough to be able to protect and defend herself out of instinct? He doubted she would answer him directly, but he would question her about her training.

He rolled to his side and faced her back. He put his arm around her and pulled her up against his body. She groaned and adjusted herself and then settled back into a deep sleep.

He took a deep breath and could smell the soap that Toreese used to clean the grime off her body and out of her hair. She had taken it upon herself to see Shelby was nursed back to health. She was a bossy woman and she reminded Kerrick of his aunt.

And now it was night again and in the dark he remembered her bruised and scratched body and her womanly shape. He remembered her flying through the air and beheading the black animal and her hair spread out like a fan. He thought about her pooling tawny eyes and the fear she had in them for the cubs. His mind would not let go of the way she smiled at him when she was near her goal of catching the cubs.

He inhaled her scent and put his face into her freshly washed hair. He needed to rest, but his body was reacting to the nearness of her warm one. He wondered if she was involved with one of his men or had been. Did she hold any feelings of desire for one of his men, or as rumored, for one of the women? He seriously doubted she liked women in a sexual manner because of the way she acted when she was accused of the preference.

He remembered her calling for one of the recruited Earth men to help her when she was caged for transport. Had that woman actually been Shelby? She was beautiful and regal. Why did he not remember that was her? No. This was something he could see through her minds' eye. Something that held the same passion she felt for the cubs; a desperation he could sense and with his mind he had somehow seen deeper into her being than he realized.

That was how it happened to him. Sometimes he could access someone's dream or see deep into their pain or joy. Usually he had a hard time knowing how he knew some things, but he was aware that he absorbed some kind of energy from people that allowed him to know details about their lives they did not tell him.

Shelby was not easy to read. Even now as he lay next to her he wondered why he could. He had tried before, but had been unsuccessful in knowing her thoughts or plans. The only other people who really knew he could do such a thing were his mother and Doc Orlie.

In his family, no men that he knew of could read minds or enter dreams. Most people would not want to wander in another's mind anyway. It is a muddled mishmash in people's thoughts and Kerrick had to train his mind to acquire only certain kinds of details and thoughts. It was something he purposely did all the time.

He was thirty when he realized for sure that his mind ran along the same line as his mother's, and that she had purposefully and subtly educated him for the possibility of such ability.

His mind finally slowed enough to realize that Shelby stirred next to him. She rolled over and rubbed her face unwittingly against his bare chest and sighed. She started talking, but he realized she was still sleeping. Her conversation made no sense to him, but she seemed engaged in scolding someone. Her face tilted up when she finished and he inspected it. She was asleep.

She had a purple eye and the knot on her forehead was going down. Her skin was remarkably clear in spite of the discoloration around her eye. Her nose was small and gently curved up and accentuated her high cheekbones. Her jaw was less defined above a long neck. Her lips were naturally deep pink and temptingly full, perfect for kissing.

His head lowered slowly and purposely brushed his nose on hers just before he pressed his lips on her soft mouth. She groaned and he continued to kiss her moving his hand through the blankets to caress her back. But her sound changed to a whimper of pain and he realized his mistake. He stilled for a moment and felt her body relax. He kissed her forehead and mentally chided himself for taking advantage of her.

Her soft even breathing soothed his mind and let him think of the cubs she was so set on retrieving. She was determined to save the little beasts. He suddenly knew he should check on them. He was loath to leave her soft curves, but he wanted to see

81

what Doc Orlie had discovered about the creatures and he needed to resist temptation.

First Time Slip / Chapter 6

Shelby lay back against the tree. She felt safe here, near the grove of her secret place. She inhaled a deep breath and felt her body gain strength and calm. One of the things she required for her well-being was solitude. The encampment teamed with people and noise; the hum of daily living and nights of fires and stories. She was not adverse to the din of life, just the constant intrusion of people wanting or needing her here or there. She tired of the strict demands Sir Kerrick saddled her with. She was constantly watched as if someone expected her to disappear.

Shelby looked at the flute in her hand. She decorated it with engraving, but credit for the sound it produced could only be given to the skilled hand that fashioned it from the wood found on this planet. One of the Alker men traded her for a haircut.

She put it to her lips and worked on a melody. Shelby heard faint howls and she shook her head. The cubs could hear her. She didn't play loud and it disturbed her they could hear that well so far away. She wondered if other animals in the area could also. The smile slipped from her face and she listened for the subtle sounds she heard before she played the flute.

All seemed fine. But, she needed to remember this area was only safe because it was occupied by Alker men. They were fierce in their ability to protect the compound from unwanted attacks now. Shelby also suspected that since her unfortunate assault from the cubs' parent, their protocol increased to include a wider span of area.

Shelby heard soft sounds approach her direction and held her breath, her body rigid. A set of wide, green eyes and furry ears twitched in the shadows before the large paws of her cub were seen. It made its way to Shelby with swift motion. Touching it did not take away the shock of seeing it.

"How did you get out of your confine or out of the compound without being seen?" Shelby stroked the creature and looked for its sibling. She could sense she was near, but neither of them should have got to her this fast, or at all for that matter. They were kept in an enclosed and secured area a long way away from here. In less than a minute, they traversed over very rough terrain and the distance of almost two miles. They must have gotten free and been closer than she thought.

The female didn't come out of hiding, but she mewed and Shelby did not try to coax her out. It would be one less thing she would have to teach the cubs before they would be able to live in the wild again.

She needed to take them hunting. She looked at the cub who studied her with intelligent eyes. The female poked her head out just enough to see her.

"Let's go hunting. You need to learn sooner than later." To her sheer delight they both trotted obediently beside her when she turned into the forest.

Later, she secured the cubs in their makeshift den and reluctantly made her way past the main dorm quarters to where Sir Kerrick held meetings with delegated leaders and conducted daily business. She actually liked the room because books of information and maps of the planet were kept there.

When she paused by the opening, Sir Kerrick, Doc Orlie, Commander Rockdurgh and Talig stared at her as if she was a devil with horns.

"Where have you been?" Sir Kerrick's voiced boomed at her. "Your cubs disappeared and men are out looking for you, again." Sir Kerrick strode toward her with anger emanating from him.

"I was..."

Before she could finish her statement he reached for her arm, but she jerked away from him. He still managed to snag her and she felt stunned as she was tugged and pulled toward the men. Only, he did not stop there. He continued on toward his own quarters and Shelby could only assume he was going to do harm to her.

"Kerrick, you need to stop yanking me around!" She said this as he literally thrust her into his room onto his bed.

He stood with his hands on his hips seething, while his jaw worked back and forth.

She quickly stood back up at the foot of the bed with her hands fisted at her side. He did not feel one punch she had landed on his person. He was built like a stone, but she still did not understand his anger.

"I was within the prescribed area and still you are angry. What is your problem?" Shelby gritted through clenched teeth.

"Being gone for two days is my problem. You come waltzing into my dome like you have been here the whole time while my men and most of the women are out searching for you and those stupid cubs." He was so livid that Shelby was more afraid than confused.

"Kerrick, I have been gone for…did you say two days?" She was so alarmed she felt the blood rush out of her head and she plopped back on the bed for safety.

Sir Kerrick just looked at her not expecting her reaction at all. He saw her face go ashen, but the likelihood of her pretending was more probable than not.

He reached down and pulled her up to look at her face. She did look shaken.

"It was only hours for me, Kerrick." Tears rimmed her eyes as testimony to the sudden fear she felt. The way she said it alarmed him more than anything.

He pulled her under his arm and quickly escorted her toward the medical ward.

Passing the men he summoned Doc Orlie to the lab. He felt her slide down toward the ground. Much to her dismay, he lifted her up and carried her the rest of the way, depositing her once again on the cold metal surface of the table.

"I did all the tests and she seems to be in perfect health. I also gave her a sedative and that seems to have quieted her." Doc Orlie talked in hushed tones so Shelby would not hear them.

"How could she not know it was days?" Commander Rockdurgh's disbelief was evident.

"Maybe it wasn't for her. That is for us to figure out before something worse happens to anyone else." Doc Orlie insisted.

"She seems to be accident prone." Commander Rockdurgh restated.

"No, more like targeted." Sir Kerrick was resolute.

"I agree." Doc Orlie nodded thoughtfully.

"Run tests again." Sir Kerrick ordered. "I want a reason for her not knowing, just in case it could be true and she is not playing us for fools."

"The trouble with men is that they are always fools," Shelby piped up through her groggy state. "And you Kerrick are as thick as a tree."

He walked back over to her bedside and looked down at her. He leaned next to her ear and whispered so only she could hear, "I will take that as a compliment. And it is Sir Kerrick." And he brushed her ear with his lips.

Shelby blushed because the way he said it was so sexually suggestive it sent shivers up and down her spine. She felt as if she was the foolish one. Kerrick was no fool, nor did he ever act like one.

Sir Kerrick noticed her face blush. He knew she understood his innuendo and he chided himself for finding pleasure in teasing her even in her distressed state.

"I want all the women marked, even Shelby."

Her head snapped at him with shock. "You are going to mar all the women just because of me?"

Doc Orlie understood her astonishment and wanted Sir Kerrick to clarify the misunderstanding, but Sir Kerrick only smiled, enjoying her ignorance.

He scowled at his godson as only a substitute father could do.

"And you wonder why the sedatives I give her never stay in her system long enough. If you constantly arouse fear in her she will never get relaxed."

Sir Kerrick turned around, but there was a sparkle in his eyes. He knew a way to relax her.

Shelby was relieved to hear the marker would be put under her skin and would not mar or scar. It was to keep the whereabouts of individuals known and it was minuscule. Still, she believed it was unnecessary. She was going to take that up with Kerrick as soon as she was up to it. That was her last thought just before Doc Orlie shot her with something a little stronger and she was out.

Warm pool / Chapter 7

She did not want to go up the ramp-like trail to the Meeting Dome. As it was, she was summoned by Sir Kerrick as soon as she returned from the excursion to retrieve samples for Doc Orlie. All day she crawled over fallen trees and pushed through bushes and trudged up hills and down and now she was tired. It was getting late and she wanted to escape to seclusion and sleep.

She assured the sentry she would go up to the dome as soon as she unloaded her personal belongings, but he held vigil until she actually started up the path. She did not get to go for her usual nightly swim nor was she allowed to change out of her work clothes.

One of the reasons she did not want to go to the Meeting Dome was she had not yet cataloged the plants for Doc Orlie and she needed to do that before she could actually give a complete report. She just did not have time to do so since her return today. Plus, she was avoiding Sir Kerrick at all costs. He constantly baited her and riled her at every turn.

Sir Kerrick's own personal quarters were attached to the Meeting Dome used as the conference room. The other side housed Doc Orlie and his assistants' area for medical and biological aspects of studying the planet.

Shelby walked to the top of the ramp and unexpectedly came upon a group of men washing their bodies, naked from the waist up, at the wash fountain constructed by the ingenuity of the Alkers. It startled her enough to make her stop for a moment. She did not know whether to proceed to Sir Kerrick's office or to retreat.

She didn't see Kerrick among the men, but he called to her to wait when she started to turn away. She was forced to look once again at the beautiful, wet bodies of the half-clad men. Shelby surmised that the warriors must have just finished their routine drills. She swallowed and tried to look only at the faces of the men, but when Kerrick came into view that didn't seem a better option either.

He was dripping wet and glistening drops slipped down his chest to his abdomen. Her eyes followed some of the droplets as they reached his waist band. She realized she was distracted when she looked into Kerrick's face and he had a surprised, yet teasing smirk on his face. She tried not to blush, but it was too late.

He saw her inquisitiveness and now he knew she was not as unaffected as she pretended to be.

Shelby closed her eyes briefly and looked away trying to remember why she was here.

"Your company returned early today. Follow me. I am finished here." His hand motioned her to the entrance of the Meeting Dome. He led the way assuming she would follow.

She hesitated before she conceded to tag along behind him. She glanced over at the rest of the men and noticed one or two of them act as if they were unaware of her presence, but she felt them observing her just the same. She looked at Kerrick's retreating back and marveled at how so many bulges could fit on a back. He looked very strong and confident as he walked into the dome.

At the entrance he stopped and looked back at her and held the flap open for her to enter under his arm.

Once she entered the antechamber, it led to the left or right; the left side was the main meeting hall, to the right led into the lab. She assumed they would go right, but that was not the case. He continued leading her through the meeting room into the antechamber that led to his private quarters.

Shelby was uncertain whether she wanted to go any further, so she waited at the entrance.

"Come in, Shelby. I need to get a clean shirt."

He said it so matter-of-factly that she felt silly for being hesitant.

"Maybe you can just tell me what you want and I can get out of your way."

"You are not in my way, Shelby love. There is a seat over there." He pointed to one of two chairs by a window overlooking the cliff into the settlement below. He went to the other side of the room and retrieved a loose-flowing shirt from his assortment of clothes. She looked like she was ready to bolt and he was beginning to enjoy making her uncomfortable.

She did not have time to clean up or change and he still liked the way she looked. He studied her for a few moments as she looked at the view overlooking the dome-village below. Her long, thick braid, usually hidden under a scarf, fascinated him, but he wanted to snatch the tie away and let her hair loose. It accentuated a small waist she kept hidden in layers and ended right where her hips flared into womanly curves. Her form was very comely, yet she went to great pains to keep covered from neck to feet. He moved to where she was and started to speak.

Shelby startled to awareness and faced him. He was really close to her. Usually she could sense or hear the approach of someone, but Kerrick seemed able to bypass her defenses. She was annoyed he was so close and she'd not heard him approach. She wondered if he was just good at being quiet or if her guard was down.

"Are you hungry, Shelby?" He looked down into her face and saw uncertainty there.

"Come, Shelby, I am dining in the back by the water hole."

They went to the back corner of his quarters and through a doorway that led to a private outdoor area. She looked up the lush bank and saw a small water chute fall into a pool area which trickled out and under the rest of the meeting hall annex of the dome. She could see a door, other than the one they came in by, that exited from the main dome. She was curiously aware this was a hidden grove for the Alkers.

Kerrick made his way to a sitting area and she followed wondering what he was up to. She was suspicious of the reason he had summoned her.

He motioned for her to sit, but she crossed her arms and made a face at him twisting her mouth. "I need to get the cataloging done for Doc Orlie and I have not unpacked from the trek up the mountain this week."

Kerrick annoyingly nodded his head trying to keep a smirk off his face. His hand went a couple of times up to rub his mouth and chin, but Shelby could see he was amused for some reason.

"What?" She tried to prod him verbally to stop.

"Shelby, sit down," he soothed. It was a firm command.

She just wanted him to tell her why she was here. Images of water dripping off his sculptured torso replayed in her mind; so sitting down to face him made her nerves jingle.

She relented and sat down next to him on the bench. They had a perfect view of the small pool and the soothing sound of running water; one of the reasons she went for nightly swims. One of the few women that worked with the Alker cooks brought in a tray of covered food and set it down on the table beside Kerrick. She and another woman returned a couple times with more food and drink. When they did not return after a few minutes, Kerrick spoke.

"I have several things to speak with you about." He looked at her and waited for her to look at him. He smiled at her. The smudge on her face reminded him of the kind of free-spirit she truly was. He worked his smile down and pointed to his own face.

"You have some dirt right there on your face."

She tried to wipe it away. He kept shaking his head 'no' when she looked at him for confirmation. After a couple tries, she stood up and went to the side of the pool.

"What else? Surely you did not call me up here to help me clean up." She was reaching for the water and realized it was warmer than the lake, a lot warmer. At the same time, Kerrick came up behind her and nudged her, clothes and all, into the water.

She was totally caught by surprise and came up out of the water sputtering. When she looked at Kerrick kneeling by the pool laughing as she wiped water out of her face, she asked the obvious question.

"Did I really have a smudge on my nose?" She splashed water toward him. He dodged it, still laughing at her.

"Yes. There are soaps by the bush over there." He pointed to a fern that adorned the edge of the pool. "I'll be back in about an hour; I have a meeting to go to. I thought you might like a warm swim tonight and this way, I know you will not be attacked by an animal. I have better things to do than carry you around half dead and bleeding." He pointed again to her clothes. "I usually bathe without garments on. You can do the same if you please."

"I don't have clothes to change into thanks to your stupid prank." She did not make any move to get out of the bath water or take her clothes off. He stood up and pulled his shirt over his head and laid it over the seat.

"I will leave this for you. I know you like my shirts." He smiled and winked at her. "When you have finished, I will be back. If not, you need to wait. You will dine here tonight, so do not go down to the women's barracks until I speak with you."

Shelby tried her hardest to keep her eyes on his face, but as handsome as it was it was not necessarily a better alternative to looking at his well defined chest and stomach muscles. She mentally chided herself. He was years younger than she was, as were most of the men, and he was just too pretty for her to feel comfortable around.

He finally turned and left after mumbling something to himself about her stubbornness. She breathed a sigh of relief. She took her wet clothes off and threw them to a protruding stone and soaked for a bit in the Alker-made bathing pool.

The soaps she used she recognized as Sir Kerrick's scent. When she smelled it, she could clearly see his face and a quirky, teasing smile. She wondered if he was aware of his sexual allure to women, to her. She was sure he was confident he had enough to serve him well, but she did question if he was even concerned about his appeal to women. He seemed uncontrived about his looks or magnetism.

She missed the cool of the lake, but the warm pool actually soothed her sore muscles and lesions from the animal attack. She decided to get out and taste some of the food left on the table. She was getting hungry.

She slipped on the shirt Kerrick left and wrung out her own dripping clothes, hoping the boots would dry before tomorrow. The Alker technology in the domes was truly remarkable, including sound proofing between cubicles and doorways. The lights were controlled by a simple touch to the wall of the dome and the heat source looked like a small rock, able to go from warm to extreme heats. They even carried these in their packs up the mountains. She would try to dry her boots near one of those instead of the open fire.

Though she was tempted to exit the other door out of curiosity, Shelby walked into the room she had passed through to the pool. She could smell a delicious aroma as she made her way through Kerrick's private quarters and looked around for the source of temptation, but couldn't see anything there, so she continued for the exit. Holding her wet clothes out in front of her, she attempted to leave, but was stopped by Kerrick's personal confidant and sentry, Commander Rockdurgh. He was a huge man and if she had not had personal dealings with him already and knew him to be a calm and mildly tempered man, she could easily have been intimidated by his demeanor now. He stood in her way and would not budge.

"You have been expressly commanded by Sir Kerrick to remain within his quarters until he returns."

Shelby just ignored him and tried to get by the lug. She got nowhere. He finally had enough of matching her moves and physically pushed her back into the room.

"Stay," he warned her.

She was so perturbed that she threw her wet clothes on the floor in a huff and crossed her arms under her breasts. She watched as he purposefully closed the doorway and sealed it. She could no longer see where the doorway was, yet she tried to touch it with her hand. It was as if the exit had never been there. The wall was solid.

She thought for a moment and decided to go out the other doorway in the courtyard by the pool. She quickly moved to the other door only to see it also disappear as the other one had. The only doorway now visible was the one that led back to the private quarters of Kerrick's. She growled.

It took her a while to calm down enough to resign to Kerrick's heavy-handed guarding. He obviously did not expect her to obey his command and wanted her kept confined. She went to the window and looked down at the camp below. It was getting dark now and some of the fires glowed. She knew there would be food down there cooking over the open fires and the women would be gossiping about the day. She could only wonder what they would say about her being up here. She groaned.

For the next hour or so, she paced and went through Kerrick's personal things and jumbled up the room, just to be obnoxious. Finally, she sat down at the foot of the bed and looked around at the untidiness. She could not stand it; she got back up and straightened everything up and put things back in order.

She was frustrated and tired now and it was clearly longer than an hour that she had been cooped up in this cubicle.

She sat down at the foot of the bed and surveyed the room in general. It was the same handsome room with rich fabrics and ornate furnishings she had been in before. The high ceiling and hung fabrics filled the area with a romantic quality. There was a long counter made of natural materials from the area that held Kerrick's personal things on top, such as a brush and a few miscellaneous items. In the wardrobe hung uniforms and accessories for his military dress, along with everyday items like the shirt she now wore.

She lifted a corner of the bed cover over her legs and snuggled in to rest. She tried to keep her eyes open and wait for the door to appear again, but she melted away in exhaustion with the smell of Kerrick permeating from the blankets and the shirt she wore.

He found her curled at the end of his bed sleeping peacefully. He had more food sent in about two hours after he left, to hopefully appease her for keeping her confined, but it looked like she had not tasted a thing.

He still had work to do that he normally would do at his desk, but he was hungry and so his first task was to eat. He debated whether to wake her or just eat alone.

He leaned over her to move hair away from her face and take a closer look. She seemed so relaxed and innocent in deep sleep. He decided to let her rest longer. He needed to be at work tonight, so he decided she could sleep until he got back in the early morning.

He touched her face and felt the softness of her skin. He was mesmerized by her loveliness. All the women here were fine-looking and beautiful, but something about her captivated him. She embodied a strength and natural allure that kept him intrigued. He wondered what it would be like to have Shelby desire him and kiss him with passion he knew she was capable of.

He lifted a lock of her thick hair to feel the weight of it. She moved and the curls slipped through his hand like silk. It was then that he noticed the bare shoulder where the over-large shirt gaped. It begged to be kissed. The bed-covering slid back from her fidgeting and exposed a shapely leg as well as cleavage.

His shirt looked so good on her he made a mental note to give this one to her and see that her clothes were exchanged for more feminine ones as soon as possible. He took another long look and thought better of waking her up.

He watched her as he ate and wondered what it would be like to sleep so deeply and not wake, even when the smell of food wafted in the air.

She felt her stomach rumble and the aroma of food was so real her eyes popped open. She wasn't dreaming. There was food close by. She threw back the covers and stretched. Shelby was famished and she remembered she was still in Kerrick's dome waiting for his return. She sat up and to her surprise he sat at the small, low table with food in front of him.

He stopped eating and watched her.

She realized he had a full view of skin and legs all the way up to her hips. Her shirt had pulled up as she scooted forward to the edge. She snapped her legs closed and pulled the hem over her knees.

Shelby blushed and he thought he had never been so enchanted in all his years. She had beautiful legs and hips and the glimpse of her feminine spot was just as enticing as how her breasts filled the shirt she had secured with a tie over her ribs. One side of his shirt collar hung off her shoulder slightly and the long sleeves were rolled up to fit her arms. Her hair was thick and curled in loose rings.

He raised himself slowly from the low table and stood waiting for Shelby to join him.

"I thought you might like to rest a while longer. Since you are awake, I hope you are hungry enough to join me."

"Are you kidding? I am starved. I would've eaten with the women if Rockdurgh hadn't forced me to stay here. You were longer than an hour."

"Not intentionally."

"I would appreciate it if you never again made me stay in your cubicle alone and hungry, Kerrick. I have other things I need to take care of.

"Commander Rockdurgh locked me in here! People will think you and I are..." She stopped aware of what she insinuated.

Kerrick raised an eyebrow at her, amazed that she would fret about such a thing.

"Sir Kerrick, I hate being locked up."

"I understand, Shelby," and he thought about the black box. "But, the women's dome needed to be made safe. The other women will not be in there for a couple nights because we are securing the area also. You can stay here for now. I will be working late with my men. After the animal attack, Security wanted to test the dome and make sure all of you are safe. New barriers are being set up so that there won't be a repeat of the incident. Most of the women would not survive such an animal attack." He looked at her to see if she understood he complimented her, but her eyes puzzled over the food.

"The animal attack was a quirk. The animal felt the need to strike, especially since it had cubs. Where are all the women staying?"

"They have been dispersed into some of the other domes."

Shelby was skeptical and her expression showed that she did not agree with the way things were being handled.

"Eat, Shelby. Do not look at me like I have ulterior motives."

She gave him a dubious look and he smiled. She changed the subject slightly.

"Why have I been locked in here?"

Kerrick was immediately bemused. "You were confined for your own safety and so that all the women would comply with the new living arrangements." He saw her scowl, but did not care she was angry. He suspected the woman before him had more power with the other women than she was aware of, and certainly more than he wanted to give her credit for at first.

"We put men and women in the same domes for security reasons. There are anomalies that have disturbed some women enough to go to Doc Orlie about. If it was one woman then it would be concerning enough, but several women have had similar dreams; ghost-like images of men that reoccur and increase in intensity. Now, with the recent animal attack, it seems prudent to take precautions; so domes are going to be unified at the upper camp."

"And you think I can assuage the women's doubt of this by complying?"

"Yes. I believe they find you to be the temperature reading."

Shelby rolled her eyes and shook her head 'no'. "I have very little influence on most of the women."

"But the women you do have influence on, the ones that have been in your dome, recognize you as the liaison for their days off, and . . ."

"You are wrong."

She was so succinct that Kerrick only stared and waited for her explanation.

It took her some time, but she finally looked him in the eye. "I am not a threat to the women because I am not a desirable mate and I am . . . expendable."

Kerrick was amused now. She really had a skewed sense of her self-worth. She held herself aloof from the larger group because she obviously thought that she was not accepted in the dynamics of the tribe.

He laughed outright. She was visibly irritated by his outburst.

"Half your problem, Shelby, is that you are not good with social settings. I get that; when you would rather swim in a cold lake instead of sit by a warm fire and talk to people. But if you ever did, you might overhear people complimenting you on the advancements you have made on their behalf. Many who are well aware that you are the one who sent the previous Lurt back to his home planet in shame.

"However, you are mistaken about your expendability on this planet, you and any other woman who think you are not desirable to the men is tragically mistaken. I know that your number of suitors is higher than any other woman in this clan." He winked at her and took a drink.

"So. Here is what I expect of you. I expect you to be the go-between for the women and to do so with respect to my position and that of my officers. I get the distinct impression that you know how to organize women and motivate them to comply for the good of the community here."

Shelby heard him emphasize 'good' and gave him a quizzical stare. How could he think she had any influence on the women to such a large degree? Then it came back to her, he said suitors?

"Suitors…for what?" Shelby was not interested in any Alkernian man here. She did not want to stay here, be here, live here or die here. She wanted to find her children and not a single Alkernian was going to keep her from her purpose.

"For the Alker Birthing Celebration. Every man is…"

"I have no desire to participate in my captor's celebration. Ever!" Shelby stood up in agitation.

"You do not have a choice."

"Yes, I do and I will exercise it. I do not like you or any other Alkernian on this planet telling me I will 'celebrate' your holiday!"

"And here I thought we were getting along so well." Kerrick bit back.

"I will not be a part of the Alker Birthing Celebration. My free-will is still mine, on this planet or elsewhere. I will not be a slave forever, nor will I, while in captivity ever, willingly participate in your 'celebration,' ever. And I doubt any other Earth woman will either."

"Which is exactly why you are here and they are down there," he gestured with his hands.

"They are not sheep, Kerrick."

"No, they are not. I am fully aware of that fact. However, you are going to stay here for a while and be my shadow. That is your lot at the request of the men in camp. When I leave, Commander Rockdurgh will be your protector until I return."

She was furious. She paced for a minute and wanted to beat on something; Kerrick more precisely. Finally she punched the door opening and stormed out of his cubicle.

Commander Rockdurgh was there almost immediately. "Shall I return her?" His mirth was palpable.

"No."

"That went better than I expected." Rockdurgh confirmed.

"Aye." Sir Kerrick was contemplative. Commander Rockdurgh said nothing more to his commander as he got up to look out the window.

"Do you think she knows, or has any inkling?"

"No." Kerrick smiled in spite of his unsettled thoughts.

"Are you going to tell her?"

"Absolutely not." Sir Kerrick retorted as he looked back at Commander Rockdurgh from the window to see if he was serious. Commander Rockdurgh's humorous look told him it was not so.

"Doc Orlie will need to know."

"Aye, he already suspects."

Sir Kerrick and Commander Rockdurgh grinned like two mischievous boys that had pulled off the greatest joke of all time.

"To work then."

"Aye.

Outmaneuvered / Chapter 8

Shelby was to travel to the mountains to do tests she had been trained for and to gather plants for Doc Orlie. By the time she was done, it would be the beginning of Alker Birthing Celebration. She dreaded the return. If she could manage it, she was going to prolong the time up there for at least the first week into the celebration, if not all of it.

She slept soundly the night before and was awakened in the morning by a man in her doorway.

"Shelby, it is time to go." A voice startled her awake. By the time she was oriented, he was turned away and she didn't see who it was.

A few minutes later she was dressed and set to eat. She readied her pack the day before and was prepared to start up the trail. It would take two to three days of walking and crossing streams before they would be to the trailhead that lead them up the mountain to the upper camp.

She was relieved to be leaving the chaos of the preparations of the upcoming Alkernian celebrations. She was actually ready to be away from so many happy people.

As soon as she stepped out of the women's dome, she was greeted by men around the fire. It made her hesitate for a moment until she realized they had been waiting for her. One of the men motioned for her to step over to him.

"Let me check your pack, Shelby."

"What for?" She grumped back.

One of the other men replied for him while her pack was lifted from her and checked.

"We always make sure the women have not over-packed before we go on a longer journey. We have found this to be prudent."

The younger man going through her stuff irritated her and she decided instead of taking the chance of being told she could not go, she would eat before she said anything she would regret. She walked to the fire and checked the food lying out on the racks. She rolled the meat with some of the flatbread and began to eat it with some gusto. She looked around and noticed some of the men smiling, not really looking at her and she wondered what the joke was, but she always needed a cup of brew before being civil in the morning, so she walked over to her pack, which was still being gone through, and snatched the cup hanging on the side.

She looked at the young man bent over her pack going through the last of the pockets and impulsively pushed him away from her pack. He fell over quite surprised. She heard the men behind her chuckle, but she squatted down level with the young man's face.

"If you tell me what you are looking for, I'll get it for you."

Her look was so direct and she was so close to him that he swallowed funny and had to clear his throat before he could answer her.

"I was told to put aside the heavier equipment you were carrying." Shelby looked aside and saw that was true as some of the heavier objects now lay beside the backpack. The young man looked at the men and then back at Shelby who seemed to be reading his thoughts. He began to blush at that thought and ran his fingers through his hair. As quickly as she came, she was back at the fire finishing her food.

To no one in particular she said, "I'll be needing that equipment, heavy or not, unless of course I am not going to be doing any tests or work."

"The men will carry your equipment. The trek is dangerous in some spots so Sir Kerrick has ordered that none of the women are to traverse the mountains unaided or laden with burdens heavier than necessary." This was from a fierce man named Torden.

Shelby looked at him directly and tilted her head to the side and then spoke to the warrior. "I can carry all that was in my backpack with ease. I'll not burden any other with the equipment I need to work with."

"And I will not argue with you as I said the same to Sir Kerrick and he still ordered me thus. You will be silent now."

"I am a woman, Sir Torden. You can try to order me to be silent, but I will not bridle my only strength any more than you would willingly be weak to please a woman. But, you may ask me and I may comply. However, you know good and well that I will talk to Kerrick about this."

He grunted and shrugged his shoulders. "That will have to wait until we get to our destination as he has already left for the other camp." To the others he ordered, "On our way." As if one voice echoed, all the men stood and shouted "hoo-ay" so abruptly that it startled Shelby. The disbursement of the men from the fire was in unison and Shelby watched in amazement as they filed past her pack and each picked up one of the objects laid out beside the pack.

Finally, Torden looked at her and walked to her pack and picked it up. Without looking back he called to her, "Let's go, Shelby."

Shelby watched the men organize the last bit of necessities into order and smiled. She was completely outmaneuvered and helpless to do anything about it. Apparently they planned all along to carry every bit of her stuff. She should have packed more.

Cliff Hanger / Chapter 9

L ong before nightfall the weather changed
drastically to pounding rain and high wind
speeds that sent gusts of force against the
wall of the craggy mountain trail. Their steps
became increasingly treacherous because visibility
was low. Sir Kerrick had doubled back to meet them,
aware they were not going to make it around the
constricted crag onto the plateau this night. They
advanced to where the trail had narrowed to a three
foot width with a dangerous drop-off on one side.

Shelby braced her step against the wall, ready to
pull up onto the higher ledge of the trail, when a
chunk of rock fell down the cliff into the tree tops
below leaving the trail cluttered with debris and
uneven ledges protruding from the wall. Before she
lifted her body up, Kerrick halted her movement with
his hand on her shoulder.

He yelled over the gale of wind, "We are going to
stop here. It is too dangerous to go any further." All
the men stopped and prepared to make shelter on
the face of the cliff using the narrow path as the
base. Shelby watched incredulously as Kerrick pulled
out clips and ropes and pounded hooks into the face
of the rock wall to create a shelter from the storm.
The other men did the same and it occurred to
Shelby they were seasoned men able to handle

dangerous situations with practiced skill. Kerrick motioned for her to come to him. He seemed to always be doing that. He lifted the flap for her.

Her hair was dripping wet and her clothes, like the rest of the men's, were thoroughly soaked. He followed behind and in the cramped shelter they had to adjust to the closeness. He pulled out a dry shirt and held it out for her.

She marveled that anything could remain dry in this weather.

"Take off those wet clothes and put this on. You will get warm faster. See this?" She shook her head 'yes'. "It is a cooking appliance." He showed her how it worked and then left her alone to go check on his men.

Her clothes stuck to her body and in the confined, narrow shelter she struggled to get them off her shaking, chilled body. She would have wrung her things outside, but the hard pellets of rain pounded against the cliffs and only in the shelter was there some protection from the elements. She dropped her clothes by the entrance and set about fixing a meal.

Kerrick reappeared and stripped his wet clothes off. He saw the pile Shelby had started and added to it.

"After we eat I will show what to do with the wet clothes so you'll know for next time." He seemed to Shelby to be totally relaxed about the whole situation. She nodded at him and he pointed over at the pack.

111

"Do you expect to be caught in a rain storm again?" She teased him while she grabbed his pack.

"Just toss me some dry things from it." When she turned to hand him his trousers he was completely naked. He was nonchalant about his nudity and kept talking to her about the circumstance they were in. She couldn't help blush.

"The other men are settled in to wait out the storm. It is dark now." He pointed to the walls of the shelter. "This fabric is great for this kind of weather. It will glow inside, outside it is almost invisible to see. This," and he held out a thin tube, "shines on the fabric and makes it visible to someone on the outside, otherwise it blends with the surrounding territory. It is an excellent camouflage tool for hunting."

He was interrupted by Commander Rockdurgh and Captain Torden who managed to squeeze into the small space.

Kerrick scooted around the food next to Shelby and motioned for the men to sit down. They were still in wet clothes and dripped at the entrance.

They stripped bare-chested to the waist, as was Kerrick

"Thought since the night was young, we would play some cards." Torden spoke for them both. "Do you know how to play 'Truce', Shelby?"

She shook her head 'no' and looked at Kerrick who changed a color of blue. Shelby was fascinated by the Alker's ability to do this. Something some of the men said was unintentional and inherently part of their makeup; attached to their emotion, which consequently made their moods visible to others.

Shelby asked several times what each color represented, but none of the men were forthcoming with any information. She noticed the other men turned color as well. Commander Rockdurgh and Captain Torden shaded to a light green on their torso, but it didn't reach their faces.

When she looked at Kerrick, his body turned a deep shade of dark brown and it did reach his face. When he turned his face to Shelby, his green eyes sparkled with amusement. She looked at the other men who had mixed looks on their faces. Captain Torden seemed amazed at Kerrick while Commander Rockdurgh had a smug look on his. What was going on?

Kerrick stirred the food and with utensils in hand all of them ate out of the pot, pulling chunks of the now heated and hydrated nourishment. Shelby felt her stomach pain ease and as the men talked and dealt their cards, she realized she was drowsy. She pulled Kerrick's wrap free of the pack and laid it out behind Kerrick and the men.

She kept bumping Kerrick, but the big oaf didn't move away. Shelby was small enough to curl behind him and rest while she discreetly looked at Kerrick's muscular form. His waist was tight with lumps and bumps of muscles that rippled when he moved even his fingers.

She noticed his body change color again.

"Are you practicing...lying?" She interrupted their banter.

"What?" The men smiled and tried to act baffled by her question. Kerrick looked over his shoulder unruffled by her as if he knew she would say something like that.

"Well, you have your shirts off. Which by your changing body colors, makes me suspect that I could never actually play 'Truce'. Not because I can't take off my shirt to be bare-breasted, but because the point of the game seems to be how to not change colors or to make the color of your body change a specific color. When you ask him a question, he always changes green. Either that is very good control or just all the emotion he has."

The men laughed now. Shelby frowned.

"You are almost correct." Kerrick seemed to have pride mixed in his voice as he looked at her with merriment in his eyes.

"The point is to turn different colors without doing the same color twice in a row. The conversation is the diversion and the cards are the direction the conversation is to be a challenge in."

"But the whole joke is that I could never play Truce." She was annoyed that their invitation was funny only to them. If she'd agreed to play, she would have been embarrassed and humiliated.

Kerrick watched her expression as realization dawned upon her. He looked at her with knowing in his expression.

"What does blue mean, Kerrick?" She looked at him curiously and he was compelled to tell her the truth.

"It is a color of dominance and is not easy to control or acquire. Very few men color a true blue shade only on their torso."

"So because you are a leader you can turn blue?" She was intrigued.

"No. Most leaders do not turn blue."

She looked at Commander Rockdurgh and Captain Torden. They turned a shade of orange.

"Why did you turn blue, Kerrick?" She was more precise this time.

"Because, I did not want you to play." He changed a light purple and Shelby just knew he was lying.

"Why really did you change blue, Kerrick?" He chuckled and looked at the other men who were trying to stay out of the way and seemed uncomfortable.

"I was practicing my color technique." He turned light purple again and Shelby raised her eyebrow.

"Same color twice in a row. You lose." The men chuckled including Kerrick at Shelby's perception.

"He changed blue because he feels protective over you and challenged us by showing a dominant color." Captain Torden was still orange on his mid-body and so was Commander Rockdurgh. Maybe it was the truth.

Kerrick said nothing one way or the other.

"We also sit in large conference groups like this so that we are sure to tell the truth for the most part. Some men can still hedge, but it is harder." Commander Rockdurgh nodded at Shelby.

115

"Do you all change the same colors for the same emotion?" Shelby looked at Kerrick who looked stoic as usual.

"Not all men are exactly the same since feelings tend to be mixed. To be honest, I like you not knowing the precise mood I am in. I believe the other men feel at a disadvantage as well since Earth women do not change color and reveal their secrets so easily." Kerrick made a point of looking directly into Shelby's face. She blushed.

Shelby looked at the men. Each of them turned back to their game, but the jest of it seemed to be gone.

"I didn't mean to spoil your fun." She was sincerely sorry.

The men together tried to assure her that she did not spoil anything.

"Shelby, the joke is on us. We thought to tease you, but you are far more astute than we gave you credit for. See I am turning orange." Captain Torden was the more apologetic of the three.

"We really do practice to hide our emotions and keep them under control, especially right before AB Celebration. The control serum that moderates our reproduction desires wears off every two years so we have emotions we are not used to dealing with. It gets better once the end of the cycle is done."

"So you are like women on their period." Shelby jested.

"Oh that is it. Beat her, Sir Kerrick. She is irreverent." They laughed.

Shelby laid back on the comfort of Kerrick's wrap and pulled part of it over her bare legs. She yawned in answer to their fake threat and closed her eyes to rest her tired body.

The men continued their debate. As their talk faded, Shelby was lulled to sleep by a deep hum she suspected was from Kerrick. How strange to be lulled to sleep by men's voices and rain pelting against the fabric overhead and to be content.

Kerrick looked down at the shapely form of his waif. How could the contrary woman be so alluring to him? The men called it a night so he slid into his occupied bag with ease and pulled her close against his body. She was a little heater and her warmth was very welcome. He inhaled her fragrant smell and moved his hand over her hips and down her thigh. She felt lush and his hand began a slow measuring over her firm belly. Just as he moved to cover her breast her hand and voice stopped him.

She turned partway toward him and elbowed him in the ribs. "Behave. I need to get some rest and so do you, so leave me be."

"I am behaving." He smiled down at her as he lifted up on one elbow. He pushed some errant curls away from her cheek and turned her around to face him. "You are so beautiful." His fingers ran along her jaw line and over her lips. He leaned down to kiss her, but she turned her face away so he gently kissed her face and began to move down her neck with slow deliberateness. He gently guided her turned face toward him to ply her soft lips.

"Stop." Kerrick heard her whispered plea, but he read something else in her eyes, passion.

"Your mouth says one thing, but your eyes say another, Shelby. Why are you conflicted?"

She frowned at him "I want you to stop, Kerrick. It is against my beliefs to have sexual relations with someone outside of marriage. You have your religious traditions and I have mine. Besides, you're too young for me." She was determined and he could hear it in her voice.

"Well, just because we have sex does not mean I will marry you."

"I never said I wanted to marry you or have sex with you." She snapped back.

He was perplexed by her refusal of him. It just went against his experience to be refused by a woman. And what did she mean he was too young for her?

"Explain." He prompted.

"Explain what?" She countered. She was confused about what he expected to be explained and now she was irritated that he would think that she would have sex with him because he was so irresistible.

"Explain what you mean by your beliefs. And what does my age have anything to do with tonight?" He was trying to be reasonable and understand her hesitancy.

Shelby rolled her eyes and coughed. "I am too tired to explain my religious beliefs to you tonight, Kerrick. But, for me it is not right."

"Are you a priestess then?" He was suddenly appalled that she was under some oath and would not be able to overcome her own moral belief to meld with her new life here among the Alkernians.

"I am not a priestess, but I do believe in one God like I told you before."

"You have never shared your religious views with me. It must have been another man you spoke to. Religion is a personal and lengthy subject which I agree we should save for another time." He pushed more errant curls off her chin and smiled down into her delicate features.

She was unpredictable and he was not sure if she was attracted to him. It had never before been an issue in his pursuits. But when he was around her, she gave very little indication she was attracted to him or any other man for that matter. So he was uncertain about his appeal to her.

"I just did not want you to feel disappointed that I did not try to have sex with you. Women often are vengeful if they are scorned by a man."

Kerrick's smirk revealed a dimple on the side of his face. Shelby could not believe he had the audacity to say that to her and look so pleased with himself. She scoffed and rolled her eyes, but she couldn't help laugh.

"You are so egotistical!"

Kerrick felt compelled to set her mind straight about their age difference. "Just so you know, Shelby, you are not older than me." He touched the tip of her nose and turned his back toward her.

"I am forty-something, Kerrick." She was unconvinced of his claim. He looked like he was barely thirty even though she knew he had been in one war at least. She expected him to look more aged if he was any older.

"I know how old you are, love."

Shelby frowned at his back. She wondered about his knowing a detail like that regarding her.

"I'm older than most of the women and men here, Kerrick."

"You are not older than any of the men here except one, and it is not me, guaranteed. Now go to sleep."

"Now that you woke me up and riled me you're content to sleep."

He smiled to himself. He knew how he could go to sleep quickly if she was willing.

With a huff she rolled away.

Shelby felt herself slip down a dark crevice in the mountain rocks. She spread her arms out suddenly to try to grab a firm hold and hit something solid. She opened her eyes and in the minimal light could feel strong arms hold her safe. Her breathing was heavy and her heart pounded in terrified speed. She woke from the dream, but it was too real to be just a dream.

Kerrick tried to bring her back to reality and gently shifted her around to make sure she was aware it was a dream. He spoke to her, but she felt immediate danger lurked just behind her understanding.

"Kerrick, we've got to get off this cliff. The men are in danger. I saw."

"Shelby, you had a nightmare. The men are fine."

"I'm going to go check." She shoved his arms out of the way and quickly put on her boots.

Her actions alarmed him. She was not given to exaggeration; still he was not convinced she was awake.

He followed quickly behind her just to keep her safe, but before he made it out of the tent he heard her scream again.

She stepped out of the tent, but there was no ledge left and where the men should have been there was nothing but deep abyss to the bottom.

Kerrick was right behind her with his hands on her shoulder looking over her head. What did she see?

"Shelby, are you alright?" Kerrick was mystified by her sleepwalking.

Commander Rockdurgh and some of the other men heard her scream over the rain and appeared out of their tents to see what was happening.

"Get back! Get back!" She wouldn't take a step closer to them.

"Sir Kerrick, is she okay?"

Kerrick looked over her head at them baffled at her obvious fear. When he tried to move around her to reach the other men, Shelby stopped him. When she looked at him he knew she was not sleepwalking or in a daze.

"Kerrick, tell the men to move down the trail four hundred yards. Tell them to do it now!" He was just about to try to calm her down when a rock rolled ominously down from above them and knocked larger material loose. It tumbled past the ledge they were on. He changed his mind about being calm.

He whistled a shrill retreat; clearly a warning and the rest of the men appeared out of their tents in seconds half clad and weapons in hand. Sir Kerrick yelled at them to get back as he started forward to help them. Shelby pulled him back to some imaginary line.

"You can't go any further than here, Kerrick!" She screamed over the rain and wind as she pulled him harder away from where she pointed.

He did yell at her then. "Let go, Shelby!" He pried her arms off his body and still she gripped his pant waist and would not let go. He was incensed at her persistence and shoved her arms away hard. He expected her to let go with the force, but he did not expect her to calmly turn and go into the shelter.

At least he could turn his attention to the men. Maybe he had overreacted in warning the men to get back. He felt Shelby go past him, further up the trail onto a higher ledge. She had a determined look on her face and pulled rope off the clip on his bag. He paused long enough to see she was safe on the ledge doing something he just did not want to take the time to figure out. He looked up where rocks had come from and decided it was safe. He started toward the other men to let them know it was a false alarm.

He heard a crack behind him where Shelby was and saw anticipating fear on her face. Her hands started moving faster at what she was doing. Was the sound from the mountain or thunder? He saw Shelby quickly pound a stake into the mountain wall and thread his rope through, knotting it to her body. He saw her look up the mountain side while she tried to shield her eyes from the pelting rain.

What happened next was so terrifying he saw it in slow motion. Part of the mountain ledge gave way and tent equipment pummeled down with the mud slide. The ground beneath Kerrick gave way so fast his hands flew up as he tried to jump over the wave of rock and debris sliding past the spot his men just vacated.

He was hit time and again on his body and face with the river of broken rocks and sharp limbs of trees floating by him. He lost the battle of staying on top and tumbled down with the speeding rubble. His plummet was halted only because he was pinned against a part of the mountain's jutted ledges. He was bleeding and broken fighting for control as he watched more mud and trees slam by him and explode with tremendous power in the deep basin below.

He looked several hundred feet above and saw his men look in horror at the catastrophe. They could not see him as camouflaged as he was by mud and limbs that covered him. There was also now no way for them to cross over to his side as a large part of the mountain was missing and most of their equipment was smashed on rocks below. The men would need to take the safer, but longer trail to the winter camp and travel several days without supplies.

He tried to move his battered and squeezed body. Excruciating pain in his head made it impossible for him to turn. Before he lost consciousness, he realized they would not be able to get to him for several days and he was sure he was too injured to last two or three days in the cold.

Shelby looked at the men stranded on the remaining ledge. They couldn't go back because the trail was chopped off by cascading boulders and a huge chunk of the ledge was eradicated. She tried to yell across the crevasse to let them know she could help, but the wind and rain carried her strained voice with it. She couldn't throw anything that far, but she could propel her rope over there possibly like an arrow and bow would do. In the back of her mind she could only hope Kerrick was somewhere on the mountain below.

She had watched as closely as she could to determine where he possibly would be. He was buried under mud and she needed help to recover his body. She had watched in horror as the slide pulled his agile body under the mass of moving rock and mountain and her heart had fainted and her body had gone weak as she fell to her knees screaming out his name. About the same time, she heard the other men's shouts and watched in mummified horror as she saw one man lose his grip and fall headlong into the grave, gurgling rubble. The other men secured, as best they could, the few remaining hand and foot holds left to them. The looks on their faces echoed her same emotions at seeing the man lose his life.

She was on a part of the trail not as affected by the rain's torrents, so she had the advantage of secure footing. She scurried up and out of sight of the men who were trapped. Not too far on the trail, limbs were blown down from the trees. She tried the flexibility of each one she thought might work for the bow, hoping one would work as well as it did when she was a child playing with her brothers. She fastened the limb taut in an arc creating the best bow she could manage under the circumstances. She shook from cold and nerves from the enormity of what she needed to do to save the men.

Shelby ran back to the edge of the precipice and wrapped the lighter rope at the end of a quickly fashioned spear chosen for its straightness. At the end of the light rope she knotted the heavier rope. She sat down in the direction she wanted the line to fly and with all her strength she used her legs to hold the arced limb and pull the bow line taut with both hands. The contraption shot the line at the men, but Shelby felt the hot burning impact of the line welting the tops of her legs and didn't see the line hit its mark.

She heard the men shout together in triumph and was relieved she wouldn't have to shoot again. She kept the rope end and looped it into the metal clip she had pounded into the rock wall, thankful it was still there.

The men at the other end of the rope were ready within minutes to send someone across. The line sagged more than Shelby would have imagined, but it was safe enough to get Captain Torden across first. Shelby was so relieved when he was across she took her first deep breath.

"Woman! You saved us! I thought you were going to run for help, but that was ingenious." He pointed to her makeshift bow. He took big strides toward her and hugged her unceremoniously and kissed her on the cheek. He let her go just as quickly and worked on the line she had tied, perfecting the connection by tightening it so that the men could slide across easier. It was less than half an hour later when they were all across on solid ground.

"Where is Shelby gone to?" Commander Rockdurgh queried. All the men at once realized she was nowhere in sight. With everyone across and the last man carrying the arrow that Shelby had shot over the gulf, they followed Commander Rockdurgh who scouted her possible trail.

Twenty minutes passed before they found Shelby lowered down over the cliff.

"Woman, what are you doing?" Commander Rockdurgh did not know whether to be angry or relieved.

Shelby lifted her head to the rock ledge she just vacated. She was tied to a rope that held her body weight secure in case she slipped in her attempt to get lower on the wet cliff side.

"I'm looking for Kerrick. I watched him go this far, but I couldn't see around this overhang." She saw the sadness in his eyes and didn't want to let it discourage her from her purpose.

"Shelby, love, come up here and let one of us look for him."

She slipped and fell a couple of feet before she landed on sturdier footing. The men yelled at her now through the steady patter of the rain. Their reaction took her by surprise and distracted her from the pain in her bleeding fingertips.

"I can see the ledge below." But, as she made her way down, the rope went taut and she could go no further without unhooking the clip. She made the decision as she found good footing to release herself.

Commander Rockdurgh was joined by a couple other men who lowered themselves down onto the narrow ledge. Others strained their necks over the edge assessing her progress.

"How can she do that? She is finding grip holds that are just cracks."

It was Bordog who noticed she untied herself. "Commander, Shelby does not have the line secured anymore."

Commander Rockdurgh took only a moment to extend the rope with a clip and more line, something she did not have until they came. Bordog held the line out from the cliff wall and swung the end toward Shelby, who snatched hold of the loose line.

She could not believe her eyes. Kerrick was just within reach of her. His motionless body looked mangled with debris twisted around him. She covered her eyes with her hands; with all her heart she didn't want him to be dead.

She heard sounds behind her. Commander Rockdurgh managed to get down to the ledge, but had to duck under the overhang to walk to where she leaned over. He knelt beside her and put his arm around her shoulders as he looked to where her eyes were fixed.

"I can't bear to see him that way." She looked up at Commander Rockdurgh.

He saw tears fall down her smudged face. He was dismayed at her distress; his own grief surging in his chest mirrored hers.

"I will go get him. You stay here and I'll hand him up."

The terrace was narrow and Kerrick was wedged tight against the wall. It was slick and dangerous on the narrow place. When he lowered himself down, he was only chest high to the level Shelby waited on.

He knelt down and moved the rubble away from his beloved friend and leader. Sir Kerrick's body was still warm and when he put his hand on Kerrick's chest he groaned. "He's still alive!"

She looked incredulously at the two men, one looked so alive and the other so lifeless. How could it be? Was his chest rising? She heard Kerrick groan when Commander Rockdurgh tried to move his body.

Shelby was joined by other men moving over to where she waited. When they saw Sir Kerrick they hugged and slapped each other on the back. No one else would fit on the ledge with Sir Kerrick and Commander Rockdurgh so they stayed close by, anticipating what needed to be done for Kerrick's recovery. Shelby scooted back to give room for Kerrick on the ledge and the men worked around her.

The overhang provided a retreat from the persistent downpour and though it was a low ceiling for the men, there was enough room for the whole group of beleaguered Alkers.

One of the men wrapped Shelby's shoulders with a coat. "He is going to be alright, Shelby. You found him in time." She couldn't help the tears from falling down at his reassuring words, so she looked away, but not before he saw the tenderness there.

Sir Kerrick's wounds were dressed and his broken arm set. In the process of making sure he was not injured anywhere else, his clothes had been removed. He was now being redressed and covered with wraps salvaged before most of the gear was destroyed.

The men started a fire from their slim trove of ingenious Alkernian inventions and shielding was attached to the landing to create a secluded resting area for the weary men. The heat warmed the enclave and Kerrick rested in spite of the subdued excitement the men expressed of his rescue.

When Shelby finally saw her chance to get a good look at him herself, she kneeled down and gazed at his disheveled appearance and wondered at how they found him amongst all the debris. He was indeed fortunate, considering that the other man didn't make it.

Unconsciously, she reached out and put her hand over his forehead to feel his temperature. Her hand drifted down over his chest and rested there as she leaned down closer to Kerrick's face and whispered in his ear, "You are a hard man to find, and a hard one to lose." She straightened her spine and closed her eyes. A song of praise began in her and slowly the sound began to make sense in rhythm.

She sang softly over him a song that floated around him, lifting him out of his cold and into warmth that eased his pain. When the song ended his eyes opened and he saw an angel leaning over him, everywhere she touched his body it burned with healing warmth. When the angel looked at him it was Shelby, her eyes welling with tears and a gentle smile turning up her lips. He tried to sit up and adjust his view, but his body weighed a ton and his eyes could no longer be held open. He relaxed and lost the dream.

Shelby moved to the back of the cave and leaned against the wall watching the group of men. Every once in a while she would catch a glimpse of someone looking at her. She puzzled over their demeanor because their reassuring smiles unnerved her. She was used to their stern looks, but not this new attitude of acceptance and gentleness. It made her want to cry and that made her mad. So she pouted and withdrew or at least tried to.

One of the men brought her something hot to drink and then he didn't go away; he sat down beside her. Another man brought her some food and talked to her and his comrade next to her. She felt like she was being drawn into something she was not really sure of, so she sat quietly and drank the beverage and nibbled at the food.

Some of the other men talked to the men beside her, but she could hardly keep her eyes open and her yawns became more frequent. In time, the men laid out bedding that would be used by all of them.

"Shelby, you will have to sleep in the group tonight. It will get cold and we are short supplies so we need to conserve our body heat." Shelby was bodily lifted by the two men as though it had been planned all along. She was brought into the group of men stretching out for the night, all side by side with Shelby and Kerrick being surrounded as though in a protective circle. The heat comforted Shelby and she felt drugged with sleepiness. Without preamble she dropped into a deep, dreamless state.

Shelby's eyes fluttered open when swooshing sounds were made from men gathering the wraps of bedding and packing up what they managed to save from the mudslide. It was very early, but breakfast was ready and someone handed her something to eat. She mumbled her thanks and when she looked into the giver's face he smiled at her.

It was too much for her in the morning so she nodded and looked around to see Kerrick sitting up with men talking to him and patting him on the back. She saw him wince then look at her and wink. She rolled her eyes.

"He is doing much better." The man kneeled down level to look at her. "Alkernians heal fast and we have excellent medicinal knowledge." Shelby nodded and sipped her hot drink.

"I'll remember that next time I get emotional about someone's broken body."

"If he had not been found when he was, Shelby, it may have been another outcome. You see, Alkernians are susceptible to cold and heat actually is a healing factor for us. That is why each of us carries one of the heat spots that you see. We can be cold but not injured and cold."

"It is the same for Earth people of course."

Not too much later the call to depart was suddenly made, yet the men anticipated the event and were ready. Shelby waited and watched the motion of the men and realized they waited for her to lead them out. Only one man went ahead, the second in command, Rockdurgh. Sir Kerrick was hoisted up by the subsequent men and the journey to the new destination was once again enroute, as if this was all part of the plan.

The Challenge / Chapter 10

As they trudged into base camp, they were greeted with welcomes and pats on the back. Loads were lifted from their shoulders and many of them were warmly embraced by others in the camp. It surprised Shelby that her load was taken off as she was heartily pushed along with the returning group to the beginning activities of the night. AB Celebration would not start for a few days, but apparently they were going to get warmed up now that the days' work had come to an end.

The mood changed somewhat when Commander Rockdurgh announced the loss of life and others began to recognize that Sir Kerrick and some of the other men were bruised and cut. It became very clear that the men's lives had narrowly escaped the same fate as that of the one man whose body had not been recovered yet.

All Shelby wanted to do was to go to her dome and retreat to her own cubicle, maybe eat and clean up before she retired. She could feel the anticipation of the other women and men as they prepared for the events of the week in spite of the sadness that hung over the loss of their comrade.

"The women think they might hold off the Celebration for the memorial of the missing man." Amy looked at Shelby for confirmation.

"Alker. No, don't count on it. Their beloved celebration waits for no one, even, I believe, if it was Kerrick's death they mourned."

"You mean, Sir Kerrick?"

Shelby looked at her and wondered what she meant. "Is there another?"

"No, I just didn't know if you meant him...I mean he's always called Sir Kerrick. No one just calls him... Kerrick. It's just that ..."

"What?" Shelby was impatient.

"It's just that when you call an Alker by their first name, it's traditionally because you are intimate and mated, and claim them to be yours, especially around other Alker men."

"Well, that's not the case."

"That may be, but no one else will think you're not."

"Not what?"

"Not mated or intimate," Amy blurted concerned.

"Oh," was all Shelby could choke out.

Other women did wonder if this sudden loss would end or delay the revered holiday, but the men seemed all the more determined to continue the sanctity of their celebration.

A ceremonial epitaph was written for the man, even though Sir Kerrick sent men back to the basin via a lower route to see if the body could be recovered. Shelby heard some of the men speak of the best way to accomplish his memorial during the AB Celebration. Apparently warriors had a 'closed to the public' attitude when it came to their fellow soldier's burial. It was very private and their custom was to bury a warrior with honoraria memories and speak to each other of his exploits or deeds, so she was surprised when Commander Rockdurgh sought her out.

"Char Shelby, would you like to be present at Sentry Makan Elong's burial?" Commander Rockdurgh's rough voice quavered.

Shelby was at first mystified by her title of 'Char', but figured because of the circumstances of her being there at his demise, she was being asked as a formality.

"I know you hold your soldiers' deaths sacred. I do not wish to intrude."

"Nevertheless, it is agreed you may attend."

"Do you agree?" She asked him.

He looked at her mystified, "I do."

She was stumped. It took her a moment to answer. "So be it. I am honored."

His head bent in approval as he gave a fisted salute; the Alker sign of respect.

So after the service and much later than she wanted, Shelby finally made it to the lake's edge. The light was fading and she would soon see the two moons and the stars that could be seen at night. She loved the quiet of the evening.

At the wood's edge, a man watched Shelby without her awareness. His job was to make sure she was safe and kept in compliance with the counsel's expectations of the mating tradition. He kept a keen look out for wild animals or sudden dangers that could threaten the woman or put her in harm's way.

To his amusement, he enjoyed her obstinate habit of being alone. As he watched, she discarded her clothes and waded into the water as naked as the day she was born. Unless he had seen for himself, he would not have guessed the waif was a beautiful, voluptuous woman---who until this moment was usually covered from head to toe with oversized, form-covering clothes that hid most of her attributes, and she did have some. In ridding herself of her clothes, her hair bindings came loose and to his amazement, her lush hair sprang to life with full loose curls. He shook his head; no, he would not have believed it.

Refreshed from her swim, she dressed and quickly went to the meeting at the main amphitheater area where the whole tribe listened to the instructions and the expectations for the coming event.

It was clear that the first blended AB Celebration would take place with fewer highlights than normal, and a day of remembrance for the their lost comrade, but since they were still in practice mode, they would have to enjoy the time with more adjustments than if they were with their own Alkernian women and all the accouterments they normally had in Alker.

It must have been an inside joke, because all the men laughed. None of the women however thought it was a compliment until the announcer spoke to the women.

"I know I speak for all the men here when I say that we feel genuinely excited to finally be able to celebrate one of our most prized holidays with women who are as beautiful and capable as all of the Earth women have proven themselves to be. You have worked beside us and now it is time to rest and benefit from this time before the final move to the winter base. I would personally like to encourage all you women to enjoy the time of celebrating with us."

The meeting continued on for over an hour and Shelby could barely keep her eyes open. She felt her head nod and she squirmed in her space. The bowl shaped mini-amphitheater had seating that doubled as a walkway, so where she sat Alkernian men's feet were on both sides of her. She looked around her and saw most of the men enjoying the impromptu theatrical performance and she sighed with impatience.

Someone came belatedly down the aisle so she automatically scooted forward to make room, but he stopped behind her and sat down with one foot on either side of her. She rolled her eyes and mumbled her disgust at being crowded when she heard Kerrick's voice. She twisted around to see if it really was him and he had the gall to smile and wink at her between jovially laughing at the antics of the stage goings-on and the conversation with his companions.

She decided she was done with the day. She got up to leave, but was halted with a firm hand on her shoulder. Kerrick leaned down and his face touched the side of hers.

"Unless you need to relieve yourself, you need to stay right here with everyone else."

"I am really tired, Kerrick." Shelby moved around him and the other men to leave, but was halted by Kerrick's grip on her braid. She stumbled back, and kept her balance only because several male hands steadied her. She was livid and slapped at the mens' groping hands.

"Calm down, Shelby, love. They were only trying to save you from landing...hard." He held both hands up in surrender or protection from her he did not know which for sure. He saw her take in a breath and glare at him as well as the other men. They sheepishly mumbled their regrets and she turned to leave once again.

Sir Kerrick reached out and wrapped his good arm around her small waist and pulled her over his lap. He heard her protest, as well as the other men's objection to his brutish behavior, but he did not care. She sat on his lap blushing and hissing at him, yet he could not help smile in spite of his pained arm.

Shelby tried to push off his lap, but his grip was firm. She was just not in the mood to be patient. She leaned to whisper in his ear a warning or plead with him, but he turned his face toward hers and planted his lips soundly on hers. He kissed her until her breath was gone. Instead of calming her, she was livid.

He realized his error when her blush deepened and her eyes filled with unshed tears. She was fighting mad instantly and took a swing at his head. He was able to block the incoming slap by stopping one arm then another.

"Stop. Stop, Shelby. I apologize. That was brash of me." He hoped to prevent the scene from escalating into a bigger spectacle. He realized he embarrassed her. Without hesitation, he lifted her up and helped her over the feet and mishaps of the path away from the commotion of the amphitheater, half carrying her. When they were far enough away he let her go slowly and she immediately slapped his face resoundingly. He stood there stunned at the sting, but not surprised at her persistence. And then she walked away without a word.

To his own astonishment he called after her, "Shelby, wait." She turned and looked at him, the moons' light illuminating her expression of disappointment and something else, vulnerability.

He splayed his hands out in surrender. He realized as he did so, that he had never in his life asked forgiveness from any woman. "I am sorry." He tilted his head to the side.

Her response was to roll her eyes. She put her hands on her hips and said, "For what, Kerrick? For man-handling me, pulling my hair like a school boy, for embarrassing me or for denying me any right to decide when I need to sleep? Which one is it, Kerrick?"

"For all of it." He had to admit when she put it like that he was not as sophisticated and smooth as he thought. He smiled sheepishly.

Shelby looked at the rakish man and knew her heart was in trouble. To have him purposely humiliate her in front of his men and the other women was too much. She knew he was just sporting with her to be obnoxious, but enough already.

"You constantly embarrass me, Kerrick. And you think just because you smile and wink it makes it all better. And what is with that kiss? Isn't that something you should do when both people are interested in each other? You shouldn't play with someone's feelings. You are so oblivious to how it looks to people who are watching you do your thing."

She put her fingers over her mouth like she said something she regretted; and then he got it. She was mad because he kissed her without being serious or as she put it 'interested'. Maybe she was saying she was not interested in him, but it did not seem that way.

"And what is my 'thing', Shelby love?"

She rolled her eyes at his endearment and taunt. He was fast falling in love with this woman even if she was not aware yet what was going on. He moved slowly toward her hoping she would stubbornly stand her ground as usual.

"To annoy me, and embarrass me, and harass me in front of every living person in this compound. What have I done to you to make you so antagonistic toward me?" The sincerity in her voice was not lost on him.

"Really? I do not feel that way toward you in any way, Shelby. I admire you in many ways and even if you never saved my life or my men's, I would feel the same way about you. You are a beautiful and desirable woman that..." He realized she was shocked by his declaration, because she uncharacteristically took steps back.

"Shelby, love, you need to not take this the wrong way." He could see it was dawning on her he was serious.

"I do not like Alkers. I do not like you. I have no desire to celebrate your cherished celebration." Her hands were fisted at her sides.

"Is that why you saved our lives, because you dislike Alkers?

He put his hands on her shoulders and pulled her closer to the warmth of his body. He put his hand behind her neck and pulled her head closer to him, his eyes reading the wonder in her striking amber eyes. When no words came out of her mouth in protest he lowered his lips slowly to hers to try the truth of her denial.

He lost himself in the sensual pleasure of her yielded body. She gave her kisses to him and made his body ache with desire in just seconds of touching her. He pulled her closer to him and the craving to make her his was so powerful he had to force himself to pull away.

She stumbled backward unstable on her own when he let her go. His hand went out to steady her, but she dodged it and withdrew from his reach.

"So, Shelby, love, you need to say 'no' with more feeling, or change it to 'yes' and mean it. Either way, I probably will not hear it when your lips and body respond like that with just a kiss."

He could tell by her demeanor she wanted to slap him again, but she tightly turned toward her dome and left him gloating. He could not remember when he had last been with a woman who could leave him bereft with a simple denial or make him so cocky with the response of her body. He shook his head and then laughed out loud.

Her dreams were haunted by the sound of a man laughing at her and caressing her face and body. She knew it was only a dream, but she was frustrated at the image of a big strong man leaving her standing in the middle of a group of people all laughing at her, while she stupidly thought he loved her. Then the image of Kerrick turned into her husband and he was not smiling.

When Shelby woke from the restless night, she was cranky and irritable. The other women were chipper and the men were polite and courteous which made her even grumpier. She did not like anyone today. All this happiness around her made her petulant.

Antics / Chapter 11

Today Shelby was told that she was to produce some kind of sketch or act that would be added to the schedule of events for the night. She really was not interested at all in participating. She marched to Kerrick's dome.

"I would like to be excused from having to participate in the scheduled events for AB Celebration." Shelby's politeness was contrived.

Sir Kerrick and his men looked over maps and schedules for the plans of the mountain city. He took his time responding.

"Really." He continued to look at the drawings with his men, barely glancing at her.

"Yes, really." She was not sure he spoke to her.

He finally looked at her with his arms crossed over his chest, "Why?"

"Because I don't have any talent and I don't want to participate in your stu... 'cherished' celebration."

"No."

"No?"

"No. You are not excused. Besides, Shelby, you can sing. I have heard you myself. It does not have to be elaborate, just enjoyable. By the way, if you are booed off the stage you will end up going back for another try at it. It is the way of the celebration traditions." And then he had the nerve to laugh.

143

When she left, other women came in to talk to him as well. Shelby knew they were not happy about being put on the spot either. She smiled in spite of her nervous fear of going on the stage. She doubted they would get out of participating either. She almost wanted to stay just to see how they fared with the stonewall Kerrick. She didn't have to wait long to see they had gotten an even quicker response from Kerrick than she had.

"Sir Kerrick told us to talk to you because you could explain why we must have something to contribute to the events tonight."

So she did, much to her dismay. She thought of all the things she hated about Kerrick and it boiled down to one thing, he could manipulate her and force her to be a part of whatever he deemed necessary without ever getting angry. His cool indifference was disconcerting to her and his assumption that she should do whatever he told her to, even if it was from someone else's lips, made her blood boil.

~*~

When night came they entered the amphitheater area in stunning dress and sat down for the evening's entertainment with a heightened sense of anticipation. The center aisles were filled with the beautiful colors of the women and the smells of intoxicating perfumes. In spite of the reason they were here, the excitement of seeing the first performances and talents of the previous evening led to the expectation of a wonderful evening tonight.

Shelby looked around at all the people and wondered at the contentment in the men and women's demeanor. She was astounded by the thought they were a community of people who worked hard together to build a sophisticated and beautiful city. Though they were not finished with the mountain capital or occupying the structures, the celebration was real enough, and so was the sense of belonging and appreciation.

For a moment she felt generous in her heart at the contentment of living in a place as beautiful as this. Though she longed for her absent children, she felt resolve rise in her to build a life here. For these next few days she would try to enjoy the moments of pleasure that were in the present and in the here and now.

The announcer of the ceremonies was Keil Augusta and he introduced the talent as it was about to happen.

So here she was tonight, resigned to the idea she would have to participate in the Alkernian Birthing Celebration. And instead of being angry she wanted to excel in something she was sure Keil Augusta and Kerrick Torrell expected her to fail at.

She was somewhat prepared, but once she decided to have fun with the challenge she knew what she would do. She waited now in anticipation of the events of the night and to her amazement, was not as apprehensive and uneasy as she should be. Tonight was proving to be as agreeable as the first night.

Sir Kerrick watched the skits and listened to the songs with amusement. He had forgotten how much civilization he left behind and as amateur as some of the offerings were, it was still enjoyable. Some of the acts were funny while others were seductive and intriguing.

He heard Keil Augusta name Shelby as the coming attraction and his ears perked up. He watched her tentatively make her way down to the stage. She was beautiful with her lush mane of curls flowing free from a braid and the airy, layered dress that accentuated her bosom and swirled around her femininely round hips. She seemed to float to Keil Augusta and whispered in his ear as the flow of the dress wrapped around Keil Augusta's legs. He smiled and nodded while Shelby's hand gracefully lifted and expressed what she was saying, as it always did when she talked.

The personal conversation was over and he bowed to her and announced her as if no one else knew who she was.

She actually curtsied to Kerrick's amusement. Then she turned to the audience and smiled. She was so engaging that Kerrick felt the whole audience wait with anticipation for what she was going to sing. Only she did not sing.

"Good evening ladies and gentlemen." She started to walk the front of the stage with deliberate grace pulling in the attention of the unsettled crowd. She was engaging to watch as she used her feminine attributes to get the interest of each and every person. What was she saying?

She gestured at an invisible line up the seating and then another and then another until she had the audience sectioned off in four quadrants. She then did an unladylike whistle and three other women and one of the men stood up and made their way to the stage.

Shelby clapped her hands together and laughed a contagious sprinkle of delight. Kerrick was smiling now, but his arms were still crossed in front of his broad chest.

"Here's what is going to happen." With that, she turned her back on the audience and began a beat that was fast and engaging. One by one the other three women added their beats and sounds to hers. They made an astonishing lyrical sound that was unusual and catchy. Then the young man named Boj sang a deep beat adding to the range of women's sounds. It was captivating and all done without one bit of musical instrument. The song came to an end and the audience clapped with enthusiasm. Shelby waited for the audience to quiet and then laughed again.

"Now it is your turn!" She went to the first division and instructed them in a beat and then to each group she gave a beat or a ditty to sing or hum. She instructed them to watch her for their cue and then motioned the other women to take a place in front of each section so they could follow along together.

"Finally, we need to hear who can sing with Boj on his part. Anyone can try but if you can't do it, then you have to follow the group part, agreed?" So Boj

147

stepped up and to Kerrick's surprise was self-assured and inspiring.

"Stop. Stop. Stop. Someone is out of tune. Try it again." The audience laughed and looked around for the culprit. Shelby walked along the audience and pointed at one man and wagged her finger at him and shook her head slowly 'no'. She smiled and winked and the crowd laughed. She pointed to a couple others and eliminated them as well. The audience enjoyed the procedure of being found out.

"Good. So here we go all together." She raised her hands and started everyone out at once. Then she waved her hands around in a 'please stop' manner. When it was quiet, she laughed and so did the others on stage. "Just joking." The audience was in a merry mood and laughed with her.

Shelby looked over at the emcee and nodded. He brought a stool out to her and she climbed up on it and sat down.

"This is to keep me out of trouble," she confided.

Someone in the audience rebuked her, "As if that is all you need to keep out of trouble!" There was laughter from the audience. Shelby smiled and blushed.

She did then begin to sing and the sound was mystical with an old world sound. As Shelby sang she had echoes of women sing from the audience as well and it occurred to Kerrick that this was a well-rehearsed moment that was magical in its movement. He saw some of the men look around as he was, awed by the reverent tone the place had taken on.

Somehow, Shelby took the song and began to add the beats and the sounds until the ballad escalated to a crescendo, where the beat was loud and the audience was fully engaged and captivated.

It was over too soon as far as the crowd was concerned, but it had been an exhilarating ride. She got an overwhelming ovation for her efforts. She was generous as she clapped at the audience, and then turned her back once again to them and bowed to her helpers and applauded them.

She smiled and thanked them and then turned to walk off the stage. Her head was slightly lowered and Sir Kerrick realized she had been acting the part of a gregarious performer. Who was this woman who could light up the stage and then walk off as though she was inconsequential? She almost seemed shy in her retreat and most definitely relieved.

He puzzled this over and smiled. It was like everything else she did. She was hiding something. Her everyday clothes layered her obviously endowed figure. Her leadership qualities she dismissed as a burden and yet she fought for her women's needs as ferociously as a mama Bilboa. Her age she used as a dismissal of any suitor and in difference to her beauty she tried to present herself as dowdy more than any woman born ugly could. He shook his head at the realization that she was good at diverting eyes from reality.

Kerrick kept a close eye on the woman as she passed by him to sit at the top of the outdoor amphitheater. He refrained from grabbing her hand

and pulling her to sit by him as she hiked gracefully up the steep steps. He opted instead to follow her.

When she sat down by some of the other ladies he moved to the aisle above her and sat directly behind her. The women whispered and one of them giggled and motioned her head in his direction. Shelby seemed aloof.

The men around the small group of women were just as interested in their huddle as he was. The beauty of the clan of women was intoxicating and such a drastic difference from their normal attire of work clothes.

His attention was drawn to Shelby's bared back. Her dress was tightened with ribbons in a vee down her back almost to her waist. Where her ringlets and lush mass of hair did not cover, he could see faint scars on her light flesh. She had been flogged. He felt his anger rise again and his protective instincts surfaced. He was perturbed by his sudden awareness of chivalry toward this woman. Maybe it was the Celebration time that made his passions stir so quickly.

Some of the women began to rise from the audience and move toward the platform. They sang from different points in the theater. It was quite beautiful and Sir Kerrick leaned next to Shelby's ear and whispered, "Why are you not singing with them?"

He could tell by her reaction that she was surprised by his nearness and she turned halfway around to look at him. How could a woman be so beautiful and so ignorant of the fact? He was sure she had no idea how she affected the men who were around her. Even the men next to him were enjoying their view of her feminine finery.

"Because they are doing a dance and a song I do not know."

He intensely studied her face and she blushed at the fact he did so with intention. He unceremoniously squeezed in beside her making the women giggle at his oafishness.

Some of the other men did the same and it surprised Shelby and made her suspicious of their antics. She gave Kerrick a disapproving look. He just smiled roguishly at her and winked. The man next to her made conversation with her and the woman on his other side, but Kerrick was so close to her she could feel heat from his body. The evening was getting cool so this was not entirely unwelcome, but she felt like she was being pinned down.

What annoyed her most was the way the men were completely casual about their nearness to her. She made great efforts to maintain a distance from any man in the compound. She was friendly enough to most of the men, but she was very aware of her space and made a point to move away from any man that tried to be near her. Sir Kerrick, of course, ignored all her protests and aloofness and boldly did as he pleased. She could almost like him if he wasn't so arrogant and obnoxious. He never said another thing to her once he sat down, but talked non-stop to the woman next to him. She evidently enjoyed the attention if her purring and touching of his person was any indication.

The ceremonies of the night were finally over and to Shelby's relief the men stood to go. She could at last move out of the sandwiched space and prepare for her evening.

Sir Kerrick watched the woman leave quickly. Her haste would not delay the inevitable. Tonight he would begin his pursuit of this woman.

He stood back from the crowd leaving and watched his charge from the shadow of the darkness. Tonight he would begin to tame his sprite and he knew she would fight him all the way. It would not matter; he was unswerving when he set his mind to a task. What he did not know was if she would ever realize she loved him.

Bewildered / Chapter 12

She sat on the bed and wished she had some wine or some of the strong auget the Alkers used to sleep. She had not had a sound night of rest in weeks and this part of the celebration was taxing her nerves.

When she looked up, she saw the scariest looking man-thing she had ever imagined. She was not even sure it was a man and a small scream inadvertently escaped her throat. She was off the bed in a flash and poised for a fight in her small space. The movement of the creature was non-threatening, but Shelby frantically looked for some kind of weapon besides her hands.

The armor of the imposing figure was black and seemed to disappear and reflect the surroundings. It looked stuck in the balance between real and imagined or here then invisible.

Her breathing accelerated to a point she almost felt faint. She felt like a rabbit scared to death unable to move if she had to. What was that thing?

It stepped into the cubicle and seemed to take the very air from the room. It dominated the small space and fear took hold of Shelby. It spoke after a moment and it took her several seconds to understand it was human, maybe.

She swayed a bit as she lowered her fighting hands and rebalanced her shaking body. What had it said?

"Woman, loosen the cog on my side."

Shelby still could not speak and her only response was to shake her head 'no'.

The creature lifted his headgear off and the enormity of it filled the crook of his arm. Removing the gear did not reveal the man-thing's identity. His face was camouflaged by the same kind of netting. Shelby realized by the exposed chin it was a very large man in a warrior's suit made to intimidate his enemies. It made her angry he scared her near to death and then expected her to undo his armor.

He looked at the exquisite woman before him, once again nearly naked. He tried to gain control of his smile before he took off his helmet. She was fierce in her stance and if not for the indicators in his mask reading her levels off, he would have guessed she was ready for a fight not ready to run. But, her levels of adrenalin revealed her fear and he wanted that for now.

"Shelby, I have brought food, but we will not eat until you have assisted me."

It took her a full minute to give in to his demand. He waited for her breathing to return to a normal level and her mind to quit racing. When he thought about following through on a threat, she slowly raised her chin and moved cautiously closer to him.

"I am Alkernian. I have lineage that I am proud of."

"Good for you," was her quiet response.

154

"I have won many battles in my service to Alker."

"Of course you have, you're here are you not?" He smiled over her head while she lowered her head and bent to see where the cog was to release his shielding armor.

"I have no mate and am seeking a woman of integrity."

Shelby paused and looked up at the man who was stone-faced and looked straight ahead. She was too close to him for her comfort. Still, the promise of food and her growling stomach made her continue on with the latches that needed release. She decided to ignore his last statement. She found a small indentation and slid her finger into it and without much effort the protective layer was free from its magnetic hold and removable.

She stepped back out of reach as the man wrestled the heavy looking breastplate and discarded it to a resting place in the corner of the cubicle, along with his massive helmet.

"I believe you are that woman."

Shelby stood motionless for a moment to absorb what he said, because she didn't know how to respond.

"I do not wish to be anyone's mate or woman." Her heart beat faster at this confrontation and she wished with all her might she was dreaming.

"Why?" The protagonist countered.

How could she tell him she had every intention of leaving this planet to find her children? That would be conspiracy against the Alkers and she would be put to death for such a thing. To even hint at it would mean all her liberties would be taken away. She would be watched even more closely than she already was. She said nothing.

"I can give you children and protection."

She was instantly angry. It was as if he read her mind and found the only thing she cared about. "I already have children and no one was able to protect them or me from you, Alkernian!" She vehemently soured his proposal with her terse retort.

She stood erect and trembled with fury in front of him and the fire in her eyes penetrated to his soul. He expected her reaction, but not his own reaction to her vulnerability. They both stood still, watching each other. Something melted in him. Was that a tear sliding down her tender cheek? He gently reached out to wipe the tear from her face prepared for her to swat his hand away, but she did not react that way. Instead, another tear started down and just as quickly she turned her head to hide her weakness.

"Woman, help me with my boots."

He decided to finish what he started. She turned around and looked indignant. The woman was unpredictable and full of surprises and he determined to know every nuance of her persona. He pointed to his feet and lifted one of them as he balanced awkwardly. She actually smiled, slightly, cheeks still wet from tears. He lifted his foot higher and started to lose his equilibrium so she swatted his foot down and slowly knelt before him.

He was shocked and humbled by her compliance. Then he heard her stomach rumble and he laughed. She was at least reasonable when it came to the basic needs of her belly. One of the things the men did before their pursuit was to study their intended choice. He was sure Shelby would appreciate food. He also discovered that she was more congenial when she was not hungry. He intended to keep her supplied with food.

He ruffed up the top of her hair playfully and she batted his hand away. Very quickly she backed away from him and his feet were free of their bindings. He stood stoic before her and she looked at him like she was suddenly aware he was there. He saw a glint of curiosity in her face.

She gradually realized this man, whoever he was, had scared her to death, had made her furious, had touched the core of her fear and loss, had offered his comfort and had made her laugh. She was very aware she felt drawn to him and she had never in her life been so caught off-guard. She began to tremble at the way she felt attracted to his magnetism. She dearly hoped he could not tell he was alluring to her. She couldn't even see what he looked like.

"Now what?" She asked blandly.

"We eat and talk." He smiled.

He turned and stepped outside the cubicle. He came back with a platter of food that Shelby was astounded by. It looked nothing short of delicious and she could smell spices that made her mouth water and her stomach growl again.

He motioned for her to sit at the small table. He smiled at her and she noticed his straight set of teeth and his full lips. Why did she notice that? She looked away and tried to concentrate on the variety of food. He began to eat off the one plate and motioned for her to try it as well. She daintily dipped her finger into one of the entrees.

"Why do all the men hide their identity during the AB Celebration?" She said this between bites of the smorgasbord he had prepared.

She was sitting far too close to this man and he smelled good. She giggled when she realized she could smell him and the food and it all smelled delicious. She covered her mouth in shock as she grasped she had giggled. Her eyes were wide when she looked at him bewildered.

He very casually told her that some of the food was an aphrodisiac and some of it was used to relax and loosen a person's inhibition.

"This is similar to your alcohol and loosens the tongue and this," he pointed to the dessert-like food she had been enjoying, "is the sexual enhancer."

It tasted very close to delectable chocolate and Shelby was mortified she had consumed most of it herself. He smiled almost wickedly and even through the mask, it looked like he winked at her.

He moved on to tell her why the men hid their identity, but she still mused over the food and wondered if it was having any effect on her reserve.

"So we can choose any woman who has not outright rejected us. So say for instance there is a woman I want to know, but she will not even talk to me. During AB Celebration I can spend time with her and as long as she does not guess who I am and reject me, I can continue to pursue her."

"Am I a woman that doesn't talk to you?" Shelby was intrigued.

He smiled and leaned closer, "No, we have definitely...talked."

"So I must know you." She thought about that for a moment. Well, she had to speak with most of the men, so that really did not help to identify this man. "What if she does not bond with the man or have an attraction to him? Does the man still court the woman against her will?"

The man across from her stopped eating and looked thoughtfully at her. "This is the whole point of the Celebration. For the man to convince the woman she is his match."

"For a man to be my 'match' it would have to happen in the real world, in my day-to-day life, not on some holiday where he is solicitous for a couple days until he gets what he wants." She was so pragmatic that she didn't realize she had set a challenge to the man across from her.

He covered her hand as it rested on the small table. Her skin was soft and he lifted her fingers to his lips and kissed them softly. "Then, Shelby love, I will make sure that in your day-to-day life you know you are desired as much as you are during AB Celebration."

She drew her hand away from him and speculated about what he said.

"You are supposing that I will be your mate and would desire you to do that. Despite the fact that this won't happen, how would you show a woman that she is cared for every day?"

"It has not happened yet, Shelby, but you will be mine because you are not going to find out who I am to reject me. After the Celebration, it will be too late. You only have until the end of the holiday to discover who I am to outright rebuff my claim on you."

"So I will be your wife even if I don't want to be?" She was aghast at the finality of the proclamation. The whole idea of being tied to someone she didn't even know for the rest of her life scared her and made her feel like she was suffocating.

"Not wife. Mate. This celebration is for a man to determine if the woman of his desire would be suitable to bear him a child. Once the child is old enough to be away from his mother, she is free to go or to stay with the child and his father as she wishes, if they are not married by Alker Tradition."

"This is totally wrong. My religious beliefs don't allow me to have sexual relationships outside of marriage. It would put my soul in turmoil to even think I would have to leave my child. I refuse to cooperate!"

Before she finished her last statement she found herself pulled up and gripped in the behemoth man's hands. "Listen to me, Char Shelby. There is nothing repulsive about being my mate or having my child. Many women have solicited me to give them a child, so do not hide behind your religion and call my traditions unholy. As far as being my wife, I reserve that for the woman I love." He let go of her abruptly.

Shelby stood momentarily shocked that she was to be an incubator for his progeny. Then she exploded over him by punching his body and kicking him. She came at him so fast that at first he just shielded his face from her onslaught, but she landed a swift kick to his groin and sent him backward off balance.

He had enough. With a swoop of his arms he tossed her unceremoniously on the bed and fell on top of her with his weight. Her frenzy was halted by the fact she could not breathe or move.

When he gained control of her arms, he lifted himself up from her lush, enticing body and looked down at her flushed face. He did not hesitate to lower his lips to hers and ply them with purpose. She tasted as good as she looked. She bucked against his onslaught; nevertheless he was persistent and continued to satisfy his growing arousal. He felt her body yield almost imperceptibly and he adjusted his hold on her to free one of his hands to feel her supple curves. Her soft moan goaded his senses, but he rallied his craving to stick to his ultimate purpose and not his immediate desire.

What was wrong with her? He smelled so good. Her mind was so against the celebration purposes, but her body was not cooperating with her ideals. His weight on her body was comforting and his lips were softer than she could have imagined a man's would be. Then he stroked her skin and she felt on fire with need. If he didn't stop soon she would not be able to keep from yielding to his onslaught and her awakening desires.

Suddenly his weight was gone and she was being pulled off the bed to her feet. He held her against him and she was confused, but she did realize even in her dazed state, she would not be stable on her feet if he let go. Her body still hummed from his touch and her breathing was heavily labored.

"My time is almost up," Shelby looked up at him with relief or hope, he was not sure, but it made him chuckle, "for the night. You will not get rid of me that easily, Shelby." Her emotions were not easy to read in her expression, yet he was sure she was confused by the way she frowned.

"I expect you to be in your cubicle every night from now on. If you are not, I will take away the liberties that you enjoy, like your swim at night, and you will go without the foods you have tasted tonight because they will be delivered to your cubicle only; from tomorrow night until the end of the celebration. And since the men do the cooking, you will be deprived of food, as is my right to do to you, if you do not behave. That means any antics you have planned will cease."

"Don't count on it. And as far as food goes, I can forage for my own meals and be satisfied without any Alkernian delicacy for a couple of weeks." She turned her back on him and sat at the far edge of the bed.

He was annoyed that she would still defy him even after he had used food to ply her and seduce her into compliance. He knew she could find food to eat. She was resourceful and knowledgeable of the surrounding woods, taking her cubs out regularly to hunt, but he was not easily intimidated. She would feel him bear down on her if she caused any trouble.

He moved closer to her and looked down at her as she sat on the edge of the bed. "I do not want you to be in misery, Shelby, but I have expectations of you during the celebration time."

He knelt down in front of her on one knee and turned her face to his. "I will protect you, Shelby, with my life, but I expect you to follow some basic laws of tradition. You do have a choice to make this time enjoyable or not. It is up to you." He took her hands and looked at her skin as it turned a bluish color. Some foods did that to the Alkers when their emotions were heightened. He did not expect that to happen to an Earth woman and it surprised him. He kissed the palm of her hand.

"I think we are good match, Char Shelby. So I will not press you any further tonight. Sleep well and good hunting tomorrow." He kissed her forehead as he stood, and then turned to leave.

"Good hunting?" Did she misunderstand him?

He turned and saw her confusion. "I assume you will try to find out who I am tomorrow so that you can cease my pursuit of you." He tried to lighten the mood with his teasing.

He saw her ponder this and was amused that she smiled at him. Soon the food she ate would reach its potency and make her very drowsy. He had noticed earlier that she had circles under her eyes and suspected she had not slept well. He hoped to rectify that and have some pleasure with the woman who definitely intrigued him. For now, he needed to nurse his black eye.

Shelby shook with frustration and fear. Did he know how close to yielding to his warmth she was? How could she possibly deviate from her deep seated personal beliefs? She had no desire to do so, but her body almost betrayed her purpose. It had been a long time since she had felt the heat of a man.

She wasn't sure what time it was, but she thought it might be late by the sound of activity in the dome. Shelby stretched and yawned.

Morning came too soon. Outside, she saw some men at the fire closest to her dome and a few women meandering around as well. It was early, because the men were half naked, exposed from the waist up. They looked at her curiously, some were in various processes of shaving and she looked around with her delicate brows pulled together. What was going on?

She scratched her messy head and tried to recall her encounter with the mysterious man. She grabbed a hot drink, took a deep breath and went back to her cubicle.

Someone swore and some of the men laughed. "I did not know a woman could wake up and look so edible." The men chortled again. Most of the men were in good moods and it showed by the humming and whistling going on.

Shelby appeared at the entrance of the dome again a few minutes later. She was looking around at all the different people.

"Is there something wrong, Char Shelby?" A man named Sims asked her solicitously.

"Am I in a time warp? What day is it?"

"It is the third morning of AB Celebration, Shelby." Kerrick stepped into the clear from the group of men.

She had not known he was there or that he would even answer a question she asked. "Why is everyone so happy? My head is killing me. What time is it?" She realized she had every one's attention and she blushed and held up her hand to stop the answers. She hurt. Her head hurt. Her eyes hurt. She tried to shield the light with her hand.

Sir Kerrick stood before her and blocked the sunlight that streamed into her face. He was bare-chested with skin stretched over his well defined physique. She almost reached out and touched his muscled chest just to see if the skin felt as smooth as it looked.

"Maybe you should go back to your cubicle and rest a little longer, woman."

Shelby raised her eyes to look at Kerrick and then around him at the other men who watched her with close intent.

She half whispered to him, "Is that allowed?"

He chuckled and crossed his arms over his hard chest. He looked at her with his head tilted and an eyebrow raised as if to indicate she had asked a silly question, but what he saw was a sensual hunger he knew well. He watched her try to hide her desire.

"During AB Celebration anything is allowed. It is like a holiday. The main things we will worry about are eating, sleeping, drinking and not sleeping." The men laughed at that and some jokes were thrown back and forth between the men. Sir Kerrick heard some of the men's talk getting more ribald and decided to usher Shelby into the dome before she caught onto the fact they were directing their charm toward her.

She protested and tried to shrug out of his hand. "Kerrick. I hurt all over and my head is pounding. Stop pushing me," she hissed at him in a whisper. "And stop talking so loud, please."

He found that amusing and he smiled condescendingly. "I am talking quietly, Shelby, love, you just have a hangover."

"I didn't drink last night. I know better."

"But, you did eat, and apparently your suitor added auget to your food. What did you eat?"

She looked at him stunned for a minute and felt confused. When he repeated himself, she grasped what he was saying. "I ate some blue stuff and some wonderful green thing, and most everything on the plate. It was very delicious and I was hungry," she snapped defensively.

Kerrick crossed his thick arms over his decidedly lumpy, hard chest and continued to grin at her. She wanted to smack him, but it might hurt her to make that kind of noise.

"The blue stuff was probably your downfall. It acts as a catalyst to some of the other 'delicious stuff' you inhaled last night." He enjoyed trying her patience and he found her amusing as she kept putting up her hands to quiet him and placing one of her slender fingers across her lush lips to emphasis he was still talking too loud.

"Okay. So I, hey! I did not inhale my food. How would you know that anyhow?" Her whisper was too loud and she put her hands to the side of her head and took a deep breath.

"Men talk. Besides, I know how you like to eat." Now he was really digging at her.

"You are obnoxious, Kerrick." She sucked in her breath again at the pain the rejoinder added.

She turned from him and strode to her cubicle to get away from him. He enjoyed the swing of her hips and the shape of her long slender legs.

He always irritated her. If she could have she would have slammed and locked a door. She sat on the bed and held her pounding head instead.

Commander Rockdurgh approached Sir Kerrick with purpose. "We need to be careful the women do not get too much stimulants tonight. Many of them had disorientation, just like Shelby. I think they have a reaction to the aphrodisiacs we normally use. Their body chemistry must absorb it differently than we do."

"Let the men know." Sir Kerrick laughed. Tonight was going to be pleasurable and he intended to be ready for whatever his nymph had in store. He loved the hunt and to be hunted.

He looked around surprised to see his match, dressed and going toward the group of women. Oh yes, he loved the hunt.

Going Hunting / Chapter 13

Brenda sidled up close to the men standing in a semi-group near the center fire of the large dome tent. She was dressed provocatively and her swaying body flitted around the men arousing their senses. She boldly looked them over to see if she could discover her suitor and she made no bones about what she was doing.

Shelby was amused the men enjoyed the attention. It was not something she was used to. Instead of being tough and soldiering, they were relaxed and coy about who was her visitor. Each of them tried to convince Brenda he was her suitor and it became a laughable game. Shelby enjoyed watching the whole transformation of the men being so solicitous to her and their reaction to Brenda's sultry laugh. She was a dark beauty and she knew it. She used everything she had in full knowledge she was very desirable. Shelby wondered if there was anyone who would refuse her, or if they could, would they want to?

Shelby looked around at some of the other women in the dome. Some were not as amused as Shelby. She walked toward a small group of women who talked amongst themselves.

"Are you all alright?" Shelby queried, her look hopefully relaying her curiosity.

"Do you see her? She is shameless!" Shelby looked to where they were pointing.

"Are you kidding? You're angry at Brenda?" Shelby clearly did not understand their annoyance.

"She is so blatantly asking for attention. She doesn't care where she gets her compliments from. Look at her!"

Shelby was surprised by their jealousy.

"Did each of you have a suitor last night?"

"Yes. So why does she act like she wants every one of those men? Isn't she satisfied with one man? It's disgusting the way she hangs all over them."

"First of all, this is Brenda we are talking about. She is one of us." At this a couple of women shook their heads 'no', but Shelby continued.

"She is getting close enough to the men to identify her suitor and dispel his pursuit. She is also very against the fact she does not get to pick her own mate and she does not want to have a child with an Alker that is not her choosing. She is just going about it differently than you and I are. Or are you satisfied with the man that was your suitor last night?" Shelby looked around again at the younger women. "She apparently is not, and the only way to stop the process is to discover the identity of the Alker who is visiting you at night. Otherwise at some point, you are going to be expected to give one of these men a child."

"What are you going to do about your pursuer, Shelby?"

"I wish I could say I don't have one, but apparently I have the same dilemma as all the women here. I have no clue as to what I am going to do. I am definitely looking for some way out." Shelby fussed with her hands. Suddenly Brenda's actions didn't seem so outlandish.

The women continued to talk about their evening with their night visitors. Shelby gathered some of the women enjoyed themselves more than they were willing to admit, while a couple of them were fine with disclosing the fact they enjoyed the whole courtship as a harmless pastime.

Shelby was curious none of them admitted to being scared by the presence of a warrior appearing before them in a tiny cubicle.

"I was wondering if any of you were annoyed that the men came in their battle armor." Shelby looked at the puzzled faces of the women.

"What do you mean, Char Shelby?"

"Why are you calling me that? Anyway, the man who came to my cubicle last night was in armor." Shelby knew the other women did not have the same experience by the quizzical expressions on their faces.

"You mean he was disguised in protective war armor?" Some of the women were amused by the absurdity of the symbolism and laughed at her.

Shelby blushed and rolled her eyes. It was a bit disconcerting that the man prepared for battle before confronting her. But looking back at her encounter with him, it was a rough engagement. She was not an easy conquest, at least she hoped not.

When Shelby got ready for today's celebratory midday meal, she did not have her own things to pick from. One of the changes her room held was a completely new wardrobe. None of her former clothes were in her cubicle, and she was agitated whenever she thought about it. But the clothing she possessed now was suitable for the events of the holiday and she admitted only to herself they felt far more comfortable than the roughness of her work clothes.

This dome was lavishly decorated for the sole purpose of eating meals here. One of the things that amazed Shelby was the men's ability to create a wealthy atmosphere from the multitude of cloth they possessed. It was one of their customs to create rooms made of the lush fabric they owned and the colors of a man's liking were ever present in his own dome. Now they adorned the extra large dome with the same flowing fabrics that made the whole huge room move with life and color.

Later that evening, Sir Kerrick watched as some of the men wandered closer to the group of women huddled near Brenda, Amy and Shelby. Shelby retreated to a place further away from the cluster of people, though from Kerrick's perspective, she was enjoying herself. She looked like she was observing the men and he recognized her predatory look. She was hunting.

She wore a dark olive-green dress tucked tight down her body embracing it like skin to flow loose midway at her hips. The strips of multicolored ribbons tied across her back wove down her bodice in such a way as to accent her small waist and round hips. He still had a hard time believing she was so beautifully built. Her presence was compelling and even though she was against the exterior wall, she was not as invisible as she believed; proof was that a man settled next to her.

She was not smiling or initiating the attention. Suddenly she looked directly into the man's face and said something he clearly did not expect. To Sir Kerrick's annoyance the man leaned over and kissed her mouth. She did not resist his attention; in fact, it looked like she encouraged his friendliness.

His unconscious step forward was brought to a halt by Commander Rockdurgh. "Sir Kerrick. It is not a good idea to act the jealous suitor so soon in the courtship."

Kerrick was irritated. If Rockdurgh had not stopped him, he would have blundered in his plan of making it to the end of AB Celebration without his identity being found out. He needed to control his impulses and not be so electrified by her erratic actions. She was looking around the area searching for something. Her eyes locked with his for just a second then moved on.

He realized in an instant she was still hunting. She knew she was being watched by someone and she was instigating a reaction from her chaser.

The man next to her drew her against him and continued kissing her. Sir Kerrick looked away to gather his thoughts on how to proceed. It came to him that annoying her in public was one of his guilty pleasures.

He turned to Rockdurgh and nodded. "I owe you one, friend."

Rockdurgh smiled, "Only one? You do not count very well, friend." They slapped each other on the shoulder and Kerrick strode toward Shelby and her kissing companion, Biat.

Shelby spied his approach and frowned at him. He expected this. He gave Biat a nod and bowed to Shelby in a respectable gesture of appreciation. They both were annoyed at his intrusion.

"You look stunning this evening, Shelby, and you seem to be enjoying yourself. Do you mind if I sit with you a while? I have something to speak to you about."

"Yes. I mean, no." She was flustered by his remarks and his command of the situation. She looked toward Biat and saw his attention was being drawn away by two women who accosted him to dance with their group. His shoulders went up in submission and the smile on his face could only be from relief of getting away from her and Kerrick's presence.

Shelby sat back down a little petulantly and felt Kerrick loom over her. She sighed and waited for him to sit. When she looked up, he held out his hand toward her. Reluctantly, she put her hand in his warm one and he pulled her back on her feet. She was puzzled.

Without any words he drew her to the dance floor and formally bowed. His suit was subtly elegant and his skin glowed, or was it the clothes that illuminated his skin? She looked toward the opening and saw the two moons were making their appearance. His hands opened out to her and she cautiously fell into

174

step with the movement of the music being played. His coaxing relaxed her and she actually started to enjoy being near Kerrick. It helped that he didn't provoke her by talking.

"Your arm is better."

"Indeed. Alkers heal fast."

"So I've been told." She looked intently at him and asked, "Can you tell me why people are calling me 'Char'? What does that mean?"

"It is a title of respect and acknowledgment that you have saved a life, or in your case, many."

Shelby was dumbfounded and Kerrick smiled down at her mischievously.

"Woman, have you any inkling who your pursuer may be?" Kerrick was aware she was not inclined to answer him. "Is it possibly, Biat?" He probed.

"No. Biat is too tall for my suitor and way too young. Plus the man was thicker."

"Thicker?" Kerrick chuckled. "I only know one man who is 'thick'."

"Who?"

"Sepoy Bordog." He jested, but Shelby was contemplative.

"Bordog is way too wide and too short. Plus, Bordog's anger permeates from him. He can't tolerate me or I him. He is indeed thick in the head, but, no. The man who pursued me last night was calm and very well built. I didn't recognize his voice, though he says I've talked to him."

Kerrick did not miss her off-handed compliment of her suitor.

"I thought you said he was thick."

"None of the other Alkernian men are heavy like Bordog."

"Oh, so you meant fat when you said thick." Kerrick teased.

"No. Stop twisting my words." He laughed and she rolled her eyes and sighed. "Why do you try to provoke me, always?"

"Because you are too serious, always." He smiled at her indulgently and winked conspiratorially.

She decided to redirect the conversation.

"I was wondering when your new wife would be appearing? Is she coming with the entourage that is expected to arrive in a few months?"

"That was the plan."

He spun Shelby around and swung her back over his arm, supporting her in a graceful back bend. He held her there until she finally looked him in the eyes.

"But, alas, she changed her mind. She took my name, but not me." He knew that would shock her, but he acted as if it was not the point. "Do all the women know my business?" He continued moving her around the dance floor.

Shelby was puzzled. Was the ship not coming, or just not his wife?

"Do they?"

"What?"

"Do they all know my business?"

Shelby looked into Kerrick's laughing eyes and shied under their probing.

"I don't think so. But all the women know some of the men's business and most want to know all your business. I get hounded all the time about you. What do you like? What are you like? Who do you like? As if I know or care!"

He chuckled at her.

"You do not care? Do you not want to know my...business?" He left no doubt in his tone that he was twisting the meaning of what she said to be a sexual suggestion.

"Certainly not," she snipped. "There are enough women groveling at your feet to keep you busy for months. I am surprised your wife is not here protecting 'your business' right now."

He whispered in her ear, "She will have nothing to worry about once we are vowed, Shelby love." His baritone voice soothed her ire.

Shelby was again surprised by his declaration, and she didn't quite know what he meant.

He saw the puzzlement on her face and smiled over her head. When he looked back at her, he elaborated for clarity in a more sincere tone.

"All Alkernian women before being mated have to go through a ceremonial process and then say vows to their husband in front of their peers after. I am technically not vowed yet, or married, as you call it."

"I was told by Rockdurgh that you went to marry your bride on Iritain. I think that's why all the women are keeping their distance from you. They were led to believe that you're now married. I guess, even if you are not technically married, or vowed, you're still not available."

Kerrick looked at her with a curious tilt to his mouth as he guided her off the floor and out the door to a private area when he heard her say his name. It was in a quiet, intense voice he heard her say his name again. She pulled against his arm and dragged her feet. He stopped and looked at her radiant skin and tried to concentrate.

"Until the vows are spoken as Tradition dictates, I can not claim my bride, nor can she claim me. We need no religious priest or priestess to guide the ritual as you do. But, alas, she is vowed to my brother. He claims her as wife."

"Oh." She didn't know what else to say.

"Did you tell the other women that I was married?"

Shelby wondered how the other women would know that, since she didn't in fact say anything to anybody.

"No. I have better things to do than to try and keep up on your business." Shelby was irritated because he had her in a private place and was cross-examining her and she was distracted about the possibility of returning to Earth. She needed to get off Aion and get to her home planet to look for her family.

Kerrick was angry.

"You must never try to return to Earth, Shelby!" His voice was terse. "Your human bodies cannot withstand the trauma of space travel within the Trough. It causes the mind to lose reality. Do you understand?" He gripped her shoulders.

"What?" Shelby realized he somehow knew what she was thinking.

He was startled by the look on her face and the slow shaking of her head. "I heard you clearly." He still fumed, but let her go. He walked several paces around her and collected his thoughts. Finally, he stuck his finger in her face and forcefully warned her, "Be careful, Char Shelby. Your body was not made to travel through the Trough or jet back and forth from planet to planet."

"Fine. But I never said anything about traveling through the Trough. I don't even know what that is."

He ignored her and went on, "This was not my home planet, but it is now." His tone calmed. "This is your chance too, for a new life, Shelby. Grab it and try to live the last of your measly, short years well. You have everything here to be happy in spite of your losses. Think about it." He turned and left abruptly.

He completely took the enjoyment out of her night. It took her a few minutes before she could calm herself as she sat down under the gaze of the moons lights.

Think about it? That was all she seemed to do. She was trying to make the best of her situation, but she still had terrible dreams of her children being torn from her arms and always she woke just as she was being put into a black box.

Then it occurred to her. Kerrick was able to leave this planet through something he called the Trough. So it was possible to space travel from here. Now all she had to know was where the thing was and how to use it. A dawning smile eased her features. Things were looking up.

179

This evening was strained for Shelby. She was aware of being watched with critical eyes from Sir Kerrick. He avoided her with such intensity it actually started to please her. His attention was often diverted to other women vying for his notice, but when she talked to other men and women and she happened to see him, his look spoke volumes of his distrust of her.

This weighed her down because of the very real probability she would be watched. Her every move would be scrutinized. She was positive she had not spoken out loud her desire to seek her children, but he assured her she had indeed said so, and how could he know if she had not said it out loud? She was angry with herself. She sunk her ship and he was not lax when it came to security around this camp, especially since the animal attack.

After the festivities, Shelby made her way back to her domicile. She was weary. She lay back on the bed and crossed her arm over her eyes when she started to weep. Her mind whirled around the anger Kerrick displayed, so out of character for him. Then she began to think of how he would smile an indulgent grin when she was angry or talked to him. It occurred to her for the first time she felt secure around him. Why?

Her thoughts wandered. Her mind slowed until she drifted to sleep somewhere between hating Kerrick and this planet and realizing if her children were here she would be content. Her heart was healing and she was beginning to feel again.

The beauty of the planet was giving her new life and hope.

He entered the dark cubicle and could sense her presence. The food he conveyed here was heavy so he touched the side of the wall with one finger and a candle-soft light illuminated the room ever so gently. He set the large platter down and went closer to the bed.

She was sound asleep, still in her evening dress. Her legs hung over the side of the bed as if she sat down on the edge and fell back on the bed without moving again.

He looked at her with unrestrained appreciation. She had no defenses or scowls on her face, so her facial features were softened by sleep. She looked young and vulnerable, but he knew she was fierce. There were so many things about her that were sketchy and unclear, but some were branded in his mind.

Up until this night, he wondered what her subterfuge was, but she was not deceitful. She had one goal, to leave this planet in hope of finding her children. Her passion ran so deep he could feel the pull as if it were his own. The two times he spoke of children, she came unglued and irrational to the point of a berserker.

He also realized she did not speak of her children out loud. He was so angry after he understood her desire to get to Earth that he did not grasp for a fleeting moment he had heard her personal, unspoken reflection. That was how it was. He was suddenly flung into the memories of another person by their intense passion or singleness of thought.

Her convictions were filled with compelling need, and he somehow visited her truth. Hidden as it was, it was apparently her true desire, maybe the pivotal desire of her happiness. He perceived she would never be able to let such a deep-seated desire die; he could not, and she was proving to be just as determined as he could be. He did not hold stubbornness against her.

He knelt down and gently removed her slippers. Her legs were slender and firm from her daily exercise. She was sinewy and lithe, but her shape was nothing short of voluptuous. He easily lifted her relaxed body further onto the bed. She rolled away from him and her long dress twisted around her body hindering her movement. He heard her sigh.

With very little effort, he loosened the back of her dress bodice so she would be more comfortable. Scars crisscrossed over her otherwise smooth skin. How had she come by those? A slow anger began to burn in his chest as he thought about her being beaten in such a fashion. A whip was the only thing he knew would bring this kind of scarring. Who had beaten her?

He knew she did not take orders well, but there were other ways to get someone to submit to commands. He still could not get her to address him by his title, not that he really wanted her to. The familiarity that she addressed him by was to his advantage at this point. The twisted thing was though, she probably did not realize that by addressing him without his formal title, she was stating clearly that she was his equal and belonged in his care.

Shelby hoped that if she pretended to be sleeping, her night visitor would go away. But as she lay there she felt that might not deter him at all. He was sitting on her bed with a hand resting on her ankle. He squeezed her leg gently and shook her body; then he spoke her name. She tried to move away from him and reject his summoning, but he was persistent.

"Go away." She whined.

"I think not. I have brought some food."

"No thank you. I am not hungry. I am tired. Go away." She repeated.

But that did not deter the boorish man. He gently pulled her over to face him and just as quickly scooped her up. The quickness of the action startled her and she squealed with alarm. She tried pushing against his chest and stiffened her body to get away from the man. He was like a rock and would not budge.

He sat down with her on his lap by the table. He held her captive until she quit squirming and then spoke to her when she groaned in frustration.

"Are you done?" He looked at her scowling face and set jaw and figured at some point she would retaliate.

She would not look at him or answer him so he held her firm and every time she struggled he caught her movements and halted her. Finally, she turned her words on him.

183

"I will be done if you let me go."

His grip loosened and she tried to get off his lap, but he pulled her back down. "I think you and I will need to settle some things before we go on."

She looked into his disguised face, and tried for the life of her to discern who it was.

He could see by her face she was unaware of his identity and that alone pleased him. Tonight he would be free to claim her for his mate. He was good at this game of pretense and he planned on using it to his advantage.

"The mask I am wearing is designed to shift my image so that the observer never quite gets a feature to hone in on."

She nodded her understanding, but she still had questions about why she could not discern who it was. "Everybody gives off personal impressions that are uniquely theirs, but even your voice is not one I recognize. So, do I not know you at all? Or are you an Alker I've been around some?"

He grinned slyly. She was determined to find his identity.

Her stomach growled from the food's appetizing aroma, but she ignored it and asked again. "How can I not recognize you from among the other men?" She sighed in frustration.

"You do realize that I have no intention of telling you until the time?" He noted her pouting lips and could not stop his thumb from rubbing across them. Her lips were soft and her skin was warm and silky. She stilled his hands and he smiled at her softening reaction. So, she was not as impervious to his touch as she tried to pretend.

He reached over the plate and lifted a portion of the food to her lips. She looked directly at where his camouflaged eyes should be and her empathic sense of need to know sizzled in her own quizzing eyes. She was devising a truce. He could see by the way she tilted her head and chewed on her lower lip that she was thinking something through.

Her eyes moved over his exterior features and she unwittingly put her hands on him and began to slide them over his body as if to coax his identity out. He enjoyed this very much.

He stood up abruptly and she slipped off his lap, suddenly aware she had awakened a sleeping giant. She pulled her hands back circumspectly. He smiled down at her and gently put her cool hands back on his chest.

"Touching is allowed." He laughed at her embarrassed scowl and spread his arms out wide, daring her to continue with a lift of his chin. She turned pink, but laughter spread to her eyes and she got a determined look in her expression.

She was so visibly uncomfortable with whatever was going through her mind, that he was afraid he had hindered her from continuing the examination. But, to his surprised delight, she tilted her head back and made a throaty laugh. Her neck was exposed to him and her body relaxed as if she let something tangible fall from her shoulders.

His arms came smoothly down around her and he held her for a few moments. He rested his chin on top of her curly head of hair and she held her hands on his hips. Ever so slowly, he felt her body relax and her hands glide up his back.

He began a slow dance of movement, plying his hands across her body and shifting their weight to move her feet away from the tiny table laden with food.

He untucked his shirt and guided her hands to his skin. Her roaming hands sent waves of pleasure coursing through his body. They moved over his body feeling his ribs and massaging his muscles. Her fingers found the waistband of his pants and followed the edge, dipping her slender fingers just below the layer of binding. She moved slightly away from him and slid her spread hands up his muscled abdomen and across his chest testing the pliability of his skin. She kept moving her hands up to his shoulders and followed the muscles down his arms as far as she could; hindered by the shirt he still wore. That was enough. He needed his clothes off and he wanted to touch some skin too.

He pulled his shirt off with a quick movement and he saw the flash of desire in her surprised expression. It gave him some satisfaction knowing she was attracted to him and that she could lust after him. Let her feel the wanting for him as he did for her. He cupped her face in one of his big hands and turned it up. He waited until she focused on him and then he kissed her, tasting her like she was a forbidden fruit he would only get once. She had aroused him just by her roaming hands and he was determined to do the same to her.

His hands found the opening in the folds of the dress he had loosened earlier. The crisscrosses of the straps held her gown securely on, but he needed only to pull the bow to have it give way to his large probing hands. When he found the flesh he desired, it heated his craving even more than he thought possible. Each taste he took of her lips made him more intoxicated with need. He held her face in both hands and looked into her smoldering eyes. She was as hungry for this as he was.

To answer his unspoken question, she lifted herself on her toes and kissed him unabashedly. His arms swallowed her body up and he lifted her off her feet and twirled her slowly around and around not losing contact with her lips. She was so responsive he nearly let his guard down.

If she found out who he was before the end of AB Celebration, he was not so sure she would accept him. In a way, he wanted to give her the choice, but he selfishly also wanted, nay needed, an heir to his name and she was well suited for the task.

He slowly lowered her to her feet before the bed. He steadied her with one of his arms when she swayed weakly. Everything slowed to an anticipated crescendo as he waited for some sign from her that she was aware of the point of no return this evening had come to.

"Shelby, I have no desire to stop, but I need you to look at me and tell me I am not forcing you against your will to be my mate."

She shook her head 'no' that she was not being forced. This man she barely knew was asking her if she wanted him to stop. Stop his tantalizing touches and intoxicating kisses and to stop the lust that was burning in her body. She did not want him to stop.

"I need you to speak the words to me, Shelby. There can be no doubt in the fact that you want me; that you agree to be my mate."

"Why? Are you recording it?" she seriously asked.

He laughed softly and pulled her against him feeling the willingness of her body separating from her inquisitive mind.

"No. I need to hear it. I need to know you will not resent me making you a part of me and me a part of you. I need to know you will not regret your decision in any part of this."

"I don't know who you are, how can I know?"

"Look at me. All I can assure you is that you have a good idea of my intentions and who I am."

She bit her lower lip. But a smile stole her worried look away.

"Something about you is so familiar. But, I know you're Alker and I don't like you because of it."

He scoffed.

"But, I also know that right here, right now, I need to remember Aion may be my home for the rest of my life and I need to belong somewhere. You could tell me who you are and then..."

"No," he assured her with a quirky smile. "I want you to say 'yes' because of what you know now, not because of what you think you know or see me as out there."

She hesitated only a little. "Then, yes. As long as you realize I am willing because of how safe you make me feel when I am with you. And that you realize I believe you claiming me as your mate is like marriage and gives me some protection and peace of mind. But, I am still going to try to stop you and find out who you are before the end of AB Celebration."

"Really? I thought you might. A simple 'yes, I agree to this' would have been enough." He said this as relief flooded through his mind and confirmed all the more that she was not easily led by her emotions. At some point this night, she determined she would willingly give herself to him. He laughed softly against her shoulder and hugged her to him. How would she react when she found out he truly was one man she had no patience or desire to be around?

He looked down into her upturned face and took the plunge into the wild depths of his churning emotions. His desire to bring her ecstasy and fear she would only give him this one chance, made his kiss deep and demanding. Her moans drove him to a sweet madness of possibility and loss. He pressed against her until she laid back, his arm lifting and guiding her further into the depths of the bed.

Her hands never stopped memorizing his body and the scar that bumped across his shoulders like a cross. How was it possible this unidentified man could make her feel so passionate and desirable? He smelled so good to her she needed to taste him. Her tongue touched his chest and she bit him and kissed his silky smooth skin. His muscles rippled as he moved over her and her body hummed with excitement. Then a thought struck her and she stilled.

"Shelby love, what is wrong?"

She shook her head 'no'. He put his forehead on hers and with as much control as he could to halt his heated body he said, "Tell me, love, what you need."

"I need you to assure me you are not a young man."

"What?" He raised his body up a little to look into her worried face.

"I do not want you to be twenty years younger than me. Can you assure me of that? There are a lot of boys in the company and I am way too old for some of them."

He laughed so hard he had to roll on his back, but he pulled her up on him.

"Woman, you sure know how to kill a mood. Really?"

She nodded her head.

"I gave you ample time to examine my body. Does it look like a young man's physique?" She nodded her head 'no' unconvinced.

He pulled her down and met her lips with his own and kissed her with such experienced kisses he took her breath away. "Woman, I guarantee to you I am not a boy or young man, but an experienced warrior and I am older than many of the men here." He saw the genuine relief in her eyes and it surprised him.

She leaned down and ardently kissed him and touched him with pure desire. He responded in kind and almost instantly he was hard for her again and in spite of his desire to make this first time last, he needed to feel the soft wet place that she offered him. His fingers found the warmth of her readiness and he plied her with strokes of temptations. He made sure she writhed with desire before he entered her and began the climb with her. She responded so perfectly to his body he felt lost in the speed his body relinquished its seed. He felt her release just after he finished and her muscles squeezed him tight making his body surrender the last bit of his strength.

He pulled her tight against him and kissed her neck. As he wrapped his arm around her, he rolled to the side keeping her against him and cradling her in his warmth.

"That was over way too soon." He was aware that she almost did not finish.

"It was perfect." She sighed and he tightened his embrace around her. He kissed her neck again and snuggled against her back.

She rested now and he was fairly sure she would sleep for a while longer. Her hair sprawled across the bed and she snored softly. He took out a knife and lifted a curl. "Tradition." He really did not need any of her hair, but tradition dictated he keep it for proof of their night together.

He cut some of his hair off and placed it on the bed. She could use it to claim the support of her baby's father. Tradition allowed the woman to claim help from the family if the man died in battle. He smiled at the possibilities of Shelby being free from him by death; a person did not almost die that many times.

He left her for the night. He satisfied the Alker Tradition. He would not return until the end and he hoped she would not be able to discover his identity and dispel his rights to her as his chosen mate. After AB Celebration he would make it public.

Shelby was disgusted with herself. What had she done? Why did she give in to her carnal desires? When she put aside her semi-guilt, she could only smile. She shouldn't feel so good, but she did. She was so confused. The man made her feel so comfortable and he was so beautifully built and his smile was very sexy. Stop! Shelby shook her head and pushed aside the delicious thoughts of last night. How was she going to walk among the men and not be a spectacle? She'd scare them if she had a smile on her face.

After the fall / Chapter 14

J ust before the end of AB Celebration, Shelby was ushered up the ramp to Doc Orlie's to help with the cubs and aid him with the plant selection she helped collect. She thoroughly enjoyed the extra time she had with the Bilboas these last two weeks. It also helped clear her mind of the lingering panic she was experiencing.

Ever since she succumbed to her own carnal desires for her suitor, she had not seen him since. She went from grumpy to giddy to even grumpier than she ever thought possible, even for her. At first she was horrified by her wantonness. Then she was dreamy-eyed about the whole experience. Then she was disgusted and ashamed by her lack of self-control.

So now, with just two days until the holiday was over, at which time they would move the camp up to the winter base, she was still no closer to finding out who her suitor was, or how to return to Earth on the ship that would be bringing newcomers later this winter.

Every man she thought might be her possible suitor turned out to be too big, too tall, too loud or too young. And whenever she could, she would scour the men when they were doing drills and working without their shirts on. Not so much to see

193

their muscular build, as to look for the scar on the left shoulder, which she felt when she had run her hands across the otherwise smooth skin of the man who bewitched her.

That was the other thing. The man she yielded to smelled so intoxicating she sniffed the air every time a man walked by. It was the smell of him she kept remembering. She must have looked ridiculous. A couple of times, men looked at her with smirks on their faces as if they knew what she was trying to do and she was some comical woman in heat. Or maybe they were flattered she sniffed after them. Either way, she tried to be less obvious after being caught a couple times.

Shelby made it to the landing at the entrance of the duel dome where she was to meet Doc Orlie. A large group of Alker men, half dressed, were washing up after an obviously grueling workout. Embarrassed, Shelby automatically turned to go back down the ramp to the main camp when she was called back by Kerrick.

When she turned around to face him, she didn't believe she could blush anymore than she already was, but she did. He was wrapped in a towel that was too small to close, and had to be held by one of his hands. Visions of him naked flashed before her eyes and she didn't know if she should run or close her mouth. Either way she was lost at the sight of him standing there beckoning her to him.

Behind him she caught other men sneak glances at her and then resume their conversations nonchalantly. Her eyes met Kerrick's and the lingering smile on his face was not the sneer she was used to from him. Instead, it was enchanting and beguiling. She felt drawn to him and it occurred to her this was the first time, since the night he danced with her, he was charming her and holding his hand out to her. All the other encounters before and since had been to rile and irritate her. When he was this way, it was easy to see what the other women saw in him. She wondered for an instant if he forgot it was her, not some other woman he wanted to seduce.

His smile broadened and he stepped close enough to her to take her hand in his. He was talking and Shelby only caught the last half of what he was saying.

"...so Doc will be in the back with the cubs."

He entwined his fingers with hers and she followed meekly behind, subdued by strange waves of clarity and bafflement. She never considered Kerrick to be her suitor. She just never saw him that way, nor did she want to be another one of his many women. But she got this overwhelming sense of strength from him, like he was pulling her into his embrace. In reality, he walked her down the hall toward the unit she was to meet Doc in, as if he was her guide and she had never been there before.

Sudden panic took hold of her and she planted her feet. She couldn't see his scar, but she had the distinct feeling he was the man she'd mated with.

Kerrick felt the jerk and resistance from Shelby. Without turning toward her he hung his head, knowing that his ruse was done. When he felt fingers touch his left shoulder, he turned toward her. She did not look happy or angry. She looked like she was going to cry.

"This will end, now." She stated flatly.

The smile was gone from his face and the mask of indifference barely concealed his hostility. He had been outright rejected. No questions, no trying to see past his faults like she said she would. She lied.

They faced each other. He could not tell what she was thinking, but he was sure she knew he was not happy.

"Fine." And he seized her and pulled her face close to his so he could see into her eyes and she could not flinch away, his lips so close to hers he could steal the breath from her. "But, I recall a woman who could not get enough of me all night long. And who kissed me like I was her salvation. Whether you like it or not Char Shelby, you gave yourself to me willingly."

Tears squeezed from her eyes and she admitted, if only to her self, that she would miss his fervor.

With finality, his mouth moved over her lips hard and angry, non-relenting in his pursuit to get her to concede to his claim. But the kiss mutated to one of hunger, born of need and desire. He pressed his towel-less body against her and felt her yield once again to his own. She still held back, but the pleasure he felt with her in his arms was alarming. His body hummed with gripping desire.

She moaned and he lifted her up and pressed his hard body against her feminine one, holding her like she was part of him. He moved toward the dark back room, and carried her further and further away from probing eyes, kissing her and being kissed.

Her hands moved over his body touching every place with fire and sensations that made him lust for release. She tasted so . . . salty?

"Are you crying, Shelby love?" He held her face in his hands now and kissed her lips, settling his passions so he could hear her over his own drumming heartbeat and screaming need. He rested his forehead against hers and waited.

"I should not do this," she whimpered.

He kissed her again and then peered at her. She looked so vulnerable. Yet, there was no way he wanted to stop, so he was not going to be the one to walk away. She would have to do it. He pulled away from her, not wanting to even know why she should not finish this tête-à-tête when it was obvious she wanted him as much as he did her. Before he even had a chance to speak his mind, she transported herself away as quickly as a passing breeze. He stood there naked in the dark for a long time wondering what he was going to do about his skittish lover who kept denying her desire.

Polotis People / Chapter 15

Traveling through the giant forest was surprisingly enjoyable. Shelby jogged to keep up with the men; their long legs covered a lot more ground than her shorter ones did. The forest of trees was very dense and old. Shelby noticed there wasn't much undergrowth and she commented on it during one of the brief breaks.

"This is because of the type of trees. In other parts of the forest there is dense undergrowth. The reason this type of tree is here is because of the shelter of the mountain and the limited amount of light it gets," Captain Torden commented.

The other men were less concerned about the forest and more interested in their hydration and rest. They traveled at a pace fast enough for the men to be tired as well, and for some reason this gratified Shelby, probably because she was nearly exhausted too.

If she ever got a chance, her job was to collect samples for Doc Orlie. At this pace she'd be lucky to pluck a few plants and pick up some rocks on the trail. Captain Torden assured her they would be at their mapped out destination in two days and she would have more time for careful observation. At this rate it would probably be only one day.

Their overall purpose was to set expanding boundary markers that would relay vital information of Aion's resources back to the Mountain city matrix and scan the terrain for water and elements that the Alkers could use.

Shelby suspected the markers also would catalog the indigenous creatures or warn of impending dangers to the Alkers, since setting them was the one task the sentries did not entrust to the women. She was not even allowed to hold one.

They camped the first night under the canopy of the forest by rolling out their wraps after eating a packed meal. Shelby fell fast asleep with men's voices talking and telling jokes around her. Their noise created a shelter of assurance she could sleep without danger.

The morning came with Shelby being one of the last ones to wake. She stretched and did some of her morning routine without the comfort of a warm fire to enjoy or a hot drink.

Hurrin handed her a cold piece of something to eat along with her pack. It was heavier than she remembered and she frowned at it as it fell to her feet. She started to examine the contents, but Captain Torden called time to leave and just like that, they were moving about and putting on their burdens.

Shelby swung her pack on, the weight making her feet move to keep her balance. She steadied herself, adjusted the straps and hoped the pace would not be as fast as yesterday's.

"I thought Kerrick said I was not to carry anything heavy." Shelby dryly remarked to all the men's backs. There was no response.

"Let's make the mountain base tonight." Captain Torden said loudly.

"Aye," the men retorted.

At first the pace was walking, even for Shelby, but by mid-morning she was sweating and panting and getting further behind the men.   Initially, she thought it was strange they would leave her behind. But after a while, she just got mad and decided to do a pace she would not wimp out on.

She caught up to the men resting and just as she started to plop down they all wearily began to get up. She looked at them unbelievingly. She could see their shirts were wet with perspiration and as she drank her water portion she wondered what the hurry was. Not one of the men said anything to her. They didn't even acknowledge her with a look or an explanation when she caught up to them.

Someone came behind her and helped her up and adjusted her pack. She thanked him, but he never looked at her once. He just turned and picked up his pack. She was at the back of the line again and this time they started out jogging. She stared at the departing men and wondered why they were so solemn and in such a man-hurry.

She determined to keep her own pace and follow the trail the men left, because the forest made visibility very limited.   If it got dark she determined to settle in until light and continue on. After several hours of being on the trail and not catching a glimpse of the men, she got the feeling she was being left behind on purpose.

Her mind was so occupied with why and what she needed to do to keep up that when she heard the screech of a dying animal in the woods a short distance away, she was shocked out of her troubled thoughts into the present. The sound was so wretched it made her stop and take note of where it was coming from.

After a few minutes, she noted the sound of a branch snap ahead of her. She squatted down to make her form appear less noticeable to whatever crossed the path in front of her. At this point her heart no longer beat fast from her jog, but she was held captive from fear of the unknown coming at her and no weapon at the ready to protect herself in case it was dangerous.

Movement ahead revealed a form of a very lean man with a shimmering coat of feathers all over its body. But, Shelby could tell it was not a man, at least not Alkernian or Earth. Her first guess was an indigenous animal of this planet.

When she saw the face of the creature, she took a quick breath and her eyes widened. The creature's strange face glowed or shone, she wasn't sure. It was beautifully colored like a male peacock's feathers, but the teeth on its elongated face made the contrast fearful.

It saw her and disappeared into the forest so quickly, she thought in the lowering light she imagined the lone creature; except her heart beat so fast she felt the flight of panic set in.

Deciding that she would take off and not wait to be attacked by some unknown thing, she jumped quickly to the trail and took some quiet, hesitant steps. Just as she was about to run forward on the trail she felt a rope drop around her shoulders.

It was so sudden she was not prepared to struggle with her heavy pack. The heave of the upward drag of the rope lifted her into open air. With jerks and pulls, the rope cut into her body and it was enough to keep her from being able to wrestle her way out of the trap. Up and up she went until she was face to face with a small and very strong little man; actually several men were atop the different limbs, but one smiled with large gapped teeth at her and held the rope. All this was done in short seconds with no sounds but her own grunts and the squeaking friction against the branches of the old growth tree.

Shelby kicked at the man and barely scraped the hand that rested on the binding that held her. His movement was so agile she understood his smug smile at her futile retaliation. The other miniature men, whom she realized actually held the rope taut, enjoyed their accomplishment of retaining her while the leader ogled his prize.

She would have laughed if she wasn't the one stuck up in the tree with little men holding her hostage. The spectacle was surely one that would cause any one of the Alker men to think her pretty silly for not being able to free herself of. Her arms hurt from her own weight against the strapping.

The little demon man said something to her in an angry accusing tone and then the other men laughed. The man's face seemed to relax a bit at his own wit and with the encouragement of his miniature men, started saying the same thing over to Shelby again.

Even though she knew he spoke in a different language, some of the words he sputtered seemed to remind her of similar words she knew. Words like territory or terror, and eat or heat and something about the continued threatening sounds of his guttural babble and the other minions' agreement as their jumps and points seemed to convey, made Shelby feel as though she might be looked upon as a meal or a ritual sacrifice for their entertainment.

She spoke for the first time and it wasn't to be nice. She wasn't known for her niceness and now was not the time. Their weaponry was real enough, and she hoped it didn't have some kind of poison that would make it even more lethal, but she wasn't going to be bullied anymore.

"That is enough!"

She swung her legs up over her head with her arms bent at the elbows. She used her hands and core strength to pull and push herself up the rope, and with her legs holding her, loosened the noose around her arms. Once that was accomplished, she quickly wiggled out of the backpack and let it fall to the ground. Then with an angry flip to right herself and face her assailants, she tried to knock the leader off the branch as she landed where he stood. He managed to move away after the shock of watching her free herself registered.

She slapped the rope end at the other pigmy men to scare them, but only managed to get slack rope. She was instantly angry she couldn't knock them back, but at the same time all she wanted to do was get away. They were to this point, harmless, but she didn't want to be anywhere near them when they regrouped and came after her en-masse.

She kicked futilely at them just to move them back so she could get down the tall tree. She dropped down to the lower branch and looked up to see one of the little men try to shoot her with some kind of dart blown out of his mouth. With quick movements, she was able to dodge to a lower branch and avoid the attack.

She let go several feet before she touched the ground and fell through the rest of the branches and brush. As she rolled toward her pack, a small arrow landed near her hand. She grabbed her backpack and used it as a shield above her head and took off running from the nervy little buggers.

As fast as she could, she ran down the trail and swung her bundle back on properly, slowing only to fasten it down so she could run without it bouncing uncontrolled around her already pained ribs. As she adjusted the weight, she felt a poke on the back of her arm. An arrow the size of a toothpick pierced her and she pulled it out and threw it to the side of the trail with an agitated growl. She hastened on down the trail, but felt queasy half an hour into the escape.

She realized then the small arrow held a bigger danger of poison in its tip.

An hour down the trail she was in pain from running so hard and her heart beat so fast she could barely catch her breath. Added to that, her vision blurred, which she suspected was a result of the poisoned tip of the little spear that found exposed flesh to pierce.

Hopping off the trail she squatted under the camouflage of a low tree skirt to check for any coming threats and contemplate what she should do with her limited choices and weakening body. It occurred to Shelby as she lay in pain, she was just as irritated with the Alker men as she was with the leering tree imps.

The men were uneasy. Shelby had not made it into camp and that was just not acceptable, nor what they expected.

"Sepoy Bordog, take one of the men with you and bring Shelby into camp. Here's her signature. Find her." Captain Torden handed him the tracking device to help him locate her in case she had not followed the trail.

Captain Torden talked out loud to himself. Most of the men were just as confused by her tardiness. "She could not have been further than half an hour behind us. Even with the added weight to her pack she was doing just fine."

Talig was assigned to fall behind and follow her into camp. What he could not explain to anyone was how he lost her.

When the two men came back without Shelby at day break the next day, Captain Torden feared for his own well-being as well as that of his small company.

"Captain Torden, here is her signature." Sepoy Bordog handed a small metal piece registered as her. "She must have decided to not continue on the trail and returned to base camp, or she may have decided to escape to go who knows where."

"Whatever reason she disappeared, we need to find her." Captain Torden looked at the fleck of metal and wondered how she found it or even knew it was there to dispel. He shook his head in disbelief. He knew Sir Kerrick was not going to be one bit lenient in their mistake. He would demand the why's and how's of what they thought they were doing taking a woman on a test trial of their own volition. Captain Torden knew Shelby had Sir Kerrick's expressed protection and would be incensed with rage at any harm that came to a woman, especially her.

Once again, the men of one accord quickly packed for the day's journey, only this time it was no game they played. They had a woman to hunt.

Shelby lay flat and sunken into the soft undergrowth. Once darkness came, she could no longer resist the relaxed feeling the poison permeated through her body. Everything felt limp and rubbery and her night vision was completely gone.

She honestly thought she saw the strange tall feather creature. And somewhere in the blackness she felt as if she floated. Even now her body was comforted by the coolness of the ground and the squish of leaves that lay over her in soft layers of insulation.

She tried to open her eyes against the stream of light that filtered through the trees, but it didn't make any sense even in her muddled state. Very little light was able to penetrate the old growth of trees when they were moving through them to the mountain trail, but here she was getting a warm gleam of morning sunshine.

Shelby lifted her arm to shield her eyes from the brightness. She was not on the ground; she must be atop some of the highest branches in the forest. And she was alone in an over-large hanging teardrop nest. She couldn't sense any other presence in her little space so she tried to open her eyes. She located the opening of the shelter and moved her stiff body toward the exit.

Once outside, she could see other hanging nests with walkways made of interwoven branches. She looked up to see more of the same. They were camouflaged so well it took her concentration to identify them. She saw the movement of some of the creatures that lived in these nests through the openings of the other hanging rooms. And they noticed her.

She stepped gingerly out onto the branched pathway shielding her eyes with her hand cupped over her brow.

A soft whispering voice was next to her and when she turned to see its source she stumbled backwards and fell unceremoniously on her backside. She looked up the length of the man-creature. He was covered in beautiful feathery fur. It looked similar to the creature she had seen move across the path. His face had colored hair that looked downy soft like a baby chick's and it was colored in vibrant hues that made Shelby want to touch it to see if it was real. It bent down eye level to her and for the faintest moment Shelby was sure it was a man with feathers.

It motioned for her to follow and she did her best to regain her composure. She looked around and the waiting feathered man creature smiled at her. She couldn't move at all. The creature must have known, because it slowly moved forward to her and a winged arm enclosed around her. He pulled her into its strength and carried her to a larger nest where others of its kind perched.

The creature whispered to another of its kind and sat her down facing a row of dignified feathered creatures. As she looked around the group, she noticed not all the feathered creatures were colorful, nor did they all have their bodies covered with the feathers. She figured the less colorful were female and the peacock-colored beings were male.

Their strange language was soft and musical. Shelby tilted her head and felt a smile ease her facial features. She looked at the creature that carried her here. He, for that is how she thought of it, smiled at her. It then gently covered her back with its feathered arm again and she could feel the warmth radiating from its comforting touch. He leaned his head close to hers and spoke softly in Alkernian, which shocked her.

"I am called Schoftastaklakla." The sound of his name was so foreign to her ears and surprised her so that he needed to repeat it again.

Shelby whispered back, "May I shorten it to Schofta?" He looked at her but didn't say anything, so she said his name exactly as he had told her and he looked pleased.

He smiled then and spoke softly to the center positioned creature. It was almost a solid green color and Shelby thought it a most dignified and powerful being. She could feel its authority and the honor it was given by the other creatures.

She watched the interactions and verbal exchanges between the man-creature and the leader. The sounds made her completely relaxed and she could tell they had no fear of her; surprisingly she was at this moment not afraid of them either. Others of the group talked softly in hushed tones showing their interest in the newcomer. She felt the curious glances, none of them with fear or distrust. That alone made her curious of them as well. They seemed almost angelic of nature and strong, if their physique was a good indicator of such. Their lack of fear of her meant they were able to protect themselves from dangers; though she didn't know how as she saw no weapons or gadgets that would suggest they knew how to fight.

"I will interpret for you. Your name?" Schofta still held his arm at her back and smiled, his tone soothing to Shelby's ears like an early morning mist of rain.

"I am called Shelby. Can you tell me how you know the Alkernian language?"

"Shelby." He smiled gently at her and leaned closer to her in an intimate way.

"Later we will have time to discuss whatever you would like." He removed his protective arm from behind her and she felt the loss with some chagrin. He spoke some more with the leader and a few other creatures exchanged discourse with him as well. As he answered he kept looking at her. She recognized her name being interspersed among the conversations.

"Shelby, our Queen Yi has suggested you stay for the night."

She looked over at the beautiful emerald creature who nodded once. "Why?"

"She says you are too weak to be on your way this late in the day and many of us are fascinated by your beauty so unlike ours." Shelby was enchanted by this creature-man.

"What are you called?"

"Schoftastaklakla." He looked at her with a lopsided smile as if this was a silly question.

"No. What I mean is, my name is Shelby, but I am an Earth human and all the other women in my clan are women from Earth too…but they have unique names. I come from another planet than this, and so what I am asking is what all of you are called? You are humanoid, but what kind? I don't even think the Alkernian men know your tribe exists."

"I assure you they do not know we exist. We are a very shy people. We are very much like you, Shelby. The only difference I can see is your coloring is unique and you are a bit naked without your feathers. We are able to withdraw our coat and look exactly as you do. Over generations this ability developed and allows us to live as we do."

"Were you humans?" She thought she offended the man-creature and covered her mouth with her hand.

They were interrupted by Queen Yi who spoke to Schoftastaklakla. He was very respectful to her and talked in soothing tones and flourished his feathers. When he did this, the other creatures changed from the waist up before her eyes into giggling, naked human beings; at least the females did. Shelby's eyes widened and her mouth inhaled with a squeak. She covered her mouth again, but she smiled and her eyes sparkled with delight. And then she giggled.

This made all the others stop and return to their original state of being feathered.

She looked pleadingly at Schofta. "You are unique humans. What do you call yourselves collectively?"

"Human." And he smiled at her with merriment. She sighed. He put his arm back around her and she felt it was intended as an intimate gesture. "What would you like to call our kind, Shelby?"

She pondered his question. Then she smiled radiantly back at him, "On Earth we have birds-of-paradise that have beautiful, colorful plumes of feathers similar to yours. Paradise also means 'heaven' where I come from, and you live up here, above the rest of us. How about 'Paradise humans'?"

He lifted his head and laughed. It was a deep and compelling sound and as she looked around the group she could tell the females were stirred by the sound of it.

She leaned her head and whispered into his ear, "Why are you laughing?"

"We are collectively, Polotis."

He spoke to the Queen who smiled at her and directed a comment to her which she looked askance to Schofta for interpretation. "She thinks you are delightfully insightful and now insists you stay." Shelby looked around and caught a few disappointed female looks in her direction.

"I think some of the females of your tribe are not enthused about my lingering here."

He smiled at her and clucked. "You may be right, faerie Shelby, but you are not to worry about them. You have been sanctioned by the Queen and that is all any of us need to know."

"Are you considered desirable in your tribe? Because I get the distinct feeling some of these females were hoping for some of your attention tonight. Maybe I should get home to my own tribe."

"You will stay and know our hospitality." This was lilted gracefully into the conversation by Queen Yi. Shelby was silenced by the shock of the Queen speaking Alkernian, having believed she needed an interpreter.

"I would be honored to stay with such magnificent and noble people. You are so curiously interesting. I have so many questions. Thank you for allowing me to stay."

"You are welcome. As for the questions, I am sure that Schoftastaklakla is more than willing to answer your questions with discretion, as he is also very curious about your existence." The Queen smiled with a pointed look at Schofta.

Shelby recognized the lift to the side of the mouth as the same as Schofta's.

"Queen Yi, are you his mother?" There was soft chuckling around the room from male and female Peacock people. Shelby realized her outburst was improper and was embarrassed by her lack of etiquette.

"He is one of my dear nephews who tends to be a bit impulsive and is very inquisitive about you."

"My clan will be searching for me so I need to get back to them before they believe I have disappeared on purpose. They will not be tolerant if I have no real excuse. I am sure you want your existence to remain undetected.

"They will search for me until they figure out what happened. They are very intelligent and persistent and it won't take them long to begin to search up and down. Their technology is unsurpassed by any I have seen before." Shelby realized she was a bit nervous now, because she was beginning to feel like a trapped and caged curiosity. She hoped they would be anxious to have her on her way.

"They will give up after a while. They have other females like you, have they not?" the sensible Queen asked.

Shelby felt troubled. As she looked at the queen and around the room, she got the distinct feeling what Queen Yi decided now or later was going to be law.

"Yes, there are other females such as myself and I am not so special that they need me."

Shelby saw the superior look in the Queen's expression and knew she needed to make sure she understood her desire to go back to the Alkernian camp.

"However, I am special to the King of our clan and am under his protection. Even though there are more women than men and I am an ordinary woman, Sir Kerrick Torrell will not be lenient with the men who have lost track of me. You know as Queen you hold others accountable for their actions or lack of them and he will also.

"I too hold myself accountable for the safety of my clan and would not want his anger to be vented on men who were deceived by myself or anyone else; so please assure me that I will get back to my people in due time or I will have to start planning my escape." Shelby looked serious and intently at Queen Yi.

Around the room the bystanders were wide-eyed, looking back and forth between the newcomer and their Queen. All was still for a moment, except for the almost imperceptible squeeze from Schofta who pulled her closer to him.

"And there you have it!" The Queen smiled broadly and chuckled. "She is truly a delight, nephew, and no doubt, contrary to what you have said about yourself, Shelby of Earth, you are of great importance.

"You do not need to plan any escape. All will be fine and time can pass as quickly or slowly as you need it to. My nephew will decide about the time, but you need to get well before continuing on your way. I insist you stay as an honored guest.

"I can see by your face you are unsure of what I am saying. We as a people do not worry about time value because on our planet we can move through some time phases." Shelby looked totally confused, so Queen Yi spoke to Schofta in their language and her head bobbed up and down in understanding. They spoke back and forth a little bit and then he looked at her with a gentle confident smile.

"Schoftastaklakla will be able to answer more thoroughly later. Let us begin the night's festivities." Queen Yi nodded and smiled at Shelby with sincere knowing in her eyes. Shelby was sure the woman Polotis could look into her soul.

The Queen motioned for Schofta to stand by her side. "I am to leave you here so others of my flock can talk with you, but when you are ready you can ask me to come back. It is our custom for all the members to speak and ask questions of every guest so they know something of the guest and have a chance to socialize with our visitors."

He moved in closer to her and completely wrapped her with his feathers isolating them from the others' view and in a conspiratorial tone said, "Not that we have many visitors like you come into our village." And then he leaned in close to her and rubbed his nose on the tip of hers. He smiled at her and then kissed her lips with warm gentle tenderness.

Shelby was silkily succumbing to his advances and had a hard time understanding the attraction. There was such a physical pull to this male that she did not feel the same ability to reject him as she normally could other men's flirting.

She was suddenly aware of noisy clucking. Apparently Schofta breeched a social rule that was not acceptable. He smiled a little more broadly as he let down the screen he had wrapped around them. He rubbed the side of her face with his and said something in her ear she couldn't understand. Then he left to stand by Queen Yi taking with him the security Shelby oddly felt in his nearness.

When she looked over at his aunt, she saw the Queen tried to shame him for his impoliteness, but he just bent down and kissed her cheek which made her puff and swat at him. Others smiled as well. The camaraderie she saw among them was something years of trust developed. Each of them belonged and had a place to be. She was a bit jealous of the relaxed and joyful way they communicated with each other.

A male Polotis sat beside her and spoke softly to her. She didn't understand a word he said, but she looked at his profile as he spoke to be sure it was her he addressed, since he didn't look directly at her.

"He would like you to know his name is Quig and he would like to know if you are hungry or thirsty." Shelby looked at the young female at her opposite side as she interpreted for the male. Shelby intently looked at this female and found she was curious as to the set-up of the conversation.

She smiled at the young female and said, "I am always hungry and I am thirsty, yes."

She interpreted to the young male who left and then the female asked Shelby another question.

"Are you considered beautiful in your tribe?" The girl was serious.

"What's your name?" Shelby redirected.

"Aurit," and then she asked the question again.

Shelby had to really think about the question because she really didn't know the answer. "I think in our society beauty is many different things and the Alkernian men of the tribe I am with do not look on women as beautiful in the physical way only, but in their abilities. The best person to ask about a woman's beauty is to ask the males of the tribe."

The girl persisted. "Do you get told you are beautiful?"

Shelby scowled at the young female. She must have thought she was in trouble because she started to be apologetic.

"I did not mean to insult you. I just do not know how anyone could be attracted to a female that has no feathers."

Shelby laughed a lighthearted snicker.

"I understand your sentiment. Only up to this moment, even I didn't know that there was such a creature as you. I, however, think your people are an exceptionally beautiful race. I can see I am plain in comparison to you."

This made Aurit nod in agreement.

"The men of my tribe would no doubt find you as fascinating as I do. Compared to you, I am not so beautiful; but maybe to the men who have not had the privilege of seeing you, I am not so ugly."

"Oh. I did not mean to say you were ugly."

Shelby was sure she did, but didn't want to chide her for such a thing.

"In our society there is a saying that 'beauty is only skin deep, but beautiful is soul deep'. What do you think of that, Aurit?" Shelby directed back to the girl.

Aurit looked at Shelby with newfound respect.

"I think that saying is confusing. What does it mean?" She had a tone that Shelby found irritating, but maybe it was because the young peacock was feeling threatened by her somehow.

"Beauty can be deceiving because people can make their hair, or face or clothes look beautiful on the outside, but what is in the heart shines even brighter and longer than the outward appearance. So it is more desirable to be beautiful on the inside than the outside. Do you agree?"

"Maybe." She shrugged her shoulders then left Shelby in peace. But, as soon as she left another sat down and began to ask her questions, which Shelby tried to answer.

This procedure repeated itself throughout the evening. One would finish questioning and then leave and another would sit down and start another string of questions. Shelby tried to remain polite and patient, but she was getting cranky and tired. All through the hours of questioning, she was not able to get any real answers about them in return.

Shelby decided she needed to get some fresh air so she politely excused herself and went out of the large room onto the path. The two moons were up and she was amazed she hadn't realized how late it was. Her internal clock was messed up.

Extricated from the community nest and hum of activity, she followed the path. She was guided by small direct lights overhead illuminating the path.

"I was wondering when you would tire of all their questions." It was Schofta's voice. He stepped out of the darkness and held out his hand for her to take. She did without any hesitation. "Would you like to go to one of my favorite places?"

Shelby smiled and he pulled her close to his side and warmed her with his feathery embrace while they walked toward the unknown destination.

"How is it your people have not been discovered by the Alkernians?" Shelby was truly amazed they were not even cataloged in the native species books that the Alkernians had.

"We are a shy people." He clucked at her so she knew he teased her. She made an exasperated sound and sighed. This made him chuckle and he squeezed her affectionately.

"Look." He pointed to the view that opened up to them.

She could see for hundreds of miles over the tops of the lush and vibrant forest. In the dark, the glow of moving bugs and the sounds of wilderness night made her feel as though she hovered in thin air. The ground dropped down over a cliff, making their treetop taller than the rest of the endless valley. What an amazing view.

The path atop the trees followed along the edge of the precipice and doubled back to a waterfall that was only a hundred foot drop to a delightful green pool with a mist that hung over it from the spray. The moonlight played across the ripples of water and rocks that made them sparkle like gold. It was enchanting.

Schofta tilted his head to see her face more clearly. He earnestly wanted her to like this treasured spot as much as he did. He put his arm around her and she looked up at him. Her eyes glowed with happiness. From the first time he spied her he felt a pull to her being as if their meeting was not enough, but needed to be lived longer. How could he convince her to stay with him? His body felt fuller and stronger in her presence. He knew she did not think of him as compatible and he pondered why this did not bother him in the least.

He wrapped both of his feathered arms around her and pulled her close to his body. Her heat seeped into his as he leaned closer to her uplifted face. She yielded to him enough that he decided to do his best to join with her tonight. That thought shocked him. He could have any one of the other females in his tribe or neighboring ones, and he had looked, but she was delightful to him. She intrigued him by her intelligence and her strength and her sexual draw was hard to resist.

She smiled at him and thanked him for showing her this place.

"I love water and this is an unbelievably mysterious place. Do others come here?"

He could only nod 'yes' to her. The moonlight touched her face and it glowed like a pink pearl. Did she know she was able to glow iridescent? He moved his face against her soft cheek and when he pulled back to look, her eyes were closed with her dark lashes tracing the shape of her eyes beautifully. Her eyes fluttered open and his heart skipped a beat. How could he be so entranced?

"Trust me." It was not a command or a question. He touched his lips softly to hers and dropped down with her off the tree top path.

She squealed in surprise as she fell backward with him through the air. Her hair reached for the sky and her hands gripped Schofta in desperation. With surprising agility he slowed the fall with his wings so their landing was an easy drop of a foot. Shelby was so alarmed and relieved that she was instantly angry at his unruffled attitude so she slapped him, and then did it again. His smile was gone, replaced by surprise.

She turned away from him and said, "Trust me. Don't you ever say that to me again and then do something like that!" He tried to look sorry, but she could tell he was conflicted and held his breath.

"Are you going to laugh?" she asked incredulously.

He nodded his head slightly and acted like he was rubbing the bottom of his nose, only she knew he was covering up a smile.

Her shoulders relaxed when she took a deep breath. She reacted out of fear and surprise and she was sorry for hitting him.

"Well, I am not going to apologize for smacking you," she retorted pettishly.

He just nodded his head understandingly trying to keep a smile off his lips. She may not have any feathers, but he sure managed to ruffle them anyway. He spread his arms out beckoning her to come and waited. Her eyes softened and he watched all her anger melt away before she lowered her head. What was she thinking now? He waited, hoping she would accept his unspoken apology. He was not used to a woman being mad at him or hitting him for that matter. He smiled when she finally raised her head and walked hesitantly back to his open arms.

"I am sorry. It was more reaction than anything else." He put his finger to her lips to still them. The touch was so intimate Shelby began to understand he was attracted to her.

"Do you know how beautiful you are to me, Shelby?" Schoftastaklakla whispered.

"You radiate something so unique from within your being I am not able to follow proper protocol. Truly, I do not normally grab women from under bushes and bring them to my home village. When I saw you lying so peacefully on the ground, my first impulse was to kiss your lips and wake you. You nearly died you know?" He touched her face and while he talked his feathery layer began to disappear, leaving his male skin exposed to the night air.

Shelby felt all kinds of emotions as he touched her and more of his human side was revealed to her. She heard his words and wondered why he would be so open about his feelings when he would not reveal anything about his tribes' ability to live without detection for all the years the Alkernians had inhabited the area.

"I was stuck with one of the devil men's darts." She looked into his eyes. They sparkled with merriment.

"I am so glad you did not die." He stroked her face.

"Me, too," Shelby sighed. She studied his face looking for guile or deception. Was he playing a game she was unacquainted with?

"Why did you bring me here? Why didn't you leave me to my fate?"

"Because, it will never be your fate to die alone or without loved ones around you. Love radiates from you, Shelby, and that means it comes from some very strong source within you that draws people to you."

Her face clued him in that she did not believe or understand what he was saying. He loved her naiveté and chuckled at her unbelief.

"Do you not know men are drawn to you?"

"I know you are extremely compelling to me, Schofta. But up to this point, I thought that you were being naturally kind to me out of respect to your culture or duty."

He put his head back and chuckled, but when he looked at her next, Shelby could see visibly he had gone from amusement to passion.

"I could not possibly feel this attraction to you out of duty."

His blatant declaration made Shelby heady. She was totally caught off guard and maybe that was why she could not resist his flirting.

"Look at the pool. It is called the Lake of Transparency." Shelby's face beamed at the irony of it being called a lake and she puzzled over the sudden change in topics.

"Why is it called a lake and not a pond or pool?"

"Because 'lake' implies depth and width, where 'pond' is shallow and murky. It is believed this Lake of Transparency is able to show the onlooker part of a future that is possible. Do you believe you can choose different paths to walk in your life?" Schofta sized up her overall reaction to his question.

"I have always believed we have different choices in life and those choices take us on paths that could be easy or hard, but at the end of my life, I believe any choice I have made in the past will bring me ultimately to the one and final choice of what my life has always been about; to obey God or to live eternally without Him."

He nodded his head in contemplation of what Shelby believed. "One God is what our culture believes also. But our God has many characters. He is Creator, Spirit, Father, Brother, King, but he is one." He was fascinated by her understanding.

"If you could look into your future, Shelby, what would you want to see? Would you change something if you could?" He knew his questions sounded desperate, but he wanted her to be open to a new possibility, one that included him.

"I don't think I am able to choose a different life just because I see it. I know there are circumstances that happen in life that leave little or no choice for a while. People would never choose to be hurt or unhappy, but some of the decisions I have made have done just that. How could knowing the future simplify or avoid such things?"

Schofta shook his head 'no' and spoke softly to her.

"That is not what I asked. What I mean is one life will have unchangeable choices and another will have another set of consequences. It is possible. Sometimes our life changes on a hinge of one choice."

Shelby only looked at him and contemplated what he emphatically believed was possible. One choice equals a different life.

"Look into the water, Shelby."

She was drawn to its pull as she watched him wade nude up to his waist in the lake and turn toward her and beckon. She followed in a sobered daze wondering if there was some magical wonder at work.

What she saw in the water mystified her. The water held images of Schofta and her in different settings, moving up and down in the depths of Transparency. Along with the images came feelings as real as any she had ever felt; joy, love, passion, hurt, pain, sadness and triumph. It overwhelmed her and finally she began to sink into the lake without any hope of escape from the kaleidoscope of emotions that took her strength away.

Bagging the Prize / Chapter 16

Sir Kerrick seethed and scowled at Captain Torden who wisely said nothing. He could not be more furious.

"None of these women are Alkernian and they certainly have not been trained to be in the wilderness alone. They carry no weapons as do the Alkernian women. Did you think of how she was to protect herself in an encounter with the wildlife of this area?"

Captain Torden shook his head, the words he needed to speak stuck in his throat.

Sir Kerrick looked at him with scorn. "You do know there are precious few women who can have children since the war and these women are the healthy ones that we were able to secure to have our children?"

Captain Torden nodded his head in agreement.

"Then why would you endanger any of them? Do you think she is dispensable? Did you know at least five men asked for her as a mate during the Alkernian Birthing Celebration? You better take care those men are not privy to your ruse."

Sir Kerrick was packing to join the search for Shelby. He knew he would not be able to stay in camp and wait for the scouting party to find her. He should not have let her out of his sight in the first place. His life-debt to Shelby included her safety.

"I am sorry, Sir Kerrick. I thought one lookout was enough."

He sounded pathetic and contrite, but Sir Kerrick knew Capatin Torden was one to do things his own way.

Sir Kerrick needed to find Shelby before anyone else so he could claim her under his sole protection. He felt desperate to find her alive. It was the only way he could hope to repay his life-owing debt to her.

He also knew from their talks she did not want anything to do with Alker traditions or celebrations and he did not want her to be forced into participating in the life-owing with any of the men that sought her out for their mate. He knew her well enough to know she would fight them with all the breath she had to remain faithful to her personal beliefs. And he was concerned for her welfare. He needed to find her and protect her.

Seven of them left together. They jogged fast and steady. Two went down the path while the others spread out from there to search through the trees and valleys looking for signs of any kind to follow. The men kept track of each other through their signals and short wave system, one of the few technologies that did work on the planet.

The men with Sir Kerrick on this trek were somber. They certainly had questions about the validity of the reason Shelby was now missing.

"If Shelby purposely left the group, then why was she allowed to be gone so long? It just doesn't seem like something she would do. She knows it would reap repercussions on the other women; it's not something she was willing to do in the past."

"I remember her storming into Sir Kerrick's office demanding the women be given rest and she was able to convince him to make it happen, albeit a few things were in disarray when she was done with her convincing." The men chuckled.

"I don't believe Sir Kerrick had ever bent his schedule to fit a woman's needs. But, she let him know the women would not be doing any more favors for the men and she had a list of all the things, too! She was unbelievable, a mere captive giving orders. I was glad to be sent out of the room while she convinced him."

The men laughed and after a few minutes quietness settled over them, each of them realized that was only the beginning of the changes she had instituted. Every change benefited the women as a whole and had in turn benefited the men as well.

She had fought several fights with Sir Kerrick with a fierceness each of them admired. She also had their heart-won approval for saving their dearly beloved and respected leader. Being reminded she was no longer a slave made their determination to find her even more fervent. She was free to do as she willed with Sir Kerrick's consent; she did not need to sneak off and they did not believe she had.

They searched for two days before they met at the base of the mountain trail. The wind picked up and the rain already soaked everything.

"I will be back in the morning." Sir Kerrick was determined to scout the edge of the river all the way to the top of the mountain if necessary. He believed she would have found the river to follow home.

"Sir Kerrick. It is getting wild out here and...," he was interrupted by Sir Kerrick.

"Char Shelby is in this cold, possibly injured and alone. I am going to check the river bank for signs of her before the rain washes it all away."

Commander Rockdurgh made moves to go with him, but Sir Kerrick stopped him.

"No. I want all of you to stay here and get some rest and watch for her possible return."

"If I go with you, Sir Kerrick, then I can come back and let them know one way or the other." Commander Rockdurgh looked determined and Kerrick saw the logic in his reasoning since communication was severely hindered by the mountain and valleys and distance.

"So be it. Everyone else can get some rest so we can start up the mountain if need be."

They traveled in the dark now and the weather was cold and bitter.

"Sir Kerrick, maybe you should do that mind thing you do." Kerrick stopped and flashed light toward Commander Rockdurgh.

He never talked of it, but Commander Rockdurgh knew. Until this moment he never thought to use telepathy. Rockdurgh was right.

"I need to be close to her and she needs to let me in. It will not work otherwise."

"Maybe if we find something of hers it will help. Here." Commander Rockdurgh swung his pack off his back and dug through it to get one of the sweet bars Shelby made. "Eat some and see if it helps. If you connected before, it's been said that subsequent connections are easier to engage and stronger."

Kerrick was miffed he had nothing of hers and yet just about every man in the camp owned something she had made or created. He realized he was jealous. That irritated him. He grabbed the bar and took a bite. His eyes closed of their own volition and he felt the smooth silky melting of the rich bar. The sweetness of it made him moan.

"I had the same reaction. It is decidedly good." Commander Rockdurgh's smile was not noticed by Kerrick who was himself enjoying the taste without pretense.

"Shelby. Shelby, love, open your eyes." Sir Kerrick's voice was next to her ear. The rain pelted her body and face making it hard for her to obey.

"I'm cold, Kerrick."

"Where are you, Shelby?" He returned.

That confused her and she tried to open her eyes, but the water on her face was persistent. "I'm here, Kerrick."

"Open your eyes, sweet Shelby." Her eyes fluttered open but it was dark. She could hear water rushing.

"Kerrick! The water is getting louder. I think it's getting closer to me and I can't get up!"

"Shelby, I am coming." With his mind he tried to reassure her of what he promised.

Sir Kerrick's eyes popped open. "She is by the river." They both ran as fast as they could see following the path toward the river, knowing they were going in the right direction when the sound of the rushing water could be heard.

"I will go toward the waterfall; you head down the river and be careful."

"Aye." Commander Rockdurgh's relief was evident in his voice just knowing they were close to recovering Shelby.

They went in opposite directions, but Sir Kerrick found her in a puddle of water halfway under a bush. He called to Commander Rockdurgh down the river. Before lifting her, he examined her with his light. She had some scrapes and bruises, yet did not appear to have anything broken.

He let out a sigh of relief and pulled her into his embrace to warm her body. She was soaking wet and he pushed her matted hair off her face. As her eyes fluttered open, he could see confusion pass over her countenance.

He brought her close to him and whispered in her ear, "I have you. You are safe now."

Strong hands pulled her up out of the cold depths of despair. She was bodily lifted and as air filled her lungs she spat and coughed water out of her body, suddenly aware of her reentry into consciousness.

Shelby was rocked back and forth and squeezed in a comforting embrace. Kerrick's smell was all around her and she cried because she missed Schoftastaklakla and she knew all she had missed by her choice.

She felt an overwhelming sense of sadness, but was so cold she welcomed his warmth. She was safe in his arms with his essence around her. He was strong and determined and found her when she was in darkness and alone.

Shelby lifted her stiff, numb hand to his warm face and whispered, "I missed you, Kerrick." After that she went limp.

Kerrick was mortified and put his face next to hers, joyously relieved she still breathed.

Commander Rockdurgh was busy busting out a temporary shelter. Sir Kerrick wrapped her in his warm coat and helped him finish the lean-to and brought Shelby under its umbrella. They were fairly secure for the night. With Shelby between them, the two men rested for the first time in almost two days. Shelby slept soundly.

Shelby was cold again, enough to rouse her from her sleep. She was alone. Out a few yards from her shelter were two Alker men. Her heart pounded faster as she realized she hadn't dreamed of Kerrick finding her. She tried to get up, but her body was too stiff to move and every muscle felt bruised. Kerrick must have heard her groan because he looked her way and caught her grimace. She plopped back and took a deep breath.

"Shelby." It was Kerrick. He and Commander Rockdurgh had smiles on their faces looking at her.

"Welcome back." Commander Rockdurgh was pleased. He rarely showed any emotion at all, especially toward her, so Shelby was warmed by his greeting. She smiled back at them.

Did he know she was gone and almost stayed in that secret world?

"I'm glad you found me. How long was I gone?" She struggled to sit so Kerrick moved to her side and helped her up. She squeaked an unbidden protest as her body adjusted to new pressures and pains.

"I hurt." She said it in such a way that the men laughed.

"Yes, I imagine you do. You have no broken bones, but it looks like you twisted your ankle and hurt your shoulder by the bruises. You have a few gashes that will need to be bandaged, but you will be fine. To answer your question, you have been missing for four days."

Shelby tried to compute what that meant in terms of her memories. She was sure she was only two days with the Polotis people, but what of the two other days and how did she get here? She was certain Schofta did not leave her anywhere near danger, so how did she lose two days? And why was she left in the rain along the river bank?

She shook her head. "I don't understand how I got here. I have no memory of the past days."

"We will talk about it later. Right now we need to get you up the mountain to the winter camp."

Finding the First Portal / Chapter 17

Shelby sat straight up. That dream was so vivid it was hard to tell the dream from reality. She was sweating and her bed wrappings were in disarray, tangled and half off the mat. She plopped back. If she didn't know better, she would have believed she just had sex. She could still see the green-eyed faceless man, smile at her and make her body squirm with desire. It was so real. But she felt unsatisfied. What was wrong with her? Maybe she was just anxious and her dreams were more vivid because of her heightened anxiety of the missing days she could not account for.

She sat up again. This was the third dream and every time she was unsatisfied. She would have laughed about being unfulfilled, but it was starting to annoy her. She was getting more frustrated and needy. It made her very grumpy and ill-tempered. She needed to put a stop to this.

Kerrick woke knowing someone was in his room in spite of the heavy darkness. He waited for his eyes to adjust to the lack of light so he could see the peril he perceived. The trespasser stood over his bed staring. He was tucked away in his corner chair hidden by the camouflage of the drape. He could see, but the intruder could not see him.

It was curious to him the prowler did not raise any warnings. The trespasser was inserted into his private domain without any alarms and looked threateningly at where his sleeping body should be.

"Kerrick Torrell."

It was Char Shelby, and her stance alone indicated she was here to fight.

He rose from his secret place to reveal his presence to her. Without a word from him, she turned toward his movement.

"Stay out of my head and my dreams. You need to stop making me frustrated." She pointed her finger at him. "I can barely tell them from reality and it's making me crazy!" She made another swirling gesture with her finger at her temple.

He took a few slow steps toward her. She was glowing, a soft luminous light barely visible, reflected off her creamy skin. He was drawn to her like a moth to the flame.

He whispered her name softly, trying to gentle her from her anger.

"I was only trying to help you, love. I can feel your desires, but you do not yield to them, so I thought your dreams would not violate your celibacy tenet.

"How did you know it was me, Shelby, love?" It was unsettling in the least, to have been discovered in such a succinct way.

"I didn't at first, but I just knew by...your eyes." She stumbled.

"There are other men with green eyes, Shelby."

"I know. It was like by the river."

"You remember?"

He was close enough to see the sallow skin around her eyes, evidence she was not sleeping well.

He was inches from her now, and she was looking at his bare chest not into his face. Kerrick rubbed the floor with his foot in a square movement and soft, low light illuminated the lower half of the room slowly.

Shelby looked around like she was waking from a dream and raised her eyes to Kerrick's green ones in surprise. His skin color was an intoxicating rich purple color that fluctuated darker and darker, almost brown. She wanted to feel if he was real or if this was a dream again, but she stood stiff.

"I can't have you moving my feelings around in my dreams, Kerrick. I am afraid of losing..."

"Control?" Kerrick offered.

"No. My mind."

He laughed appreciatively.

"Are you losing your mind because you can't tell it is a dream or because I leave you wanting more?"

Shelby looked up at him again with pleading eyes. She didn't want to admit to wanting more. She sighed and groaned, thinking how he knew exactly how to play with her body, even in her mind, and bring her just to the point where she was not finished. The dream ended without a climax.

"Do you feel it too?"

"Yes."

She understood now his reason for entering her dreams.

"Do you enjoy frustrating me?" Her accusing tone, though delicately regulated conveyed her hurt and disappointment.

He put his forehead on hers and his hands found her small ones. He squeezed them gently.

"Not as much as I enjoy this." His large hand slowly moved up her bare arm and over her shoulder feeling the soft skin beneath his calloused palm. He slid his fingers around her neck and into her silken curls. He breathed in her scent and moved her head back tenderly so he could gaze into her enchanting eyes. He waited for her to accept her need and his desire. He had never turned a deep brown before; he was sure she was the only woman who could do that to his chemistry. Her nearness made his body hum with energy and stimulation.

Shelby looked into the man's deep-green eyes fascinated by the warmth she felt and the odd sensations her body felt, like a craving for his body, to make him part of her and to keep him within her. She groaned as she realized she was already connected to him in ways she would never be able to escape.

"You won't stop, will you?"

"Do you want me to?" He studied her to see her reaction.

Her eyes filled with tears and she lifted her hand to his smooth face and touched him gently with her finger tips, sending a tingling sensation through his body. Suddenly her hand pulled his head down to her lips as she lifted on tip-toe and tasted his lush

mouth, savoring the feel of real skin and scent. She
inhaled deeply moving her nose against his flesh.

He tasted the sweet salty kiss of her mouth and
knew he would never be able to let this woman go,
not tonight, not ever. She was magical to him.

Tears continued to fall from her eyes and he
wondered if she even knew she was crying.

"Do not fret, Shelby, love. I will not leave you
wanting tonight. I promise."

She nodded and continued to place kisses on his
sensitized skin.

Kerrick pulled the woman up against his hard
body and felt her warm legs wrap around his hips,
fitting her body perfectly with his. There was no
frenzy to her embrace, but a solid complete taking of
him to her womanly body. She satisfied her need to
feel his real body and he knew they were mating in
such a way that he would never want another woman
after her. He felt his body guided by her emotions
and was contented inexplicably to the fullest by
satisfying her need.

Strangely enough, he was more than satisfied.
He felt complete.

Then both of them fell asleep and the palm
markings on Shelby's hand began to glow and fade.

Shelby reluctantly got up, not really knowing
what she was going to do with her pent-up
nervousness. It was very early and the two moons
were still in view. She made her way to the lake
edge, the trail was hard to see but she was guided
by familiarity and the subtle light of the two moons.

In the clearing, she could see glistening soft ripples on the water. She was surprised to see something or someone was in the water swimming and splashing at this late hour. She found a place to perch and wait out the time until she knew for sure who or what it was. After a few minutes she determined it was human and so she had less trepidation of entering the water herself, but still she hesitated.

The night visitor made his way back to the shore and Shelby watched curiously from her place in the shadow of the boulder. Something about its form was not right. It was too elongated and the head was covered with some kind of helmet of feather and snout. The body was deformed, the arms and legs bending like a four legged beast's would be. It dropped down on all fours and swung its head back and forth, sniffing the air.

Shelby gasped. It heard her. She thought it might not be able to see her, but it turned toward her and stood up on its hind legs and walked like a man, swinging its arms. Shelby was paralyzed, unable to move her feet. She unconsciously stood shakily to her full height using the boulder as support.

The Egyptian god, Thoth, for that was what it reminded Shelby of, came very close to her, but seemed unaware of her presence. Shelby held her breath and waited for it to pass by. Instead, it stood eight paces between her and the water facing the solid wall and looked past her to survey the surrounding area before it hopped up through the cliff wall. Shelby saw the creature disappear in increments.

She pushed away from the boulder and took some steps away from the facing wall, prepared to run back to the compound, but she was compelled to look closer. How did it do that? Her curiosity urged her forward instead of away.

She could see wet footprints left on the layer of rocks where the being stood before the cliff wall and they ended there. It was strange; there was no crevice or space to get through the wall, and yet the indigenous creature did not go up and over this barrier that jutted out from the ground and pointed almost vertical to the sky.

Shelby put her hand on the place where the disappearing act took place. Nothing. She put her feet in the same positions the wet prints appeared, then she gazed up the extended rock and puzzled for just a minute what the humanoid had done. She glimpsed a shadow of the creature across the rock wall and it made her jump back and away from the potential danger behind her.

There was nothing there and she realized it was not a shadow, but an image in the rock itself. It was so faint it was like she saw through obscure glass that moved and continued to fade.

Working up courage, she moved close again and put her feet in the same position, keeping a close eye on the sinister image. As she suspected, the figure appeared again, so she put her hand cautiously on the murky wall. To her horror, the image reached out and pulled her into the rock while she shrieked wildly.

Feed the cubs / Chapter 18

"**S**ir Kerrick."

Kerrick looked up only briefly to see the young centurion soldier saluting him.

When Kerrick was finished he stood to his full height and looked at the young man with resolute eyes.

"The Bilboas are squalling, but Char Shelby is nowhere to be found."

"You entered her quarters?"

"Yes, Sir Kerrick."

"You queried her comrades?"

"Yes, Sir Kerrick."

Kerrick heaved a sigh and looked to Commander Rockdurgh and Captain Torden.

"Do you know of her whereabouts?"

They stoically nodded 'no'.

"Monitor the boundaries and maintain the woman's quarters. That woman is never were she should be, and no one seems to be able to keep her out of trouble."

"Sir, she is trouble."

"I have to agree."

"Sir. What about her pets?"

"Feed them."

"What, Sir?"

"Food." He was so abrupt, the centurion left to do his bidding immediately still not sure of what to feed them.

"Did you find it, Sir Kerrick?"

"Yes. It alludes to the markings as a key to the rise and fall of Alkernian power and the demise of the planet, basically the end of our kind."

"Are you sure it was not just an impression from the rock?"

"What does it matter? The symbol was exact in measurement, whether it was a birthmark or impression from the rock."

"Well, is it still on her hand?"

"Yes and the prophecy does not distinguish the way it is presented, only that the 'marking would appear and not be visible to all, all the time.' Since she is not here, I can not tell you if they are still visible."

"What is the importance? She is not on Iritain. So how could it affect our future or have any consequence now?"

"Prophecy has a way of happening whether we understand the origin or significance."

"What exactly does it mean?"

Doc Orlie entered and heard the last of the conversation.

"It means, warriors, we have entered a time of change and fulfillment of something that can not be reversed or stopped. It means we have somehow become an integral part of prophecy. All we need now is the star to appear." Doctor Orlie was more enthusiastic than the rest of them.

"I believe the star has already appeared."

"I have not seen a new star in the sky nor have I heard of one emerging in Iritain atmosphere."

"The prophecy does not say it has to appear in the sky or where, only that it would appear in the midst of Alker."

"What are you talking about?"

"Char Shelby." Kerrick talked more to himself than to the other three men.

He looked up now at each one and tried to gain some confidence in his newly developed convictions.

"Shelby glows in the dark. She actually sparkles."

The other men looked at him like he was a lunatic.

"It is probably some kind of lotion she has concocted." Commander Rockdurgh was disturbed by the thought an alien of Iritain could be part of its prophecy. He did not want to believe the very woman who despised their traditions and did not embrace the men and was a holy terror, could be the same woman foretold of who would bind wounds and heal their world with power.

"Impossible. She is the least likely to have any compassion for the Alker Nation. We did destroy and annihilate her culture, temples and whole world existence."

The men looked at each other with concern.

Finally, Sir Kerrick had to agree. She was after all, not of their culture or civilization. How could she possibly be integral to its fulfillment?

But if she was, would she be the Destroyer or the Healer?

Meeting Nemesis / Chapter 19

Shelby pulled herself up from the coolness of the ground. It was unnervingly black thickness all around her, and she could sense emptiness. The darkness was surprisingly warm, so she felt as if she was in the belly of a great beast, minus the wet gooeyness. She stood erect slowly and reached her hands out from her. Nothing. She wondered at her ability to stand steady without reference to her surroundings. She turned her whole body slowly around to search for some kind of reference. Nothing.

She put her hands on her hips to think for a moment and bit the corner of her mouth. A panic moment came and passed in a flash. She was more disturbed by the fact she didn't know the course she should take than by the darkness. Deciding that taking a step some direction was better than standing in complete darkness, she placed a foot out, feeling for solidity. As soon as she moved, the walls in the beast of darkness came to life with a starry, speckled illumination.

She stood at the entrance of a small pathway leading to a tee just a few feet away, where she would have to choose to go left or right. The short hallway was quite high and it would have taken four of her arm lengths to span the width of it. Shelby moved forward to investigate. She could hear no movement of other people or creatures, though that proved to be just as unsettling.

She was inside an invisible gateway of some kind that bridged over the lake. The larger hall continued without any ending left and right. To the left there appeared to be some kind of dais. She wanted to investigate.

When Shelby stepped onto the platform in the main hall, the walls of the tunnel appeared to vanish and become clear glass giving her a view of the lake and beach below. Her vision of her surroundings did not end at the walls of this structure. Instead, as she looked to her right and moved forward her view was that of a bird flying. She could see the planet surface as if she was moving over it. When she looked down at her feet the flight of her vision slowed to a stop. When she looked around her from the new position, it was as if she was there. This was so confusing to her she felt more panic than when she was standing in complete darkness and didn't know which course of action to take. Was she really here? Or was she seeing the planet area from the hallway?

She took a step back. The picture did not change. She hovered over the spot, suspended in an invisible bubble. She looked down at her feet and saw some kind of markings at knee height. She took another step back and the picture receded, another step and she was quickly back in the main hall of the alien tunnel. The walls arched around the hall pathway were back in place again. Shelby felt uneasy and woozy.

"That was weird!" She spoke and it echoed down the hallway vastness.

She moved a few feet toward the pedestal and stepped to the wall on the opposite side of the tunnel. The same thing happened again. She saw for miles and her body seemed to be transported toward the direction she looked. She wanted to slow down, but the view seemed to go faster than she could look. Her eyes closed and her hands went out from her sides, spread. She immediately slowed down and the symbols that registered at her shoulders slowed as well.

This was a chute made by alien technology that appeared to let the user view the planet from above. She wondered if she could get closer to the ground. Her hands went to the symbols and made as if to push them down. Her bubble of view went closer to the ground, and kept going down beneath the surface. She moved the translucent emblem to the left and her sight was directed that way. She glimpsed a tunnel, but was more interested in the ability of the bubble. When she pushed the motifs up again she rose higher. This was fascinating.

She wondered if she could see the camp. Immediately she was being moved in a new direction and stopped without any provocation from her, hovering just above the camp. She could see the men and women moving around for their morning activities. So, this technology could be used by the mind as well. She visually moved her thoughts to the hallway and she was instantly back. Shelby stepped away from the wall. She felt the same tingling sensation and lightheadedness as before.

She realized for the first time, the floor of this contraption was colored with different hues. The pathway to the dais was white and she decided to follow it straightaway.

As Shelby walked toward the dais, her thoughts settled on the creature she witnessed stepping into the boulder wall. How had this amazing portal been kept secret all this time? Who made this? Was this how Kerrick and his men traveled back and forth to their home? She somehow doubted it. This know-how was strange and the markings on the walls and bubble transports were different than Alkernian language and representation.

She was beginning to believe the creature she followed here was only an apparition of a past age. It didn't make sense. Shelby thought for a moment. It was because the creature was opaque and had no scent.

She stepped up on the dais and turned around on the platform. She waited for something. She did not know what she expected to happen.

Nothing. What was she thinking would happen? When she turned back toward the pedestal on the dais, the same Egyptian god-form that led her here appeared.

Shelby gasped and a small cry of surprise won out. The creature stood there and its eyes seemed to acknowledge her and appreciate her fear. Though she was quite different from the being, it seemed familiar.

"Who and what are you?" Shelby whispered.

"We...Nemesis. You called we...Nemesis. I Nemesis.

Shelby's consternation of facing this adversary in his own domain unsettled her.

"We...caregivers...this...planet...We...lived...here eons...we...exiled...We...eliminate...kind,but...planet ...protected...you...Now...we...Nemesis."

"What were you before you were called Nemesis?"

"To...own...people, we...called...Cauble."

"How did you learn the Alker language?"

"Crenulate...planet...connects...Cauble...Al Kerking...Deminuses...Alker...Polotis...more...Now exiled...We...dying.

"Dying? Why?" Shelby was trying to grasp what she now heard from this native being to what she suspected.

Nemesis stomped and swung his huge head in agitation. "Not connected...planet Crenulate."

"Please explain this better. Not connected?"

"Crenulate connects...not connected then Cauble die. Healing, too late." The Cauble sighed and hung its massive head.

"Why then are you here?" Shelby lifted her hands to indicate the tunnel and structure they were now in.

"Are your people dead or gone somewhere else? I don't understand. Some of your people are alive somewhere else?" Shelby queried.

"If exile...place. Planet...divide. Divide...wants... whole. Divided...exiled."

"How does the planet divide and exile?"

"Connected...all things live. You connected...else you not live. Aion...connected...you. Other... division."

Shelby tried to understand his unique way of expressing his knowledge. Some of it she did comprehend but she wondered about the division of the planet.

"Nemesis, when you say division of the planet, do you mean another continent or another part somewhere?

"Place...time...continent...zone...point...in...time. Where on planet does not matter. Nemesis...alone. Bring...Cauble...back."

"You're talking about dimensions. How are you going to do that if you don't know where they are?"

"Destroy evil Al Kerking...Nemesis connected... again."

"How do you know destroying what you think is evil will make you connected again?" Shelby wondered if she was at a place where a decision or verdict had been made.

Shelby felt she was falling into some type of vortex emotionally. She was aware a decision was beginning to come from the humanoid Cauble, but she was very afraid of the assessment of its data.

"Nemesis, how can I help you? Tell me what evil do you want to destroy?"

"I...must destroy...Al...Kerking."

"Who is the Al Ker King? Do you mean my clan?" Shelby tried to discern what the Cauble said. "Is he close by? Can you show him to me?" Shelby felt with all this amazing technology, the Cauble could destroy the whole planet if he was not careful.

She wondered if he was sane. He seemed to have been alone for a long time. His dialect indicated he was from an era or two before her time and the Alkers she was with.

"King...Al Kerking...in Diminishing zone...Al Kerking...wants...back, but we stop him...his kind. He evil. Almost destroyed planet. We...exiled...here. We...alive, but we...exiled." He hung his head again and swung his Ibis-like head back and forth in agony.

"I am sorry for your loss, Nemesis. Please tell me how the King's zone is diminishing and how you stopped him from coming back."

"It...secret. You can not know unless...chosen."

"How would you know if I was chosen?" Shelby countered.

"You...Creation Crenulate."

"You said the planet connects with all things on it. So, Nemesis, you and I both must be connected."

"We...exiled. We stop Al Kerking return."

"What will the King do if he returns?"

"He must not."

"Nemesis, I will help if I know how to and if the King is supposed to be stopped. How do I know if you are not the one the planet has exiled? What did the King do to hurt and destroy your people?"

The Cauble sighed and swung its head in agitation. "Very...terrible...thing.

Terrible, terrible, terrible." His anxiety was palpable and Shelby became even more leery of its state of mind.

"Tell me, Nemesis. What did the evil King do?" Shelby wanted to assure the creature of her support without losing the crux of the point.

"He stole our Crenulate! Most precious...sacred. Gift from planet. Now...woe...is we...Gone, gone, gone!"

"Nemesis, your Crenulate is gone? How do you know?" Shelby was sorry for the Cauble, but still she did not understand the loss.

The Cauble held his hands out. For the first time Shelby realized though his hands were hairy and clawed, they were similar to her formed digits. Its body was animal like and its feet clawed as well, but it stood on two legs like a man. It was an incredible creature and its strength and power were implied.

Shelby walked down off the dais and reached for the creature's hands. She lifted her eyes to the Cauble's and saw an intelligent, cunning creature not bereft of its senses. Was she being tricked? She backed away from the Cauble and stood just beyond its reach. She looked around the tunnel and tried to identify some sense of what she should do.

When she looked back at the Cauble, it looked at its hands, but nothing was in them. Shelby considered this for a moment and then put one of her hands over Nemesis' and looked into its eyes again.

"If you get it back, will you still destroy the Al Kerking?"

"I...must...King reason world divided. Soon...memory...one planet...gone...chaos. Planet wants...whole. Evil destroy race."

Shelby tried to understand Nemesis' words, yet they seemed so strange to her and her grasp of what he said just seemed like gibberish.

"Nemesis, if the Al Kerking is the cause for all the division and the loss of your world, I will help you. But I do not know how."

"King stay diminishing zone...until...no more."

"How long will that take, and how do you do that?"

"You can not...help...unless...Creation Crenulate. Only planet give."

"If that is true, then how did the King take your Crenulate?" Shelby seriously wondered if this Cauble was sane.

"When Cauble...perished...King stole Crenulate. Before perished sometimes King...perished...them."

That she understood.

"He would kill your people?"

"King evil...deceitful evil. We exiled...in separation. We not take care evil. Evil...stole from planet."

"Did the King take the Crenulate off the planet?" Shelby was exasperated. She just did not know what Nemesis was capable of.

"Tried...but Crenulate connected to planet. Divided...planet...Crenulate from King. Now... King"

"Is in a diminishing zone," Shelby finished for Nemesis. "So the King keeps trying to get out of the zone, but how does he do this, Nemesis?"

"Clever evil. Fractured...division. He fractured ...Connected being perish...takes. See division... steal more Crenulate...if gets being."

Shelby's head started to hurt. She feared the Alkers she was now with would be in grave danger if Nemesis wanted to destroy them. What if the Cauble decided she was a threat to the planet, or evil? What if her understanding of the evil was skewed from the Cauble's?

"Nemesis, how long do you have to wait until the King's zone is gone?"

"Not long now."

"How do you know?"

"It is...foretold."

"So, you are here now keeping everything right. How do you do that?"

"When connected being goes through division...Nemesis stop King stealing Crenulate. King...crafty...evil."

"I am so thankful you stop the King from stealing the Crenulate, but have you ever failed?" She wondered how he could stop the intrusion if the King's technology was so powerful.

"Crenulate selective...know King evil...Do not show power yet...Soon. King...evil...no match. Planet at peace...we exiled...we pain."

"Nemesis, I am connected and I travel into other divisions." Shelby hesitated before going on. "I think you mean dimensions, but different ages, too." Shelby tried to remember something just out of the reach of her recollection.

"What...called?" Nemesis was now curious of her.

Shelby thought for a moment of all the Cauble said and wondered if she could be honest with the creature.

"I am Shelby. Char Shelby of Earth and now Aion. I was taken from my planet and brought here by Alkers of Iritain. But, the ones I came with are new to this planet. So I wonder how long ago the Alker King came here. If I help you, are you going to kill the innocent Alkers?"

"Innocent? Al Kerking...ageless. Here...long time ...still live."

"But are the new Alkers destroying your planet? Maybe the planet has not rejected the new Alkers and if you destroy them, will the planet punish you?" Shelby tried to bargain with the creature to preserve the lives of the ones she knew and cared about.

"Show me...connection," it insisted.

Nemesis was unreadable to Shelby. She was not sure how to produce Crenulate for the demanding Cauble.

"King must destroy. Nemesis...not promise." Nemesis' frustration weighted his words with conviction.

"I agree, Nemesis. But I must know you will not harm my people. The Crenulate can destroy the King if it is supposed to. You still have not shown me the King."

"Can not. If you...Crenulate...King sees...Take it. Understand?" He was getting exasperated.

"I am sorry Nemesis. This is hard for me to understand because I am new here."

"Then how Shelby Crenulate? You must...belong. Planet have...Crenulate. You must connect. You lie! Show Nemesis Crenulate!" His voice grew loud with his ire.

The Cauble was angry and Shelby felt panic rise in her as she realized he was agitated enough to attack her. Just as quickly, she threw her arm over her head and took the stance of a prepared warrior. Her hand instantly grasped a beautiful, gleaming sword and her other hand produced a shield of exquisite detail.

Nemesis was overcome with shock. He fell to his knees and stared at the amethyst colored armor Shelby now had covering her whole body.

Shelby was just as stunned by the sword and shield in her hand and the covering on her body. Her memory cleared a bit and she understood she had a part to play in the Cauble's restoration. She relaxed slightly.

"Nemesis, I need to get back to my people. They will be anxious if I do not return soon." She stepped back, aware of the danger that still hovered in their difference of what should happen to stop the King.

"Wait. You...would give us Crenulate? We return to our division...our people...if Crenulate."

"I will keep my word, Nemesis. But you must meet with the Alkers to see if they are the ones that harmed you. Then I will understand more. But I do not know you or if you are the evil one. Maybe you will harm the planet more."

"No...Not Nemesis! We not harm...Aion."

"But if you have no Crenulate then you are the one not connected."

"No...here...but...weak."

"No, Nemesis. The Crenulate is not weak. It is connected. I came into your division, but you can not come into mine. Why?"

Shelby was suspicious of the suppressed rage and anxious behavior of the creature. She was aware of heat surging in her veins and she extended her arm as the Crenulate formed a glove around her hand. At the same time, she heard noises like a recording in her ear and she knew she was gleening historical data about Nemesis. The Crenulate was somehow relating to her its past through the process of anamnesis. Knowledge was being transferred to her.

"Help...Char Shelby. Nemesis desire planet whole again." He was on his knees begging.

She felt compassion for him and yet her armor did not disappear. She wondered if the Crenulate in her was aware of who the Cauble was.

"Come with me to the camp and meet my clan. Then we will see if you are telling the truth, Nemesis. I want to help, but if the Crenulate rejects you, I can do nothing else for you."

"I...can not leave...Nemesis division. I...can not."

"Okay. Then I will come back when I know more about what you speak of. I desire to help, but I will not if you are going to destroy my people."

"I...not harm...you."

"But, you may need to harm my people and I do not want to help you do that, Nemesis."

"But...you connected. You...save Nemesis people. Bring...back."

"And I will, if I know how, Nemesis." Shelby took some steps away from the Cauble and when she sensed it was not going to attack her, she turned to leave. She hesitated and turned back to the Cauble, she stomped her foot and a piece of amethyst stayed on the floor.

"If you are worthy, you can pick this up and it will awaken the dormant Crenulate, Nemesis. It will also direct you to your own time so you can share with your own kind. Be careful, Cauble." Then she strode out the exit she came in from.

She landed with a thud in the sand below the boulder. She forgot she had been pulled up the equivalent of a couple stairs. Shelby looked back at what she thought was the entrance to see if the Cauble followed, but no form or opening appeared.

She gazed at the lingering color on her skin and softly stroked it with hesitancy. How could something like that happen? She was examined many times and no one had said anything about Crenulate or what it was. But weirdly enough, she seemed to understand its function instinctually.

Shelby held out her hand and thought of the sword that magically appeared and now was gone; and the shield too. Evidence of it really happening lingered in the color of her skin.

She wanted to hold the sword again, but a gem rose in her palm. Shelby stood up and made the stance of a warrior and the sword instantaneously formed in her hand. She looked at her other hand

and willed the shield and it too was there. Without thinking she slapped the sword at her side and it formed into a delicately embossed belt that wrapped around her waist and swung with the grace of her movements.

She examined the shield to understand the markings on its surface. She could not decipher them. She instantly thought of Kerrick. She had an inkling he was fully aware of all that was going on within the radius of their camp. She wondered how much she would actually have to tell him and at how much he would just nod and smirk with his arrogant smile and wait for her to make a fool of herself.

Isolation / Chapter 20

Shelby carried the shield into the camp bringing all eyes toward her as if she was some kind of strange being. She was anxious to show Kerrick her findings. "Kerrick Torrell!" She yelled looking for him with desperate eyes while taking in the disorder in the camp. "Kerrick!"

She felt his presence behind her though he spoke not one word. She turned with gratefulness welling in her. He was accostingly handsome and the thought to run to him and hug him was overwhelming.

"Where have you been?" His cold accusing voice broke through her joy and almost jolted her back physically.

He looked at her appearance and was aghast at her. "You are gone for a month and come waltzing into camp as if you owned the place! Where have you been?" He eyed her suspiciously and kept his distance from her.

Shelby was confused by his demeanor and suddenly comprehended he thought she was a threat.

"Take her to the isolation hold and let Doc Orlie know she has returned."

Two men grabbed at her arms to capture her and others immediately surrounded her, though she tried to twist out of the grasp of their hold. In her wrestling, her grip was lost on the shield and it rolled ironically to the feet of Sir Kerrick. He seemingly did not notice and watched her arrest with passive disinterest.

"What is going on here? Stop! You need to listen to me! Kerrick!" Shelby tried to get his attention enough to stop him from walking away, but he seemed distracted by some kind of disturbance behind him.

Other men and a few women were armed and battle ready, talking in hushed tones to Sir Kerrick.

An explosion went off and everyone ducked.

"What is going on?" She asked the men who still held her fast and pulled her away from the commotion. She looked around as best she could and wondered at the upheaval of the camp quarters. "I was only gone for a while," she spoke aloud to herself.

"That's what you call a month?" Sepoy Bordog retorted accusingly.

"Really?" She was incredulous.

Though she persisted, they treated her like a pariah and were rough with her, pushing and pulling as if they would tear her apart. Not one civil word was spoken to her for the rest of the night and she wondered if she would ever know what had befallen the Alkers in the purported month she was gone, though to her it was a mere hour.

She was put in isolation and was surprised by the actual comfort provided. There was a large cot and some accommodations not usually given a prisoner; at least what she thought would not be given one. Her food was of excellent quality, but she was aware she was not welcome in the company of Alkers any longer. Not one person came to see her, not one acknowledged her, not even her personal group of women.

Days passed and the only contact, non-verbal, she had was when a woman or sentry would bring food in. They were unidentifiable in the protective clothing she had seen Doc Orlie use, though she could distinguish between men and women. When she tried to speak or get some response, she was warned by the outside guard to be silent.

Shelby struggled with her knowledge. She felt her emotions get the best of her. Depression hit her like a ton of boulders and she unwittingly cried when she fell into a fitful sleep. She was clueless as to her crime, other than being gone supposedly a month.

She had no idea what was going on outside the cubicle. No one had any intention of letting her know either. She was greeted with silence and contempt whenever someone brought in her food. The scorn she felt was tangible.

She finally had enough and attacked the bearer of food at the door, throwing the food back out the entrance. She was beaten for her assault and suffered bruises and pulled hair.

And that became her vigil. She stopped eating and every person who brought food into her confinement was met with hostility from her, though she was beaten again and again for her behavior. She would fall asleep only to wake whimpering pitifully from the despairing dreams she had of losing her only hope of happiness.

"How long are you going to keep her confined, Kerrick?"

"A month. And you will address me properly," he succinctly replied. Absolute resolution and righteous indignation made his reply irreproachable. "I have had enough of her rebellion."

"Is that what you think she was doing when she disappeared...Sir Kerrick?" Doctor Orlie was totally opposed to his indifference.

"Did you speak to her? Let her know she was guilty and being held responsible for her animals attacking the camp and the elusive deadly creatures cutting off the women's hands? Or do you assume she knows all this and actually planned for it to happen? Do you even know if she meant to be gone? Some said she was trying to tell you something. Do you even know what it was?"

Kerrick stood up angrily, his vehemence radiating from him. "Get out!"

His rudeness shocked Doc Orlie and took him a moment to recover. But he decided to ignore Kerrick's outburst.

"Anyone in isolation for a month goes a little crazy. Is that what you want her to do? No one is allowed to speak to her and only the ones who seem to hate her are allowed near her. You should at least speak to her, find out why she was gone."

"And say what?" His temper barely recovered. In fact it wasn't. In a menacing voice he said to his guards, "I want him out, now."

And to Doc Orlie he warned, "If you come in here again about her, you will end up in isolation yourself."

The guards tried to respectfully usher Doc Orlie out, but he was indignant and furious at being treated so disrespectfully by his godson.

Childishly he said under his breath, "Wait until your mother hears about this." But it was loud enough for Kerrick to hear and surprisingly he did envision his mother's horror of his treatment of his godfather...and a woman.

"Get out! All of you! NOW!" He bellowed and threw his papers off the desk.

Rockdurgh kept his mouth shut, but he had seen enough. Even though Sir Kerrick ordered that Bordog had authority to control her, he heard enough to know she was going to die soon. She refused to eat.

"Just in case you really do not know, Shelby has not eaten in several days. She's been beaten to a bloody mess. She attacked Bordog after a week of being locked up and now she lies there not caring who comes in. She will most likely die within the week, since you expressly told Doc Orlie he could not treat her. The month long isolation is working just fine if killing her is your intention."

He paused before he said anymore. He couldn't tell if Sir Kerrick heard anything he said. He watched him handle some artifact he examined.

"You should tell Bordog to kill her. It would make him happy, put her out of our misery and apparently solve all your problems." His tone dripped with sarcasm and hinted contempt for Sir Kerrick.

"Get out." It was redundant, Commander Rockdurgh had already exited.

Kerrick was left with his own remorseful thoughts beside those implied upon him. Most everyone in the camp detested Shelby for their own reasons, reasons he was not sure she could be blamed for, but somehow were laid at her feet.

It started with the animals she left behind who howled and cried in her absence until some of the people in the camp decided to kill them, sick of their awful noise; believing they would bring other animals of their own kind into the area. Others had taken the stance to let them go back into the wild. All of them agreed Shelby was to blame for the disturbance.

What was more was those who helped feed them were no longer able to calm the Bilboa cubs. Their constant cries agitated the men in the camp who were done with the cubs' annoying howls. Everyone was on edge. Someone finally did let them go without his sanctioned authority. He suspected it was Doc Orlie.

It was decided since Shelby was gone the animals would do more harm than good in the wild; they were to be destroyed to avoid any possible retaliation or attack later on. A week later, though no one actually saw the animals, there was plenty of evidence they did come back. Things in the camp were shredded and destroyed in places where no one was present. Food was destroyed.

After that, one of the women disappeared with paw prints of the animals clearly around the last sighting of the woman. She was found dead by the river, a hand chewed off.

That set the quarters in an upheaval, even Kerrick was determined to kill the beasts. Then another woman went missing, evidence of her being drug by the animals was again present.

So in less than a month, with Shelby missing on top of all the other things, she was guilty for the deaths and at fault for the feral animals. Some even believed she was systematically going to kill everyone in the camp because of some imagined evil she thought had been done to her or that she had gone insane.

Shelby abandoned her clan. She abandoned him after he trusted her. He really believed she found a way to get off the planet and he was incensed he allowed her to use his feelings so she could get access to the Trough.

And then she entered the camp in some kind of strange covering and the relic shield he now held.

He gave Bordog the command to see to her discipline, knowing he himself could not withstand her pleas. And then he walked away. Bordog did not need to report to him on her status. She was to be broken and made to feel the wrath of her waywardness.

He wanted to know only two things, where her giant Bilboas were so he could kill them and where she had been so he could eliminate any lingering doubts of her innocence and punish her for her truant behavior.

His goal was to stay the hell away from Char Shelby. His men demanded her punishment and he knew he would be too biased; but not in her favor. He felt she played him like an instrument; like how she petted her cubs and then just abandoned them. Just when he thought they were coming to some understanding of each other, she left him.

Simple as that. She seemed to have no regard for his rank or person or anyone else in the camp. Even some of her confidants worried she had gone feral like her animals.

But, she was caged now and being broken, trained to obey. Commander Rockdurgh seemed to think it was wrong to teach her a lesson. That she would die before being coerced. Surely he exaggerated about her dying in a few days. He did not care. Rockdurgh was right, if she was dead, his problems would vanish, almost.

Over the course of the weeks she was gone, he convinced himself she was a traitor. That she intentionally trained the magical beasts to terrorize the Alkers and to bring them all to ruin. It was strange he even thought she had that kind of power and he knew it was strange. But something in him just could not forget the eerie howling of the Bilboa cubs and the wild displeasure they had of being locked away from her. She brought this on herself.

~

She brought this upon herself.

Shelby got up off the floor of her cubicle confinement. She was done feeling sorry for herself. She walked over to the captured trickling water and picked up the scantly filled saucer she left there. It was not enough to clean with, but she was thirsty and the metallic flavor of her bruised and sore mouth felt some relief from the wetness.

"I thought I was supposed to heal quicker with Crenulate in me," she mused. Apparently, that was not true. She wanted to cry out in agony. She had been beaten by a masked man and she chose not to fight back. Her reasoning was she did not want to take the risk of killing one of the good Alkers, though she did jab the man with some direct kicks to the groin.

But, the real reason was she was spooked. She could already do much harm on her own, but not knowing when the Crenulate would materialize made her second guess her own motives.

She held her hand out and the amethyst gem appeared. She willed it into a blade and put the blade to her throat. At that moment, one of the men appeared at the doorway to the cell.

"Where did you get that blade?" The man's caustic growl reverberated in her ears.

She looked horribly dejected as she barely stood upright with the knife at her filthy discolored neck. She would be able to slice her own throat before he ever got close to her. Suicidal was how Rockdurgh described her, though not eating was somewhat less permanent, at least in his mind, than slicing one's throat.

Standing there with her clothes hanging off her bones, he realized she was not healthy. It was four weeks since her return and the little meat she had on her was gone. She looked like it had been a year since she bathed. Her hair was matted and she smelled. She looked like she came out of the box. His revulsion of what she must have gone through in the last weeks to look this bad made him sick.

"Get cleaned up." He ignored the fact that she had a knife at her throat. How she got it would not be left unanswered. He reveled in the fact her eyes flashed with anger at his injunction. He was well aware she was not ready to die yet.

Shelby wanted to throw the dagger at the unidentified man, but she knew it would be lethal and she didn't want to lose this Crenulate as she did the shield.

"If you decide to use that knife on your neck, I won't stop you."

"What knife?" Instantly the Crenulate went limp and she fastened it around her neck as if that were her original plan.

"Where did you get that?" The man was dumbfounded.

"I made it." Her voice was gravelly from weeks of crying and not talking.

As he neared her to take a closer look, the round rocks appeared to be woven grass. How did he think that was a knife?

He looked her in the eyes and saw her defiance. Some nasty, arrogant part of him wanted to beat the defiance out of her and break her will once and for all, but a nagging part was relieved she was not completely lost or mentally broken. She stood there in her weakened state strong and determined.

She could not tell who this man was because of the mask covering, but she despised him. How had it come to this? Was there some way to resign from this path of destruction?

Shelby slumped to the floor and her disheveled hair hung around her face hiding any more defiance she might have wanted to display. She fell slowly to her side and passed out.

She wanted to get up because she could hear all the commotion, but everything spun and she was nauseated when she opened her eyes. She did not care. She was miserable and the hate radiating from the people who transported her was nothing less than loathing.

She did not even get a trial or a chance to know what changed everyone's attitude from at least accepting her to outright hostility and disgust. She wasted time thinking of Kerrick's betrayal in not even talking to her or treating her with some trust. He was after all the one who condemned her to isolation under Bordog's command; Bordog whom she detested for his constant harassment.

Finally, in all her distress she came upon a saving shred of truth; people are fickle. She needed to believe in herself, no matter what others thought. That was when she picked herself off the floor.

But she was weaker than she thought. Even now in her distress, she discerned the tumult she heard around her was not about concern for her; but something happened in the camp that caused the people near her to emit real anger and fear toward her, even in her weakened state. She struggled to open her eyes, but slipped once again into oblivion.

The cubs could smell their own and followed the scent, their bodies translucent as they passed unseen through the camp. Even by the fires their miraculous coats of fur were ever-changing to the passing of their presence.

The hairs on the back of the necks of some of the people in the compound stood on edge, but the danger could not be seen, only felt. The sound of the animals' movement was barely audible, passing as a rustle or a crackle of the fires. That did not stop the vigilance of the guards. They relied more and more on their sense of smell than sight and something did not smell right.

Shelby woke alone in the barely lit cubicle and knew she could smell the cubs. She felt their breath before she actually saw them next to her cot. Shelby felt the warmth of her cubs and heard their hissing before she could audibly respond to their cries. One of them licked her face with its rough tongue and waited beside her as she tried to open her eyes. They were much larger than the last time she saw them. Maybe a couple months had gone by.

Shelby felt so much relief at being greeted by the Bilboas she almost cried. Her arms wrapped around the backs of them and she breathed in their woodsy scent. They smelled like freedom. She felt the warmth of their bodies and sensed their mutual angst of seeing her locked up and smelling of death, but she gained strength from them.

The cubs' heads simultaneously focused on the doorway. Shelby also felt the urgency to go for freedom, but she could hear people's anxious voices getting closer. The Crenulate formed into a beautiful ornate knife in Shelby's hand and needing no further impetus, she went to the back wall.

Revelation / Chapter 21

She felt the urgency to get them out of here, but she had no strength and guessing from the sounds coming toward her, the Bilboas were not any more welcome than she was. She struggled to her feet and walked toward the open doorway. Instead of going out, she decided to go into another room with the cubs. Her forming idea was that she could slash a way out through the dome walls.

Their sharp claws scraped down the partition and did nothing but glide over it. Shelby panicked when she heard noises coming closer. The Alker men evidently deduced the Bilboas would try to find Shelby and came to secure her prison.

She used the Crenulate sword to easily slice through the structure of the isolation dome into another room. A screeching alarm sounded and Shelby covered her ears. The cubs yowled at the sound, but followed her escape as she tried to remember which way was to the woods. Shelby looked up and could see the textile locking and reinforcing itself from the incision. The next cut was vital as the technology of the dome inferred it adapted to any assault on its integrity.

Which wall? She panicked again, the need to protect the cubs imperative. She cut a final slash and to her utmost relief was next to the cliff, it was outside the dome to freedom. She sent the cubs out and signaled them to hide. She had trained them to act on certain commands and they were intelligent. Shelby saw the tail-end of the second cub escape before she was caught unexpectedly by hard, pain inflicting hands grasping her weakened flesh.

She used her weapon to cut off the offending hands, but the Crenulate did not harm the man. It appeared to flow through and around his wrists and remain intact as a knife. It made Shelby furious instantly; to be caught and to have this Crenulate betray her!

In her disgust she tried to throw the Crenulate away, but it slipped into her hand and disappeared. No crashing sound from being flung away or scream of pain from the man who now held her fast in his vise-like grip. She was undone and just as she was going to scream in her frustration, she heard the cubs howl their mournful agitation of her not escaping with them.

She was shaken. The man was more than angry with her. She tried to fight back but she was so weak from not eating that her attempts were fruitless. She felt a sharp stab in her arm and then just before she once again slumped into oblivion she saw the storming green eyes and realized the man she wanted to maim was Kerrick.

He let her fall to the floor. The other men picked her up and took her back to the cubicle.

"She tried to cut off my hands!" He looked at his hands in wonder. He still had them attached, much to his surprise.

"A lot of that going on here lately. Yes. But it didn't work. How come?" Doc Orlie was unmoved by Sir Kerrick's concern. He was so fascinated by the outcome of the encounter everything else seemed irrelevant.

"You are lucky she did not kill every last one of us. Something in her did not want to harm you, Sir Kerrick. You should at least be glad for that. Look at the dome wall. She cut right through it like butter!"

Kerrick bent down to witness the textile wall close the breach and negate the effect of the assault. The readouts would calculate the make of the weapon and design an effective control for it the next time. In all the years he had used these domes, not one thing had been able to even scratch the textile of the dome structure.

"Get that knife from her," Kerrick demanded of the sentry.

"What knife?" The guard was skeptical of the command from his leader.

"Why does everyone keep asking me that?" The irritation from Sir Kerrick made the young sentry step back out of his way.

Kerrick looked for himself and only detected the rough necklace he queried her about earlier. He lifted her palms and arms and rolled her over noting she was thin and battered, but still no sword was evident. He looked around the cot and went back into the room she almost escaped from. Nothing. He went back to the room Shelby was now being tended in.

Kerrick noted Doc Orlie's demeanor was indirectly cool toward him. Clearly not concerned, Kerrick addressed him.

"You saw the sword."

"Yes." Doc Orlie busied himself with Shelby's well-being. It was nearly two months since he had been allowed to see her. He missed her like a long lost friend. He knew he should have confronted Sir Kerrick and freed her immediately upon hearing of her misuse. This charade had gone too far. She was nearly expired. This was a tragic case of injustice.

"You know, preventative maintenance is much more effective than after the fact." Doc Orlie was clearly disgusted at the shape Shelby was in.

Kerrick looked longingly at the unmoving woman. As long as he did not think about her as a person, he was fine. It was when he remembered all the other accomplishments and kindnesses she had done that his resolve was almost undone.

So how did she get here? Because of his suspicions. Suspicions of her being part of a prophecy. In the back of his mind he remembered the markings on her palm.

Even with prophetical warnings, he could not have expected any of this to happen. What was more, he loved her.

"Sir Kerrick?" Doc Orlie called him back to reality.

"Is she coherent?" Kerrick's gruff voice cut him short.

"I believe she will be out for a couple hours, which leaves us some time to figure out what just happened."

He and Sir Kerrick were alone now and so he felt he could speak a little more freely.

"Let us look at what we were trying to determine." Doctor Orlie coaxed.

Sir Kerrick gave his godfather a scowling look, showing he was not interested in clearing the board just yet.

"Try," Doc Orlie cajoled. "Did we at least prove that she was loyal to the Alkers?"

"I do not know what we proved." Kerrick was despondent.

"You said your objective was to determine if she had made contact with the natives and if she was collaborating with them because of her disappearances. You also wanted to know if she could possibly be the 'star' that blazed and fell to the ground to devour the evil Alkers."

Doc's mocking did not sit well with Kerrick.

"That was close Doc, but you should leave the quoting of prophecy to the one who actually said it, or to the one who actually heard it and knows it."

He felt compelled to quote the actual prophecy for good measure and confirmation of the point.

"A star will shine without divine, the purpose sole to make it whole. Upon the truth a pledge wilt thou make, but not without the Alker sovereign break. One will be, then two, then three, to unite the broken and rebind the free. Look to truth trust not the eye, the star will grow without a lie, but two will know the truth beyond and four will be the tie that bonds."

"How do you remember or make sense of it?" Doc Orlie was flabbergasted.

"My mother. She made me memorize it and speculate about what it might mean. I finally realized she could not tell me what she thought it meant for fear of interjecting some untruth or misguiding me from the natural course of the prophecy, which by the way, she never did tell me directly that it was prophetic. But for the first time since I can remember, it is starting to make sense."

"Do you believe the prophecy has come true?" Doctor Orlie was confused.

"Some of it. 'A star will shine without divine' was very obscure until the night I saw Shelby without her clothes on."

He looked at the shock on Doc's face and smiled. "It was not what you are thinking. I actually was curious about what she was up to. She does have a way of sneaking off."

Doc Orlie looked somewhat relieved for the simple fact that he had never suspected his godson of voyeurism. Sir Kerrick continued his revelation.

"The designs on her body you showed me glow in the moonlights. It struck me we think of stars as celestial or needing to be in the sky to shine, but she radiated on the planet or 'without divine'. That is when I suspected the prophecy would not happen on Iritain, but possibly here on this planet."

"Since 'without divine' could mean 'non-heaven', I believe this planet may be in danger of being destroyed. 'Not whole' could mean it is parted or in..." Kerrick was having another revelation and Doc Orlie was lost at the moment, believing there could not possibly be answers to the vague prophecy.

"What did Shelby say to the men when she walked into the camp?" Sir Kerrick said as a way to remind Doc Orlie.

Doc shook his head, but a voice from the doorway intervened.

"She said she was only gone for an hour."

Both the men's heads turned to Commander Rockdurgh, and Captain Torden who stood behind his massive shoulders peering at them and the limp form of Char Shelby.

"How much have you heard?"

"The prophecy and some of the interpretation. Is there more?"

"Possibly."

Both of the intruders approached the cot where the other men hovered and waited for more.

Sir Kerrick thought about Shelby's response to his rejection of her when she returned a month later. Then his mind stumbled.

"To make it whole. To make it whole." He repeated it again.

"She truly believed it was an hour, we know it was a month."

"The planet has fractured time dimensions." Commander Rockdurgh surmised.

"Yes. That is how she does it!"

"Does what?"

"A star will shine without divine, the purpose sole to make it whole. Upon the truth a pledge wilt thou make, but not without the Alker sovereign break. One will be, then two, then three, to unite the broken and rebind the free. Look to truth, trust not the eye, the star will grow without a lie, but two will know the truth beyond and four will be the tie that bonds." Kerrick said it out loud again.

"She disappears. She disappears by transporting through the broken time zones of the planet. How, may have something to do with the glow on her body," Kerrick asserted.

All the men looked at Shelby who was not glowing at all. In fact, her body was not there.

Dirt / Chapter 22

All the men did a quick survey of the room. She was just simply gone. There was not even a hint she had been there a second ago.

"This is getting strange. Where did she go?" Rockdurgh was not amused.

Sir Kerrick and Doc Orlie looked at each other and then back at the vacated bed.

Kerrick growled and a rage he had never felt poured out of him. How was he going to keep track of a woman who could evaporate into thin air and then reappear a month later? He thought through the prophecy again saying it aloud, hoping it would reveal something.

"A star will shine without divine, the purpose sole to make it whole. Upon the truth a pledge wilt thou make, but not without the Alker sovereign break. One will be, then two, then three, to unite the broken and rebind the free. Look to truth trust not the eye, the star will grow without a lie, but two will know the truth beyond and four will be the tie that bonds."

"We are going to find out why and how she vanishes and where she goes. Get a reading on the place and take an echo reading on the other room where she used the disappearing knife." Sir Kerrick ordered.

"Oh, I almost forgot! The reading from the incision to the dome walls gives us little information except that Shelby's genetic writing is now incorporated with the technology of the corporal textile." Captain Torden looked at Sir Kerrick as if he understood what the implications meant.

"Which means?" Sir Kerrick was obviously irritated and impatient.

"It means that she can now access all our technology."

Kerrick was quickly moving down the path of that disclosure. He was not worried about Shelby getting into it. For some reason he was certain she was not the threat, but more likely a pawn.

"Then anyone who knows this and uses her blood can eventually access our technology as well, and destroy us, or at least attempt to."

"That is assuming someone knows she is a key to such a thing," Doc Orlie interjected hopefully.

"I believe the reason she is gone now, is because someone or thing does know she has power they can use. 'Not without the Alker sovereign break'," he quoted.

"But, the next part of the prophecy says the broken will be rebound," Doc Orlie tried to quote again.

"No, it says 'unite the broken and rebind the free' which like all prophecy could have a double meaning; it is obscure to me," Sir Kerrick corrected.

"Well, what do you think it means?" Rockdurgh pushed.

He sighed. He had a feeling whatever he said would be wrong.

"We just need to do what we have to. The prophecy will come true without us. We need to do what is necessary. So get to work and get the women in here to prepare for emergency evacuation." Sir Kerrick was not going to wait for an attack. He was moving the clan to the safe haven in the mountain structure.

Kerrick wondered how the culprits were able to snatch Shelby within the dome of the Alkers, provided she herself did not do it. He knew of no species that could move through the tent without detection. Even unseen, her Bilboas were immediately discovered upon crossing the barrier of the protected area. So he suspected something more sinister than an escape or abduction.

Only Alkers could use technology within the dome or else the alarms would sound. None had when Shelby evaporated. This mystery reminded him of the twenty or so women that reported to Doctor Orlie about their dreams being so realistic they could smell or taste what they remembered. It was so unsettling to them they let Doc examine them. The reoccurring dreams had also been described by each woman as if they dreamed the same thing.

Kerrick turned to Torden.

"Captain Torden, since we have her signature we will single in on that genetic indicator and scout the area to pick up recently left markers from her. We know she has not been out of this dome for over three weeks, so there should not be any recent genetic prints.

"Also, take her markers out of the Alker technology base."

"But Sir, then she can be a threat again." Commander Rockdurgh was sure this was not a good idea.

Sir Kerrick paused for a moment. "We had her confined for almost a month and she was not able to get out. What made today different?"

"The cubs."

"Possibly. But I believe something made the cubs desperate to get to her and Shelby felt threatened enough she used her vanishing knife and almost within the hour she disappeared.

"It was not the cubs that brought the disappearing act, just her use of the weapon she hid. After she was seized, I could not find her weapon again, so either the Bilboas were able to carry it off or she still has it hidden here or whatever or whoever took her now has power that can be used against us."

Doc Orlie thought about that and it seemed possible she had some technology they were not able to identify.

Sir Kerrick continued with the facts.

"I personally examined the rooms she had been in and could find nothing unusual. She had nothing in her hand or on her that..." He thought about the way the 'knife' had changed into a necklace.

"The necklace or thing she had around her neck! She said it was something she made."

Doc Orlie pulled the thing out of his pocket. "You mean this?"

Sir Kerrick grabbed it from him and began inspecting it.

"It is made of organic materials." He was surprised.

He could hear pieces of things shaking in the hollowness of the shapes. Everyone watched as he peered into one of the beads.

"Dirt?" The men were baffled.

Doc Orlie examined it with magnification and concluded within a few minutes that it was the very dirt they walked on. Kerrick scrutinized a few more globules and the same thing was found.

"So the whole time she was here she had this around her neck, but within..." Sir Kerrick tried to think of the time frame.

Doctor Orlie spoke up.

"Minutes. I took it off and within minutes she was gone." He was dismayed he had not realized it sooner and may have caused this fiasco.

"But what is so special about this necklace with pebbles in it that..." Torden struggled to piece together the significance.

"She could have taken it off at any time or escaped if the necklace was something magical or had some kind of power," Commander Rockdurgh concluded.

"Or maybe it was like a charm to keep bad things from taking her."

"Or to keep her here," Sir Kerrick concurred.

"Once off she was either traceable or ungrounded." All the men nodded their heads thinking about any more possibilities.

"This planet is alive with strange uncharted, potential phenomenon and we need to accept the fact Shelby has tapped into something we are barely aware of."

"Maybe she is not aware either."

"She had a necklace she did not take off. I think she may have been somewhat aware to her dangerous situation."

"Let us find the woman and get her back here where she belongs."

Sir Kerrick Torrell, High Lurt of Aion, contemplated the recently found shield Shelby dropped in the scuffle on the day she arrived back in camp. It was a work of art and he wondered how she came by it. The strange thing about its markings was their familiarity; ancient Alkernian he judged. Older than anything he could recall owning. The weight of the shield was extraordinary; light as a feather.

He wanted to test the shield and laid it down on his desk. With all his pent up rage and self-loathing, he swung his sword across the shield with such force that the hefty table under it shuddered and sank inward from the blow.

When he looked up, he knew Commander Rockdurgh had seen and heard the antics and was a bit appalled by his illogical action.

"That is disturbing."

"Yes," he consented. "The shield should have broken, yet there is not a scratch on it. The desk probably was not the place to test its strength, however. Come look at it and see if you can read the symbols on the shield."

Rockdurgh moved over to the unstable desk and looked down at the ornate shield. It was too small for his body, but for a woman it would work nicely. The markings proved to be too covert for him to decipher, yet he recognized its representations as very old Alker.

"This was what Shelby had in her possession when she first came into camp. She kept telling me she needed to tell me something, but I was so furious with her for waltzing into the compound after all that time, I wanted to punish her.

"Every day she asked to speak to me. I realize my resentment was fueled by what I thought was betrayal. Now, I do not know what to believe."

"Sir, do you think she actually lied to us about where she was?"

"I believe she was not sure where she had been or for how long. But I know she has not told us all she does know."

"Sir, maybe when she came into the compound she had decided to do just that."

Kerrick looked at the shield and noticed some of the magnificent colors matched the beaded necklace. He wondered how the dirt was inserted into the carved beads and pulled the necklace of Shelby's out of his pocket and examined it more closely.

"Sir Kerrick, what are you thinking?"

"He is thinking what a jackass he was to an innocent woman."

Sir Kerrick's head popped up. "As irritated as you make me, I can not disagree." He pointed to Doc Orlie, "But I will not tolerate disrespect for my position.

"I see you think that upbraiding me in front of my Commander is going to endear your cause to me."

"Doc Orlie." Commander Rockdurgh addressed his elder properly and Sir Kerrick could see he was going to ignore any knowledge of hearing their jabs to each other.

It was not like Doc Orlie to keep his opinions to himself and he was sure others in the ranks knew of their opposite stance regarding the punishment of Shelby. Sir Kerrick straightened up and looked both men in the face.

He needed to admit his wrongdoing and enlist their help to squelch any backlash her disappearance was going to have. He was just not ready to admit anything right now.

"Is the entourage ready to make the trek to the mountain location?"

"Aye."

But what of our wayward waif? What if she returns to find us gone?" Doc worried.

Sir Kerrick had to admit now that it was his intention to stay behind in hopes of snatching her back should she return, though they all knew in their hearts there was no reason she should come back to be confined again.

"This necklace and shield are the key to Char Shelby. I have already discussed with Commander Rockdurgh that he and his men are to see the women get to the Mountain city. Commander Rockdurgh can take the clan and get to safety. Our comrades from Iritain will be coming within the week. I want all things in place."

"Understood."

Sir Kerrick watched him leave knowing Doc would berate him more for his insolence.

"You still believe she is a threat. You need to find out what is driving her to these extreme actions. What is her goal, her purpose? Does she want something and is she looking for a way to get it?"

Kerrick had to think about that for a minute. He remembered one time when she had disclosed she wanted to get off the planet to get to her children. Little did she know she was never going to be able to find them in the same point in time as she left them.

This planet slowed the aging process compared to Earth. Eventually, she would approach the same age range as her children. That was the sacrifice all Alkers knew they were making. In the scheme of things it was not a drastic compromise since the ages on Iritain reached hundreds of years. Alkers would not be as affected as the Earth women who barely reached a hundred.

"She desires to see her children, no doubt."

"Could be."

Sir Kerrick put his hand on his godfather's shoulder and looked into his piercing grey eyes.

"I am sorry that we appear to be at odds. My heart's desire is to get Shelby back and to secure her safety."

"I blame myself. As soon as that necklace was off she was gone."

"Don't." He looked at the beads again and then remarked, "Why is there dirt inside some beads and pebbles in others?" He held the beads up and shook them.

Doc Orlie shrugged his shoulders.

"I think it's because the dirt is from different places."

"Yes. That makes sense. Maybe even different time dimensions. Which is why she disappears and returns at random," Doc Orlie concurred.

"Which is why she can return...or could. What will draw her back this time?"

Captured / Chapter 23

Shelby stood shaking in complete darkness; her legs frozen in indefinable restraints. She groaned and the sound of her own voice was foreign to her ears.

"Wait one moment and you will get your bearings." It was a woman's voice, soft and pliant in the emptiness of the space.

"I can't see," Shelby's voice scratched.

"It will take some time," the unseen voice replied.

Shelby put her arms out. She felt for some kind of palpable and identifiable surface.

"Where am I?" She heard her words fall quietly around her body. There was an absence of echo or delay in her voice and she sensed she was in some kind of capsule. When her arms returned to her side, she felt as if they were numb.

"Quickly now before we lose her again. She can not be lost this time!" There was urgency in the male voice. Shelby felt she was in a precarious situation she couldn't understand.

The woman's voice was close to her ear and talked to her while the hubbub in the background grew more distinct.

"Listen to me, Shelby. You may only have a few minutes to grasp what I am saying to you. You have a special bond with the planet you are on. Somehow you picked up a minute piece of Crenulate and it bonded with your anatomy. It's like a parasite, except it is controllable; it interacts with your thoughts. No genus of humanoid that has come here has been able to accept it biologically like you have. It is like a baby in your system right now and you need to train it as it grows. Call it out of you. It hides by your bones and is like a protector of your body."

"She is fading." Someone in the background spoke.

"Shelby!" The woman's voice commanded her attention again. "Do you want to know more?"

"Yes." She found her voice.

"Then call the Crenulate to embrace your body."

"What do you mean?" Shelby whispered back.

The woman's voice desperately coaxed her, "To cover your body with a coating or to form into a sphere or something tangible."

"Why?"

"So you can stay here."

"I do not want to stay here. I want to go home!"

"Noooo!"

The voice faded from her ears, but not before she heard the wails of other voices together crying out in anguish and a sole voice of the same man she heard earlier booming his voice in anger, "Get her back! The others are gone!"

Bright lights exploded around Shelby and even with her eyelids closed she could sense them. It hurt her head and she moaned without meaning to. She was no longer strapped down so she was able to put her hand over her eyes, sitting up as she did. She tried to adjust her vision, but it took a few minutes.

She recognized Nemesis' voice before she could actually see him.

"Char Shelby...Earth...Alker...safe."

"How did you get me here?" Shelby squinted able to focus a little. She tried to get a bearing on what happened.

"You   experience...confusion...rest. Crenulate...Char Shelby gave Nemesis." He held the amethyst gem in his hairy hand and smiled at her. It scared Shelby because of his decisively large teeth, but he seemed harmless at the moment.

"This," Nemesis held the gem up, "save Char Shelby...Creation   Crenulate!   Oldest...anamnesis ...elements each division...Shelby gave."

"Nemesis? Division? What are you saying?" Shelby was once again lost by the Cauble's explanation.

He came close to Shelby, so close she was tempted to lean back away from the large hairy head that filled her vision.

"Nemesis   track   different   divisions existent...Aion... See?" He took the amethyst and it formed into a tube which the Cauble then inserted into the dais structure. He came back to help her up to the platform. They visually moved in a bubble. She literally felt like she was flying and she grabbed the wrist of the creature.

"Nemesis, does this take us to your zone?"

With a nod of its massive head it turned and slowed above a beautiful city of stone and natural growth. The Cauble knew how to navigate with much more control than Shelby thought possible.

"Nemesis, why have you not returned to your own kind if you can navigate this?" Shelby said this as her eyes were transfixed on the gliding view through the lovely city. Waterways and buildings were ornate and full of natural colors. Animals and birds were evident, but sudden realization dawned on Shelby, there seemed to be no Caubles.

"Where are your people, Nemesis?"

"Gone. Exiled." His head shook back and forth and hung in despair.

"Do you know where?" Shelby was dismayed.

"Al Kerking…Yahatamah division. No…Crenulate …dying…pain."

"How can we help them Nemesis? How do we save your people?"

"Key…Aion whole…Shelby…Alker…boy key."

Shelby did not understand the Cauble and she could see he was troubled. Nemesis took her and moved her over the planet and suddenly they hovered over the Alker camp. He pointed and Shelby could see people she knew. She yelled at them with no response.

"They can't hear me."

Nemesis shook his mighty head. "In…no…Out …Yes. He pointed to rings on the dais.

"If I step off the dais I will be with them?"

Nemesis shook his whole body. "In…no…Out…yes…Boulder." He whisked them away and Shelby cried out in dismay.

Suddenly, they were in lofty ancient trees moving among branches and swinging ramps high above the ground. He moved to a group of small humanoids with feathers. They were playing some kind of game, but a small boy stood out from among them. He had no feathers like the rest.

"Polotis division," Nemesis pointed. "Nemesis found...Alker...boy...Shelby...Polotis...division...key Creation Crenulate."

Shelby just frowned at him. "Polotis division?"

"Boy not Polotis...Alker...Shelby Alker." Nemesis insisted.

"Yes, I can see the boy is not...Po-lo-tis." Shelby tried the word on her lips.

"Yes...boy Alker...Shelby Alker...Boy Shelby's." Nemesis concluded.

"No, Nemesis. I have no boy on Aion. I've only been here two years. That boy looks like he's seven or eight." Shelby disagreed.

Nemesis stomped his large feet and swung his head in frustration.

"Polotis division...seven years...Alker division...two years...Shelby Polotis division...two years."

"Nemesis. I was not in the Polotis..." Then she remembered faintly a dream she had of these bird people, the Polotis, and the missing days she could not account for. And time. Was it possible? Why did she not remember? How could she not remember?

Nemesis brought her up close to the boy without feathers. He looked familiar. He looked like...Kerrick. In her mind his face superimposed on the boy's and

Shelby could see similarities, the shape and color of his eyes and his mannerism of crossing his arms over his chest...and a dimple. She felt faint.

"I was in the Polotis division for two years and had....a boy?" Her voice rasping what she thought Nemesis was telling her.

"See..." Nemesis swung his arm toward the boy as if that was proof enough.

"Is that where I was?"

The Cauble looked at her again with pitiful eyes. "Two years Polotis...Seven past."

"I have a boy in the Polotis division, in a different time zone...dimension." Shelby was incredulous.

"IzTaln." Nemesis grinned.

And then Shelby impulsively stepped out of the ring off the dais.

Shelby's Bearing / Chapter 24

Shelby went through some kind of cold again and then warmth wrapped around her. She was afraid to open her eyes, but her body felt cocooned in softness and she floated in and out of consciousness. How strange to dream of...

Shelby sat up, suddenly. She was fully alert and looking for familiar bearings. She recognized this place. Shelby was in the realm of the Polotis people, Schoftastaklakla's clan. Was she dreaming again?

As if to confirm her revelation, Schofta came into view, beautiful in his clamorously feathered body. He seemed surprised by her presence, but he quickly recovered his astonishment and dropped to her side. He was as shocked by her presence as she was his.

"Shelby?" His warm hands held her face to peer at her more closely; to examine her and determine if she was indeed truly present.

"I never thought that you would be back in my realm. I thought to never see you again."

Shelby put her hand on one of his and kissed it tenderly. "I have missed you, Schoftastaklakla. I see you always in my dreams, your green eyes pleading with me."

Shelby was a little taken back when he pulled his hands away abruptly.

"How is this possible? You should not even know my name! That should have been taken from you." His voice faded, contemplating how someone like her could remember what should have been forgotten.

They were interrupted by a young boy who greeted Schoftastaklakla without realizing she was present. He exuberantly hugged Schofta before he noticed her.

Something tugged at Shelby's heart, a soft longing, an ache that grew as she saw the young boy and he saw her.

"Is this my mam'a, Da?"

The boy's hope turned to confusion and Shelby recognized the same frown she often saw when looking into a mirror.

Schoftastaklakla hurried the boy out promising to talk to him later. The lad was obedient and left with such a look of trust, Shelby was ashamed she had intruded into their lives.

Schoftastaklakla looked Shelby over again. Her beauty to him was perfection of all that she was. Her heart was so good and so devoted that he was comforted just by the sight of her.

"Do not cry, Shelby. IzTaln is a strong, young boy and is well suited for this life.

"He is contented here and very gifted."

"I am bouncing back and forth to places and I am not sure why or how or when it is going to happen again. I am having a hard time knowing if I am dreaming or in reality."

Schofta hugged her and she felt her fears being absorbed and lifted away from her.

"You'll be safe here, for as long as you need to be away from the turbulence."

He wanted to make her stay forever, but she was not of his realm and he knew he had only a short time before she would need to go again. But for now, he did not want to retell her again all the things she would need to know.

He had tried to spare her of the memories she had made in their short life together. Two years was not enough, not nearly. But she had given him a perfect son. And he had rejoiced when she had done so willingly.

Time warped differently for them than it did for her. Years here would only be days in her realm if entered at a certain place and time. They had lived in this realm safe from the foul creatures of the other zones. They could pass by different zones if they studied the stars and the laws of the planet. Centuries old, the laws of the planet were steadfast for them, predictable, accurate and limiting.

Shelby was one of those rare creatures who could transcend into their time zone.

But her mind had somehow retained the ability to hear or be aware of the other things in her dimension without her seeing them. It nearly drove her crazy. The only way she believed she could quiet the extra noise was by going back into her own time era.

She had done so to keep her sanity and Schoftastaklakla had known she would never be able to make it back before he had grown old and ugly. But he had been astonishingly mistaken.

Even with a ceremony to withdraw her memories so the transition would be easier, his heart had bled with regret of losing their love. He assured her it would be best for her happiness, but she had obviously retained a deep-seated memory that he was selfishly glad for.

"I left my son? A baby with you?" Shelby was mortified.

"While you were here you had IzTaln. His body was too small to cross the dimension barrier with you. You knew you had to return, but to return with a two year old child would reveal our dimension to your Alker clan. You agreed to keep our existence secret until you knew for certain the Alkers were not the ones responsible for Aion's dimension disparities. We really didn't know crossing into a different dimension was possible until you appeared. We knew it had been possible at one time, but the knowledge was forgotten and died with one of our Ancients, until you."

Schofta soothed her, murmuring into her hair. She smelled so good and memories flooded back to him of her sacrifice to leave her child with him, and her sincere regret of leaving her family. He pulled her into his embrace; his feathers enveloped them in privacy.

Shelby looked into the face of this beloved man and knew she was being coaxed into a serene state. It was something vaguely familiar to Shelby. She remembered the calm he would bring with his presence, and strength. He reminded her of Kerrick. She saw again his eyes and clarity dawned on her.

The green eyes she saw in her dreams were not the light ones of Schofta, but the disturbing ever-changing green ones of Kerrick Torrell. That was the reason she had gone back. She loved that man and Schofta had tried to dispel her memories of him.

She pulled away from him. She did love Schofta, but not because he was the only one she could love, but because she had been lulled onto compliance and her thoughts of Kerrick had been dulled by the persistent and attentive Schofta.

"I will see IzTaln. Then you and I will discuss what I know you are withholding and trying to evade."

Schofta felt the jab of anger directed toward him. He was losing her again, and this time more quickly. He could not use his siren coaxing for his beloved Shelby. He needed to remind her again of the comfort she felt here in this place.

Shelby headed for the exit from the teardrop nest. Outside, others waited for her appearance. The unique cooing of their sounds, so like birds and creatures of the forest, erupted like a disturbance of warning or awareness to the community of Polotis peoples.

Shelby bowed in respect and without much thought instinctively made a throaty sound that came from somewhere in her forgotten recollection. She was caught off-guard by the echoing sounds of approval. She was going by instinct alone and so much of what she sensed was just beyond her understanding.

She saw IzTaln come forward hesitantly. Shelby walked quickly to him and picked him up and hugged him fiercely. She kissed him and then put him down to look at him with wondering eyes. He looked so much like his father she had to take on faith that he was hers too.

"I am Shelby and I have some things I must say to you. When I passed the barrier into my homeland, I forgot what I should know. Here," her hand encompassed the whole view of what she saw, "I begin to remember what I have forgotten. Do you understand what I am saying?"

She looked at this very young progeny of hers and wondered how she was going to save their idyllic wonderland. She looked at the trees that were occupied by such supreme beings and wondered if they would fight for their own survival, or if they were so passive they would wait too long to rise up to the challenge of their ways.

She looked at the males and knew they were strong and very intelligent, beyond her imagining. Behind the passive facades they possessed extreme warrior capabilities.

Shelby watched IzTaln's reaction and still he looked at her with awe. Schofta came behind her and looked over her shoulder at their son.

"IzTaln. Speak your mind; you usually never quit asking questions." He chuckled at the blank expression on his son's face.

"I must leave very soon. Before I was drawn here, I was in a place where people could somehow detect the Crenulate in me and they were trying to take it by force. I think they need it to survive in their world. I don't really know, only that they are going to try to find me again and if they detect this time dimension, it will be very bad for all of us. They have learned how to harness it somehow."

She was only now realizing the danger she put them in.

"You never spoke of any of this before."

"I did not understand it before. I still know very little. I met a Cauble and it seemed to know some things about the ones who wanted to take the Crenulate. The Crenulate I have hides except in times it needs to protect me. But I am starting to remember things... know things instinctually."

Schofta looked at Shelby with new understanding. She was indeed going to help his people. She may not remember all the things that happened before she left, but she had gained knowledge somehow through the passing of her very short time in the Alker dimension.

For now, he needed to tread softly. She did not remember all the details of why she went back, but he was sure she would regain some sense of the reasons the longer she stayed.

She held out her hand to IzTaln. He took it hesitantly and Shelby turned to Schofta.

"I will speak to your aunt and Ancients."

Schofta nodded in assent and started to leave. He was stopped by Shelby's voice echoing out over the top of the trees. As he looked around, he saw the draw of all his people to Shelby. Where had all her composure come from?

"Dear Polotis people. You are beloved. I have a deep longing for your safety, but I fear I will bring only bad to your way of life. I have lost much of my memory, but I sense your care for me and I look at you and know I should say something to encourage you. I will try again to help, but I am limited by my inability to cross into the phase of my own time without losing memories. As I look at each of you, I know you, and things about you, yet names are lost.

"Please forgive me and be patient. I do have hope though that all things are going to work together and will be for the good of your survival. I will talk with the Ancients before I say more."

Shelby's voice was like a melody to Schofta's ears. He had missed her so deeply he felt weak from the loss of her leaving. Even worse than that was his part in removing her memories of this place and time, and his knowing that she was lost to him even if she came back.

"Schofta." Shelby addressed him now and he put his hands on her strong shoulders.

"Before I go back..." Shelby was interrupted by Schofta.

"I need to speak to you about this young man and our time together."

"Yes." Shelby's sad look on her face spoke volumes. She was remembering and not all of it was good.

"Schofta, the feathers that you can grow and that disappear back into your body?"

"Yes?"

"Do you realize that it is the same Crenulate microorganisms that can form into this?" She touched her luminous belt.

Schofta looked at her without saying anything one way or the other. His hand touched her silken hair and her face with tenderness that only a lover could do. His forehead bent to hers and he spoke very softly.

"I will love you, Shelby, until the day I die. I will fight for you and I am honored by your trust in me, and know this, I do not want you to leave; but I love my family also and will not take sides against them or their safety."

Shelby pulled her head back and looked at him with an uneasy look.

"I do not understand."

"You think that our feathers are the organism. How can that be?"

"Let me show you, Schofta." She put her free hand on his arm and pulled back from him.

To everyone's amazement, Schofta's beautiful feathers fell off of his body and puddled at his feet. Even Schofta was mystified by her ability to take his adornments from him.

"Da, your colors are off." There was astonishment in the eyes of those observing and some fear of Shelby's ability to accomplish such a thing. Clucking distress vibrated in the community ranks.

Shelby put her foot in the mess of feathers at his feet. She stood very close to him and could sense his extreme calm. She looked up into his face and saw the love he had for her, a sense of pride and admiration. His arms wrapped around her and within seconds, she was embraced by his warmth and strength. She started crying. She could not stop. Her emotions flooded her body's ability to contain the relief she felt in his hold; the comfort. His feathers re-emerged and enveloped them in privacy. She kissed his chest and turned her ears to his heart to hear the strong steady beat of it.

"You are beloved, too, Shelby. And I know you need time to heal. That can happen here."

"No. I need to leave before the Shadow creatures find this place."

"Shadoubles. They cannot. It is a protected area and one of the reasons people are not lost here. Remember those that you helped back? They spoke of the same Shadow creatures that you have, but they were only discovered outside of the realm of this protected area."

"Where are the boundaries?" Shelby mumbled back.

"They are marked by the water ways and the rock formations. We are aware of them now."

Shelby looked unconvinced. Schofta laughed softly and unfolded his arms from around her.

"IzTaln, go and tell the others she is ready."

"Yes, Da."

He left and Shelby felt the loss of his going. She watched him run and leap from place to place going to the community loft; and Schofta watched her.

"He is very strong and agile." He reminded her.

"I see that."

Schofta led her to the meeting and sat beside her. Many things were discussed but Shelby had the nagging feeling some things were purposely left out of the dialogue.

Shelby's fatigue grew and she yawned as she listened to the debate of her presence and the return of the threat. Mostly, Shelby listened and tried to keep up, but she was drained and still needed to talk with Schofta.

"I may not be able to stay awake very long, Schofta. I am exhausted." He only nodded and handed her something to drink. She took a small sip and felt the burning of it going down her throat. It was familiar and yet different from what she expected.

"I need to talk to you, privately," she asserted.

He nodded. "There will be time later. Rest. You look very pale."

Against her will her eyes closed and she fell fast asleep, leaving many things unanswered and fearing she would never remember to speak them.

Married / Chapter 25

Shelby removed her shoes and sat at the edge of the ramp. She was in a morose mood. She loved being with the Polotis people, but she missed her clan. When had she begun to think of them as 'her clan'? Shelby leaned her forehead against the roped handrail and sighed. How was she going to get home?

Shelby looked out over the treetops of the magnificent ancient growth. Birds of all kinds and way too many bugs and insects for her liking lingered and crawled in a dizzying array of movement that meant the feeding time had come. There was so much life above the ground. This planet was full of beauty and danger and peculiarity. Some of the differences she could relate to, but some of the animals were so strange and the bugs so bizarre she was nervous of them. Thankfully, her growing knowledge of them lessened her alarm of their strangeness.

She felt a shift in the ramp she sat on and looked for the culprit.

"IzTaln. Come and sit with me." Shelby beckoned him with an outstretched hand and motioning fingers. He hesitated for the proper amount of time while Shelby waited.

"Why are you sitting here?" He apparently did not see grown Polotis sitting on the ramps very often.

"I love the view. And I was waiting for you because I would like to talk to you." Shelby smiled at him and then turned back to the vista not knowing if her action would make him feel dismissed or comfortable enough to join her.

After a while she thought he had gone and she lowered her head, surprised to feel tears well up in her. A soft shuffle at her side delighted her. He had stayed in spite of her doubt.

"There are better views down the path." His surly response scolded in a grownup tone.

"But not as much privacy. IzTaln, did you know your father found me in the forest of Lanhan?" He looked at her puzzled. "I was near death and I was also pregnant." She waited for this to sink in, but he did not seem to understand the relevance.

"Did you lose the baby? That is what happened to Narcila when she fell during the storm." He was obviously aware of the dangers of the treetops.

"No. The child was a boy and I lived here for almost two years with the Polotis. I believed I would live here for always."

IzTaln was quiet for a while. Hesitantly he asserted, "You should not have left. It is a good place to live."

Shelby nodded her head in accord. "I need to explain something to you. Would you like to know more about why I left?"

"Yes," and then hesitantly, almost a whisper he said, "mam'a."

Shelby smiled at him with pride showing in her tearing eyes.

"I can tell IzTaln, that you understand many things. Your Da told you about me then?"

He held his head high and shook his head 'no'.

"How did you know, IzTaln?"

He shrugged his shoulders.

"Do you wonder why I did not stay with you and your Da?"

He looked at her with doubt. Did she know these were things he had already asked his Da?

"Am I going to have to answer questions without knowing exactly what you want to know?" Shelby was intently watching his reactions and still he looked at her with awe.

"It's okay. I will speak my mind and then if you have any questions, you may ask them then."

Shelby reached out to IzTaln and brought him closer to her.

"I may not be able to stay long or I may stay for a very long time; it just depends on the catalyst that pulls me home." She looked at this beautiful boy and realized he understood what she meant.

"I am going to give you something. Hold out your hand." He did as she commanded.

Shelby held out her hand and in her palm a small square of clear amethyst grew and the boy's eyes widened in astonishment.

She put the gem into IzTaln's palm, and then she asked, "Do you trust me?"

The marvel in his eyes was testament to his anticipation of what she would do next.

"It will hurt one time then you will be all right." Instantly the bottom of the square gem changed into a sharp point and Shelby put her palm over his and squeezed hard. The boy cringed and tried to pull his hand back out of instinct, but Shelby held on pulling his hand back and opening it.

There was no mark and the gem was gone.

"Call it back." Shelby commanded him.

He looked at her with the hurt look of one who had been betrayed, but Shelby laughed and he looked back down at his palm. Shelby grasped his other hand.

"In this one." He looked at her with puzzlement as she pointedly looked at the opposite hand she held.

"Look." The cube began to grow again in his open palm and the boy was startled and tried to shake it off of his hand. It stuck like glue.

"Think of a different shape." Shelby quieted his movements and soothed his alarm with her calm admonition.

The boy stilled and was captivated by Shelby's intent gaze.

"I remember how horrified I was when I discovered I could produce a knife or sword just by reaching my hand out." As she detailed her learning experience, she demonstrated a knife and then a sword and then she put the sword to her neck quickly so it looked as if she would cut off her own head, but the sword warped into a beautiful necklace that wrapped around her throat.

"The creature that now inhabits your body also is in your father's. It connects us through the planet's energy. It will grow in you as it does in me. It has chosen you and that is why I am here. It cannot grow in Schofta, and I don't know why.

"Each of the clan probably has a piece of the Crenulate microcosm in them as well, but your body will at some point collect it from them. And when you are grown, the Crenulate will draw all its parts together and that means you and I will come together and it will be free to protect the planet again.

"Now it is split by time zones, but the planet wants to bring all of its inhabitants onto one plane. But for now, the Crenulate microcosm is safer from the exploitation of corruptible powers, powers that almost destroyed this planet. But the organism in our bodies, though small, is connected to the planet and more powerful than the ones that tried to harness it.

"So, now it selects its hosts, and protects us. If you are worthy, then you will have the ability to shape it. It will protect the host it inhabits, but it will go back into Aion if it is being destroyed or used in destructive ways. Do you understand what I am telling you?" Shelby looked at the innocent boy and wondered what she was thinking explaining such things to one so young.

"Yes, Mam'a. It was used to do bad things so it divided itself into a lot of pieces to get away from the bad people."

"That is probably true, IzTaln. It probably, at that time, split the world into different zones as well. It will reveal to you things it may not tell me, so you need to pay attention. It will teach you things that are important, and when the time is right I will see you again. But I can not live with you or else the bad people will find us."

"Are you leaving soon?" He sounded impatient, as if his life was halted by her appearance and he wanted it to move on.

"IzTaln. I know you think I have no right to interrupt your life here. I just want you to know I am sorry."

"It's okay. You are not really my mother. Zeryl is my mother. She always takes care of me and is going to be my Father's mate."

He was cutting and it hurt, but she felt it was right for him to be resentful. Who was she to disrupt his peace and security?

"I want to tell you something, IzTaln. I have other children that are not with me." Shelby saw the surprise in his eyes.

"I do not tell you this to hurt you. When I was taken off my home planet, they were taken from me; I had no choice but to adjust. I miss them more than is good for my heart. It causes me physical pain and I wake up nights knowing I can't see them."

Shelby's voice broke as her mind flashed to scenes she could not forget. She bit the corners of her mouth trying to quell the quivering and looked directly into IzTaln's face after she took a moment to regain her composure.

"Just because I am not with them, does not mean I do not love them. My desire is to have all my children with me, here or there, it does not matter just as long as I can be with them.

"I know I probably will never see them again, but I am still going to try to find them. I don't even know the way back to them or if they are alive, but if I ever get a chance to see them, I hope they remember me and are..."

She caught her breath as she looked at IzTaln. He was intelligent; she could see it in his eyes. He was years ahead of his age. His mannerisms looked so much like Kerrick it distracted her.

"Are what?" He prodded.

"What? Oh," she tried to retrace her thoughts. "I hope and pray they are happy and honorable people." There was a pause.

"So I have a brother?"

That put a slight smile on her face. "Two and a sister."

"How old are they?"

"Older than you," she teased. "But really I can not say for sure, IzTaln. Your time zone is different than theirs. I calculate that when you are thirty you will be older than them if you stay here."

He was considering her math and smiled. He understood. "I will be older in years and younger in age, fascinating. I will have to get Maxcob to help me figure that out. I could be older than you at some point?"

Shelby laughed out loud at that. In her camp, she was one of the older women already and the more time she stayed here, she would age more, but the time for them would be slower. She just kept getting older! Now she was depressed. But a thought occurred to her.

"Unless your time zone is more like theirs, and I am going to be younger than them when I see them."

IzTaln looked at her with some confusion. "You could be younger than all your children? Strange! I could be older than you some day!" He repeated again. "That would be strange."

Shelby looked at him with wonder. "No kidding."

She loved the way he looked and the way he held his head. If he did not look so much like his father, she would not have believed him to be her child. There was nothing of her features in him. She smiled at that.

"I will need to leave soon, bud. I fear for the Alkers and I desire to help Nemesis find his people. He is all alone and it is not good for humanoids to be without companionship."

"Do you love him?"

"Who? Nemesis?" She saw the question in his eyes. Shelby shook her head. "No. I just feel compassion for the Cauble. And really, IzTaln, I do not know if it is male or female." She made a face and they chuckled.

His dimple was exactly like Kerrick's. She was beginning to understand the reasoning she had in keeping him here, but she was going to have to make this right somehow.

"I am glad Zeryl is a good mom to you. Schofta promised me he would take care of you and the clan would always call you their own and take you under their wings." She smiled at her pun while IzTaln did not get the humor, but he did not disagree either.

"I tell you this because I know you love your father and your family is always going to be here for you. They are very good people. But I do not want you to think I lied to you or deceived you when you are grown. I love your father; actually, I love both of them. You look like your biological father, but he doesn't know about you, yet."

The boy looked at her with hurt and anger so she waited, not trying to push him anymore.

"If you don't want to hear more, I will tell Schofta as much as I can, and you and he can talk about it later, when I am gone. I know there will be a time when you will need to know more about your other father and you will have questions."

"What is his name?" He was so direct Shelby was taken back and it took her a moment to respond.

"His name is Sir Kerrick of Torrell. He is the leader of the Alker people here on Aion."

"Are you married?"

Shelby shook her head 'no'. "Not really."

"Are you going to marry my father?"

Shelby knew he meant Schofta. She did not know what to say to him. But she considered for a moment her options.

"Schofta is peace to me and security and when I was here, I didn't know I could be anywhere else. But after a while, as you grew, I realized I missed your real father and I felt an urgency to be with my Alker people."

"Schofta is my real father." IzTaln was indignant.

"Yes. He is a real father to you, but we were never husband and wife, nor mated. But he loved you and he believed you would be like a beacon to me and bring me back to him. And you have. But, I worry that you..."

Shelby was deeply concerned her emotions would get the better of her. She already sensed Schofta was listening in the background. She did not want to speak for him, but maybe make him tell IzTaln a little more detail about their relationship because she herself was not sure of what they had together.

He looked at her with furrowed brows and yet he was far more patient than she expected a young boy to be. "What do you worry?"

Shelby sighed. "I worry so much about what is going to be the best solution for a difficult choice. I have always loved Schofta, from the moment I laid eyes on him. He is very wise and kind. But before him I loved and still love your biological father, Kerrick. And that is complicated."

"Why don't you stay here and marry Schofta?" He was so hopeful.

"I believe your father Schofta is in love with Zeryl. The reason I needed to leave last time was to keep this part of the planet dimension hidden from the Alkers I came with so that I could determine if they would harm your family and clan."

Beneath the ramp, a lone girl listened with earnest at the revelation she now heard. Schofta's boy was really not any part of the clan. This would change everything for her. Now her sister's son would be heir and not IzTaln, the adored boy of the Polotis. Everyone believed he was of the hallowed prophecy of the Polotis lineage, but now she heard with her own ears the truth from the woman who had the whole clan in an uproar. She would let Zeryl know she would be able to claim the throne for her own child if she married Schoftastaklakla. IzTaln would never be able to rise to power now, and Zeryl as Queen would be able to bring her brother to power.

"Does the Crenulate help you?" He understood as did all the Polotis people young and old that the Crenulate was the symbiotic entity that made time dimension possible on this planet.

"Yes, but I believe it needs me to go to my own time zone so that it can grow strong. Does that make sense?"

He shrugged his shoulders and looked away.

"When I knew I had to leave, I asked if there was some way to forget what I was leaving behind, or else I knew I would not be able to endure the loss. The Polotis people are very intelligent, and they wanted to take my memories not only to protect their existence, but it would also help me to go back to the life I had left.

"I had to decide if I wanted to bring you back with me and try to explain your age discrepancy or leave you behind and all the memories that would otherwise lead to their safe haven. It was one of the hardest choices I had to make, and the clan was not going to force me either way, which shows their loyalty and trust in me.

"I am sorry, IzTaln, if this forgetting makes you sad. I did not think I would ever be able to come back. But once I was in my own zone, I did not even remember the existence of the Polotis people because my memory was taken."

"How do you remember now?"

"There are embedded triggers the Polotis Ancients left in me. The longer I stay, the more I remember and can fill in."

"Polotis people are the wisest and most knowledgeable on Aion. They are the oldest living clan on the planet."

Shelby nodded assent to his bragging of his clan. She could see the pride he had in the people of this tribe. They were a unique race and she admired them almost as much as IzTaln.

"You should stay."

Shelby wanted to, oh, so very much. But she still felt a deep urgency she was not where she should be and time was running out.

"I wonder IzTaln, if you and I could exchange memories through the Crenulate? I could give you some of my Crenulate and you give me some of your memories through the Crenulate." She held out her hand to IzTaln. He took it hesitantly.

"No! You must not do that, Shelby." Schofta scared both of them and Shelby stood to her feet without even knowing she had taken a defensive stance. Mother and son both looked at him with concern.

"You may cause more harm than good." He tried to back down the alarm, but it was too late for not arousing consternation.

"I take it, you have been listening?" She looked at him with disquiet eyes.

"I am sorry. I did not want to interrupt." He looked at his son and felt anguish at the development of their lives. Then he looked at the woman who was certain to leave again and break not one heart, but two this time. The counsel was right. The sooner she left the better for all concerned.

"I need to talk with your mother for a while. Go to Zeryl and wait for me."

He put a strong hand on his son's shoulder and for privacy encircled them with his feathers. Shelby saw the shield as evidence of her exclusion from their circle and she dropped her head in sorrow. She turned away from them and started to walk away to somewhere, she did not care, just away. She heard her name being called and she ran.

She ran fast and jumped from one ramp to another like she was born to it. She leapt into the air and landed on her feet each time on some limb or ramp, not slowing until there was no more place to run.

Still, she needed to go so she descended the treetops as she had seen the Polotis people do, using the vines and dropping to lower branches. She slipped easily down as if the vines and branches were designed to accommodate such an escapade.

Her feet finally touched ground and to her amazement she took off running again. She kept running until her lungs felt like exploding drums in her chest.

She was waist high in undergrowth, scratches and droplets of blood squeezed from the slight slashes and sweat beading over her body. She slumped down and rested unwillingly. She raised her eyes and let her mind catch up.

When Shelby looked around and saw no one, the bugs caught her attention with their buzzing and she saw the beauty of the growth surrounding her. As if in a trance, she zeroed in on the sound of water and moved toward it.

The kaleidoscope of undergrowth and vegetation opened up under the eaves of the mammoth trees to a dropoff overlooking a fall and pool down below. It streamed out not far from the ledge she stood on and continued weaving its way into the lower vegetation. It was such a private place she could almost imagine it had never been discovered until now.

Shelby made her way down to the pool edge and sank to her knees in exhaustion. The spray from the fall misted her hair and skin with beads of coolness. Shards of light made their way into the nook that cast shadows and created the illusion of mystery. She sipped the water cupped in her hand and when she was done she laid back and closed her eyes.

Shelby realized she may not have complete memories of her time with the Polotis people, but her heart had not forgotten a thing. She was never supposed to have returned and now since she did, she could not change what pain she was going to create for those around her.

Her heart remembered love and happiness here. Her mind was confused and so many questions nagged at the back of her mind. Why did she leave? Was she in love with Schofta? Did he love her? What about IzTaln? Did Schofta know he was not his child? Would she be that deceptive? Could she truly leave her own child with someone that was not the father? Why would she do such a thing? Her mind went round and round until she found she was crying quiet sobs.

The warmth of the sun touched her misted skin like a warm blanket and she stilled her mind so that the spiral of sadness would not consume her. One thing she knew for sure that surprised her was that she loved IzTaln very much and she would have done whatever she thought was best for him. She also knew for certain that she loved Schofta deeply. She was almost certain she had never told him so though she did not know the reason for it. Maybe it was because she always knew she would leave, even as she knew now. Or maybe it was because he was in love with someone else as he seemed to be now and she knew it would be of no avail. Whatever the reasons for her decisions, she was certain of who she was and that it would have been for good reason she left her child behind.

Even reasoning that now, she could not stop the sadness in her heart. She drifted off to sleep with the soft mist hiding the salty tears sliding down her face.

He looked at the woman in her stillness by the pool of reflection. He had brought her here many years ago it seemed, to show her their possible future. Why had she come here? Did she remember this place? She wasn't supposed to.

Schofta had tried to harden his heart and mind against this woman so that he could fulfill his tribal duty and marry the woman who was pledged to him. Zeryl was a beautiful and kind woman from the sister clan of Polotis people. She was betrothed to him since her teen years as was the custom for the future leaders of the people. He loved Zeryl when he laid eyes on her and knew he would be blessed in such a union.

Even knowing this did not change his mind after he met Shelby. He was drawn to her like a moth to the flame and he tried to woo her to him but to no avail. She resisted his flirting and though she finally did give in to his sexual advances she never let go of her conviction to leave. He remembered believing that if he could get her to love him she would stay and be his mate. He did not then realize her resolve and conviction of going back to her own people.

He was to be ritually mated with Zeryl within the year, but up to now they had only been courting as was allowed. She was to live with his Aunt the Queen since his mother was deceased, and to become a member of the clan learning her place and her role in the tribe and accepting Schoftastaklakla's position.

His was a unique situation in that he already had a child. The clan had adjusted to his decision to raise a child by a mother who was no longer his mate and gone. What they did not know was that IzTaln was not even his progeny. But he had been determined to protect Shelby from the negative sentiments of his clan. His one purpose was that she belonged here.

But fate would not have any of it. She started hearing voices.

She finally understood that she was feared by the clan more than welcomed. She also had a physical pull causing her to be restless and in pain. Schofta knew she would not be able to stay, but the child she bore was going to make her lack of memories incongruent to the time span and would eventually lead her Alker clan to the conclusion that the Polotis people existed; something that at the time seemed to be an important factor with her return.

They did not want her tribe to come looking for her either. There were other reasons also, but she was put in a position of no choice. Either she left the child willingly or they would be forced to protect their secrecy. He knew she suspected his clan of being capable of killing her to keep their secret, and she was right. Even now at her return, she was thought of as a liability and was treated as if she was creating a rift in their security.

The Ancients knew this was not so, but he was still under orders to escort her to the return portal and to close it permanently on her, as if he would.

The sun waned and she woke to the realization she was not going back to the Polotis nest. Her memories though unclear heightened her senses enough to conclude she was not welcome in their midst any longer.

In a moment of clarity, she realized that she was a prodigal in both worlds. She did not belong here with her son and the Polotis people and the Alkers did not want her.

She pulled herself up to a sitting position and rested her arms and head on her knees. In alarm she heard a soft shifting of movement and twisted to the direction of the sound. It was Schofta.

He sat down next to her, careful to keep his distance. He noticed her calm return and felt more than heard her sigh. They sat like this, neither one spoke for some time. It was as if the air enclosed around them and weighted them down with all the unspoken heartache of what was to come. They could sense it, feel it, even taste it, but words would not have explained it.

"Before I go, I need to know some things. I hope I can remember them when I go back, but if I don't, it won't be because I chose to forget."

Schofta looked at her and wondered which questions he would be able to answer and remain true to his clan and personal resolve. It was getting late and he was expected to expel her from their world, permanently trapping her in one of the in-between worlds, neither in his nor in hers, alone for the rest of her life. He had no such compulsion to do so. It was traitorous of him, he knew, but it was a fact he would never do so, though he adopted an attitude around the clan as if she were unimportant to him since her return.

"Does IzTaln understand about his real father?" She watched Schofta carefully for indications he was going to evade her question.

He looked directly at her after a moment and shook his head 'no' slowly.

"Were you going to tell him?"

He looked at her sideways and smiled mischievously, "Not until I had to. The clan does not know either."

She hesitated. "So they think you and I mated?"

"At least once." His smile was quirky and she couldn't help smile back.

"Did we?" she asked uncertainly.

He laughed at that and looked her directly in the eyes and said with the same endearing smile, "At least once."

Shelby was really not sure who she was to have lived with such a man. Truth be told, she was ashamed of her unorthodox behavior. It took a few moments for her to grapple with what he proclaimed.

"Why did I really leave him, Schofta?"

Tears brimmed at her eyes and he saw the vulnerability that he loved so much in her. He would not lie to her.

"Because it was either that or both of you would be exiled to the land of the forgotten. Polotis people do not want their existence revealed to any outside people, that is the way we have lived for hundreds of years and we have survived and outlived the advanced nations that have tried to control this planet with force.

"This planet chooses who will live and thrive and who will be banished. You have experienced this with the Cauble and the Al Kerking. Crenulate is the connecting force and without it, no one survives for very long."

"So you would have sent us into exile?"

"Without Crenulate. If you would have returned to your people with a two year old child, there would have been questions to answer. Even without your memory it would not take long for your Alker leaders to conclude a time difference and then the discovery of an adjacent world."

Shelby understood. They were far more advanced than they appeared or purported. "You have the technology to remove the Crenulate?"

He gave her a small negative nod. "Only death removes Crenulate, or going into a dead zone. The Crenulate returns to the planet at such times, that is why it is called the dead zone."

"So once in the dead zone, one can not get out of that dimension; which is why everyone laughed when I asked if they could get out of there with the Crenulate. It does not exist there."

He looked at her with a forlorn expression. He could not answer that truthfully. But he would try to explain some of it. "You would be forced into the dead zone where the Crenulate would leave your body, thus rendering you unable to return ever again to your time zone or leave that zone. The Al Kerkings are in the dead zone. You've heard about the Yahatama region. You need the Crenulate from your own time zone to travel back." He did not want to say more.

"Why did I not want to stay?"

"You did. But your body and mind could not distinguish the difference and it caused you physical pain."

"Why?'

He looked at her with intense clarity and spoke with conviction. "Because Shelby, you are destined for more than this kind of life. Something about you causes the Crenulate to react differently and shuffles the lines of dimensions when you are close to them."

Shelby looked at him. "I just want you to know that IzTaln is a wonderful young boy and I am so thankful that you have taken care of him and taught him to be strong."

"He is my son and always will be." That made Shelby a bit uneasy.

"I must have known that or else I would not have been able to leave him."

And then quite suddenly she confessed, "I must have loved you deeply, Schofta." Shelby spoke quietly, so much remorse filling her words with misery.

Schofta's look was one of honest surprise that did not go unnoticed by Shelby.

"I thought so. I never told you, did I?"

"No, you did not." His smile was peculiar to Shelby. He looked pleased but distressed at the same time.

"My heart feels it, a longing and sadness at the same time that pulls at me physically when I see you. I must have felt that to tell you would make things harder or worse somehow."

Schofta looked at her with quiet intelligence, a slight furrow on his face. He did not say anything, but continued to look at her.

She pushed on trying to get through the uncomfortable place her admission brought them to. "Was Zeryl betrothed to you then? I am just trying to understand why I could ask you to keep my child and not tell you how I think I must have felt."

"No, Zeryl and I started our courtship after you left, though she was presented to me when she was an eligible woman." His gaze never left her and she felt a dawning of realization.

"Oh, Schofta, I am sorry for making you uncomfortable. I assumed there had to be someone else. I didn't realize you just didn't love me in return. I must have known it back then."

Shelby felt supremely idiotic and looked away. How could she not have realized he just did not feel the same way she did? Of course he did not love her, so why did she stumble so blindly into this situation? Maybe she misunderstood the pain in her heart.

He stood up and Shelby looked up into his face before she realized he was holding out his hand to her to help her up. Their conversation was over and she would not be able to find any more answers for her present dilemma of her past decisions.

He helped her up and surprised her by cupping her chin in his hand.

"I would see you go almost transparent, like your Bilboas. We never spoke of it to anyone, but you understood it more clearly each time you got close physically to the edge of our dimension. You lost your ability to withstand the pull. You started hearing things we thought at first weren't there. It is why you had to go back. When you left, I knew you were gone forever."

"Why did you not come with me to my dimension?" Shelby realized her error when she spoke it. He couldn't. He had responsibilities. Beside the fact none of the Polotis could travel across dimensions, the secrecy and preservation reasons were still factors in their choice. But, he did not seem to notice her faux pas and smiled, leaning into her with clear intent.

"I was forbidden by my clan, but that was not enough to keep me. It was IzTaln's small body that would not have been able to endure the slip stream, especially the one that would take you back to nearly the same time frame you left. You would return almost as if you had never been gone. It could have killed IzTaln."

Shelby thought about the days after she had been found on the other side. She was sure that without the Crenulate she would not have healed so quickly, but she did suffer searing pain for the first couple days. She understood the decision, though she wondered if she could make the same one again.

"He is still too young."

"Yes. But the Crenulate is strong in you now and not weak like it was before."

"So, I could take him now?" Shelby was almost hopeful.

"Possibly. But the same problems remain. Come." He took her over to a small rock outcropping. He hopped up and pulled her to his body. His wings appeared and expanded as he tilted into the breeze to lift off. Shelby was astonished at how easily he soared higher, even with her added weight.

He was beautiful to Shelby. She did not know why or where he was taking her, but she loved the freedom and almost wished she could do this herself. On second thought, she liked being with him; soaring above the trees would not be as exciting alone.

He followed a canyon that widened and fractured into other divides before he twisted and twirled in a spiral down into the shadow of the chasm. He deftly turned her around to face him in mid air.

His flight seemed effortless and he paid more attention to her than she deemed was safe. His kiss was consuming and she completely succumbed to the overwhelming explosion of passion she felt. Had it always been like this? She felt her body tingle and the sensual pleasure she experienced was so intense she almost cried out.

She pulled away to catch her breath and to look at Schofta to see if his reaction was as powerful. It must have been written all over her face, the illogical reaction she'd just felt. He released something in her she craved and wanted more than anything she could imagine.

His smile was so self-assured and perceptive that she knew he was pleased with her reaction. Shelby was breathing like she had run a long race.

He gazed intimately into her eyes.

"It must be the lack of air up here," she mused.

He laughed breathlessly. "There's plenty of air up here." He kissed her again and Shelby felt the same fervor instantly, like her body and mind remembered all too well their previous couplings.

"Ah, Shelby. You have no idea how irresistible you are." Their feet touched the solid rock outcropping before an enclave.

She had no idea he could make her feel this way. She felt desperate and her principles seemed to evaporate with every kiss. She was so thoroughly enveloped in his embrace that she felt she was part of him.

Then she remembered IzTaln, and Kerrick and she knew this was a ploy to manipulate her somehow.

Shelby pulled herself away from the warmth of Schoftastaklakla and looked around. The shadows were long and waning on the small ledge overhang they had landed upon.

He stood and wrapped his arms around her, pulling her smooth back against his body. "Be still for a moment, Shelby." He kissed her shoulder and nibbled at her ear then whispered to her, "You and I are mated in all ways that matter. I know you think there needs to be some words spoken by a holy orator, but," he turned her gently around to face him, "I am heart and body, soul and mind yours. I am stronger with you." He kissed her lips tenderly and held her close and still.

She found some comfort in his calm, but she knew this was not where she would feel whole. She had so much at stake in taking more time here, yet she was reluctant to leave. It had been a long time since she had felt the warmth of another person. She was lonely.

Her hand went up to his face and she memorized the lines that creased at his eyes and willed herself to remember this moment in time.

"You are to marry a beautiful woman and fulfill your obligations as a leader of your family and I want you to be happy and not linger over what could never be. It would be too complicated."

"Shelby, you have not complicated anything for me, only clarified.

"Shelby, love, sit down." He pointed to a spot in the last remaining rays of the sun and knelt down opposite her.

Shelby watched as Schofta's plumage appeared. The shimmering off the surface of the feathers looked more like a shield and it occurred to her the Crenulate was beautiful in the different forms it took and yet so indestructible.

He pulled two matching feathers from his ribs and to Shelby's surprise his skin bled around the vacancy.

"Char Shelby of Earth and Aion, here and now I claim that these are part of me and just as the Creator made male and female, and took from the rib of man and formed a help mate for his creation, I offer these from my body to you to as a symbol of my protection and love from my strength and soul. Will you accept them to your body?"

Shelby looked at him and felt this would somehow seal her fate. Did she have any right to do this? She leaned forward and looked into his face to search for the truth in what he was doing.

"Are you sealing your life and fate to mine, Schoftastaklakla? Are you in essence taking me as your mate?"

"If you will let me, Shelby, I will again." He leaned forward and lifted her top to touch the plumes to her ribs.

Of their own volition they attached to her skin. She marveled at the infusion of the feathers into her own body. How could she unite with him and still be true to her own convictions of setting the planet at rights with itself?

"If there were not all these extenuating circumstances, Schofta, I would not hesitate. But, I can not stay here."

"I don't expect you to. When IzTaln is grown enough I will bring him to you, but I want to remain with you then."

"That will be years from now, Schofta! I do not expect you to go without companionship. For me it will be hardly a moment, but for both of you so much will happen."

"No. There is another way.

"When you get to your own dimension, take one of the feathers I gave you and stick it into the ground and bury it. It will cause a connection in the

335

dimension, a slip stream and it will be my magnet to you. Do you understand? The Crenulate is connected through the planet and touches all dimensions. I can cross the boundary if I have a beacon to you in your own dimension."

Shelby looked at him and wondered if it was true. A beacon?

"Do you want to leave your clan? How do you know it will work?"

"It will work because it is supposed to. I want to be with you, Shelby. There is no happiness so complete than when I am with you."

"IzTaln, how will he get here?"

"He already has your Crenulate in him. He can probably go through the slip stream if he has a focal point, which you can give him. If I bring him to you, I can't go back. My clan expects me to deliver you to the Yahatamah zone. It will be known I did not do that if I deliver IzTaln to you."

Shelby found tears forming in her eyes. She was conflicted in what she felt and what she knew.

She embraced Schofta and whispered into his ear, "Thank you, Schofta."

Schofta saw that she looked at him with such trust that he nearly hesitated. He did not want to deceive her.

~

"Do you feel it, Mother Queen?" Letchell urged her to acknowledge something had transpired that was changing their surroundings.

"Yes, Letchell. It is the mating of two dimensions. The boundary is melting and connecting ours with another dimension."

"Was this supposed to happen?" Letchell always asked the most ridiculous questions the Queen ever heard.

"It is not what the Ancients wanted to happen, but apparently my nephew has gone with his heart and not what was expected of him."

Queen Yi tried to keep her face as neutral as she could. No one could have predicted that the woman that drew her dear nephew's attention and desire was so powerful. This was historical. In all her many years she had never seen a person come into her camp that was from a different dimension, and yet Char Shelby of the Alkers had walked and lived among them for many months and had born a child.

If she was responsible for the rift in the time zone, then the planet was indeed revolting against its imprisoned borders. Was Char Shelby the one that was prophesied about? Surely that small woman was not the powerful instrument the planet Aion christened for prophecy fulfillment.

Beautiful Markings / Chapter 26

Schoftastaklakla of the Polotis clan, future leader of the whole region of Umtulah and Yahatamah lands that were as vast and lush as any in this world, looked at the beautiful markings on Shelby.

They would eat and in the early morning, he would dutifully take her to the boundary dimension. He just didn't know which one, to the Yahatamah dead zone or the Alker one.

"I love the markings on your back. They are enchanting." He watched her halt her motions of preparing a place to sleep and turn to him with a baffled expression.

"What markings?"

"The ones on your back." She looked so disturbed he was sure this was something she didn't know about. He thought it comical, however, when she tried to look at her own back.

"Come here and sit down. Lift your shirt up." His hand went out to assist her and she looked at him with serious concern.

He turned her back towards him and drew the depiction in the layer of silt on the cave ledge floor. He did a fair representation of the design; however, it was much more stunning on her body. When she turned around to view the drawing she was aghast.

"Have you never seen it, Shelby?" He was aware of a shifting of her mind and wanted to know her thoughts.

"I had no idea that was on my body. I can't feel it when I reach my back. Is it a tattoo or colored or what?"

"It glows underneath your skin, so I guess it would be considered white, but it looks a little blue or green. It truly is intriguing."

"I've seen the design before, but I can't remember where. Did I have it when I was here the first time?"

"No. But then again, you weren't wandering around in nothing when we were in the home enclave." His roguish smile embarrassed her so she leaned over the drawing to inspect the intricacies of it and hide her blush.

"How would something like that be on my body and me not know about it?"

"Perhaps the Crenulate has something to do with it," he suggested.

"Have you ever heard of such a thing?" Shelby looked at him with trust, deferring to his knowledge of the Crenulate.

"I think, Shelby faerie, that you come with a whole new set of plans. What was true is now added to and what was once thought impossible has been disproved." He stroked her jaw and felt the softness of her skin and he was not sure he would be able to send her to her home.

"Shelby, the Crenulate is able to cover your body, just like the feathers it forms into on mine. Touch the feather and think of clothing or covering your skin."

"I do not want feathers all over my body, Schofta." She was so blunt she feared she might have insulted him, but Schofta did not seem offended.

He smiled at her with assurance. "That is up to you and your ability to convey to the Crenulate what covering you want."

"You can do other forms than feathers?" She did not know that.

He nodded 'no', "With exception. I am limited to a few varieties of the layers that are seen on my body from bare skin to wings. Not all the Polotis can fly. It seems to be a genetic marker passed on in my lineage. It is one of the reasons that I am..." He hesitated because he did not want to sound boastful.

Shelby waited for him to finish, smiling at him. He figured she probably knew what he was going to say, but he did not want to go on.

"Attractive?" She suggested with some humor dancing in her eyes.

"I was going to say, 'desired as a mate'."

"You think you are desired for your feathers?" Shelby murmured a soft sensual sound of pleasure.

"I am irresistible to most."

"I can see that," she smirked.

"Come on now, and try."

"Oh, very well. How do I do this?"

"How did you produce a knife?" He countered.

Shelby realized he had been watching her and IzTaln for a while before he had made his presence known.

She stood up and turned in a circle. When she opened her eyes, she looked down at what appeared on her body. The Crenulate formed several layers of milky fabric that looked more like lingerie than clothing. Her Alker clothing lay in a tattered pile at her feet; the Crenulate sheared it as it formed a layer over her body.

She was embarrassed, but when she looked at Schofta, he was ogling.

"Stop," she warned him. He brazenly grinned at her.

"I didn't think anything could top naked on you, but that is pretty close." When he saw her disappointment in the outcome he prodded her.

"Keep trying."

For some reason, she could not ever completely cover her back or stomach in all her tries. She finally conceded to a compromise she would feel comfortable in. Still, she begged Schofta to sneak back to the village and retrieve her some real clothing.

"Why are you resisting going back?" She groaned.

"Because, Shelby, when I leave you I fear that I will come back to you being gone and I am not ready yet to let you go."

So he stayed and when the night came he took her with him gliding through the canyon and over the tree tops and held her close. Shelby melted against his strength and absorbed as much of his being as she could. Still, she knew this was a dream and her real life was in her own dimension. Her heart longed to stay but her mind desired answers as to why she shifted from one zone to the next.

Eventually dawn fingered its light into the canyon and Schofta brought them to a soft wooded area.

"Schofta, I know you are holding things back. Is there something you need to tell me?" Shelby's concern was palpable.

"Love, I have many things I want to tell you, but I don't know which are important and I do not know if I can tell you knowing you are going back to your Alker clan."

"You think I'll betray your clan?" She was saddened by this.

"I think they will hurt you when you return and force you into things, telling you that you are betraying them if you do not."

Shelby looked at him and understood his disquiet. She remembered their treatment of her for being gone. For over a month she was kept in isolation and away from kindness. It nearly killed her.

He pulled her into his arms and covered them with his feathers. Even though they were alone, this was his way of showing his intimacy and vulnerability to her. He wanted her to feel the security she had in his strength.

"You must not return here again."

"Why? Do I pose some sort of threat?"

"You are unpredictable, and that creates fear. You are powerful, Char Shelby." She was shaking her head 'no' as he said this.

"Whether you know it or not, you are more powerful than you are aware of. There are so many things the Crenulate does within your body that you can not learn all at once. Just like this covering. I have never seen the likes of it."

"Well, feathers are pretty spectacular. Maybe I should be afraid of you." She was contrary now.

"You do not know how to be afraid, Shelby."

"Of course I do, Schofta."

He held a berry out to her. "This will make the transition into your dimension easier. It's a pain deadener and sleep derivative."

"Will it kill me?"

He chuckled and kissed her forehead, then her eyelids and lips and then her neck and she succumbed to his tantalizing, sensual warmth where he held her.

He waited until she was sound asleep before carrying her to the entrance of the slip stream. His energy was sapped as he approached the place, some of his feathering falling off to indicate he was in the right area and exhausting his power.

For this reason, he could not go through the dimension rift. He would not be able to come back and he did not know if the Crenulate would once more enter his body. He would likely be naked as the day he was born with no hope of ever possessing his power again for the rest of his life if he went through with her. He feared his appeal to Shelby would be gone then and that she would no longer recognize or desire him.

He backed away from his sleeping beauty and saw her dissolve away and into his dreams. Then he knelt down and cried silent wrenching sobs and he asked his God above to let her remember him and to bury one of his feathers into the planet's dirt in her dimension so that he could follow her.

And then he waited. And waited.

Shared Memories / Chapter 27

There was no help for it. Shelby needed to move on and she almost could not remember how she had last left the camp of the Alkers; it seemed ages ago. Her memory was a bit slippery, but she knew she had been tricked. She went to sleep in Schofta's strong arms and woke in a mossy nest of wet undergrowth all alone. She groaned aloud, "treacherous son of a blistering fiend."

She looked down thankful the reason she was not shivering was her covering was still on in spite of the dimension she traveled to. It looked too feminine for her taste, but she could not get the Crenulate to comply with her mind's eye. She assumed it was because deep down she must have wanted to be more womanly, or at least feminine.

She rose to her feet and looked around. Relief flooded her when she recognized the surroundings. She was close to the foot of the mountainous region near the Alker base camp. She had been in this area before. She took a deep cleansing breath and started out on a slow run, increasing to a full swift run. She could be in base camp by evening.

He had been keeping vigil too long. Everyone else was in the higher based camp gearing up for the winter months and boosting safety measures at the borders. What he saw coming at him was surely an apparition. The woman was faerie-like with silvery hair flowing under the moon lights and her body lightly reflected the glow of the moons off her skin. She glided across the fallen branches and overgrowth as if she was flowing like water and she was coming straight for the camp fast.

He sounded the silent alarm and readied himself for the meeting. What he did not expect was for the woman to be unarmed or alone. He assumed she would be accompanied by others whether he could see them yet or not.

"Halt!" His voice erupted.

She slowed, startled by the lone voice. Usually she was allowed to enter without the sentries' making their presence known.

"Char Shelby?"

"Aye." She looked at the young man, hesitant about what would happen to her again.

"How long have I been gone this time?" She was grieved she had to ask.

"Too long. Much has happened and I know some men who are going to be glad you are home."

"And some that won't," she agreed.

Sometime later they entered a strangely empty camp to Shelby's disappointment. The young soldier made her nervous looking back at her with wonder in his eyes.

"Is something wrong?" she chided.

"You look," he stumbled, "I would not have recognized you if..." He was having a difficult time explaining his behavior.

346

"I mean with the clan. Most of them are not here."

He looked uncomfortable and just nodded his head indistinctly. She was almost to the community dome where the Doc resided and Sir Kerrick's office was situated anyway. Hopefully she would not be put under lock and confinement again. Maybe this time they would listen to her before sentencing her to isolation.

The young warrior led her to the entry guards who looked stricken with mortification.

"We thought you were dead, Char Shelby. Is that really you?"

Before she could answer, she looked past them to see Kerrick coming out of his chambers, unaware of her as yet. Her heart thudded hard against her breast and she felt fear, real fear for what he could do to her. She did not know if she could be imprisoned and bereft of all kindness again. She shifted on her feet to take a stance of defense if it came to that, but then she saw his face and the astonishment there and she relinquished her fear somewhat.

"Shelby." The strangeness in his voice and the catch in his throat made her name sound whispered.

"I don't know how long I've been gone, Kerrick. I'm sorry to put everyone through any distress if I did. Please forgive..." She did not have to finish her apology. Kerrick whisked her into his embrace and held on to her as if she was his lost and found friend.

"Two months, six days and ten hours." He mumbled into her hair and rocked back and forth to feel the weight of her in his arms.

She was crying with happiness and relief. He held her face in his strong hands and looked down at her like he was memorizing her features. He hugged her again. Maybe this time she could tell him the truth of things. Suddenly the other men were patting her and she felt their delight in her sudden appearance.

Kerrick stood before her when they were done and solemnly returned her necklace to her, reaching around her and clasping it securely. If this was the way to keep her here, he was going to make sure she possessed it.

Then to the others he commanded, "Pack up the remaining equipment and ready the rest to leave for the heights in the morning." He turned to size the woman up and down.

"Shelby, you look different. I have decided that until we find a way to keep you here, you are going to be with me at all times."

Shelby was relieved not to be alone for a while. She heard howling in the distance and she looked at Kerrick with wonder.

"Most every night they have mourned and howled like hungry babies."

"It is how many of us feel right now," one of the guards revealed uncharacteristically. Shelby saw a strange fear in his eyes and wondered what could make such a valiant man cringe and gape at the surroundings as if there where phantoms that snatched their very souls away.

"What has happened here, Kerrick?"

Kerrick scowled at the men and they reluctantly dispersed to do their commander's bidding. He held his arm out for Shelby to lead the way back into the dome.

When they were alone in the expanse of the community area, he turned and looked at this wanderer. What was she wearing? He knew he had no right to her affection, because he could feel the guilt of his mistakes burdening him down with regret.

"Kerrick, I must tell you many things, but I am so weary that I need to rest and eat first. May I use the pool first?"

He could only nod. He watched as she quickly left in the direction of the retreat. How had it come to this? She looked stronger than she ever had. She looked like a warrior with the poise and grace of her Bilboas. She seemed different to him. Like a woman with total determination and focus. Of course, she had always seemed strong willed, but she acted as if she knew something needed to be done and only she knew what it was.

He heard her fall into the pool with a loud splash and it disturbed him enough that he strode to the back to see if she was alright. What he saw was a woman laughing and crying at the same time and it troubled him.

"Are you alright, Shelby?" Kerrick heard her groan and watched her turn around to face him.

"I am far from alright, Sir Kerrick. I keep going to places as real as this and I am loath to understand where my place is."

He walked toward her and slipped into the pool, clothes and all, walking toward her with purpose.

"Your place is here with my people, your people. You are as much a part of our lives as anyone else we have brought with us. I am beginning to believe in fact, that you are the reason we have survived this long here."

Shelby looked at him with furrowed brows. What was he talking about?

"When you left we were attacked by gothic, deformed creatures. They appeared within our territory and left just as quickly, but not without apprehending some of the women. When we surveyed the damage and the surrounding area we realized the shield that belonged to you was glowing and those within the radius light of it were protected from their grasp.

"Some believed at first that it was because you were doing the damage." To this Shelby hung her head. "But others who were closer to the initial attack were convinced the strange beings were trying to get to the shield and could not. The monsters were somehow thwarted by the light of the shield. We don't understand why, do you?"

He was fully clothed in the water and standing before her with his large, rough hands on her bare shoulders soothing her with his touch. He watched her shake her head 'no'. He wondered if she was aware how beautiful she was. The steely way she gazed into his face, searching to see beyond his words into his inward thoughts, made him feel exposed to her. She seemed to penetrate beyond his eyes and pull his hidden feelings from his heart.

"I believe you are playing a focal part in the resurgence of these creatures; when you are gone they are free to move from place to place. What they want is the shield but, for some reason we do not understand, they can not gain it.

"All the equipment you saw in the compound is to analyze their approach, but we know they are not made of flesh and blood, but some other form of life."

Shelby listened with interest, but she was vaguely aware of what she said next.

"They are flesh and blood, but not of the same dimension," she repeated. "When they approached the shield they must have forgot they can never possess Crenulate in another time zone. The shield is constructed of what was matured in my body so it belongs to me, in my time. The Al Kerkings do not want the planet whole because they will die. Their…"

He interrupted her to ask, "What is this Crenulate you speak of? What do you mean it was matured in your body?"

"Hold out your hand, Kerrick." She removed one of his hands from her shoulder and held it in her own. A droplet of amethyst formed in his palm then melted away.

When she looked up into his face, he saw the hesitation in her stare. She did not have any reason to trust him. He had not understood in the past and she could not know that he was forever more going to regret his actions of distrust.

He lifted her hand to his lips and kissed her palm. He was aware of her revelation as being groundbreaking in their relationship. He wanted to return in kind somehow.

"I am sorry, Shelby, for misjudging your actions. Betrayal is always on my mind, it's been necessary, but I have never had concrete reason to suspect your intentions as mercenary or evil."

Shelby looked at him with concern. Was she hearing an apology from the arrogant and skeptical Kerrick Torrell? Guilt flooded her mind and heart. She was uncertain that when he heard all she had to say he would still feel sorry for his actions; though the ill-treatment of her sentence previously seemed a precursor to her now guilt-ridden conscious and deserved mistreatment.

"When I've told you all I know and you need to hear, I wonder if you'll remain apologetic or if you'll throw me into isolation again or have me put to death this time."

"I have thought of the many things you have done, but none seem to indicate the nature of your character is betrayal or revenge. Every time I hear what you have done and it seems wrong or angers me, circumstances have proven your intentions were only admirable, though misguided in effort.

"Tell me what you must, and I will try to keep my temper. But," he hesitated for effect, "Maybe you should ply me with tenderness so that I am weakened by your words all the more." He winked at his own jest.

Shelby laughed aloud at that thought; Sir Kerrick of Torrell weakened by her? She looked at him and saw a tenderness there she had disregarded for a long time. Had he concealed his feelings for her all the times they had clashed? Was he not toying with her even now, as he did with all the other women, trying to bend her to his will?

Shelby looked at his clothes, wet and cloying to him with revealing appearance. He was beautifully formed and his heat made the cool air wisp spirals of steam off his body. He was angelic looking, in a dark and fiery way. She felt herself waver in her convictions of being elusive to all Alker men. How could she reconcile her convictions from her desires when they were sliding together into one design? She suddenly realized she needed this man to keep her sane and she knew he was the one man who could blend her desire and his will into one.

She was frightened by the revelation. Needing someone would make her vulnerable. Needing Kerrick would open her up to all kinds of heartache and weakness. She steeled her heart and mind and moved to go around this temptation. What about Schofta? Would she ever be able to be with him again? Was he a dream? For that is what he felt like when she was in her own time zone and his for that matter.

He could sense, almost physically, her desire for him and her refutation of him. It took him only a second to realize she was afraid. His arm caught around her waist and he pulled her back up against him gently. He rubbed his face against her hair and lifted her slightly off her feet. She was helpless against his strength, but then she was not fighting him either. He moved her through the pool to the edge and lifted her out of the water with him.

Still holding her against him, he turned her around to face him. His forehead found hers and he calmed her with soothing hands.

"It will be alright, Shelby. You and I will be stronger together than apart. I am done doubting your intentions." He pulled the towel off the rock and wrapped it around her wet body. She stood there watching him remove most of his wet clothing and waited.

"How do you know what to say to me? I think you can read my mind sometimes." She was in wonder at his words.

"Sometimes, Shelby, you speak words without saying a thing. I can understand what you feel by the vibes you give off. It is part of your allure and your strength."

He slowly lifted his hand to her shoulder and pulled the towel off her covered body. He pointed to his own chest at the same time his fingers touched under hers and she gasped as she saw the same feather formation she had, mimicked on his body.

"When I tried to read the writing on your shield, I fought with the formation of the words, but they eluded me. I also tried to break the shield. It is still whole." He assured her as he laughed at her look of displeasure. His hand moved to her cheek and rubbed it softly.

"You are so beautiful in all your expressions, Shelby. I never tire of your company." He put his forehead on hers again, and then whispered more of the story.

"A piece of the shield stuck into my skin and I saw memories, your memories. Flashes of those memories took me to an understanding of what you had gone through. I do not know how, but it was like you were telling me the story; but there were gaps. I know things about this planet and the entity that belongs to it, but your connection is the one thing that I have grown to understand better. You are going to have to trust someone, Shelby, and it might as well be me."

Her stomach growled and he chuckled at her embarrassment. He took her hand and led them to the table of food.

Shelby finally understood, as she stood by the table and next to Kerrick, that this seduction was purposeful and intentional. His design was to prove beyond a doubt that he was offering his protection and help.

She looked at him brazenly. What was his limit? Would he accept refusal? What if what she needed to tell him turned him completely away from her forever? She still did not want to go back to the Polotis people. This was her clan, her people. She loved these men and women and she loved this land and the planet. It was nourishing and restorative to her senses and she felt joy.

But, even with things at a critical point and her stomach gnawing at her, she sat down at the edge of the bed and waited for him before she began her tale.

She told him of the Polotis people, Nemesis, the Al Kerkings (whom she thought were related to the Alkers, but was relieved to know it was not so), and the evil that the Al Kerkings were trying to do and their notorious ugliness.

She told him of the dimensions and the chutes of time travel and pockets that caused people to be able to be sucked into the Al Kerking's grasp. Then she came to the more sensitive parts of the story.

"I am going to be blunt now. Please bear with me and let me finish with all the rest. If you interrupt me, I fear I will not be able to finish or be clear about my part in all this, and my choices. Agreed?"

Kerrick nodded. He was an intense man and to hold his attention this long made Shelby feel too intimate with him. He was also a gorgeous man and when she looked at him, really set her eyes on him, her heart made annoying stops in her chest.

How was she going to say all that needed to be said?

"Kerrick, where is everyone?"

"I have moved them up to the high mountain base, where we are headed to tomorrow."

"Why?" Shelby was wondering if she should wait until others were able to hear as well.

"It is the only place that our technology does not work, so it can not be used against us as we believe it has been compromised. It is also, according to

Doc, time to get to high ground for the coming winter months to avoid the waters and floods that are followed by high winds."

"I think I should wait until then to tell you and the others what I know."

"I want to know now where you were for two months and what is going on. We need to get the other women back and maybe what you can tell me will help our success."

Shelby nodded at his logic. "When I was gone for those four days and you found me by the river, I had actually been gone for over two years as best as I can remember. But, at the time I did not remember any of the two years. This time I can remember. When I returned again to the place I'd been, I came to realize that I had a son there."

Kerrick's eyes widened in dismay but Shelby continued. "I was pregnant with your child. I know that now because he looks like you. He has a dimple and your stormy green eyes. He is with the Polotis people and he loves them. They love him also."

She waited for Kerrick to deny such a possibility and she watched for Kerrick's reaction to this revelation. His jaw twitched and he searched her face for the truth.

"I realize there are many questions so I will hurry with the rest of the story." And so she told him of their son and why she had to leave him for now and of her hope for their future together and of the planet time zones and dimensions.

"I think I am married to the nephew of the Queen of the Polotis. Schoftastaklakla has claimed me as

357

his mate. Because of his protection our son is safe. I lose some memory when I go from this place to Lahata, so I need to assume some things.

"The Polotis peoples are covered with feathers, but your son, IzTaln, is bare. I think once he hits puberty the Crenulate will be strong in him and he will cross the borders as I do."

The whole time Shelby talked of her time away she watched Kerrick for cues for his reaction and to see if he heard what she said. It unnerved her when he would only glance at her now and then and the whole time she talked he said nothing, but he worked his jaw. She did her best to tell him everything except the more intimate details with Schofta.

"Do you love him?" Kerrick whispered and steadied his gaze on her.

"Kerrick, it seems like I have only seen him for a few days, but he is so smart and…"

Kerrick interrupted her, "No. The man."

Shelby was numb. How could she explain his magnetism and the desire she felt when he was near her? She felt his desire as if it were her own. Outside of his dimension the pull was not nearly the same nor were her own feelings. Now that she thought of it, it could be that he was able to succor her emotions with his own, overriding her real feelings.

Kerrick was a patient man, but her sullen quietness irritated him. Finally, she spoke again.

"I absolutely love him, when I am there."

Kerrick scoffed at her proclamation and he could not hide his displeasure or his hurt.

"Seriously, Kerrick. He has a magic ability to dull my senses and heighten my..." She trailed off wondering why she would tell him this.

"I want to see my son."

His features seemed to harden when he looked at Shelby.

She gasped as she realized her error.

"Before I left, Schofta told me the only way he could cross to my dimension was if I put one of the feathers he gave me into the ground. I think you should be prepared to meet a group when I do."

"You did not plant it?"

"I wondered at the possibility of what it could do to us."

"Are you suspicious of his intentions?" Kerrick was confused at her reluctance to bring her lover into her own dimension and couldn't stop his derisive jab at his unknown adversary.

It struck Shelby that she had the leverage to strike a bargain with Kerrick, one that would set her back on course of finding her own children left on Earth.

"When I was brought here against my will, I never dreamed I would fall in love..." she stumbled over her words but continued, "with this planet and the creatures that inhabit it. I never dreamed of the possibility of being content ever again, not until you admonished me to live in the present.

"I can't forget the past, but I've learned to embrace the beauty of this planet and the diversity. And yet my present happiness is clouded by my memories and dark dreams of children I'll never see again. Why should I help you see a child you did not even miss until I told you he existed? You've never helped me to even locate my children's existence, let alone give me hope of ever seeing them again. Why should I help you? I should never have told you anything about him," she blurted.

Kerrick cringed at her regret and accusation, but he had never been in a position where he could not get what he wanted, until now, until Shelby. Until now, he did not understand the frustration of being at someone else's mercy or power just to have what was his.

The idea of not seeing his own child was unthinkable to him. He was Alker and the conqueror of weaker people and worlds. Though he had protocols and traditions that he abided by, he could justify his actions if he could lay the guilt at the feet of the greater goals and purposes. His commitment had always been to honor his family and the Alker nation.

"I can not help you go against my orders or defy Alker sovereignty. It is forbidden to send a captive back once exiled to another planet or to help such a one reestablish family ties." Kerrick stilled. In his mind the prophecy rang loud and clear, "Upon the truth a pledge wilt thou make, but not without the Alker sovereign break..."

Shelby saw hesitation in his face.

He looked at her with regret in his eyes that mirrored her own. "He is your son, too."

"Yes. And I can see him again, but without my help you'll never see him, just like without your help

I will never know what happened to my children on Earth. I need to know they are safe. At least you know IzTaln is safe. I have no assurances about my other children," Shelby protested.

"I can not even assure you they are alive," Kerrick sighed.

They sat for awhile, each lost in their own thoughts.

"I want him here," Shelby finally conceded.

"Who?" Kerrick didn't know if she referred to Schofta or IzTaln.

"IzTaln."

"Will he come or is he stuck in the other dimension?"

"I think that unless I connect their time zone with ours it will be impossible, unless he is able to use the Crenulate I gave him."

Kerrick willed Shelby to look at him. He needed to clarify some things with her first.

"How do I know that you are not lying to me about a son?"

Shelby just looked at him with consternation, but she acknowledged that if she was a dubious woman he would have every right to believe she was capable of such manipulation.

"Were you my suitor at AB Celebration?"

"Yes." Kerrick affirmed.

"If I was pregnant, then only you could be the father."

"Or that Scotchbla." Kerrick wanted to hear her deny it for his own sanity.

Shelby knew he was purposely mimicking his name. She didn't play into his riling.

"He could've been if I wasn't already with child at the time. But he looks like you at any rate."

He had no right to expect her to be exclusively his, but he did anyway. He did not like thinking of her in someone else's embrace the same way he had held her, close and possessively.

Shelby continued. "You need to realize that there is more at stake than just seeing our son. The time zones are fluctuating and the boundaries are unstable. That is why the Shadoubles from Yahatamah are able to cross into our time and steal the women away."

"What has that got to do with you opening the way for me to see IzTaln?" Kerrick tried to understand her track of thought.

"When I open the way, it will signal the boundary has been unsealed. The Al Kerking will take the opportunity to seize control of the Crenulate. If they manage that, our time zone will be unsafe again and they will destroy and kill to control the time zones and our dimension will revert to their own.

"In their dimension, they are the conquerors and have unlimited power. They are not from here, Kerrick. They are a species of unbridled wickedness and they do not die. They have lived for ages."

"How do you know this?" Kerrick was not convinced of her convictions.

"The Polotis people know this from their history and legends."

Shelby was at a loss as to how to tell Kerrick she was in danger and so was her son if they came together.

"Opening the junction between our worlds will also endanger the Polotis people and our son. It will become a beacon to the Al Kerking. They can track the opening of dimensions and steal Crenulate from the host at that time.

"If I can't keep the portal open or unite it with ours, the Polotis will be like ducks in a pond, unable to escape the destruction from the invasion of the Al Kerking. I will have betrayed what I promised to keep safe. If they open it, then they are ready and IzTaln has grown and become stronger.

"Alone I can do nothing. I have no memory of how this planet was, but IzTaln is learning and will become that knowledge. He has access to their legends and memories. They can share that with him."

"Why did they not share it with you?"

"They would not. I am not their people."

"Neither is IzTaln. He is yours and mine."

"Let's hope that this secret remains with his Father Schofta. As long as the secret of IzTaln's heritage remains, he is safe. For you to see him and claim him as your son will negate the possibility of IzTaln becoming a leader of the Polotis. And the healing of our planet will be at jeopardy. We need the Polotis people to be our allies not foes.

"To make the planet whole again, we will need to fight and destroy the Al Kerking. But they are thousands and we do not know their weakness. That is what you and I need to find together, before the Polotis people cross over to here and they will. Even if I do not open the way, IzTaln can, but he doesn't know that yet.

"You and I will not see our son until the day he has this knowledge. If we do not get it, the Polotis will kill us and take our Crenulate so that they can be strong enough to defeat the Al Kerking. They will have no choice but to do so to keep the planet whole and to bring all the dimensions into unity again."

Kerrick was reeling with the wonder of how this could be true. He had already experienced the effects of the planet being different from his home world, but he thought it was only from the time and space difference between the worlds, not actually a product of the world.

"The women will be dead if the Al Kerking have taken them, I think. If they need them for the Crenulate and they don't have it, I don't see why they would keep them alive."

"Unless," Kerrick countered, "they could become hosts to the same Crenulate that grows inside of you. Then they would be invaluable and the Al Kerking, as you called them, would no longer need to invade the dimensions to get it. Until they were ready to destroy all the other powers on this planet, they could harvest the Crenulate."

"But the Crenulate can leave their body if it chooses," Shelby assured him.

"How?" Kerrick pushed her.

"When they touch the ground it goes back into the planet and waits for a worthy host."

"But what if they never touch the planet? When the necklace with the dirt inside of the beads was taken off of you, you were spirited away. Your Crenulate had no ground to slide into."

"It could have gone through the floor of the dome if it fell."

"Yes, but maybe it remained in you to protect you. Or maybe it needs you to actually touch the dirt to retrieve the others of its kind or to exit your body."

"What do you mean, Kerrick?"

"Only that if the host must be connected to the planet for the Crenulate to exit, then maybe the Al Kerking live somewhere where once they have captured the Crenulate it can not exit from that place.

"I have some knowledge from the piece that pierced me, but I only saw your knowledge and memories and yet I know there are parts of those memories missing. Maybe your shield has more memories for you to retrieve."

Shelby thought about it for a moment. She had given pieces of the Crenulate to IzTaln and taken some from Schofta, but she had given it back to him. Could she possibly have given some of her memories to Schofta?

"When I was in Lahata with the Polotis people, I was going to share Crenulate with IzTaln and take some from him. I knew it would be like sharing pictures of who I was with him, but Schofta forbade it. I wonder if he thought I would gain memories of some secret that IzTaln was privy to.

"His reaction was like he knew I could take some of IzTaln's power with me. He said it might harm him or scar him." Shelby thought about Kerrick receiving knowledge from the piece of shield. Maybe her missing memories could be retrieved in the same manner. Maybe the Crenulate had separated memories and stored them so that the Polotis people or the Al Kerking could not steal them from her.

"Where is the shield now?"

"It was carried to the winter camp with my possessions."

"Then we will have to wait to retrieve those memories. One more thing."

Kerrick looked at her with trust and it filled Shelby with hope.

"They must be in the Yahatamah region. The Islands float above the planet and the gravity is weak. We must go there and find a way to close the link between their world and ours. Maybe all that Alkernian technology you keep hidden is going to be tested to its limit."

Kerrick crossed his arms over his chest and looked at her with a speculative grin. "And how would you know about that?"

"You are not the only one with new memories."

Answers / Chapter 28

Shelby was frustrated. It was going to take at least three days to get up to the Mountain camp and she already had several bad experiences going that way. Then she remembered the boulder and Nemesis.

Kerrick was packing the remaining items when Shelby came upon him breathless.

"Let's go. Leave everything and come with me. I'm going to show you something you never let me explain the first time I came back. Bring the men, without weapons."

Kerrick stood up and put his hands on his hips to look at his little boss. He had no desire to reject her or to leave weapons behind, not in this dangerous climate.

"All of you are coming or else it will be like I left for a month again." That got his attention. It was risky to go into the portal, but Shelby had no desire to go alone.

She took them down to the lake and stood at the entrance of an unseen doorway and scratched the tip of her nose thinking.

"I have to get us all in there and I do not know if we should hold hands or walk in individually."

While she pondered this the other men looked at her like she was insane. Where did she think she was going from here? There was a hundred foot high slab of smooth rock in front of her connected to the cliff wall. The lake was a few feet away on this narrow beach. Were they going to scale it with no ropes or tools?

"Okay." With that Shelby ran at the wall and jumped up as high as she could. Some of the men started laughing thinking she had gone crazy, but her body was sucked into the solid rock.

Seconds later an arm and a smiling head appeared waving them in. Each man took her hand and was pulled into the illusion and stuck in the darkness with only her voice to calm them.

"Just stand still. The light will come on when we step forward."

Kerrick was the last man in and still held her hand. Shelby bumped into one of the other men, but true to her word the lights came on. Just as before, she was in an anteroom connected to the immense hallway that led to the dais.

"Listen to me. Once we are in the main hallway we will start to catch up to the time zone here. I believe we will enter the stream of time and eventually you will see a creature called a Cauble. His name is Nemesis. Be very careful not to say too much. "We will go to the dais and use the machine to transport us to our camp, hopefully in the same time zone."

Shelby was really unsure, but she looked at Kerrick and knew he was not intimidated at all. She sensed he expected something like this. Before she could question him, he took the lead and headed for the main hall.

Shelby looked for Nemesis, but she did not see him. Was he hiding or did he manage to get to his people? She had no way of knowing.

The men were engrossed in the technology. Shelby showed them what she knew and then they tested what else they could learn.

"We need to be quick. My experience here has been that a lot of time transpires while we are in this hallway."

"You are evil! You have brought others to destroy us!" Nemesis wailed.

He appeared so quietly beside her she almost did not see him swing, with deadly force, the weapon at his side. She dodged, but even if she had not been so quick, the swing was halted by Kerrick's quicker reflex. The Cauble was pounded upon by the Alkers and Shelby feared for its life.

"Stop! Stop it now! Let him go." Shelby was crying. The creature was pathetic. Shelby tried to pry their hands off it. Nemesis whimpered.

The men held the Cauble forcibly and looked at Sir Kerrick for their orders.

"Nemesis, it will be okay. These men are not the Al Kerking. We are only passing through. I thought you were gone to your people," Shelby soothed.

Kerrick nodded to the men when he saw the Cauble had calmed, but the men still kept a wary eye and weapons ready.

"I told you not to bring the weapons, Kerrick."

"I did not say I would agree to that." He was unapologetic. To Nemesis he said, "You will come with us and we will see if what you have claimed to Shelby is true."

"Nemesis...saved...Shelby...Al Kerking," Nemesis reminded her.

"Nemesis, this is the Alker I wanted you to meet. Sir Kerrick Torrell." Shelby spoke softly to him like he was a child.

"We are going to our upper camp. Is that possible from here?" Kerrick's voice was gruff. He saw a glint in the Cauble's eyes and instantly did not trust him.

"Go...Nemesis...show." The Cauble was instantly helpful and even Shelby was leery.

When all was set Nemesis stepped backed from the dais. Sir Kerrick nodded and the men trussed him up and pulled him onto the platform with them. Shelby was dismayed but said nothing.

Nemesis however was frantic. "Can not go...outside ...dimension. Nemesis...lost."

Sir Kerrick leaned into the face of the creature and said bluntly, "You can not go because you think you have sent us to our doom."

Shelby was going to correct him, but Kerrick gave her a quelling look that let her know he knew what he was saying.

"So Nemesis, you will explain what is happening, because I know there was supposed to be a ship arriving, but on the shield over there," he pointed, "I see floating islands and a ship, my ship, caught in the time warp you are controlling."

Shelby was aghast at the deception, not only Nemesis', but the Alkers' as well.

All the men stood around Shelby, who looked from Kerrick's determined and enraged face to Nemesis' cunning and calculating one. She did not know which was more frightening.

Nemesis was frigid. He was resisting the command of this weaker enemy.

"You will go first, Nemesis. Then you can warn your own of the coming doom you created." That got his attention.

He went limp and back to the lost and forlorn creature Shelby had first come upon. Nemesis was a traitor. Shelby saw it in his eyes the first time they met, but she doubted herself. Kerrick discerned the Cauble's deception immediately and she saw it again and recognized it. Without hesitation he sent the Cauble off to the same place it had intended to send his men and Shelby.

"How did you know?"

"I read your mind."

"My mind? How could that help you?" She and the others were mystified by Kerrick's answer.

"And I took its Crenulate."

Shelby gasped at the cruelty. "You have doomed it."

"Not if it was truthful. The place it goes will be on the planet and if it was being honest, which I doubt, the planet will supply the Crenulate. At any rate, we are going to make this planet whole and bring everyone and everything back to its intended dimension.

"We will soon follow the Cauble if we can not set things right. But seeing this," he looked around the massive hive, "makes me realize we have all the resources we need, along with our technology and you, to reset the planet's dimension."

"How do you know this stuff? And what do you mean 'me'?" Shelby was worried.

"I have your memories, remember? And I have some you do not. I am almost two hundred years old, Shelby, but you have more power and understanding than you realize."

"What are we to do next?" Shelby countered still thinking about the quandary she was in.

"We are going to make some new friends, and I just might meet my..." he looked at her with pride and tenderness, "our son."

Interpretation / Chapter 29

Shelby, Kerrick and his men transported to the winter Mountain camp and surprised everyone by their sudden appearance. Amazingly, the Alker men were able to surmise the time difference and put them there almost on the day of the others' arrival. Shelby did not know how they could figure such details out on another life form's technology, but apparently they were smart enough.

Kerrick took Shelby aside. "I know you are confused about my tactics, but when I studied the shield you dropped at my feet, a lot of the memories you already had were embedded in the shield and somehow conveyed to me in dream-like impressions. So, you and I need to translate the information you somehow stole away from the different dimensions you have gone to."

Shelby looked at him like he was daft. What did he think she could possibly have repressed and put into Crenulate form? She was never even aware of it most of the time.

"Shelby, I have something I would like you to hear first. You may be able to give me a different perspective.

"I was given prophecy with no clue what it meant. Now some things have happened that I think you may understand more fully than I do. It is possible it is about you."

Shelby looked at him with complete consternation.

"You think prophecy given to you pertains to me?"

It was ludicrous. There was no way Alker traditions, celebrations or prophecy had anything to do with her. Then she heard him rhyming.

"A star will shine without divine, the purpose sole to make it whole. Upon the truth a pledge wilt thou make, but not without the Alker sovereign break. One will be then two, then three, to unite the broken and rebind the free. Look to truth trust not the eye, the star will grow without a lie, but two will know the truth beyond and four will be the tie that bonds."

"You are that star," Kerrick offered.

Shelby would have denied it, but she recalled how Schofta said she glowed like a star in the moon lights. She already knew the planet was divided and needed to be made whole. She thought about the similarities she had in her own life. She felt divided and split, certainly not whole. Going to different dimensions made her feel divided in body and mind.

She did not want to tell him that uniting with IzTaln would probably bind them to each other, each of them as of right now was free. The whole prophecy seemed to truly be about Kerrick's life. His life was now on Aion, so it also doubled as a far deeper repercussion of his life here, while pertaining to the planet as a whole.

She knew the only way she would see her lost children was if Kerrick broke his own Alker law and allowed her to find them. When she'd told him the truth about IzTaln, she felt certain he would relent and promise her a chance to find the truth about her own children. But he had not done so yet. So she did not know how the 'pledge' part of the prophecy related.

"You are one, I am two and IzTaln is three." She looked at Kerrick certain he understood this. It was a surprise to him. "Without uniting we can not close the separation of the planet. We already know that."

"The next part, 'Look to truth trust not the eye, the star will grow without a lie' is about IzTaln. You can not trust what you have not seen with your own eyes, but I have told you the truth; that he is your child and he is the star in this part of the prophecy."

"I believe you, Shelby."

"Good. Because the next part about the 'lie' means that I told him the truth when I saw him last, so he knows about you and he will grow up knowing the truth. He is not deluded about who he is.

"Finally, I am sure the last part 'but two will know the truth beyond and four will be the tie that bonds' means that two others know the secret about IzTaln who should not."

"Well it could mean that Schotchbla and IzTaln are the two..."

Shelby caught the slur and couldn't help but smile.

"No, Kerrick. Whenever there is a 'but' in prophecy, it is contrary to the purpose of the warning given in the prophecy."

Kerrick understood the logic and respected her firm conviction, but the last part 'and four will be the tie that bonds' was still hugely vague to him.

"I don't give much to prophecy or fortunetelling, unless it is from a true prophet; one that has never lied or been faulty." Shelby leaned in to look at Kerrick more closely because she wanted him to understand her next statement as well.

"You need to remember that this prophecy was given to you. So it is your personal interpretation that matters, but this prophecy is twofold. Do you know what that means?"

He shook his head looking into her amber eyes and felt drawn to her irrevocably. He knew so many personal memories about her that he felt his heart was connected to her mind, body and soul. She was his star.

"It means that your life is somehow coinciding with what is happening on this planet and the meaning of the prophecy has two distinct interpretations. One meaning is personal and the other is global. You need to be careful to not give too much importance in following or trying to make this happen on your own."

"I know that. You seem to know a lot about foresight."

"No, just interpreting. Prophecies are not meant to enlighten as much as to caution the hearer of what will happen." His snort made her restate what she meant.

"What I mean is that to 'enlighten' is an after effect, to 'caution' is to warn so one can prepare. You have been treating this warning as proof or confirmation this is really happening when you should be focusing on stopping what should not happen."

Kerrick thought about what she was saying and realized he knew instinctively that IzTaln was in danger, just as he knew Nemesis was lying, and just as he knew the planet needed to be whole.

"Let's get your shield and figure a way to get IzTaln home."

Shelby was ready for that.

Preparing / Chapter 30

Commander Rockdurgh watched Sir Kerrick and Char Shelby converse back and forth, Shelby's hands doing as much talking and hip resting as Sir Kerrick's.

Amy stood before Rockdurgh and put her small hands on his folded forearms.

"What are you smirking about?"

"Them." He indicated with his nod.

Amy followed the direction of his gawking and saw Sir Kerrick with her dear friend Shelby in a locked stare, Shelby's hands on her hips and Sir Kerrick's arms braced across his chest.

"I've never seen that color on Sir Kerrick in the hundred and seventy years I've known him." Amy's eyes widened in shock; not at his observation, but at the years he admitted to knowing his leader---at how old he was!

"I believe my High Lurt Kerrick Torrell is completely, helplessly in love with that woman."

"I don't need to see any color on Sir Kerrick to tell you that. It's been obvious for a long time." They both laughed.

All the men were positioned and Sir Kerrick took them to the area he deemed was best for the confrontation with the Polotis People. Over three hundred Alkers were prepared for battle. Shelby looked at the men and a pride she did not know she had for them swelled in her chest. They were magnificent.

Kerrick looked at the gleam on Shelby's face and knew how she felt. He felt the same way about these men. He could trust them with his life and had.

"Are you ready, Char Shelby?"

"Aye." Shelby pulled the feather from under her breast and layed it on the ground. She materialized the amethyst sword and stuck it through the feather into the ground driving it hard and deep. There was a shuddering that rocked the men off-balance for a moment and then a searing sound that made all of them cover their ears for another moment.

Shelby and Kerrick watched the sword seemingly melt into the ground like ice and instantly a wall of another dimension was visible. They were all looking into the landscape of another realm. They could see other people Shelby recognized immediately as the Polotis Clan.

"They are moving faster than normal," Commander Rockdurgh observed.

"As they get closer to this entrance they will slow to our time." Shelby knew this intuitively, but when Kerrick concurred Shelby was reassured.

Instantly, there was a band of Polotis Warriors at the wall. Shelby did not know how they did not see them approach, but it scared her and she backed away from the overwhelming display of military force. Kerrick was right beside her and held her steady. The men behind her were getting their first glimpse of the colorfully feathered tribe and she could sense, more than see, the reaction of their awe and assessment.

Like a snap shot of pictures in time, Schofta and Zeryl came in phases to the front line and stood in regal poise.

Kerrick spoke to Shelby in her mind, "Make the introductions."

Char Shelby stepped to the flowing opaque wall and put her hand on the energy that separated them from the Polotis. She walked until she was standing in front of Schoftastaklakla and Zeryl, the obvious leaders of the clan now. She bowed with respect and looked around them to the enforcements they had come with.

"Are you expecting war, Schofta?" Shelby jested with a smile.

"It is King Schoftastaklakla," Zeryl demanded, her voice whispery but cutting.

"Greetings, Char Shelby," Schofta replied with eloquent gentleness.

"You remember, Queen Zeryl, my wife." Schofta was letting Shelby know that time had indeed passed and things had changed.

"I do remember you," Shelby had a moment's hesitation to address her formally, "Queen Zeryl. May I ask how Queen Yi, your aunt is doing?" She turned back to King Schofta.

"She is deceased," Queen Zeryl affirmed with exaggerated pouting.

Shelby saw the blankness in Schofta's eyes and was sorry for his loss. She indicated it with a Polotis gesture.

Sir Kerrick stepped forward next to Shelby, making her feel his support and protection. He was obviously sensing something Shelby was not.

Kerrick did not bow. He stood regal and balanced in stoic form, his eyes assessing all that was happening around them.

"This is High Lurt Kerrick Torrell of Alker and Aion." There was immediate rumbling and dissent behind the Polotis royalty. They did not like his title at all. Shelby continued.

"This is Commander Rockdurgh. This is Doc Morrell Orlie."

Shelby stepped back to let the commanding leaders talk. Shelby knew it was only a ruse to appraise the power of each force. She knew there were thousands of Polotis and had told Kerrick so, but he only smiled as if he knew that did not matter. Knowing the ratio, she still would put her bet on the supremacy and cunning of the Alkers, too.

Shelby kept looking for her son through the barrier and could not stand it any longer. She went back to the group of leaders and waited for Schofta's attention. She did not wait for long.

"How many years has it been, King Schoftastaklakla?"

Queen Zeryl was seething and Shelby could see it was a sore subject.

"Ten years, almost to the day," he replied generously.

The others in the small group watched the exchange, especially Sir Kerrick, who noted the tenderness with which the king attended her words and presence. He also glimpsed the gloat in the Queen's eyes.

"For me it has only been three months."

The king of the Polotis had a sorrowful look in his eyes. Shelby stepped back and burst out IzTaln's name and whistled a high piercing sound. It made everyone jump.

"Shelby," Sir Kerrick chided with a knowing smirk. But he expected she would do exactly as she had. He was counting on it.

She yelled again. She kept calling his name. No response from any of the Polotis, as if they also had expected this. She stepped in front of the King and Queen again.

"Bring him forward, Schofta," Shelby insisted.

Queen Zeryl stepped closer to the barrier and looked down her nose at Shelby intimidatingly.

"You will address the King of Polotis properly or not at all."

Shelby's look was mutinous. She looked over at Schofta and said again, "Where is our son?"

"You mean your and Kerrick Torrell's son do you not?" the Queen incited furtively.

Shelby looked at Schofta and knew that their secret was a leverage that Zeryl had used to her advantage. It fell into place in her mind. Zeryl had somehow overheard her conversation with either IzTaln or Schofta and had used it to assure her place in the hierarchy of the Polotis. She would keep the secret if she was wed and titled as Queen.

"I see you understand the secret is not so secret. All I have to do is let the right Ancients know that

IzTaln is not Schoftastaklakla's and he will be put to death, and I do mean your son as well."

Kerrick was infuriated by the threatening witch.

"As long as you do as I say, IzTaln will be safe," the Queen bargained. Shelby understood that the Queen of the Polotis was more powerful than the men and she now comprehended Schofta's surrender was for the safety of her son's life.

"What do you want?" Shelby heard Kerrick gruffly ask.

"I want power of course. You see my son?" She motioned for the little boy to come forward.

"He is King Schoftastaklakla's and mine, not like your imposter son. He is entitled to the throne and I do not want that to change. I can assure that by having IzTaln's Crenulate given to my son, but he refuses to do so. I would kill him and take it, but it doesn't guarantee the transfer of power. Besides, it is not the Polotis way and it would cause too much resentment from my husband."

Shelby hated the woman. "My son said he wanted to stay because you were good to him."

"I am good to him. He is protected. Here is what I want from you, Shelby. You will convince your son to give up his Crenulate willingly and I will let him go."

Shelby looked at the others backing their new Queen and wondered at how quickly a leader could alter the dynamics of her citizens. She stepped in front of Kerrick with her back to the assembly of Polotis and put her hands on his hips. His arms were crossed over his chest and he was looking over her head at the Polotis with distaste in his eyes and his jaw flexing in repressed hostility.

"Speak, Shelby love." He watched his adversaries.

"The Alkers are my clan. My place is with you." She spoke so out of character.

"I know." He did look at her then. "Why are you telling me this now?"

"I need you to trust me."

He hesitated, for he knew she would probably do something he would not like. He put his forehead to hers. "Do not disappear on me, and do not do anything foolish."

Shelby rolled her eyes.

She turned to the Queen and spoke to her and King Schofta.

"You are not going to like this." Shelby pulled out a feather and showed it to them. The Queen laughed, but Schofta seemed to come out of his stupor and the men behind the Queen got edgy.

"A feather!" Queen Zeryl exclaimed. "You threaten us with a feather?"

"I do." Shelby moved to face Schofta and said again, "It has only been three months for me," and she moved her hand unconsciously to her belly, gently covering it with her hand, indicating a treasure. The gesture did not go unnoticed by Kerrick.

"Some of you recognize this feather. I will take every last one from you and drive it into the ground. After I do that, I will open this barrier and the Alker warriors will pass through to your side and take what is already mine. Do you understand? None of you will have your protected zone or isolation and none of you will fly or have your covering as you do now. Your King and Queen will be powerless to stop my clan.

"But I propose a deal. Give me my son and join us in conquering the Yahatamah region and the Al Kerkings, the Shadoubles, who are killing both our people, and I will generously let you keep your region and boundaries for your lifetime. But know this, once the boundaries are down and the differential zones are combined, you will no longer have a choice.

"Bring me my son or I will take your boundaries down now and the Al Kerkings will annihilate your clan." Shelby was determined.

Queen Zeryl was infuriated. "You think you have won with a feather?"

"With that feather, dear Queen, she can strip us all from where she stands. The Crenulate will flow to her through the planet energy and she will be more powerful than any of us. They have seen her strip me of my feathers and Crenulate by a touch. She has Creation Crenulate," the King confirmed.

"That is a myth! She would have to kill you to take it. We will kill her first."

"How? We can not cross into her zone, but she can ours. And that is not a myth. She only needs to touch one of us and it will happen like wildfire. You know the Crenulate is connected and once it is in motion it remembers when commanded by Creation Crenulate."

The Queen looked at the men around her and dismissed the idea of Shelby being that powerful or able. She was not used to being denied.

At that moment Shelby spied her son, who looked so much like Kerrick, being escorted forward by Polotis warriors. She walked right through the barrier. The Polotis men fell back from her giving her a wide span of room, knowing now she was dangerous. She strode right up to IzTaln who was surprised to see her. She took his hand and walked him through the barrier to the side of the Alkers. It happened so quickly that everyone but Shelby was astonished, especially the Queen.

Shelby pulled the astounded young man right up to Kerrick.

"Sir Kerrick, this is IzTaln your son."

"Our son," Kerrick corrected. He greeted IzTaln with a respectful nod.

The outraged Queen ordered her soldiers to cross the opaque stream. When they hesitated, she shoved one of them through the barrier. He stood on the other side with the Alkers and everyone watched with suppressed wonder. When nothing happened, two others stepped through and then some more, but before a full minute had passed the first Polotis to step through the stream disintegrated into a bloody puddle. The ones stuck on the Alker side joined their fellow Polotis in quick death. The energy stream of the barrier had separated their cells thoroughly.

Everyone on both sides of the barrier looked simultaneously at Shelby and IzTaln with renewed admiration. IzTaln's face widened in horror.

"You'll be okay," Shelby assured him with a laugh. "I am impulsive sometimes and don't think about explaining my actions."

"I could have died! You could have died!" IzTaln was mortified; his hands waved expressively like his mother's did when she talked.

"Not hardly. I gave you some of my Crenulate so the anamnesis of the Creation Crenulate is in you as well. Plus," she pointed to an amethyst ring on his hand, "I made sure you had Creation Crenulate."

IzTaln's eyes were drawn back to Kerrick who watched with pride his son's reaction to his new circumstance.

Kerrick raised his hand. The same color ring was on his finger and, as he looked, on all the hands of the Alker warriors.

"What now?"

"Now we rebind the free."

Yahatamah Up Close / Chapter 31

"You should have let me get him."

Kerrick and Shelby stood side by side, flanked by Commander Rockdurgh and Captain Torden, at the edge of the Yahatamah region looking at the floating islands through the energy wall.

"No, I should not have. You would have drawn your weapon and I did not want blood shed. Besides, they did not know you have the same Creation Crenulate and it would have been a bloody mess."

"Did you not see the red pool of Polotis guts?" Kerrick chided with gross humor. Shelby rolled her eyes.

"Pay attention you two. I still think we should have used the portal." Commander Rockdurgh was petulant about the disuse of the technology.

"The Polotis do not need to know about that device either," Kerrick warned.

Shelby pulled her shield into view. The map ensconced within the embellishment of the shield turned out to be the path that all people with any kind of Crenulate could walk within and not be harmed. It was a map the Polotis were well aware of. They were now on that invisible path, directed by the glow of the two moons' light reflecting off the Crenulate shield.

For the populace to rid themselves of the murderous Al Kerkings and free the planet from the inflicted spatial and time discord, according to the writings on the shield, they would have to diminish the territory of the Yahatamah region to nothing, just as Nemesis had insisted. This could be done only one way. Collectively the energy of the Crenulate would be used to fight and weaken the Al Kerkings and then the Crenulate would be left within the borders of Yahatamah at the weakest part of the planet; the place where the gravitational pull was evident. The Crenulate would strengthen the planet and it would heal itself.

If they did not succeed in using the Crenulate to mend that section of region, all of them would be doomed to live within the fluctuating and destructive zone once inside. The only probable hope of getting out of this alive if they failed was the Creation Crenulate being gifted back to the people of the planet. Shelby sincerely hoped that Kerrick's, IzTaln's and her accumulated knowledge were enough to understand the truth.

Kerrick looked down the ranks of the thousands of warriors with King Schofta and his own men strategically positioned. Shelby had rolled the barrier down true to her ability and the invasion was ensuing.

"You will wait here until I return." Kerrick held Shelby's shoulders, appraising her.

"I will not." She was indignant.

"I do not want to worry about your safety, Shelby." Kerrick was firm and in charge. King

Schofta came up to them at that moment and noted Shelby's agitation.

Kerrick protectively stepped between them blocking his view of her.

"She needs to come. My men will not go into the Yahatamah land without her presence. I will protect her."

Kerrick scoffed. "This is not your decision." He did not like Schotchbla.

"Father." Both men turned at IzTaln's voice. "Without all of us, the Crenulate will not be whole. All of us need to go. One person alone can not contain the entire organism of the Crenulate at once."

Shelby looked at her ornate shield and noted the oval center needed a colorful stone to make it complete. Why would she fancy such an idea now? Is that what they would need? Did the Al Kerkings already have a stone?

The men saw the baffled looked in Shelby's expression. "What is it Shelby?"

IzTaln answered for her. "It's the shield. It's missing a center stone." He watched Shelby move her fingers around the indentation.

"That shield must have the key to annihilate the Al Kerkings' power. Where is the missing stone?"

"What is the missing stone?" Shelby spoke hollowly. "This must be how the Al Kerkings were able to track the Crenulate. They have a stone that connects to this shield, the oldest formed anamnesis of Aion's energy, Creation Crenulate."

"Then we need to get it and put it back into the flow of the planet's energy." Kerrick was beginning to believe that unless they found the stone and united it with the shield, killing the Al Kerkings would not stop the destructive crux the planet was now at.

The shifting of the time zones, as they powered their armies through, had been shaking the ground and the tremors were distorting the process of entering the Yahatamah territory. He feared the closer they brought the shield and the elusive stone together, the more the focal point would ignite the process of regeneration of the planet. Somehow, being at ground zero did not seem like a rational idea.

"Let's go then and woman," Kerrick looked at his waif and warned, "do not disappear."

They entered the kingdom of the Al Kerkings at dawn, but not unnoticed. They were met at the borders of the central city by the ugliest creatures Shelby had ever seen. The specimens displayed black wart-like nodules over their entire oily bodies. The heads of the Shadoubles were shaped like a Cauble's with bone distortions protruding and pushing the transparent skin and veins in a gross display of disfigurement. Shelby looked around at the men with her. They smelled it too, the smell of dead flesh.

"Now what?" Shelby heard herself say.

Kerrick looked down at her and smiled.

"Now we do what we were born to do, conquer."

The Shadoubles' ear-piercing warcry was countered by the clang of thousands of warrior swords and weapons springing to life. The rush of power and adrenaline surged through the ranks of the Alker and Polotis warriors with acrid speed.

The Polotis took bites out of the sides of the brigade of deformed Cauble, slicing, cutting and killing in strides; while the Alkers kept a tight nucleus around Shelby and IzTaln and chomped at the front battalion of Shadouble, moving the quest toward the floating island castle, the suspected control center.

Shelby's presence was like a magnet to the Shadouble. She had the shield they wanted and the force of their might was directed toward her. She was surrounded by Kerrick's hundreds and then the Polotis warriors all the time she was moving forward through the city toward the tower that reached the furthest to the sky. It was positioned closest to the floating island. As they closed in on the tower, she could see connections to the island from it. They would have to use that route to get to the power source.

Kerrick pulled to a safe spot, blood running down his arms and from his hands. He shook his head 'no' to assure her over the noise of screams and clanging that he was not hurt. He pointed to the island and Shelby understood that they needed to get there.

All of the entries of the tower were well guarded, but the Alker warriors were one unit of brutal force and determination. They were good at conquering.

As they cut through the stationed Shadouble guards, a lone creature saw its chance to secure the coveted shield in Shelby's possession. While the other men were fighting off its comrades, it slammed her against the rough wall of the tower and tried to bite her neck with its razor-sharp teeth. She slugged it with the handle of her sword and it morphed into a knuckle of teeth mimicking the creatures, more suitable for this close encounter. She wedged the amethyst teeth under the jaw and willed the Crenulate to form into a knife.

The Shadouble's claws scraped against her side and around her arm, trying to dig into her body, but the Creation Crenulate formed impenetrable armor around her.

She grappled with the handle of the newly formed sword and pulled outward with both hands, splitting apart the gruesome head of the Shadouble. She now held an identical sword in each of her bloody hands. Shelby looked around slowly. Tears streamed down her face. She saw men she knew sliced down and lose limbs and she felt sick.

Shelby looked around at the carnage of the fight and knew they were winning, but the battle was not the victory of this war. They still needed to take the power away from the Al Kerking and deformed Caubles to win their ultimate goal.

The nucleus of Alker fought their way to a tower-island connection. Their own sentries defended their position, resisting the invading attacks of incoming Shadoubles who were closing in on their little group.

Shelby looked at the covering on her skin; metal hard. She wished she could set up a mini-barrier that would allow them the same kind of protection from the incoming attacks of the Caubles streaming down from above as well as up from below their location.

She was abruptly pushed inside a portal with Kerrick, IzTaln, Commander Rockdurgh and Captain Talig and jetted to another location. She could see the Alkers left behind fighting their way through the Caubles.

The portal had taken them across the span to the island and deposited them in a room inside the castle. It was eerily quiet.

"Shelby." Kerrick and the men had made it to the inner sanctum and now they needed her contribution.

"Shelby, we have gone as far as we can. We're on the floating island."

"Shelby." Kerrick was trying to be patient but they had little time. The locked doors would not remain so for long. He held onto her arm to keep her stable on her feet.

This all seemed surreal to her and she struggled to focus.

"Tell us what we need to do next." Kerrick was looking to IzTaln and Shelby for some kind of direction.

Shelby took the shield off her back and placed it on the floor. She motioned for IzTaln to grab her hand like they were going to arm wrestle.

"So, you brought it to me." All of them turned at the sound to face a woman of obese proportions. She was not disfigured in any other way. Shelby recognized her voice.

"You," was all Shelby said.

"I have waited for a long time to acquire that shield. We could not cross over the threshold, but you have brought it to us just as the Cauble said you would."

Nemesis appeared at her side. His head swung back and forth in remorse. He was not here of his own volition, but a traitor nonetheless.

"He is a silly creature. He thought he could destroy me and my people."

'So maybe not a traitor to us,' Shelby considered.

Kerrick spied the stone in the center of the dais and realized that if the stone was connected to the shield it would give the Al Kerkings what they wanted, not destroy them. The stone was how they controlled the Crenulate.

"Shelby, the stone, they have it."

She understood the conflict. They had been duped into entering the Yahatamah with the Creation Crenulate. To unite it here would give the Al Kerkings what they wanted, the power and control to conquer the rest of the planet.

"Yes. And now we have everything we need to subjugate this planet and use its resources to rule like gods. The Creation Crenulate was the only thing we could not extract. It had to be transported here by a trusted vessel, that vessel being you, Char Shelby. Nemesis, bring me that shield."

He hesitated for dread of being bound again by the Alkers. Her guards came out from the surroundings of the room on cue. They were not disfigured in any way like the ones below. They looked like Caubles.

"You are not like the creatures below."

"Oh, yes we are. The only difference is that we do not live on the planet. Those below us are Al Kerkings and Caubles that do not have the symbiotic Crenulate. We found out very quickly that we needed Crenulate to survive on this planet."

"The problem is that we dug the Crenulate out of this part of the planet not realizing it was sentient and able to expel us or trap us. But we have corrected our mistake and can harness its power. The stone is the antithesis made from the extraction and separation of the Crenulate from the dying bodies of its hosts."

"You seized it for your own evil machinations," Kerrick rebuked with disdain.

If fusing the stone to the shield was the controlling power for the Al Kerking, then what could they do to stop the melding of the two? What did the Crenulate need to be powerful and free? A living, breathing host and connection to the planet itself made energy potent enough to break down the barriers and move through time.

Shelby fumbled her necklace nervously wondering how they could bond the disconnected Crenulate to the planet and balance the energy of the planet to its natural state; taking the power away from the Al Kerking.

Dirt, not a pretty stone was the connection, but they were above the planet on a floating island severed from the planet and its energy.

Kerrick was in her mind at the back of her thoughts, pushing. How did he do that?

Shelby knew that as long as she kept dirt from her timeline she would be pulled back to it. That was why she always kept this necklace filled with dirt on. It grounded her. What if it ground the shield and made it impervious to the manipulations of the Al Kerking? She could think of no other way to save them from losing all their power except to rid all of them of Crenulate.

"Nemesis, get the shield from her," the massive Al Kerking woman repeated. The Al Kerking sentries held back as if they knew there was danger.

Shelby looked at the men, her son, his father, their friends.

"It is time to relinquish all our power; Crenulate to dirt and dirt to dimensions. It's time to unite the broken dimensions and bind the free Al Kerking and Shadoubles."

Shelby yanked her necklace off and filled the filigree of the shield with her beads and willed the shield to absorb the substance. Kerrick also added his soil as did the other men.

Shelby lifted her shield and took up a fighting stance. Her amethyst sword grew and glowed. Beside her the Alker men and arriving Polotis raised their defenses for the final battle. Shelby threw her shield with all her might at the Al Kerking representative, slicing through the woman's body like water.

Shelby's skin was intricately filigreed with Crenulate as she ran full force at the Shadouble soldiers that had emerged from the sidelines.

The men passed her and swarmed to intercept the onslaught of swinging battle weapons and shooting lasers. Shelby looked for a chance to retrieve her shield. Each time she moved she was shot at or hit and knocked back with the force of the impact. If not for the Creation Crenulate, she knew she would be dead.

The Alkers were outnumbered but prevailed against the Al Kerking and Cauble, killing more than she believed possible. Still, she could not reach the shield. She was stymied each direction or course she took. Helpless to get to the shield, she pondered if she could get the stone to it.

She saw the commanding Al Kerking grab the shield and to her dismay he held it aloft in triumph. The others of his kind cheered in victory.

Sir Kerrick sent a sword flying through the air to pierce the Al Kerking in the chest. He slumped to his knees and the shield wobbled and rolled closer to Shelby.

She motioned to Kerrick and threw one of her swords to him. He caught it in the nick of time to deflect the claws and teeth of a frenzied Cauble attacking him.

Shelby now turned her attention once again to the shield. She wasn't the only one who was after it. Behind a line of defense, an Al Kerking in an embellished uniform shouted commands to the Cauble soldiers under his authority to advance.

The quest would be lost if she did not succeed. She felt Kerrick at her side and just as quickly, IzTaln was there too. Shelby put a hand on Kerrick and one on their son to stop them from going out into the open. At her feet, a web of amethyst flowed on the surface of the floor toward the shield, unnoticed by any but the three of them.

The Al Kerking and Cauble soldiers moved unstoppable to the shield, protected by a force field of energy.

The web of amethyst reached the shield just as the Al Kerking commander picked it up off the floor. All was lost.

No. Shelby saw the thread of Creation Crenulate still attached to the shield and connected to the floor webbing, and to her. She and her men watched from their blocks of protection as the shield dissolved from Al Kerking hands and then appeared in Shelby's.

"Shelby, now!" Kerrick urged. He pulled her to her feet and wove his way around the refuse of broken machinery and wires and metal and stone. Shelby tripped and caught her foot in a pile of wires. She was yanked roughly up by Kerrick's strong arm and hauled once more onward to the platform.

Her shield worked against the blasts of lasers, but the soldiers were closing in.

They made their way around the dais while deafening fires exploded around them, making gestures the only way to communicate.

Across the area, IzTaln and Rockdurgh and the other men attacked the Cauble and Al Kerkings with renewed force to create a distraction for Shelby and Kerrick. The momentary reprieve gave them time to set the shield on the stone. At once, a force of power and heat surged outward knocking everyone back off their feet.

Instead of working for the Al Kerkings, the introduction of the dirt into the shield gave the Crenulate a channeling force to move through the surge of energy connection and dissolve the boundary of the Al Kerking territory.

The force of the merging gravity and power stream shook the building with terrifying tremors and rolling. The floating islands free fell in chaotic form, listing and undulating toward the planet.

Shelby was seized firmly and heard Kerrick's baritone voice bellow, "There's only one way out! Jump!"

Shelby ran hand-in-hand with him out to the terrace and into thin air avoiding the falling chunks of collapsing building plummeting toward the ground. All Shelby knew was the landing was going to hurt.

Shelby was snatched from behind and whisked away from Kerrick who was himself ensconced in the grip of another Polotis. Each of the Alkers had been rescued by gliding Polotis, but the island disturbance of the convergence caused thunder and lightning to strike to the ground and explode. The sound of the earthquake was swallowed up by the crashing of the islands impacting the planet. The plume of debris and choking pollution was suffocating.

Shelby was dropped some feet from the place they had entered the territory. The ground was still shaking and men everywhere were either flying to safety or running. In the confusion, Shelby strained to see her son or someone familiar. She and her Polotis companion had flown blindly through the cloud of grey soot, so she feared others might be trapped.

Over the thunderous noise she heard her name being called. Kerrick and the men with him had full smiles on their grimy, bloodied faces and they looked handsomely pleased with themselves.

Shelby ran to Kerrick and wrapped her arms around him tight. "You saved my life, I think."

The Polotis that carried her stood behind and shook his head with a sigh. Shelby looked up at Kerrrick and wondered if he was as amazed as she was to be caught by the Polotis.

"I told you, I knew how to conquer. The saving part was purely accidental." His robust laugh caught the attention of the other men. Hearing their leader laugh made them realize that the worst was over.

That night they all rested at the border, unencumbered by strife or fear. The women who had waited for the men came into the mix of the thousands of victors celebrating.

The rumblings of the planet were lessening and the scouts gleaned the rubble for survivors and enemies, with different groups returning to the boundary with reports of complete triumph.

Shelby had assumed all the Crenulate would return to the planet when she had fused it to the dais and the balance of the energy was achieved. She presumed the others would no longer have abilities like flying and swords or armor, but that was not the case.

She now speculated that the isolation of the Polotis allowed the Crenulate to behave differently from her own symbiotic Crenulate. They could still produce feathers and weapons, but no sword or shield formed for her. No covering or intuitive sensing came to her either. She had given it all back to the planet.

After the Battle / Chapter 32

Shelby contemplated the loss of her shield and sword. It was mysterious to her that she felt no different, only sad at the loss of protection she had gotten used to.

"You look deep in thought." This came from an unexpected source.

Shelby looked up to see the handsome King of the Polotis. He seemed different to Shelby, more melancholy than normal. She indicated a seat next to her. He sat across from her.

"I need to explain some things to you," he started out.

Shelby shook her head but blurted, "I want to apologize for threatening you and your clan."

"I would have done the same," he replied courteously.

Shelby observed that he hesitated. Finally he decided to plunge into his real reason for visiting.

"I know that you were surprised by my appearance with my Queen wife. I want you to know that I had no choice but to assume you had changed your mind about us. I thought I could compel you to call me over, but you never opened the barrier.

"Zeryl was also threatening to reveal IzTaln's true identity and disinherit him altogether. We struck a bargain for the welfare of my clan and son.

"IzTaln is my son; I have raised him as such. I know you sacrificed your relationship with him for his safety and for the security of my clan; that will never be forgotten. Still, I would ask one more thing; that you give him Creation Crenulate so he can travel back and forth as he wills."

"That is not going to happen," Shelby stated succinctly. "He is not going to need it for one. The boundaries are healing and you will no longer be invisible to us or isolated. We will respect your borders for now, but everything else is going to change."

"You must understand our dimension is fractionally different than yours because our place on Aion is connected to our home planet." Schofta noted Shelby's frown.

"Think of Crenulate as a path to our home world that only works one way. You have thought of it as a different dimension, but the border that you just walked through to Lahata is really a different planet than Aion. That is why there are time differences and that is why it is miraculous you did it.

"Once the path was disconnected, there was no way back to the home world. Lahata is disappearing. Creation Crenulate will make a new path to our world. We could stay here, but Creation Crenulate gives us power to return home. Something we have never been able to attempt since being severed when our technology failed us many years ago. If Creation Crenulate can empower IzTaln to travel over the whole planet and beyond this one just by a command from him, then it will work for us too."

"You could abuse this power. Besides, what if your home world is ruined or strange now after all this time? Remember, your dimension speeds by in comparison to Aion. Who knows what the difference will be if you reconnect with your home world?" Shelby queried.

"We survived because of our ability to hide. You see how valuable it is to my people for protection. IzTaln could be that door for the Polotis to return if needed."

"I can not give him Creation Crenulate because it no longer resides in me, nor would I. It is too much power for an already powerful people. Besides, I gave it all back to the planet to destroy the power of the Al Kerkings. I can not help you nor harm you, so you need not fear me taking your feathers." Shelby bit the corner of her mouth and looked away. She was vulnerable now. So if he wanted retribution, he could drive a knife through her heart.

"You're pregnant." Shelby was caught off-guard by the sudden change of subject.

"Maybe a little." She made a Mona Lisa smile. "How did you know? Kerrick doesn't even know."

"By the pride in Sir Kerrick's eyes when he looks at you, and the last time we were together I knew you were pregnant. I tried to tie you to my dimension, but it was too late."

"I didn't even know then." Shelby was astounded. Maybe that was the only reason she was able to make it back to the Alker camp, the connection she had with Kerrick.

"He knows?" she marveled.

Kerrick came gloating into the circle at that moment with Shelby's shield of Crenulate, not caring one bit he was intruding.

"A present for the Star of Aion, discovered in the rubble of Yahatamah." He presented it as others gathered around the scene smiled.

Shelby looked at it dumbstruck.

"I believe this calls for a celebration."

He turned intentionally toward King Schofta.

"You and your clan are welcome to celebrate with us a week hence in our territory. We welcome the chance to extend our hospitality to our new allies and neighbors. We are pleased to fight with such mighty warriors."

"And we will be there in all our fine feathers, to celebrate the Star of Aion." He bowed to Char Shelby and then to Sir Kerrick and waved at the crowd of listeners.

There were shouting and loud whistles from the spectators hearing the promise of festivities and even more cheering when the King of the Polotis announced his acceptance.

A little while later Shelby approached Kerrick with the shield in her hands.

"I saw this destroyed in the shift." Her open statement solicited a reply.

Kerrick smiled down at her with a quirky grin.

"You are not the only one with Creation Crenulate. Seems only fitting to give you something, since you keep giving me children," he teased.

Shelby gasped. He knew too much. And how did he still have Crenulate?

"How?" was all she could ask.

"Because, Shelby love, you are a part of me and I am a part of you. Together we are finally whole, 'and four will be the tie that bonds'."

"You finally figured that out, huh?"

"All by myself."

"I guess you're stuck with me, Kerrick."

"I know."

Shelby rolled her eyes and Kerrick laughed and held out his open arms to her.

Life-Debt / Chapter 33

Shelby was going through the woods looking for the prescribed plants that Doc Orlie had enjoined her to seek. He was, in some respects, like a mentor to her knowledge of the indigenous plant life on Aion. She sought out the plants with a curious pleasure and gloated whenever she found one of the species before he did, and when she found more.

"You are extremely competitive, Shelby, I dare say." Doc Orlie laughed as she rolled her eyes.

"I have very little competitiveness in my bones, Doc. I just get excited when I find the very plants I need for my collection. I can't help it if you are old and slow and need me to remind you of why we are here." She laughed with him.

He snorted. She teased him again, but he found her a pleasure to be around. Even though she would taunt him with relentless jibes, he was quite fond of her cheerfulness and enthusiasm. He found her to be good company.

"See this," she brought it to him to inspect, "it is perfect for scenting the soap the women make. It is one of my favorite fragrances and they have no more, so this is my lucky find today." She waggled it in the air and then went back to picking the wildflowers, storing them in the pouch separate from the medicinal plants he was seeking.

They had started the day quite early and he decided he needed a break from the heat. She was in a busy mode and had to be called several times before she actually quit looking for the herbs. They sat down companionably at the base of a grove of trees.

They both heard noise and rustling coming toward them and both were equally relieved it was an Alker soldier that appeared. Shelby and Doc Orlie looked at each other with a sheepish grin.

"I miss my Bilboas. They kept me safe from the varmints. Now they run amuck."

Doc Orlie gave her a reproachful look. She just laughed.

The young man saluted Doc Orlie and then proceeded to deliver his message. "Sir Kerrick Torrell has requested Char Shelby attend the meeting today. I have been assigned the..." here he hesitated a bit, "pleasure," he emphasized, "of escorting her directly to him." Satisfied he had made the delivery, he smiled, pleased with himself.

Shelby didn't know what to make of it, but anything Kerrick wanted her to do she immediately balked at. She thought about it for a minute then reluctantly said, "Fine."

All the bravado of the young man escaped in a relieved sigh.

"I suppose he gave instructions to bodily carry me if I refused."

This she said slightly under her breath as she picked up the sachets that held her prized finds.

"Yes, Char Shelby, he did."

Shelby hadn't expected an answer, but she was ticked that Kerrick was so blatantly forceful and arrogant enough to expect his word to be carried out to the fullest.

The young man continued. "I have brought a ride to carry you back."

"Is there room for Doc Orlie?" She waited.

"No, Char Shelby."

"Then I will walk back with him, directly." She thought that would be acceptable.

"This is where I will bodily pick you up if you do not conform."

Shelby's ire was immediately at the ready to do battle, but Doc Orlie's calming assurance helped the situation resolve.

"Shelby, dear, I am not ready to go back quite yet. Please go on and see what the man desires of you. It may be a good thing, yes?" He patted her shoulder and pushed her toward the young soldier.

"Fine." But it was not a happy agreement.

Shelby arrived and was, as commanded, directed to Kerrick's domain where the main cubicle was large enough to accommodate any meetings Kerrick had with his men. She stood beside her sentry waiting for Kerrick to recognize her presence, but he seemed too occupied with what he was reading at his desk to acknowledge them.

Shelby walked over to the window bay that overlooked the camp. As far as a vantage view, this was perfect. She could see beyond the spacious ledge outside, down into the camp. The only domains she could not see were a few men's quarters. She could even glimpse a light shining on the paths outside the mountain city trail.

She could see the fires and the women milling around and wondered if they were starting the evening meal or setting up bread for morning.

Kerrick knew the moment she entered the cubicle. He wanted to be fully informed of the procedure before he approached her with his duty.

She was at the window when he motioned for the guard to be excused. His movement attracted Shelby's gaze and she turned as the guard was leaving. She stood where she was waiting for Kerrick to tell her what was so important.

He moved around his desk and leaned against it with his arms crisscrossed over his well developed chest looking at her as if he were still deciding something. He looked at her budding belly, barely showing the babe inside. He smiled with satisfaction.

She wondered if he knew how striking he was or if he posed in such a way to leave the impression he was easygoing and affable.

"It has come to my attention that you have not been properly awarded for saving my men's lives. Since it is no secret to anyone that you, by Alkernian law, must be acknowledged for such a feat with some kind of reward, I am pressed on every side to do so.

"There is a board of Elders and peers that have been assigned to delegate what, if anything will be done to acknowledge your bravery. It will happen here tonight."

His hand made a sweeping motion of the room. On top of all the other challenges of the newly arrived delegates and people, this impromptu meeting was being thrust upon him now. He would not even have time to prep Shelby for the inquisition.

"You will need to come dressed properly and present your request with decorum that is acceptable to high ranking dignitaries. It will be a celebratory occasion, but on a small scale. Do you understand?"

His head tilted slightly and he looked at her with seriousness.

Shelby did not say anything. She detected he was not pleased about the situation and she wondered if he had been reprimanded by his superiors. He was being so formal.

"Why are you annoyed by this?" Shelby had to ask.

He stopped his movement and looked at her with unveiled sincerity. "Because, Shelby, under normal circumstances, you would not even have a hearing before the board. But because several of the men here have rehearsed the ordeal to their families, an inquiry has been made as to what happened. They want to speak to you personally. You are to be given a formal hearing and an opportunity to request a reward. I expect you to comply and try to behave."

"Fine. I will be properly dressed and ready to present my request to your board tonight."

He was clearly in need of some better manners, accusing her of not behaving. At that thought she almost giggled. Who was she to be giving anyone lessons on good manners? She was so rotten at being polite; it would be irony to point out someone else's obnoxious behavior.

She decided to seek out Amy and see if she knew the proper way to ask for her reward. She was sure it would be in the book that held all the secrets of the Alker traditions. And then she needed to get dressed for the presentation itself.

When Shelby entered the meeting room, he felt like he had been kicked in the stomach. Shelby was in a pristine gown of her own design, the very one he had seen in her cubicle being worked on. It flowed around her like soft clouds fashioned to accentuate her womanly round shape.

Nothing about her dress was ornate, but the elegant emerald green, simply embossed with designs of swirls and beads accentuated her waist and shoulders. Nothing of that dress was Alkernian. Part of her hair was pulled back with ringlets cascading down to her waist, complementing the swirls on her dress. The final touch was her simple hair comb that acted as a crown, highlighting the small glittering jewels in her hair. He stood dumbstruck, unable to move.

She entered into a transformed room. Hours earlier it was an ordinary work and meeting room. Now it was decorated and filled with Alkernian men dressed in military formals. There were women following her that she was determined to bring into the meeting for moral support if nothing else. They were appropriately dressed and acting as her entourage for the night.

Rockdurgh moved toward the women, very pleased that they accompanied Shelby this evening. Now it would be a little more entertaining, though he expected this evening would be anything but dull. He anticipated fireworks, and the way Shelby was dressed to kill, his expectations were growing.

There was a surge toward the women that annoyed Kerrick. As soon as Rockdurgh took Shelby's hand and kissed it, she said something that made him laugh. Then another man stepped forward and another all vying for the women's attention, especially Shelby's. She finally spoke up.

"Stop, stop, stop." Her hands were held in a manner that made the men hold off a bit.

"I am still the same Shelby that needs space," and then she laughed and extended her arm out in front of her with her hand gently bent. The eager young Biat took up her hand and kissed it. She laughed again.

Kerrick had made his way to the cluster of women by this time; the men moving back respectfully as he approached. He stood directly in front of Shelby, the other women held back a ways, flanking her.

He bowed respectfully to her and held out his hand. She looked at it and then got a mischievous look in her eyes and asked, "Do you want me to kiss your hand?" Behind her the women giggled at her teasing.

Kerrick smirked at her, still holding out his hand, "You can start there if you like."

She rolled her eyes very non-elegantly. She took his proffered hand however, and he immediately pulled her closer to his body and wrapped her arm around his elbow.

The warmth of his body and the intoxicating way he smelled made her giddy. He was a controlled and complicated man. There were depths to him that she had not imagined. He radiated a confidence that comes from a man who has conquered hardships and possibly some of his own demons and won. He knew who he was and was proud of it.

He walked her ceremoniously toward the far end of the meeting hall. Seating had been set up for the attendees and she found herself being sat down right in front, facing the newly arrived delegates.

She thought Kerrick would leave her there, but he sat down beside her, crossed his outstretched legs at the ankles and waited.

She looked behind her. The seats were filling up with men who had been anticipating the ceremony. The women she had brought were directly behind her, but only she and Kerrick occupied the front row. She felt conspicuous. She looked at Kerrick, but he seemed unperturbed by the event.

She was nervous.

"Do not leave me, Kerrick."

He took her cool hand into his big warm ones and kissed her fingers. "Are you serious? There is no other place I would rather be, Shelby love, than right by your side." He smiled and looked directly into her eyes. "Have no fear, Shelby. Every single person in this hall is on your side."

The Assembly of Elders entered the room and went to the platform. As soon as an austere man in white appeared and moved forward to the empty seat at the table, all the men in the hall stood up. When he sat down, there was a salute and loud cheer from Kerrick's men. The people at the table smiled with warmth and greeted the men with respectful salutes.

The elder man looked at Shelby with unveiled admiration.

"Son, you did not prepare us for how beautiful she is."

"I knew it did not bear any precedence on the facts, Sir." The two talked as if no one else was in the room hearing their comments. Shelby was blushing to Kerrick's amusement.

"How are your assignments progressing, son."

"We accomplished all the plans on schedule, Sir, in time for the celebration and in anticipation of the next arrivals."

"Yes, yes. And how is my old friend, Morrell? Are you behaving and keeping out of trouble?"

"Aye, I am, you old geezer! Spouting off about behaving, when you know quite well that it is you that needs watching. You need to respect your elders, Elder." Doc Orlie smiled at the man in spite of the rebuke.

"That is true, Morrell, as my wife constantly reminds me."

The people at the table were enjoying the chatter. His attention was back on Kerrick who was smiling at him.

"Now, son, you have quite a bit on your shoulders, though I know you are capable of carrying any load you are given; that aside, what is your assessment of the progress on Aion?"

"Sir, quite frankly, we are in uncharted territory here. Earth women are not Alker women as you will be able to assess for yourself shortly."

"Yes. Let us get to it then, shall we?"

His eyes turned on Shelby and she waited for whatever was happening to unfold.

Kerrick pulled her fisted hand from her lap and held it comfortingly on his leg. He felt her try to tug away but did not let go. Instead, he gently pried her hand open and entwined his fingers over hers.

"Let us begin, Char Shelby, by introducing ourselves to you." With that all the delegates gave their names and she answered appropriately.

There was a mixture of men and women on the board, which surprised Shelby. And then it began.

"Young woman, it has come to our attention you are a very gifted and knowledgeable asset to the men on Aion. We actually have had frequent updates on the happenings here and your name has come to our attention more than once; though sometimes it was not good." He raised an eyebrow and looked sternly at her.

Shelby said nothing, but Kerrick gazed at her with speculation. She bit her lip and then put a calm mask over her features. She would address that later no doubt.

"I suppose you know we have the custom of gifting our men with honors and such for their bravery beyond the normal expectations of military life. Our military is exceptional, do you not agree?"

Kerrick bowed his head. He did not think it was wise to engage Shelby in giving her opinion of his men. Bad idea.

Shelby gracefully stood and gave a respectful bow to the Elder Lurt; then she turned back to the men in the hall and addressed them first with a respectful salute. She stood looking at them for a moment and the men held their breath in expectation. She looked at Kerrick who smiled with such a curious look, she smiled back. She turned back around to face the Elder and the board members.

"I do, Elder Lurt. They are fierce warriors, but more than that they are honorable, loyal and chivalrous men. They are my friends."

The men saluted her and stood to bow to her.

Shelby gave a faint smile and bit the corner of her bottom lip. She turned away from the men so they wouldn't see any weakness.

One of the women spoke up from the other side. "We have no doubt she is not an Alker genteel lady, Sir Kerrick. She is, however, a woman who evokes loyalty from your men for some reason."

There was uncharacteristic murmuring from the men and shuffling of feet. She was sure the men did not like their loyalty to be questioned or accused of misplacing it.

Shelby was insulted to the core that some woman who was in society had the nerve to say she was not a lady of culture. She glanced at Kerrick with anger in her eyes and then to her amazement he winked at her.

"Lady Rightell, you are indeed correct in that my men give loyalty to Char Shelby and rightly so."

Shelby was shocked Kerrick would say such an outrageous thing. She looked back at the men and some of them gave her a nod of acquiescence. She was suddenly warmed by such a thought.

Kerrick continued, "I sometimes think that if it came right down to it they would choose her over me; hell, I choose to be loyal to her."

He stepped up to the dais so he was very close to the woman and he bore down on her with his sheer presence. She was visibly squirming back from his directness.

"Let me explain some of the reasons why."

He turned back to Shelby and made a slow perusal of her. She got the look on her face that meant he had better be careful. He chuckled.

"The woman is fearless. She has never backed down from me or what she believes is right. She has been attacked by an animal and killed it, without a weapon I might add. She has rescued thirty-seven of my men; when as a captive, it was not in her best interest to do so. She has to my chagrin saved my life." Shelby voiced a fake cough and held up two fingers when Kerrick gave her pause.

"Well, I was not awake for one of them so it does not count." He grinned at her and the audience laughed.

"Actually, Lady Rightell, she also has the devotion of many of the women here because she is a fierce advocate on their behalf. I am not easily swayed by complaining women, but Char Shelby has the ability to express very strong reasons for change."

One of the men behind anonomously blurted out, "And she wins most of the time!" There was agreement in the ranks and Shelby was disconcerted by it.

"Aye, she wins most of the time, but we," he indicated with a sweeping motion of his hand toward his men, "have been made better by the changes. We are learning better manners. You will be happy for that, Mother."

Shelby couldn't see his mother, but apparently he knew she was there.

"This is the woman who has been referred to as the Star of Aion from our very own prophecy. Her exploits are the reason you were freed from the grip of the Al Kerkings. We all have a great deal to thank her for.

"We are here, however, not to decide whether she deserves recognition, but to give her a chance to make her requests before us as to what she deems is the cost of our lives to her. It is the least we can do."

He looked at Shelby and gave her a respectful bow. Some of the men in the audience stood and saluted her as well. She recognized them as the men that had been on the cliff that fateful night. She marveled they even conceded to her their thanks because not a word of the accident had been spoken to her since. Most of the men had come to her directly after the incident and mumbled their gratitude, but that was it. She never even spoke of it to the women, though they knew.

Both of Shelby's hands covered her surprised expression. Kerrick moved toward her and gently pulled them down from her face holding her hands between their bodies. He was pleased and his heart beat faster as he witnessed unchecked tears roll down her cheeks. Her back was to the audience of men and his large body shielded her from most of the panel.

He moved his face close to hers and whispered, "Here is your chance, Shelby love. Ask for the moons, and make sure the price is equal to the gift of life."

Shelby looked at him not sure what he meant, but she finally understood he was truly her ally.

She raised both her hands to the sides of his face and really looked at him. The moment seemed to slow and she wondered if she was truly seeing what she thought she saw.

"Thank you, Kerrick," and to her amazement and his she softly kissed his lips.

There was throat clearing from the panel and Kerrick slowly straightened to his full height. Shelby looked up at him and he looked back down at her and winked again!

She blushed and laughed softly not caring a bit about how it looked or what anyone on the panel thought. Apparently Kerrick didn't care either. He bowed to her and the panel and then sat down leaving her the floor to speak her mind.

She turned to face them with as much decorum as she could muster and began to speak her requests.

"Ladies and Gentlemen, I, Char Shelby Deit Demine, Lady of the former house of Port Angeles on Earth, stand before you to make my requests known."

At the announcement of her heritage, Shelby was startled at the commotion it caused. She turned back to the men and spoke up loudly.

"Be quiet! I can't hear myself think. This is hard enough." She looked at Kerrick whose color had gone ashen. "What is wrong with you people?"

"Madam, this is an outrage! You can not possibly be a Deit Demine. They are of the lineage of kings and queens on Iritain."

"Sir, I assure you I am not of that lineage. It's the name I was given at birth by my father and since I was born on Earth, it is probably a coincidence. My father loved nuances and was notorious for bad jokes, so I apologize for any similarity. I however, assure you my name is mine; so may I continue?"

It took a few minutes before the meeting got started again, and in the meantime, Shelby sat down next to Kerrick. He would not look at her.

Finally she whispered at him, "Friend or foe, Kerrick, friend or foe?"

He just shook his head, but would not look at her. She could see his jaw work at grinding out his frustration.

"You sure are fickle for a friend, Kerrick. Have some faith."

He snapped his head in her direction. "Be careful, Shelby love, I am more than your friend. Stars can fall from the sky."

"What does that mean?" She was totally at a loss at his anger and his change of spirit.

"Later," was all he said.

"Shelby, who you are at this point, does not diminish the debt that needs to be paid for the lives you saved. You may continue." This was said by an Elder after some time of confused chaos.

"I apologize for any misunderstanding I caused. I am not quite sure about the nuances of your language, so I do express regret at the unintended insult."

She looked at the panel of people and realized they were now very unlikely to concede anything to her. But she would try anyway.

"I realize that as a captive," she heard Kerrick get up and leave in a huff, but she continued as best as she could, "it is unusual to be given the opportunity to even talk to a board of Alkers."

"Then make it short, so we can get on with our other duties," Lady Rightell quipped.

Shelby felt as though this whole meeting was of no value now. Did her name really insult them so much? She sighed and looked out into the hall of men behind her. Did they turn as fickle as Kerrick?

What was the nuance she missed? She searched their faces and didn't see one smile, only worry.

"Do you have a request or not, Shelby?" This came from the Elder Lurt.

It angered her enough to put backbone into her and she immediately quit feeling sorry for herself and turned to face her daunting task.

"I do indeed. First, it is suddenly very clear to me, that as a captive, you have the idea that what you reward me with, though very small in nature, would be plenty; since I am a captive. I ask you this; is an Alker life worth more or less than a captive?"

"More of course," was the retort from several on the panel. Shelby nodded.

"Ten times more or equally so?" She queried further.

"At least ten times as much," Lady Rightell repeated.

"So if you had a choice to keep one Alker alive or ten captives, you honestly can say that you would choose the one Alker?" she pressed on.

"Yes. I would give up one hundred captives for one Alker." One of the elder men spoke agitatedly.

"Have any of you actually done that, I mean, allowed a hundred captives to die for one Alker?"

No one spoke at first. Finally, one of the women who had not said anything yet stood up so Shelby could recognize where the answer came from. Shelby walked toward her and looked directly across from her.

"We are in agreement that at least ten captives' work or value, are less than what we value our own

Alker people. We have far more knowledge and strength than a mere captive."

Shelby felt no insult at her words. She realized she did not need their approval. She wanted to keep to the course she had taken.

"Fine. For every Alker man I saved by my own benevolent actions I request, no, I demand ten captive women to be given complete freedom from all laws, traditions and expectations, henceforth to be complete citizens of the Alker Nation, to come and go as they please from this time forward!"

There was a loud unanimous outburst of protests and shouts and it took Shelby a moment to realize that the ones from the men behind her where shouts of joy! Shelby's mouth was open and she realized they had hoped for something and got it. She wasn't quite sure what it was that they got.

When the rumbling started calming down, Elder Lurt started to say something. Shelby didn't care what he wanted to say, she wasn't finished.

"Excuse me, Elder, I am not nearly finished. This will release all the men from the life-debts owed to me. By my calculations, ten times thirty-seven is three-hundred seventy. We have only around three hundred women. So that takes care of all the women here on Aion, with seventy more to go.

"I propose you allow Sir Kerrick to choose some of the women among your captives equal to the number I have earned."

The panel of elders sat dumbfounded and in fact Shelby noted that they looked as though they still had a right to refuse her. For this she called Amy forward to present the traditions out of their very own book. She smiled sheepishly when Amy was by her side.

"I apologize for not being able to read Alker myself to you. She is much better at the nuances than I am and the things that are relevant.".

Shelby stepped back and Amy matter-of-factly stated the page number and quoted roughly the law of Alker in regard to a woman saving a man's life. She reminded them that it clearly stated if the person, male or female, saved the life of an Alker, they would immediately be remanded their own freedom, if marriage to an Alker was not possible or preferred.

"In addition to said person's freedom, they will be allocated for life, substantial finances owed for life by the indebted recipient to the life-saver, until marriage or agreed upon debt was acquitted by the life-saver."

"Thank you, Amy. If these terms are agreed upon, all the men will be acquitted of their life-debt to me."

Shelby waited until Amy sat down again and then saw Kerrick in the back smiling with satisfaction. She frowned. He abandoned her here and now he was smiling. She wanted to kick him so hard. She was still incredibly angry. He kept smiling like a proud peacock.

Again the Elder started to speak and again Shelby had no mercy for him.

"I apologize again, Elder, but I am not finished. I still have yet to address the two times," she held up her fingers, "I saved Kerrick's sorry neck at the peril of my own safety.

"Once I had to climb down a rocky cliff to find him, and another time I had to cut the head off a creature to save him from his stup...his chivalrous tendency and avert his certain mauling of claws bigger than the stupid knife he brought to the fight."

There were chuckles from the men and women in the meeting.

She put her finger up to her lips and tapped them thoughtfully. Kerrick had the audacity to come from hiding to the front to face her.

He loved the way she looked. Her hands were on her hips and she stood there ready he was sure to do him harm. She was livid. But he could tell she was debating what to do because she was biting her bottom lip. He looked her directly in the eyes and repeated, "Ask for the moon, but make sure the price is equal to the life."

She still didn't know what he meant. But she wanted to teach him a lesson not to lose faith in her. She stepped up to him and slapped him hard across the face. She left marks on his otherwise handsome face. A gasp of shock went through the entire room and shocked the Elders' side as well. A hush fell over the crowd.

He had fire in his eyes of anger but she did not care. She stood before him. Only today did she realize the extent of her power over him. Because she saved his life, he would forever be indebted to her until she was given her gift, whatever it was, or married. But because she saved him twice, he potentially could never be rid of her.

She did not even know what to say to him. How humiliating that he had to marry her or keep her financed so that his debt to her would be paid. No wonder he did not want her to address the Alker panel. He would have to pay his debt.

"Focus, Shelby. I know where your mind is going. That is not the right path. Come back."

She looked at him and realized he was communicating to her without speaking out loud. She tilted her head at looked at him with amazement. How did he do that? She moved closer to him and his hands went up to keep her at a safe distance.

"Focus?"

He nodded slightly at her question.

"I mean no disrespect to the men of Aion, but..." She was interrupted by a beautiful woman that appeared from the darkness behind the panel of interrogators as Shelby now thought of them.

"Who do you think you are, to hit Sir Kerrick like that? Never in my life have I done so. You are not worthy of any blessings this court could give you. To hit the prince like that is punishable by law!"

"Woman, sit down! You have no idea what is going on here." This came from the Elder Lurt. He commanded the people behind her to settle her down.

"I have been here just as long as you have, Elder Lurt Torrell!" She spouted.

Shelby looked at Kerrick and just shook her head. In a low voice directed only toward him she declared, "I do not care if you are the king of Iritain and Aion and Earth. You deserve that for all the deception I have had to muddle through. But specifically, that slap was for abandoning me when you said you would gladly be at my side."

"Did I say 'gladly'?" He smiled mischievously and rubbed the side of his face where it burned red.

How could he be so flippant in light of this whole procedure? She was to the end of her wits on how to proceed.

"I would like to finish this. Sir Kerrick's life is substantially more important than ten captives, according to you."

She stopped for a moment and lowered her head. Her curls fell forward and covered her face for a moment. She took a deep breath.

"But my children are lost to me somewhere on your planet or back home on Earth."

She looked up at the panel of Alkers.

"In return for Sir Kerrick's complete freedom from any life-debt ties to me, he will find the whereabouts of my children and bring them here to me if at all possible. When that is done, he is free to live as if he owes nothing in the world to me."

He leaned into her and whispered, "We are bound by more than life-owing. You will not get rid of me that easily."

Shelby was acutely aware that the child she was having was of great value to Kerrick. IzTaln was grown and living here now, but this new one would stay with his father Kerrick, if he so desired. She did not want to be any where else either.

"Do you include yourself in the counting of the women who will be granted freedom?" This query came from Elder Lurt and brought Shelby back to the present turmoil.

"I do not."

There was again hushed whispering from the men. She raised her head high and looked Kerrick in the eyes.

"I may be called a captive, but I have always been free. I do as I need to and I yield where I must." She looked at the panel. "But I do not need your permission to live. I do not live on your planet, I live here. I have done what I want and will continue to do so. I only want freedom for the women to be able to move freely where they wish."

She turned to Kerrick who was looking at her with admiration in his eyes and hope. "I have no desire to leave my friends. I only ask that if my family is living they be allowed, on credit of Sir Kerrick's life, to come here if they choose to."

"You have requested an incredible thing. Why did you not ask for freedom for yourself?"

She looked at Kerrick and thought about it.

"There are several ways this could have gone. I could have made Sir Kerrick indebted to me for life by asking for my own freedom with the first life-debt, whereby I would be a free woman and he would have been obliged with the second debt to marry me or provide for me.

"But I would never enslave anyone to a life of servitude to me or force them to pretend to care about me. Besides, Sir Kerrick would not make a very good slave." She was laughing at him, "He is far too much upkeep. He needs constant attention and he just does not do things he doesn't want to do."

Kerrick was shaking his head, but the smile he tried to hide just did not go away.

"I also know that if I were to ask for my freedom, then my life would cost more as a free woman and you could ultimately grant me only my life. So my life is worth more as a captive. Now that is irony, isn't it Lady Rightell?"

She laughed a full and hardy laugh of joy. It was contagious as she looked at the men and women that she so dearly had come to love and respect. They were laughing with her.

She turned back to the panel and gave a sweeping, graceful bow and said with concrete authority, "I have done my worst. I request all this knowing full well that I must remain a captive to receive what is indebted to me."

"It is indeed unfortunate that your request can not be granted as you have specified." This came from an Elder at the table as he was motioning the rest of the panel to huddle with him. There was some debate done in hushed tones, but got louder at points. Finally, an agreement must have been made because they all came back to the table.

Shelby sat down. She was emotionally exhausted. She could put on a show, but that was all it was.

"We will allow you to go with Sir Kerrick when he begins the search for your children."

Shelby gasped and jumped for joy. She looked at Kerrick to see if he would balk, but he was smiling as if it was a triumph for him as well.

"As for the amount of women that will be freed, this is a substantial request and we will need to present it to Bestoch de Lurt Proh before it is sealed. I believe we are finished with the bequeathing for right now. But we will recommend the request as you have laid it out."

Shelby was weeping grateful tears. She had never been more relieved than at this moment. She was suddenly engulfed by the other women and the men gathered around her. She couldn't make out what anyone was saying, but she heard her own voice calling for Kerrick.

How silly. Did she actually think he would come to her if she called? A warm hand touched her arm amidst all the commotion. She felt that. She turned to see who it was and another hand touched her face. She was lost in the moment and knew for certain that Kerrick was right there. Her eyes were blurry with tears, but she welcomed his perusal.

"Kerrick," she couldn't say it. She could not say in front of all these people that she loved him. Everyone loved him. Her heart was melting into fragments. She said his name again, "Kerrick." It came out more as a whisper and the throng around her was still celebrating with whistles and shouts.

He heard her the first time. He was waiting for her to admit she needed him. He wanted to be vowed to her but it would be a tough sell not because of his lineage and the expectations and responsibilities that came with his title, but because she needed to believe he wanted to wed her.

He heard her again whisper his name like a prayer.

"I am right here, Shelby."

She stood on her tip-toes and wrapped her arms around him. She kissed his cheek and then his neck and whispered in his ear, "I love you, Kerrick Torrell, with all my heart. I know I have never loved anyone the way that I love you."

His head tilted back so he could look at her face. Tears were streaming down and she had an odd hesitant look on her face, like she was not sure he would care.

"Finally!" He said it so loud people looked their way. "She said she loved me. Did anyone else hear that? Say it again, Shelby, loudly." She rolled her eyes. People were shouting jubilantly.

He kissed her with an unabashed desire that took her breath and her knees gave completely away. He held her up against him and continued kissing her neck and face as she clung to him for support. He walked her to the corner of the hall to try to escape the chaotic celebrating as more and more women heard of their new-found freedom and made their way to the celebration.

"Shelby, love, you could not make me any happier than at this moment. You have just said your vows to me in front of my peers and yours." He kissed her and looked into her sweet, tear-stained face. "You are the woman I have hoped for all my life, Char Shelby. You need to acknowledge me as your husband, wife." He kissed her and she laughed in his mouth.

"Okay, Kerrick, but there are things you need to do for me, before I make any commitment that is so binding."

He nodded his head 'yes'. "There are things I definitely need to do to you, but you are going to have to wait until later." He purposely derailed her.

"Let's not do any more requesting tonight. Let's just dance," he jested.

She touched his face where it was still marked. "I am sorry."

"I love your passion. You are the only woman that will fight with me and not relent just because you can get more with sex."

"Well, that's going to change." She promised with a Mona Lisa grin.

"I doubt it."

Kerrick kissed her again and swept her into the room, twirling her around the floor.

~

Kerrick's mother stepped out from the shadows up to her husband's side.

"Ah, husband, they make a wonderful pair. She will never let him get away with anything. Did you see how hard she hit him?"

"Yes, my love, I 'heard' how hard she hit him."

"Do you think she really is a Deit Demine?

"Of course she is. Did you not see her luminous amber eye color when Kerrick opened the windows to let the moonlights in?"

"Of course. I just wanted to know if you saw it too. So, are you going to tell her or am I?"

"What? That she is higher ranking than anyone here, or that he thinks she hung the moons?

"Well, she is the Star of Aion."

THE END